Owner
Of
A
Lonely
Heart

Eva Carter is a pseudonym for internationally bestselling author Kate Harrison, who worked as a BBC reporter before becoming a writer. She lives in Brighton on the south coast of England and loves *Grey's Anatomy*, walking her dog, and running very slowly on the seafront. *Owner of a Lonely Heart* is her second novel.

Also by Eva Carter

How to Save a Life

PRAISE FOR *OWNER OF A LONELY HEART*

'Heart-warming, immersive and hopeful . . . A beautiful read'
Julie Cohen, author of *Summer People* and *Spirited*

'A truly moving, uplifting story about love, connection and finding the courage to start over'
Rowan Coleman, author of *The Memory Book* and *The Girl at the Window*

'Heart-warming and full of insight, this book will lift your spirits and make you smile'
Katie Fforde, author of *A Wedding in Provence*

'The perfect holiday read – wonderfully plausible characters, dark secrets and a fabulously teased-out love story. When I got to the end, I gave it a hug'
Josie Lloyd, author of *Lifesaving for Beginners*

'A gorgeous novel about messy, scary, wonderful love in all its forms'   Katy Regan, author of *How to Find Your Way Home*

'Sensitively and beautifully written. This is a book that will stay with you long after the last page is turned'
Milly Johnson, author of *The Woman in the Middle* and *Together, Again*

'One of the most beautiful books of the year. Brilliant'
The Sun

'I adored this incredibly moving and touching tale, with an unlikely hero who will steal your heart. Deeply emotional but with a light touch, this should be the love story of summer 2022 – an absolute delight.'
Veronica Henry, author of *The Impulse Purchase*

'Eva Carter has done it again. The perfect book to relax, unwind and warm up your heart.'
Suzy K Quinn, author of the Bad Mother series

PRAISE FOR *HOW TO SAVE A LIFE*

'*How to Save a Life* is so rich and fully-rounded – a sweeping, brave, epic love story. I was hooked from the very first page. I loved it. All the stars'

Josie Silver, author of *One Day in December* and *The Two Lives of Lydia Bird*

'A gripping love story that doesn't shy away from the mess and complexity of real life. I couldn't put it down until I reached the final page' Beth O'Leary, author of *The Flatshare* and *The Switch*

'We fell head over heels for this sweeping love story'

Fabulous Magazine

'Couldn't put it down. Gripping, unflinching, honest and dramatic' Jill Mansell, author of *And Now You're Back*

'A sliding-doors tale of life and loss' *Woman's Own*

'A heart-stopping, heart-wrenching and heart-warming story that kept me reading well into the night. I loved it'

Clare Pooley, author of *The Authenticity Project*

'A beautiful love story' *Bella*

'Impossible to put down, I adored it. *How to Save a Life* is heart-rending and uplifting, tragic and triumphant. It pulses with pain, passion and exquisite pleasure: I don't think I've read a love triangle which has been so addictive'

Cathy Bramley, author of *The Lemon Tree Cafe* and *My Kind of Happy*

'A heartwarming page-turner' *Closer*

'A fabulous story of the strength and fragility of life, love and friendships' Milly Johnson, author of *My One True North*

'Moving, gripping, with unforgettable characters, *How to Save A Life* is a beautiful page-turner with a very big heart. I just loved it' Eve Chase, author of *The Glass House*

EVA CARTER

Owner Of A Lonely Heart

PAN BOOKS

First published 2022 by Mantle Books

This paperback edition first published 2023 by Pan Books
an imprint of Pan Macmillan
The Smithson, 6 Briset Street, London EC1M 5NR
EU representative: Macmillan Publishers Ireland Ltd, 1st Floor,
The Liffey Trust Centre, 117–126 Sheriff Street Upper,
Dublin 1, D01 YC43
Associated companies throughout the world
www.panmacmillan.com

ISBN 978-1-5290-3889-7

1 3 5 7 9 8 6 4 2

A CIP catalogue record for this book is available from the British Library.

Typeset in Sabon by Palimpsest Book Production Ltd, Falkirk, Stirlingshire
Printed and bound by CPI Group (UK) Ltd, Croydon, CR0 4YY

Visit www.panmacmillan.com to read more about all our books
and to buy them. You will also find features, author interviews and
news of any author events, and you can sign up for e-newsletters
so that you're always first to hear about our new releases.

This book is dedicated to my father Michael (1939–2021),
for teaching me about love, and about dogs,
which are pretty much the same thing.

Chapter 1: Gemma

Sunday 1 July

'My Little Gem waited a long time for the perfect person. But then, suddenly, there he was.'

And here he is. Andrew Boxer. The love of my life.

Our guests whoop in response to my father's words, and a blush spreads up my new husband's neck, above his stiff collar and along his square jaw. I reach for his hand.

Dad hasn't quite finished. 'Before we accepted him into the family, this young man faced quite an inquisition. I call it "being hauled over the Coles" and it's extremely rigorous. After all, her sister has interrogated Somerset's most hardened criminals, but Andrew charmed her instantly.'

Laura nods to confirm it.

'And after decades as a medical receptionist, my wife can sniff out a fake or malingerer at fifty paces, but the worst thing she uncovered about this man was his passion for jigsaw puzzles.

'I liked him on sight. Which was a relief, because daughters are precious, especially when you delivered them yourself, on the kitchen floor. Look at the bride and groom. Aren't they wonderful together?'

Yes. We really are.

'It's time to toast the happy couple. To Andrew and Gemma!'

'*Andrew and Gemma!*'

The ring of crystal echoes around the function room, and Dad's dewy smile makes my own eyes smart. I brush away the hint of a tear before the wedding videographer zooms in too close.

Andrew stands up. The anticipation makes me catch my breath.

'Love is the biggest puzzle in the world. You'd all expect me to say that. But it's true. You can't see it. You can't hear it. You definitely can't buy it. Yet finding it is the key to happiness.'

The glow spreads through me. The speech has taken him weeks to perfect and it is Andrew to a T.

'So what *kind* of puzzle is it? Maybe it's a treasure hunt. The fun is in the seeking. Making mistakes – and, as many of you know, I've had plenty of practice in that department. Following false trails. Reading the map upside down. Gemma is a specialist at that.'

Everyone laughs. My terrible sense of direction is a family legend.

'Or perhaps love is a crossword, with cryptic clues that make your head hurt. There are millions of words that might fill in the blanks, and there are millions – *billions* – of people out there who could be The One.

'Finding love could also be a numbers game, like Sudoku. When you meet the right person, *everything* suddenly adds up.'

He turns and his surf-blue eyes lock onto mine. He's perfect. I know I'm biased, but I'm also right.

'For me, though, love is actually a giant jigsaw, but with no picture on the box. You make the frame first, learning about yourself. Sometimes it feels like you'll never be able to see what that image is – what it means.

2

'And then it happens. That person comes into your life. That missing piece. I knew the moment I saw Gemma that she was The One. Compared to some people, we took a long time to find true love. But the trickier the puzzle, the more incredible it feels when you complete it.'

Love surrounds us, warm and buoyant, like the thermals that lift a hot-air balloon into the sky. I can *almost* smell the tea-rose arrangement on the table, *almost* taste the biscuity bubbles of the champagne, *almost* feel his hand around mine, and the unfamiliarity of my wedding ring.

But not quite.

Andrew's face fills the frame.

My handsome, living, breathing husband.

I press pause. How many times have I watched this? Two hundred? No. More. And this is where I always freeze the recording. Andrew is the picture of health: his frame still broad, not fat. His face tanned. His lips soft. His dark hair thick and glossy.

Everything about him seems vital. It will be seven months before his body starts offering him clues. Another three months before the most dedicated puzzler I've ever met joins the dots and 'bothers' the doctor.

I press play again, but with the sound muted. Jed's best man's speech goes on a bit, so the video editor has cut it short, panning the room, showing polite smiles as people get restless. My bridesmaids try out Princess Elsa poses before my sister gives them a fierce stare and they freeze. Even in her turquoise taffeta maternity dress, Laura looks as if she might have handcuffs stashed under her skirt.

I didn't want a video, but I'm grateful for it now. When Andrew proposed, we imagined an intimate ceremony in a wooded glade, barefoot, wild flowers in our hair, with a handful of guests sitting on hay bales. He would have written poetic vows to make *everyone* sob, and I could have worn something folksy and smocked.

Instead we ended up with the works: silver service, tuxes and tiaras, plus the incredible view from the pier's ballroom, suspended on iron struts a quarter of a mile out to sea. Andrew's an only child, and his mother Isabel travelled to Paris for her couture outfit; she would never have forgiven us for not doing it 'properly'.

And we obliged, because one day seemed like nothing, when we had many thousands more ahead of us.

Or thought we did . . .

Shit. I can taste the tears, but I won't let them out.

The shot returns to us again.

My face hasn't changed much. It is only three years ago, after all. But *I* can see the difference. Video-Gemma seems girlish and naive. Her face glows with unfiltered expectation as Andrew takes her hand and she treads carefully around the pooling layers of fabric of her train.

I glimpse the silk jigsaw-puzzle waistcoat under Andrew's morning suit, can remember how cool it felt as I touched it, and how I was counting the hours till I could touch the hot skin underneath.

As we gaze at each other, we're trying so hard not to giggle, because *marriage is a serious commitment.*

Again we look like children. We have no clue what lies ahead.

Laura would accuse me of self-indulgence if she knew I was watching this, but I'm not a masochist. This fortifies me for the next twenty-eight days.

A loud snore to my left makes me turn away from the screen.

'Boring you, am I?'

Bear opens his eyes, sighs and stretches out his legs so

4

his hairy body takes up almost half the sofa. He got up with me at 2 a.m., after I woke needing the loo and realized that today is when the rigmarole starts up again. I couldn't sleep after that, and he joined me on the sofa. He's been dreaming ever since, whiskers and paws twitching, in pursuit of imaginary squirrels.

It's hot already, so I open the doors onto our tiny balcony. I crane my neck towards the suspension bridge. A shimmering golden balloon rises above the trees, the first of many.

'Come on, dude! Let's go out now, before it gets too hot.'

Bear could happily snooze until midday, so when I grab his lead he opens only one eye, not believing I'm serious about going for a walk this early. I reach for his favourite of the many balls he's abandoned on the floor. He opens the other eye. The ball only bounces once before he leaps off the sofa with a delighted bark.

'That's more like it.'

I glance at the TV screen, which shows Andrew whispering in my ear. The sound is still muted, but in my head I can hear the opening bars of our first dance song, 'One Day Like This'. A long, uplifting anthem, which brought all our guests onto the dance floor to join us.

And I can hear what he whispers: *Thank you for solving the puzzle.*

We thought we'd found the solution to everything, because we'd found each other. But with him gone, nothing adds up any more.

Chapter 2: Dan

'Which trainers will impress her the most?'

Vijay squints at the box-fresh pair I'm holding, then down at the scruffy ones I'm wearing and all the others lined up on the bedroom floor.

'I'm still trying to get my head around the size of your collection. How come I never knew this about you?'

'I like trainers, OK? It's not a crime.'

'No, but neither is it entirely normal for a grown man to own this many.'

'Says the man who has collected more vinyl than Elton John. Anyway, stop taking the piss and tell me which she's going to think are the coolest.'

Vijay snorts. 'You're in massive trouble if you have to ask *me* for advice on fashion or girls.'

Too right. I am in massive *trouble.*

I flop back down onto the bed and the astronaut-tested layers mould to my shape. Vijay's mattress cost more than my jeep, and I imagine the memory foam swallowing me whole.

'The Queer Eye guys haven't returned my call, so you're all I've got, Veej.'

He frowns. 'OK. How about the Vans? Or go for Converse if you don't want to seem like you're trying too hard. But I bet she doesn't even look at your trainers. It's the *real* Dan she wants to get to know.'

'Not comforting.' I've got sixty minutes max before she shows up. Enough to change my shoes. Nowhere near long enough to transform my entire personality.

'Come on. You are Dan the Man, great laugh, with not just one but *two* cool jobs, a posse of outstanding mates . . .' Vijay grabs my hand to help me up from the mattress. 'Not to mention your amazing bachelor pad.'

I grin. 'Yeah. Thank you again for letting us stay.'

He shakes his head. 'No sweat. I wasn't going to be here much anyway.' We walk through the living room and out onto the terrace. The day's barely begun, but it's gonna be a scorcher. The water shimmers and I reckon the view of Bristol Harbourside will blow Casey's mind.

Except I don't know that. I know nothing about her.

Vijay reaches under the pizza oven for the emergency packet of cigarettes and offers me one. I shake my head: nicotine breath won't impress Casey or her mother.

'OK. I need small talk. What are the cool kids chatting about these days?'

He strikes a match, lights his cigarette. 'Harrison is obsessed with *Minecraft*, which by definition makes him one of the *uncool* kids.'

'Like father, like son.'

'Which means your daughter should be the epitome of cool, if she takes after *you*. How about music?'

I groan. 'We've already had that conversation on FaceTime. She basically thinks all music recorded before 2010 is rubbish.'

'TV then? Harrison likes *Stranger Things*. And, inexplicably, *The Great British Bake Off*.'

I shake my head. 'I'm not a cupcake guy. Oh shit, Veej. I am not cut out for any of this.'

Vijay places a reassuring hand on my arm. 'What you never seem to see, Dan, is that people can't help liking you.

I'd kill to have ten per cent of your natural charisma, you lucky bastard.'

He's wrong. I *do* see it. I'm that laid-back guy you meet at a party, or a gig, the one with the right playlist to match the mood, or the funny story about your favourite band. You warm to me instantly, easily. An accident of biology means that I am easy on the eye. You might even fall in love with me for five or ten minutes.

And then I'll walk away and you'll forget all about me, because that's easier for everyone. My charisma is a smoke-screen, and I learned it from a master illusionist. No one knows what I'm really like, not even Vijay, and we've been friends for twelve years.

Though Vijay knows a bit more now than he did three weeks ago. We were on a night out with the festival gang when Casey's message popped up on Messenger. I'd had a couple of drinks, and I almost deleted it without reading. But something made me open it, and as the words sank in, I couldn't breathe.

Idoia noticed I'd gone pale and she grabbed my phone, read the message out loud to Veej and Eddie, and the questions started. I recovered fast enough to tell half-truths that didn't reflect as badly on me as the full story. Yes, I'd known for a while that I had a daughter, as a result of a fling thirteen years ago. No, I'd never met her, because her mother had asked me not to.

But in that moment everything changed. Casey had found me on Facebook and messaged me with terrifying news: she had a brain tumour and was coming to Bristol for specialist treatment. And she needed help.

Of course my gang rallied round, because that's what decent people do. We all got swept up in the drama. Including me. Even I could handle four weeks of fatherhood.

Except that I've already crossed a line by lying to her. Or, at least, not been brave enough to tell her the truth. Casey and her mum needed somewhere to stay, so I offered my flat on Messenger, though I warned her it wasn't very fancy.

But she instantly sent back a wild tsunami of excited emojis, along with a screenshot she'd taken of a tagged photo showing me at Vijay's place:

Looks super-fancy to me!

I froze, staring at the picture, as I realized two things: first, that she thought the penthouse was *mine*. And second, that she must have spent hours on my timeline, building up an idea of her long-lost dad in her head, before summoning up the courage to message me.

I tried to think up a way of breaking it to her, but I couldn't burst her bubble on bloody Messenger. When I told Veej about the mix-up, he instantly offered us this place for the whole of July. He loved the idea of making her fantasy come true, so she can enjoy all the buzz of the harbour when she's not at the hospital. And doesn't Casey deserve *this*, instead of my poky 1980s flat, with its view of the A-road?

More than one of my exes has called me a man-child, and I can't disagree, but as soon as Casey and Angelica settle in, I'll tell them the truth, like a grown-up.

'Ready?' Veej stubs out the cigarette, tucks the butt back in the packet.

I follow him inside. 'As I'll ever be.'

'Gotta split,' he says, doing a geeky hand-movement to match. 'But as soon as I'm back from Berlin I want to meet her, OK?'

Not a chance. 'Sure.'

9

Vijay gives me a doubtful look. 'You're not going to back out, are you?'

'Too late for that.' And it is. The harm I'd do by backing out now goes beyond the emotional.

After Vijay leaves, I check the spare rooms. Clean all the surfaces again with the hospital-grade antibacterial wipes Angelica told me to buy. Anything to stay busy. I'll get this bit right. Keep Casey and her mum safe. It's the least I can do.

But it's four weeks only. Like I always say, we're here for a good time, not a long time. When August comes, they will go their way and I will go mine.

Chapter 3: Casey

Me and Mum are on the road, the Ka windows wound all the way down, singing to 'Toxic' on the radio at the top of our voices.

Everyone says we're like sisters. Mum hasn't got an actual sister and I don't think I'm ever going to get one of my own. But when she's happy, even just for a few seconds, we don't need anybody else.

'Last services before we get to Bristol,' she says. 'Do you have to stop?'

Mum hates service stations because of the germs. Usually I cross my legs and wait till we've got to where we're going. But when I check my face in the mirror, my eye make-up has run, so I look like a fat panda. I can't show up looking like this.

'Yeah, I think I do. Sorry.'

The faint lines between her eyebrows pinch together. 'Don't apologize, sweetheart. When you gotta go, you gotta go.'

Luckily she lets me go into the loos on my own, so I don't have to pretend I need an actual wee. The lights above the washbasins are even meaner than the ones in hospitals. My face is fat and my skin's grey-yellow, like the yolk of a hard-boiled egg.

I get out the contour palette *all* the YouTubers use, but I still look horrible. Back at the car, I ask Mum to open up the boot so I can unzip my suitcase. I pull out the long chain strung with my beads of courage, and the acupressure wristbands that are meant to stop nausea.

'Mum? You did pack my wig, didn't you?'

'Yes, but only in case the therapy affects your hair—'

'Found it!'

'Oh, Casey. You don't need to wear that *today*. You can't even see the scars any more.'

She's lying. I've got stitch lines that look like I've been struck by lightning, and my real hair hasn't grown back enough to cover them.

'I've got to look right. For Bristol.' I stop myself saying *for my dad*, but she knows that's what I mean.

She sighs and starts the engine again. 'What about one of your scarves?'

I didn't even know headscarves were a thing till I got sick. But the tumour vloggers swear by them, so Mum and me went on eBay to find ones printed with meerkats and dachshunds and cacti. After my surgery I learned 'seven cool ways to tie a scarf'. My favourite is no. 4, with a 'rosette twist'.

But I can't wear a scarf for an entire month, not when they're forecasting the hottest July *since records began*.

I take my wig out of its special bag and tug it on, zhuzhing up the hair that once belonged to a stranger, trying to make it less flat. I check my reflection. Better. Except already my scalp is itching around my scars.

'Do I look ugly?'

Mum turns towards me. 'No. Never. You're gorgeous. I love you.'

The car's little engine revs as she reverses out of the space and drives, faster than usual, towards the slip road. We flash past a sign reading: *BRISTOL 18 MILES*.

Bristol, where my father is waiting for me.

12

My scalp tingles, but in a good way.

I'd rather not have a brain tumour. But if it means I get to meet my *actual dad* at long last, then this was *meant* to happen.

Mum's frown gets deeper as she drives the last couple of miles. The only thing she hates more than motorways is city centres.

'Yeah, you can piss off too,' she shouts, giving the finger to the driver behind us who tooted when the lights changed. 'Why are people so aggressive?'

I try to ignore her temper as I take in Bristol for the first time. I already know I'm going to love it. I've lived in the same village my entire life, but here no one knows me. I can be anything I want.

The satnav takes us down a narrow lane and the car bounces on the cobbles. 'I hope this is right,' Mum says. 'It's changed a lot since I was here.'

'Since two weeks ago?'

'No. Before that.'

'You've been to Bristol before?' She's never told me that.

'I'd forgotten. We, um, passed through, came shopping for wellies, on our way . . . on our way to Glastonbury.'

Mum can't have forgotten. She remembers every detail of that weekend, because if she'd never gone, her life would have been *totally* different. There'd have been a law degree and a well-paid job and a big house and a husband.

There would definitely *not* be a me.

Suddenly the alley ends and—

Wow! The harbour! There are boats and cafes and cinemas and restaurants and people – *so* many people – and music pouring out of every window, so many voices and rhythms, and I want to jump out of the car and join in.

'Does my dad live near *this*?'

'Hang on, let me get my bearings,' she snaps. 'See that building?' She points to a warehouse on the other side of the water. 'That's his place.'

My head is literally about to explode. It is the coolest building I have ever seen, Kardashian- or Manhattan-cool. My dad lives *here*. And, for the next month, *so do we*.

We cross the bridge and park in a spot marked *MERCHANTS' LOFTS VISITORS*. Getting out of the car, I almost get run over by an e-scooter rider.

'You need to be careful here,' Mum says. *Like, when am I ever* not *careful?* I turn and see the famous bridge that was in every photo when I googled Bristol and, floating over the top of it, *so many balloons*, against a sky so blue it makes me think I've never seen real blue before.

But before I can show Mum, I smell doughnuts and curry: right next to my dad's building there's a pile of shipping containers with shops and cafes *inside* them! Can't wait to WhatsApp Molly some photos. She will be *mega-jealous*.

'Ready?' Mum says, taking two cases out of the boot. 'Your father can get the rest.'

When she buzzes the intercom, he answers immediately. 'Hey, welcome to Bristol, you two.'

Of course I've spoken to him on the phone, but his voice sounds different today – kind of American. 'How did you know it was us?'

'There's a camera.'

Ugh! When we've FaceTimed I've always added filters or bunny ears, but now he's seeing the real me. Too late I tilt my chin, the way Molly's taught me, to hide my fat face in photos. The skin under my wig is sweating and I hope it won't run down my forehead.

'Take the lift, it goes all the way up to the penthouse,' he says, like the word *penthouse* is one he uses all the time. I've never said it in my entire life.

Hospital lifts are wipe-clean and dented from trolley wheels. This one has wallpaper of huge green leaves with parrots and birds of paradise in turquoise and gold, and it smells of fruit, not sick people.

The doors open.

There he is.

Dan Lennon.

My father.

He's taller and better-looking than his photos. He could be an actor on *Hollyoaks* or a singer in a band.

Oh. In his picture, his eyes seemed blue. But they're actually grey-violet, with long lashes. He's got *my* eyes.

Or, I guess, I've got his.

Doors closing, the lift says, bored with waiting. Mum and I are still inside it, but my legs won't work.

'No!' Dan says as the doors start to shut. Before he disappears completely, he puts his foot into the gap – *how ultra-cool are his Vans?* – and his arms stop the door closing and *he's got so many muscles.* No one else's dad has muscles like those.

'Come on, let me help you.' As he takes the bags, I step through the doors and see his flat, and everything else stops mattering.

'Wow.'

IRL it's even more amazing than the Facebook photos. We're in this gigantic room with a massive L-shaped black leather sofa, metal beams holding up the ceiling and windows that span the entire wall, with a huge balcony beyond that. I step forward. What a view! Shops, ships, people. From his sofa I could see more life in a day than I've seen in the previous twelve years.

15

'Like it?' my father says, sounding worried. 'Go ahead, open up the doors.'

Mum's saying something about pollutants, but I zone out as I step onto the balcony and the city's warmth hugs my whole body. Down there, the harbour explodes with colour and I want to climb over the glass edges of the terrace and shimmy down to the waterside. To freedom.

My head spins with *all the feels*. Happiness and excitement and, yeah, a bit of fear. But right now, on this terrace, it's like I'm on the edge of the biggest adventure of my entire life.

Chapter 4: Dan

She stands with her back to us, taking in the view.

My *daughter*.

When the lift doors opened and I saw her face, I couldn't speak. She looked so much like the one photo I have of my mum as a young girl.

Angelica marches over to the edge of the terrace. 'That's enough, Casey. It's not a good idea for you to spend too long outdoors; you're not used to such poor air quality.' I hear the criticism – of me, of my adopted city – in her voice, but also her concern for her daughter.

Casey turns round and the familiarity of her face shocks me again. Of course I've chatted to her twice on video. But the first time she used digital rabbit ears, and the second she hid her features behind showers of sparkling hearts.

Angelica warned me not to say anything about her plump cheeks – *that's the steroids* – or the fact that Casey is small for twelve – *they think that might be the tumour delaying her growth*. But what I notice most is how pretty Casey is, with my eyes and Angelica's smooth skin and long blonde hair.

'This place is amazing. It is giving me *all the feels*,' Casey says. Her soft Midlands accent reminds me of her mother's when we first met. *The music is amazing. Glastonbury is amazing.*

Angelica was amazing too.

'Hmm. If I'd known this was how you live, I'd have asked for more child support over the years,' Angelica says, and though her voice is light, as though she's joking, her pale eyes are glacier-cold. What happened to her?

Stupid question: I know *exactly* what happened to her, and who is to blame.

'I only moved in very recently.' Should I say tell them it's Vijay's place, get it out of the way? *Ugh!* Not now. Things are awkward enough already.

'Lucky you.' She turns round to inspect the iron units that line the brick wall, then runs her finger along the rungs of the ladder to the mezzanine. She frowns, like she's pissed off there's no dust. I used half a pack of antibacterial wipes on that.

No one says anything and I feel like the silence could last the entire month. I'm lost for words. Where is the charm Veej always bangs on about? My irresistible banter and legendary ability to read the room?

I *am* reading the room. That's the problem – the vibes Angelica is giving off would make George Clooney tongue-tied.

'Let me show you where everything is.' They follow me as I open the door to the main bathroom. 'Power shower OK for you both?'

'That's as big as a tractor wheel!' Casey says when she sees the shower head.

'I know you like to stay clean,' I say. What kind of idiot statement is that?

Angelica corrects me. 'It's not about cleanliness. It's about avoiding threats to Casey's immune system.'

Don't react.

'And this is your room, Casey.'

It's the smallest room, but also the nicest, with a tiny porthole window overlooking the harbour and a roof light that lets in sunshine. I went shopping yesterday and bought new stuff to make it just right for a young girl: fairy lights and a rose-gold mirror and a fluffy rug and a new duvet cover, a woodland design covered with foxes and floppy-haired rabbits jumping around a forest.

But now I'm worried it's too babyish. 'I hope this is all right.'

She glances at her mother – the curve of their pouting lips is identical – and shrugs. 'Fine, yeah.'

I ignore the brief stab of disappointment. Huh. *I bought her a quilt.* What was I expecting, a Grammy Award? The Nobel Prize for Parenting?

Angelica's room is bigger, but it's crammed full of office stuff and record boxes. She dumps her bag and we go back into the hall.

'Where do *you* sleep?' Casey asks.

'In there.' I point at the door but don't open it: too many questions, too soon.

Angelica looks at me suspiciously. 'You're not hiding a girlfriend, are you?'

'No. I'm not seeing anyone right now. And even if I was, I've cleared the entire month for Casey. Making up for lost time.'

'I think it'll take more than four weeks to do that,' Angelica says pointedly as she walks back to the living room.

OK, I guess it's time to mention the elephant in the room. 'Listen, guys, I'm not trying to muscle in on your lives after all this time. I'm just grateful Casey got in touch, so I can do something practical for a few weeks.'

Casey gives her mum an apologetic shrug, tucks her hair behind her ears. Why *did* Casey message me? They'd have

19

got free hospital accommodation, and it's obvious that Angelica would rather sleep on the streets than be here.

She opens her mouth and I wait for something venomous to come out. But she sighs, as though it's too much effort. Casey touches her hair again: a nervous gesture.

But it's not the gesture that startles me. I look again at her hair and realize: the poor kid is wearing a wig. So much for inheriting her mum's blonde hair. The shock makes me look away.

'Are you guys thirsty?' I say, trying to distract us. 'I've got juice, Coke, whatever you fancy.'

'I told you in my emails, we don't drink Coke,' Angelica says curtly, what little patience she has for me clearly already wearing thin. 'Have you seen what it can do to a coin? Imagine what it does to your insides. I asked you to buy organic juice.'

'I did.' I'm heading for the fridge to prove how I almost cleared out Wild Oats wholefoods store when I stocked up yesterday. Except somehow I already know it won't be enough.

'Is that a coffee machine?' Casey points at Vijay's pride and joy: a silver Rocket Cinquantotto that takes up most of the marble kitchen island. 'Because Mum and me love our cappuccinos.'

'Caffeine? I'm amazed that's allowed.'

'It detoxifies the liver,' Angelica says.

'That's the best news I've heard all week.' I try to channel charming Dan, the one my mates would recognize. 'Bristol runs on caffeine. So let's kick off your stay with the best cappuccino this side of Roma.'

Casey giggles and I want to hear that more, because I'm getting the distinct impression that life with her mum isn't bursting with LOL moments.

Chapter 5: Gemma

Monday 2 July

Bear pulls me along, nine kilos of strength and extrovert enthusiasm.

'OK, mate, I get the message – you want to get cracking.'

I always shudder before we enter the hospital building, even though it has changed almost beyond recognition. The sculpted metal panels glow in the afternoon sun, sending a mosaic of light particles onto the paving under Bear's paws.

Inside the glammed-up foyer the security guy has a treat in his pocket, and the receptionist wants 'a lick from Dr Dog', plus we have to pop into the shop so the volunteer can give Bear a tummy rub. And in the lift one of the consultants takes a selfie to show his kids.

Outside the classroom Jed grins at me through the glass and gives the thumbs up, so I push open the door and go inside.

There are five kids in school today, and I recognize four of them from last week. Bear approaches each one differently, as though he can tell what they need right now. The youngest girl is barely old enough for school, never mind what she must go through here, and Bear cocks his head to one side, making happy snuffling noises as she scratches between his ears. Next, Bear jumps on the spot, to say hi to the boy with the biggest brown eyes I've seen outside manga.

The newcomer is the eldest: a girl wearing a dark-blonde wig, with luminous grey-violet eyes that widen when I smile at her, before her glance drops to the floor. She's pretty, though her face has that telltale steroid plumpness, and her body language is fiercely self-conscious. I remember being on the cusp of adolescence, and I want to give her a massive hug and tell her it'll all be OK.

'Casey! Come and meet Bear. He's a key member of the team,' Jed says.

I smile, but the girl – Casey – backs away, her face twisting with disgust. 'There's no way a *dog* should be allowed into a hospital,' she says, her voice tight.

'It's OK, I promise. He's been assessed by the therapy-dog charity to make sure he's got the right temperament,' I say.

Casey rolls her eyes. 'I'm talking about *germs*! People here are *sick* already, and animals carry horrible diseases that could make them worse. Or cause allergies. Or even zoonoses – that's illnesses that cross the species barrier.'

Whoa! Who has filled her head with these scary ideas? I stay calm as I reassure her. 'Well, the doctors love it when we come in, and we have very strict rules. We stay away from vulnerable patients, and Bear always has a bath before he comes, even though he *hates* it.'

But her stern expression hasn't changed.

Jed stands up, arms relaxed, all open body language, to diffuse the conflict. 'Tell you what, Casey, you could go and see the play therapists down the corridor? You could make something, or paint your new treatment mask, just while Bear is here.'

Casey tuts. 'I'm twelve, not two. You can't fob me off with poster paints, or building a dinosaur out of egg boxes.'

'We're all out of egg boxes. But we do have a top-of-the-

22

range Mac next door, if you fancy making an animation or recording a vlog?'

Her eyes dart to the right. 'I guess,' she says, trying *not* to sound interested. Jed always seems to find a way to relate to the pupils who come here, whether they're a scared tween like Casey or a tiny child learning their alphabet in between surgery or chemo sessions.

Jed's pretty good with adults too. Volunteering here was his idea. He'd been reading about the benefits of therapy dogs, and Bear has loved people since I adopted him. It took almost six months to get through the volunteer red tape, but interacting with these kids has calmed Bear down *and* stopped me from retreating completely into my little nest of sorrow.

'Can I read him a story?' the brown-eyed boy asks.

'I'm going to brush his hair,' the girl with pigtails announces in a cute Welsh accent. Kids come from all over the UK for treatment at the unit. 'You always have to brush your hair before going to school, and his is a right mess!'

'He'd like that,' I say, removing his red Assistance Dog tunic and taking his brush out of my bag. Bear *hates* being groomed by me, but accepts it stoically here.

As he settles down with a tremendous sigh, the boy starts to read a story about wizards storming a castle. I glimpse Casey through the glass window into the art room. I've never seen any of the kids look quite that lonely.

When school finishes, she shrugs off Jed's offer to show her where to find Scanning and Diagnostics for her next appointment. 'I *can* read signs. I'll work it out on my own.'

After the door closes behind her, Jed raises his eyebrows at me. 'Another satisfied customer.'

'I remember what it was like to be twelve,' I say. 'Bad enough, even without cancer.'

'It's actually a benign brain tumour, but it's still making its presence felt. She had treatment last year in Birmingham, but the tumour is growing again, so she's come down here for proton-beam therapy.'

I shake my head. 'Poor kid. Still, you'll have her figured out by tomorrow and a fully signed-up member of the Jed Porter fan club by Wednesday.'

'She could be the toughest nut yet. There's all sorts going on in Casey's head, and I don't just mean Bob.'

'Bob?'

'Her tumour.'

'Oh?' I try hard to rein in my nosiness, but it's been ages since I've felt this curious about anyone. 'So what's the story?'

'It's no secret – she's given the other kids a blow-by-blow account.' But Jed still leans in conspiratorially. 'Yesterday she met her father for the first time in her life!'

'Wow.' I lean in.

'According to Casey, her dad's high up in the music scene. Lives in some swanky penthouse down by the harbour. Those warehouse conversions cost at least a couple of million. She showed us pictures on her phone. She obviously thinks he's the coolest dad on the planet.'

Inside my body, somewhere between my heart and my belly, a flame of indignation ignites. I try to ignore it. 'But if he's such a great guy, where has he been for twelve years?'

'Apparently he didn't know he had a daughter for the first couple of years. It was only when the child support people tracked him down that he started paying towards her maintenance.'

'But he's never met her?'

Jed shakes his head. 'No. It's only happening now because she's sick. Casey thinks it's fate – written in the stars, that

24

kind of vibe – because she's always known he lived in Bristol. So when the doctors referred her here, she messaged him and the prodigal dad has finally got involved. She thinks it's happy ever after.'

That flame grows. 'I can't even . . . How could you have a daughter and not want to be in her life? When so many people never even get the chance.'

Jed sighs. 'Gemma . . . Shit. Sorry. I should have thought – sorry.'

'No, don't worry. I wasn't thinking of Andrew,' I lie.

Jed is the most perceptive of my husband's friends. He was Andrew's best man, and the two of them were founder members of the Puzzlers' Club, which met every Thursday in the kind of authentically rough back-street boozer hipsters love. They ended up recruiting thirty members, playing retro board games and competing to source the trickiest jigsaws.

In Andrew's last weeks, when he was too sick to leave the house, Jed even re-created the vibe in our living room, complete with warm beer, a tobacco-scented candle and a 1970s prog-rock playlist.

'You can always talk to me,' Jed says.

But where would I start? We decided not to tell anyone outside the family about the embryo transfers, and now there's no point mentioning it, because it probably won't work.

Please let it work.

'Gemma?'

'Sorry, I was thinking. About work.' A white lie, for my own sake.

'Has it picked up then?' He gets up, starts tidying the classroom: piling up beanbags, turning off the soothing music he always plays in the last session of the day. I'm in awe of how he's turned these hospital rooms into a haven for the kids who come here.

'There's a commission that's right up my street, but after last time, my agent's asked for more spec sketches than usual. To make sure I don't screw up again . . .'

Jed nods. 'You seem calmer to me. A lot more like the old Gemma.'

'Yeah, I'm almost back to being the girl whose idea of a crisis was getting the Pantone a shade out on a packaging mock-up.'

'It's what he wanted, right? For you to be happy again. As happy as you were together?'

'That's a tad over-ambitious.'

'Is it? Because I'm determined to be happier than I was with Niamh.'

The comparison irritates me, but I try not to let it show. 'But Niamh was wrong for you, so *of course* you'll be happier when you find someone better. Andrew was perfect for me. The One.'

'You think there's only *one* person out of the world population of seven-point-six billion that you could love? Andrew would take issue with your numbers.'

He is right, technically. 'OK, in the entire world there might be two or three more. But the chance of me bumping into one of them on the Downs is statistically low, and I don't have the energy for a global manhunt.'

Jed has the patient expression he uses on children who refuse to learn Very Important Lessons. 'Even if you *did* bump into the right person on the Downs, would you actually notice them?'

'OK, Teach, I think you're forgetting I'm not one of your naughty pupils.'

Jed laughs. 'Sorry. Occupational hazard.' He turns off his

laptop and the projector. 'I won't put you in detention. But how about a drink? It's the perfect weather for the deck at BayCaff.'

Except that BayCaff was *our* place – mine and Andrew's – so now I only go there alone. 'Another time. Sorry, in a bit of a funny mood tonight. You know how it is. By tomorrow I'll be my usual sunny self again.'

I give him a quick hug before I leave the classroom, and the solidity of him surprises me, as it always does. I grew used to skin and bones.

Bloody hell, it is scorching out here. Bear blinks in the bright sunshine and stays within the shadow cast by the hospital building, so his paws don't burn on the hot paving. Oh, I miss BayCaff evenings: the lapping of the water against the side of the boat, the chink of ice cubes in a tall glass of iced mocha.

I try to breathe it out. Must be the oestrogen I started taking yesterday, triggering Too Much Emotion. I guess it's OK to be pissed off that I have to do this alone, when shitbags like that girl's father take the gift of having children for granted.

When we get home, Bear drinks an entire bowlful of water before stretching out on the wooden floor, half his body in shade, half in a pool of sunlight.

I reach up to the very top of our shelves and take down the book that's the best antidote to my negativity.

The Amazing Book of Us was our fertility counsellor's idea: a book for the kids we hoped to have, explaining how they'd come into the world. We started treatment when Andrew went into remission, full of the optimism of those who have 'sent cancer packing'. We kept the scan of my ripe ovaries and I drew smiling embryologists, and Andrew wrote about how love and science would come together to make our family.

27

But then he got sick again and I was too busy doing medical stuff to face working on the book. So he took it over completely. He was determined to keep going until he finished writing.

He died four days later.

HELLO!

This is *The Amazing Book of . . . US!* Written by Daddy (with drawings courtesy of Mummy*) long before you were even born. If you're anything like me when I was a little boy, you'll be extremely curious, and I expect that you are full of questions. I've written this book to answer them. It's a guessing game for me, because I've no idea what your questions will be. I wish I could be with you in real life. This book will help explain all the brilliant things that happened before you came along, and why I'm not around to tell you how excited I was by the idea of becoming a dad. This is definitely a celebration, not a sad story. It's about how to be happy and full of hope and laughter — just like your mummy and daddy are right now, as we're dreaming of making a family.

Our wish is that this is a book you'll love to read as you grow into a truly unique and special person. To help you, I've written down what I believe in 'Daddy says' sections. You can find them next to the speech bubbles, like this.

Every word and picture comes with all my love. I have had a wonderful time creating *The Amazing Book of Us* as a gift to you.

* In fact the only drawing Mummy didn't do is on the front cover, which I drew. Perhaps you can tell why I didn't do the others! The creature with the massive head is a dog, and the other shapes are meant to be us: Mummy, Daddy and you. Every time you look at it, please remember families are amazing, which is the reason for this book's title.

Chapter 6: Dan

Tuesday 3 July

The workshop thermometer hit thirty degrees this morning and the testosterone is soaring too. I had to break up two fights before lunchtime. But then I hear that one of our trickiest trainees has landed himself an apprenticeship and I decide to reward myself with an ice-cold can of Arbor Lager as soon as I get home.

I'm halfway there when I remember.

Bollocks!

I turn the jeep round.

The lift purrs as it takes me up to the penthouse. Will they notice I'm late? There are *no* excuses for forgetting your own daughter.

As the doors open, a wave of heat hits me: Angelica has closed the bifold doors to keep the pollution out, but it's turned the penthouse into a greenhouse.

I get this insane urge to call out *Hi, honey, I'm home,* like in a fifties sitcom, but I stick to 'Hello?' I don't sound like myself. 'Hello?' Louder.

Nothing comes back.

I sigh with relief. Has Angelica 'accidentally' forgotten I've arranged a treat for tonight, and taken Casey out herself? She probably finds it infuriating, even threatening, when I flash the cash. But I'm not trying to take over; I just want to spoil them both, to distract them from the stress and worry they're facing at the hospital every day.

Still, if they're not here right now I'll be able to relax, pour myself a cold beer, sit on the terrace, breathe in the non-existent city smog.

Except the door to Casey's room is opening and she's bursting out – is she going to hug me? Every muscle in my body clenches and she skips right past.

'Hey, how *you* doin'?' she says in an American accent.

'I'm doing *goood*,' I say, matching her.

We're laughing as we go into the living room, but the expression on Angelica's face makes the laughter stop. She hates me. Which is fair, but it's tricky occupying the same overheated room with someone whose loathing is so poorly disguised.

Casey launches herself onto the sofa and the leather cushion *oofs* when she lands next to her mum. They could almost be sisters. Except that Casey seems more like the Angelica I remember, because she actually *smiles*.

I'm breaking my first rule: *don't look back in anger.* Don't look back *at all*. 'What have you been doing with yourselves today, girls?'

'The same as yesterday,' Angelica says. 'And the same as we'll do tomorrow. Hospital, hospital school, home. Not that this place feels like a home.'

Casey fiddles with her wig. 'But on the way back here we went to that market, the one in the old building, like in *The Muppet Christmas Carol*.'

'St Nicholas?' I'm a bit put out; it's one of the places my friends recommended I show Casey. 'Did you see my favourite record store?'

Angelica sighs. 'I couldn't believe people pay a tenner for

31

old records. This lot must be worth thousands.' She waves at the shelving units packed with Vijay's albums.

Tell them, now.

But already Casey is speaking again. 'We don't have a record player at home,' she says. 'I'm surprised they're allowed any more. Those needles look very dangerous.'

'They're not dangerous! Let me show you.'

But Angelica is frowning. 'Aren't you meant to be taking us out? It's not good for Casey to eat too late. It interferes with her sleep, which is vital for her recovery.'

God, she's hard work. Except I can hear how *tired* she is, and I know it must have been bloody relentless, as a single parent, coping with Casey's illness. I should cut her some slack. 'Yes, I booked for six thirty and it's not far to walk.'

Angelica sighs again. 'Well, I've got a migraine coming on, so you two will have to go alone, if you think you can handle a couple of hours in sole charge of your daughter.'

'I've got headache pills you could take,' I say, but Angelica scowls at me as if I've suggested rubbing cocaine into her gums.

Casey gives her mum's hand a squeeze. 'Have you tried your lavender stick?'

'It's the heat. I'll be fine after a lie-down. Go on, you deserve to have fun.'

Casey gets up. 'I need to change. Are we going somewhere fancy?'

'No. More of an upbeat, happening place.'

Casey thinks it through. 'Got it. Back in ten.' She disappears, leaving me alone with Angelica.

'Shall I bring you something back to eat?' I ask.

'I'm not hungry, thank you. And I don't know where you're going, but I hope it's not fast food. Please encourage her to choose plant-based. The vegetables help fortify her immune system.'

She's told me this at least half a dozen times. But I won't get wound up; it can't be easy to relinquish control of any aspect of Casey's life, especially when she's sick. Besides, it's the first time I've been alone with Angelica since they arrived, and I need to find something out.

I go to the fridge, pour two glasses of water from the dispenser and sit down opposite her. 'Angelica, what's the deal with Casey's wig?' I speak quietly.

'Shh. She's very self-conscious about it.'

I get up again, push the living-room door shut. 'Does she ever take it off?'

'She hadn't worn it for months before we came here. Then, guess what, on the drive down, she put it back on before we got to your flat.'

'She's wearing it for me?'

Angelica stares at me, pityingly. 'You must see how desperate she is to impress you?'

I shrug. 'That's crazy. She doesn't have to impress me.'

'I've told her that. But I think she's hoping that you're going to fall in love with the idea of having a daughter – and then you and I will fall in love into the bargain – so we can all live happily ever after.'

Shit.

She continues to stare me down. 'You've got no intention of staying in touch with us after this, have you? A month of playing at parenthood and you'll be laid-back Dan Lennon again, not a care in the world.'

'Which is what Casey asked for. I haven't promised any more than that.'

'Even if you had, we both know you don't take promises seriously. But I worked very hard so that Casey would never have to find that out.'

'Angelica, you're right. I'm not into commitment. Which is why I never wanted to get involved, because I knew I'd let you both down.'

'How noble of you. How *self-aware* you are.'

'I'm not noble. But I understand my limitations.'

She shakes her head in disbelief. 'No, Dan. You believe that you're special, that you're exempt from the normal rules of human contact. But that's not special, it's . . . empty.' For the first time she doesn't seem to be trying to score points; she sounds genuinely bemused.

My ears start ringing and I want to turn on the stereo, put on the hardest of hard rock to drown out another voice that's repeating: *I can see through you. You're a charmer but there's nothing underneath.*

'I didn't ask for any of this,' I say, but it sounds even more shallow than I meant it to.

'And I didn't ask to be a single mother. Your daughter didn't ask for a brain tumour. But we muddle through.'

'Casey's a credit to you.'

'She's her own person. A survivor. And I'm scared you're going to hurt her, because I *know* she wants more than four weeks of fancy meals and shopping trips. But she'll survive, and get stronger as a result, just like I did. That's what living is about.'

'I'd rather avoid the pain.'

Angelica sighs. 'I almost feel sorry for you. Don't you get lonely up here in your penthouse, looking down on the little people and their messy little lives?'

Before I can answer, behind us the door opens and Casey strikes a pose. 'Ta-dah!'

She's wearing bright-yellow dungarees, a funky headscarf around her wig and a pair of copycat Converses the same blue as mine. She reminds me of the women in wartime posters, doing their bit. She breaks my heart – which would surprise Angelica, who doesn't believe I have one.

'You look awesome!' I say, and Casey beams back at me.

Is that another mistake? It felt natural to pay her a compliment. But what if every kind word makes it even harder when August comes and we go our separate ways?

I know I've fucked up my past. I do *not* want to fuck up *her* future.

On the quay Casey falls into the same walking rhythm as me, but her eyes dart everywhere, hungry, taking in the late-afternoon mayhem.

The little people and their messy little lives . . .

'Can I ask you a question?' she says, as I toss a couple of quid into a busker's guitar case.

'Yeah. Anything.' *Shit.*

'Are you *sure* you don't have a girlfriend?'

Of all the questions she could have asked, this is getting off lightly. 'Totally sure. Why?'

'Loads of girls are checking you out. You're . . . you're not ugly. You don't smell weird. And your flat's amazing. So what's the problem?'

We pass the shipping containers and she hesitates, as though she's expecting to go into one of the pop-up restaurants on this side of the water. I hope I've picked a place she'll like.

'There's no problem. I've had girlfriends. But nothing serious.'

'Don't you want to get married?'

'Ha. My friends are always on at me about that. No. I like my own company.'

'What about kids? Most people your age want kids.'

'I've got you, haven't I?'

I see Casey's cheeks colour and her eyes sparkle, reflecting the shimmering water. Is that another false hope I've given her?

'Don't you miss having a big family?' she says. 'I've always wanted one.'

I remember how disappointed she looked when I chatted to her on FaceTime and had to tell her there was only me: no grandparents, no cousins or uncles or aunts. And how quickly she switched to sympathizing with me because I'd lost both parents.

'I prefer friends, because they're the family you get to choose,' I say.

We cross Prince Street Bridge and walk past the Arnolfini. Casey gazes at the skateboarders over on the other side, kids her age doing amazing stunts that make me worry about broken bones. *Have I ever worried about broken bones before?*

She wants to watch, but we're running behind, and I have a hunch that Angelica will go nuclear if I keep her out too late. We cross Pero's Bridge, and Casey runs her fingers along the padlocks bolted to the sides.

'What are these for?'

'I think they're meant to symbolize love. The council regularly has to cut through them to stop the bridge from getting overloaded.'

Casey pulls a face. 'That's awful. What if it jinxes the couples who left them?'

I'm about to say something about humans being more than capable of jinxing themselves, but what do I know about love? 'I guess it's more about the symbol than the locks themselves.'

She nods, satisfied, and now she's touching the horn shapes on the centre of the bridge and taking a photo to send to her best friend. On this side, the vibe's more corporate. But there are still cool cafes, and I point to the Watershed, with the funky posters advertising French and Spanish films.

'It's like Paris. Or Barcelona,' she says.

'Great cities. Have you been?'

'No. I don't even have a passport.'

People drink and smoke and vape at outdoor tables and I hope the smell doesn't linger on her clothes. I stop at the place I've chosen. You can't miss it, thanks to the huge glowing parrot that's perched outside.

'This is us,' I say.

Her face falls, which isn't quite the reaction I was hoping for. 'We're eating *here*?'

I try to ignore the disappointment in her voice. 'Yup.'

I give my name to the server – *Siobhan*, her name badge says – and she leads us past a bunch of families. *Families.* Is that what Casey and I are? Our table is laid with paper mats for colouring in. I scrutinize everything through Angelica's eyes and imagine the crayons are crawling with deadly germs.

Siobhan hands Casey a kids' menu and gives me a slow, sexy smile as she passes me an adult one. I *was* getting checked out all the time as we walked here. Who knew a kid could make you hotter?

Unrelentingly upbeat music and rainforest sound effects blare out of speakers hidden behind plastic trees. Creepy primates hang from the ceiling and their dead eyes make me feel I'm dying inside, too.

'Hello?' Casey says loudly to Siobhan. 'Sorry to be awkward, but I'm not a child. I am nearly thirteen and, tragically, a brain tumour has stopped me growing properly. So can I have an adult menu, please?'

Ouch.

37

Siobhan flinches like a startled wildebeest. 'Oh. Oh no, of course, so sorry.'

I'd usually smooth over any awkwardness with a funny comment, but I'm not sure that's what Casey wants. Instead I check my menu: it's all terrible puns and ethically sourced quinoa and avocado.

'One of your regular places, is it?' Casey asks.

'Not exactly. I asked friends with kids for recommendations.'

'No shit.' She's testing me, seeing if I will tell her off for swearing.

'Seen anything you fancy?'

She drops the menu on the table. 'No. The food here is rank, anyway. There's a branch ten miles away from me, in the retail park. We went there for my best friend's ninth birthday. The waiters sang to her and then we all had a go at the chocolate fountain and four kids threw up.'

'OK, right. I can see why that would tend to put you off the menu.'

She sighs. 'Plus, you're meant to be into music, so how can you bear it? The playlist is *literally* torture and it's making my head throb. I want to go home.'

Head-throbbing doesn't sound good. *Is it the music or something more sinister?* I don't have any idea what to do if she collapses. 'Are you ill, Casey?'

'Don't panic. I'm not about to die on you in a plastic rainforest.'

'Casey—'

'I'm fine. I just don't want to stay *here*.'

'But you need to eat.'

'Mum got some shopping in. I can have beans on toast.'

As I stand up, Siobhan is heading our way, her *what can I get for you?* smile faltering. My stomach growls – I hadn't realized I was hungry – but the noise blends in with the soundtrack of angry silverbacks. I apologize to Siobhan and she gives me a wink that says: *That's kids for you.*

'I messed that up, didn't I?' I say once we get back outside. Drinkers and couples skirt past us, and Casey refuses to look at me. 'But you could cut me some slack maybe? I don't know you yet, and I want you to enjoy being here. So how about you tell me the kind of places you'd like to go and I will sort it.'

'Stop pretending,' she says.

'What do you mean?'

She tuts – exactly like her mother does – and steps back onto the bridge, ignoring the locks this time.

'Casey, wait.' I catch her up. 'Tell me what's the matter.'

'Like you care.'

'I do care.'

'You feel sorry for the poor brain-tumour girl. So does everyone. It's not the same as caring for me as an actual person.'

'Casey, I like you a lot.'

'You don't even know me. We're not in some ancient Hugh Grant movie where we do "fun stuff together" and you get to feel better about yourself, and when I'm gone, you can tell your mates or your secret girlfriend how you gave your secret daughter the best month of her life.'

'That's not what this is about.'

That's exactly what it's about.

'Good. Because why would I want to spend time with some random sperm donor? In fact it'd be better if you *had* been a sperm donor.'

'I get why you're angry with me. But I want to make your treatment as comfortable as possible.'

'Yeah? You haven't even bothered to come to the hospital with me.'

'I'm at work when you're having treatment.'

39

'Whatever.'

'Do you *want* me to come to the hospital with you, Casey?' The ringing in my ears gets louder as I think about what it would involve.

She scratches her head. She must be so hot in that bloody wig. 'That's not the point. The point is whether *you* want to. And you don't. I wish now that we'd gone to London for my treatment instead.' She's out of breath, and I'm scared she's making herself sicker. No. That *I'm* making her sicker.

'Why *did* you choose Bristol over having your treatment in London, if you didn't want to meet me?' I put my hand on her arm to slow her down.

She turns and that's when I can see her eyes are magnified by tears. 'You want the truth?'

'Yes.' But I brace myself.

'Because we needed someone as backup. Mum's been my mother *and* my father for so long and she does the best job. She's amazing. But she's struggled since they said my tumour was growing again. She hates cities, and having to live in a strange place for a whole month is her worst nightmare. I was worried it'd be too much for her.'

A strange place? So Angelica hasn't told her anything about living here. 'And that's the real reason you contacted me?'

She shrugs. It's bad enough that this kid – *my* kid – is having to cope with a tumour. But it's so much worse that she feels so responsible for her mother. In the sunshine Casey is so much like the Angelica I saw thirteen summers ago at Glastonbury, and I understand how much better her life would have been if she'd never met *me*.

And I also realize why Angelica had such a go at me earlier, because my clumsy attempt to 'do the right thing' might make it worse for all of us.

'Do you think it *is* helping your mum, staying with me? You could still swap to the hospital accommodation. Whatever you both want, it's cool.'

Am I thinking this for their sake or because it'd make my life easier if they left, so I wouldn't be reminded of my failings?

'Nothing is cool. Stop using that word. My brain tumour isn't cool, it's not cool that my mum's mental health is bad, and you're not cool if your idea of a big treat is that stupid little kids' restaurant!'

There's nothing I dare say in reply, but I stay close because the Harbourside pulses with people and I can't risk losing her. We cross the other bridge and I bet it'll make Angelica's night when we come back so soon. I can't even care for my daughter for a single hour without upsetting her.

The smell from Cantina Rio on the roof of the shipping containers wafts towards me: barbecued meats, deep-fried bean patties, little rolls with melted-cheese centres. My mouth starts to water.

Casey has noticed it too.

'Have you ever tried Brazilian food?'

She scoffs. 'Not unless you count the rainforest restaurant.'

'Would you like to? See the place up there – it's one of my favourite places to eat.' I point towards the roof and her eyes widen, despite her scowl.

'What is Brazilian food like?'

'*Delicious*. A lot of meat and deep-fried snacks. Your mum wouldn't approve and they might be fully booked. But . . . they know me. I could ask.'

It's *her* belly that rumbles this time. 'We still could tell Mum we ate vegan, couldn't we?'

This is a test. Would Vijay advise lying to the woman who has raised my daughter single-handedly?

No way. The fact I'm even considering it proves I've learned nothing.

But right now this isn't about what Angelica or I think Casey ought to do. It's about the hopes and dreams of a bright, confused kid who is in a new city, surrounded by possibility. She deserves to forget her tumour and her treatment and this whole messy situation, and be happy right now.

'We can decide what to say later. Let me see if they can give us a table – you get an even better view from the rooftop.'

Chapter 7: Gemma

Wednesday 4 July

After the still, sanitized air of the fertility clinic, the world outside smells of summer and the sky is an unbroken blue. In another life I'd be heading to the Observatory, where I'd lie down next to Andrew on the hot grass, drunk on love and sunshine and the English sparkling wine he always packed for a picnic.

But that's not how I roll these days. I drink elderflower cordial or – if I want to live on the edge – I get my kicks from kombucha.

And when I lie on the Downs, it's with Bear at my side. That idea cheers me up a bit, so I walk faster, taking the shortcut that'll bring me out on the other side of the uni campus. Despite my shocking sense of direction, I've been here so often I know the terrain as well as any junior doctor or PhD student.

My phone rings: Dad, wanting an update after my appointment. He loves understanding how things work, whether it's a circuit board or my uterus. There's no such thing as TMI in his world.

'So it's the same plan as last time?' he asks, after I've told him what happened.

'Yup. I've been given hormones to take, but it's a natural cycle, so the less they mess with it, the better.'

'Right, right. I suppose they are the experts,' he says, though I can hear the doubt in his voice.

'It wasn't their fault last time.'

'No. But you *were* pregnant. I can't help but think that if they'd given you the right drug or something, you might have *stayed* pregnant.'

'Dad. We talked about this. It was a chemical pre—' I'm too superstitious to say the P-word out loud, 'a chemical result. Not a real positive. There was no other way it could have ended. And the time before that was the luck of the draw.'

He sighs. 'I'm sure you're right. But I so want you to get what you want.'

My throat tightens and I don't trust myself to say any more. 'I know. Got to go now, but I'll see you tomorrow.'

I slip the phone into my pocket. *Tomorrow.* How many hours are there to fill between now and then? I'm in limbo till the end of the month. What I *should* do is focus on work. The deadline for the bank commission samples is Monday, so I should ditch the Downs walk and get back to my drawing board.

I step up my pace, determined to *stay* determined.

Only to run right into the back of a crocodile.

'Keep moving, Year One. That means you too, Kyle Bannister.'

This crocodile consists of at least twenty children and five adults, carrying a neon rainbow of backpacks and swimming bags. They must have been to the university pool – the air around them smells of chlorine and fruit juice.

There's no way I can squeeze past and no point turning back, as I'm more than halfway along the cut-through now.

Anyway I don't *want* to go back because these children are *adorable*. Even Kyle Bannister, who turns round to pull a grotesque face at me, fingers stretching his mouth wide, nose wrinkled up so his join-the-dot freckles merge.

When I pull a face back at him, Kyle laughs so hard that I join in.

Their noises envelop me: giggles, shrieks, sandals slapping against paving stones. The kids are gloriously dishevelled, socks wonky, damp patches leaking through their school shirts.

And now I'm imagining the child Andrew and I might make together. A chatterbox daughter, like the girl whose voice rises above all the others, sharing every thought that pops into her head, asking why dolphins are shiny, why soft-play is stinky and why beans on toast are *the most boring food in the galaxy*. Or a son like the tallest boy at the head of the line: Andrew would have taught him chess and Scrabble and tag rugby.

Any child would be a gift. But the journey from the lab freezers holding our last two embryos to these earthbound individuals seems as hazardous as a trip to Mars.

I hear a tut, a long sigh, another tut. Somebody behind me.

I turn, expecting a grumpy old man, but instead—
YOU.

I'm sure I've never seen this man before – I've a good memory for people, and I'd certainly remember him – but the recognition is instant.

The sounds and smells of the kids fade until all I'm aware of is me and this man, whose face is criss-crossed with stress. Despite the frown, it's a breathtaking face.

He hasn't noticed *me* at all.

I try to look away, utterly discombobulated. He is extra-ordinary: movie-star beautiful, with the features of a troubled hero.

Right now, though, he's not being very heroic. He's scowling as he tries to dodge past Kyle and co, before realizing it's a lost cause.

'I bet you didn't expect this kind of traffic jam,' I say. It's meant to be a joke, but it sounds deeply unfunny as soon as it's out of my mouth.

'I'm so bloody late. It's a nightmare.'

His strained voice doesn't match his laid-back clothes: fancy trainers, loose jeans, an artfully washed-out *Primal Scream* T-shirt. Already I'm doing my Gemma thing of making up stories for him: he's a bank robber on his way to a heist. No, a tech billionaire running late for a make-or-break meeting to sell his business to the Chinese. Or a dad-to-be missing his wife's labour?

For many reasons, that one hurts.

'We won't have to wait much longer. But you can't hurry crocodiles.'

He looks at me properly, his lips – full, dark – curled downwards with irritation. But now his pale eyes are widening, as if *he* recognizes me too. Perhaps I was wrong and we *have* met before. Why else would those grey-violet eyes be so familiar?

'Crocodiles?'

'That's what the teachers called it when they lined us up like this. Not sure why. Though children can get snappy.'

He smiles, but only to be polite, and takes out his phone, peering at a map on the screen, then back up at the surroundings. Exhales in frustration.

'Where are you trying to get to? I know the campus quite well.'

'Oncology. I left loads of time, but it's like a maze round here.'

Oncology.

46

One of the kids has started singing – a K-pop tune – and her classmates are joining in. I try to focus on that, not on this man and whatever his story might be. It's none of my business.

Yet I can't help myself. Is he a patient? He still looks well: lithe, feline, with skin the colour of wet sand. But if he doesn't know where he's going, it must be a first appointment. Perhaps they've caught it in time.

'Don't panic.' I make my voice as reassuring as possible. 'The unit's very close. Once we get to the end of here, it's two minutes away, maximum.'

'But I should have been there ten minutes ago.'

'I volunteer at the unit, so I'm happy to show you the way. Try not to worry, it's better for your treatment if you're in a calm state of mind.'

So much for not getting involved.

'I'm not the patient.'

'Ah. Well, sometimes that's even harder.'

Ahead of us the children reach the end of the path, and the teaching assistant at the back smiles a thank-you at us. It's sunnier now we're out of the alleyway, but the man's entire face seems to be in shadow.

'I shouldn't have told her I'd go. I don't think I can. Seriously, I'm not cut out for this—' He's panicking, the words getting faster and his breathing shallower. I take a step towards him, worried he's about to faint.

'OK, listen to me. The first thing to do is breathe. Do it with me. A deep breath in . . . hold it . . . and now a nice, slow breath out. And again. In . . . hold . . . out.'

He does as he's told and his grey skin turns pinker.

It's only as my own heart slows that I realize how fast it was beating. 'Better?' I ask and he nods. 'You know it's not that unusual,' I say gently.

47

'What isn't?'

'Being scared of hospitals.'

His eyes focus on mine. 'How did you know?'

'I'm good at reading people. But the unit is amazing.' We're walking now, my reassurance distracting him enough to keep moving. 'And the reason I understand is not only because I'm a volunteer. I've been in your shoes. Supported someone who was having treatment.'

'For cancer or . . . ?'

'Cancer, yes. That's how I know how tough it can be for everyone involved. But you're showing up, and that's what matters.'

We're almost at the hospital entrance, but he's still holding back. I rack my brains. What do I wish someone had told Andrew and me at the beginning?

'The other thing is . . . when you're supporting someone, there are times when *they're* the strong one and you're vulnerable.'

'She's way stronger than I am. She's beyond brave.'

She? His wife? His mother? 'No one can be brave all the time. If you tell her you're scared, it could free her up to admit she is too. Honesty will get you through this.'

'Honesty is overrated.'

I hear a sharpness in his voice, maybe even self-loathing. 'Well, you've been pretty honest with me just now and it seems to have helped. Listen, I don't know anything about you. I don't even know your name.'

'Dan.'

'OK, Dan. I'm Gemma. So we only met minutes ago, but it's completely clear to me how much you want to do this. To be there for this person you care about, so they understand they're not alone.'

Dan stares at me, like he's about to run. I wouldn't blame

48

him. First I gawp at him like a love-struck teenager, next I'm giving him an impromptu TED Talk. It must be the heat, or perhaps the artificial hormones I've started taking.

'I'm way too late,' he says.

'Only a couple of minutes.'

'No. I'm twelve *years* too late.'

The drama beckons me again. Part of it is nosiness. But also: *I don't want to let him go before I know where I can find him again.*

Where did that thought come from? OK, I need to move on before I do something weird. Say goodbye *now*, then walk away.

'Trust me. It's never too late to be there for somebody.' That wasn't what I was expecting to say. 'I could come in with you, Dan, if it'd help?' Neither was that.

Dan turns to look at the unit and, as he does so, those incredible eyes light up and his face softens into the most astonishing smile. 'She waited. She's still there.' He turns back to me and the intensity of his gaze makes my pulse race again. 'Thank you, Gemma, for being kind.'

'I'm happy I could help.' I peer through the glazed doors into the lobby, curious to see the woman this amazing man cares about so deeply.

And instantly all the warmth drains away.

The woman he's meeting isn't a woman at all.

It's Casey. The new patient at hospital school, the scared girl with the grey-violet eyes.

The child whose father never wanted to know her, until now.

49

Chapter 8: Dan

Casey looks tiny, dwarfed by this enormous building.

I rush towards the glass doors. She's had to hang around on her own and I don't want her to wait a second longer.

'Hey! Casey!'

She looks up and grins and I wonder who is behind me. No one. It's *me* she's grinning at.

She holds up her hand for a high five. But I don't want to high-five. I want to *hug* her. As I approach, my arms wide, her eyes are wary and I almost chicken out, but I whisper, 'Is it OK for me to do this?' and Casey nods, and for the first time since we met on Sunday, I am hugging my daughter. Her hair – no, her wig – smells of baby shampoo and her arms only just reach around my back, but she holds on tight. 'Is this awkward?' I check.

'A bit. But nice too. Though I'm getting cramp in my leg, so I'm going to let go now.'

When we part, I spot that woman – Gemma – staring through the window. I smile, but she doesn't smile back.

'I can't believe you came!' Casey says, but then she puts her hand to her mouth. 'Is Mum OK? Has something bad happened?'

'No, everything is fine. After what you said yesterday about me not coming here, I asked your mum if I could come instead of her. But then I got lost.'

Casey is waiting for me to explain how I got lost in my home city, or why I didn't leave enough time. I need a good excuse . . .

Gemma's still staring at me through the glass. I never normally tell people the truth, but when I risked telling her, it *helped*. So could I try the same with Casey?

'OK, the thing is, I'm nervous about hospitals. So when I said before that I couldn't come during the day because of work, it was an excuse. I'm sorry. I know it sounds wimpy.'

Casey seems to be weighing it up. 'Not really. Loads of people are phobic about hospitals, especially *old* people.'

'Oh. Right.'

'But you shouldn't worry. I don't like some of my *actual* treatments, but everyone here is so nice.'

The matter-of-fact way she talks makes me speechless. When I look back up, Gemma has gone.

'I could give you a tour,' Casey suggests. 'Things are never as scary in real life as you think they're going to be.'

Did you make her this brave, Angelica, or was she born this way?

'That could be good,' I say, even though my head's pounding and my ears are buzzing already.

'So this is the newest hospital in the whole country, which is why it's so cool! We're in the atrium – and that's the coffee cart, which you have to pay for. You can get free tea and coffee in the patient lounges, but me and Mum have worked out that the cappuccinos from the cart taste much nicer.'

'OK.'

'Out there is the garden area, which is good when you want fresh air if you're waiting for treatment or a scan. And up there,' she points at the glass roof, 'that's a sculpture they had specially made for the new unit. Can you tell what it is?'

'Those balls are like planets, so is it the solar system?'

51

Casey shakes her head patiently. 'No. It shows how proton-beam therapy works. So that's a hydrogen atom, and you see the sparkling thing in the middle? That's the proton, which they fire at top speed at the tumour in my head – hopefully missing my actual brain. Like a bolt of lightning that only hits the bit that needs to be destroyed?'

'Wow.'

'They have a thing called a cyclotron in the basement and I'm one of the first kids in the country to get treatment here. You used to have to go to Florida. Some of the kids I met in Birmingham went and were treated like VIPs. Got taken to Universal Studios and SeaWorld and everything.'

'Maybe, when this is all over, your mum can take you.' I remember what Casey said last night about not having a passport. 'Or there's a pier at Weston-super-Mare. They don't have rollercoasters, but there are dodgems and slot machines.'

Casey is unimpressed. 'Huh. After the rainforest restaurant disaster, I'm not wild about trying another of your recommendations.'

'Sorry.'

She grins. 'Joking. I love piers, but we live miles from the seaside.'

'I'll take you in the jeep one day.'

'Really?'

I nod. 'It's a promise.' One I can keep.

'Shall I show you the lounge now, and my school?'

'You have to go to school?'

She pulls a face. 'It's totally unfair, right? But I only do a few hours each day, because I get tired otherwise.'

I follow her into the main part of the hospital. The buzzing's getting so loud now I can barely hear what Casey is saying to me.

I close my eyes, trying to block it out. Instead I hear someone else's voice, one I know can't be real:

'Come on, kiddo. Chin up; the sooner we get you seen, the sooner we can get home. We're missing Noel's House Party.'

This woman sitting opposite us is knitting super-fast, even though her nose is bleeding onto the yellow wool. Dad's tried to talk the receptionist into letting us jump the queue but, for once, the charm's failed.

On the plastic chair we've lined up snacks: Hula Hoops and Toffee Crisps and Dr Pepper, because Dad knows this trick that lets you get six items from the vending machine even though you paid for one.

It's past midnight and I doze against my dad's shoulder and I can smell Extra Strong Mints in his jacket pocket. Dad's biggest fear is bad breath, because you only get one chance to make a first impression.

'Darryl Lennox?'

Everything gets scarier after they take me through. Tests and phone calls and a procession of frowning doctors. And at the end of it, the lady doctor says, 'We'd like to keep him in overnight', even though it's already morning.

'He's not seriously ill, though, is he? Nothing a giant bar of Dairy Milk won't fix?' Dad says.

The lady doctor smiles, but one half of her mouth doesn't turn up. 'Until we diagnose the problem we can't be sure, but we'll have answers for you soon.'

The ward's so noisy with other kids crying or coughing, and there are more doctors and still no one gets what's wrong with me. And when Nadia finishes her shift and comes in, she bursts into tears.

'Why didn't you say you were so ill, Darryl?' Like I've done it on purpose.

53

'*I only fainted once. And I feel OK now. Can we go?*'

'*Not till they make you better.*'

'You OK?' Casey stands close to me, her face full of concern.

'Sorry.' My head pounds and I try to breathe away my panic, like that Gemma woman suggested. But it's not working this time.

'Have you had enough for today? You've gone pale and weird.'

The last thing Casey needs is to worry about me. 'You're right. Let's finish the tour next time I pick you up,' I say. 'Plus it's lunchtime. Why don't I take you to my favourite cafe and you can tell me all about your treatment.'

'Ugh, it's boring enough having a tumour, without having to talk about it the entire time.'

'OK, we'll talk about anything *but* the tumour. Like all the places you could go in the next three and a half weeks.'

'This favourite cafe doesn't have inflatable parrots, does it?'

I shake my head. 'No kids' menu, either. And definitely no chocolate fountain.'

'Bring it *on.*'

Once I'm out of the hospital, the buzzing stops, just like that.

'I need to ask you something,' Casey says as we walk.

'Sure.' My jaw tightens. Did I give something away while I was freaking out back there?'

'What can I call you? Not Dad – that'd be weird, and Mum would hate it.'

I smile. 'My friends call me Dan or Danny or Lennon or Lenny.'

She shakes her head. 'Too weird.' We turn onto Christmas Steps and she skips down so fast it makes *me* dizzy. At the bottom she dances to music coming out of a hair salon and

I'm surprised by how elegant she is, as her mum has two left feet.

'Do you have a middle name?'

'No.'

'So you're DL. Daniel Lennon. DL sounds mega-cool. Will you hear me if I call you DL?'

'Hear you?'

'Earlier, when you were freaking out, I thought you were going to collapse and I couldn't seem to get you to hear me.'

So the real reason she wants to give me a name is because she feels she needs to care for me, as well as her mum. I want to make things easier, not have Casey getting stressed out about me too. I must try harder.

'DL it is. I can get used to that.'

After taking her to BayCaff – where she eats a huge BLT, plus half of mine – we go back to the penthouse, which stinks of bleach. Angelica's been cleaning again. She scrutinizes Casey, like she's terrified even a couple of hours alone with me could have done irreparable damage.

'How was your day, sweetie?' she asks.

'Boring. But good boring. I'm tired now.'

'What do you want for your tea?'

'We had sandwiches at the cafe. I don't think I'll want much tonight.'

'What kind of sandwiches?'

'Vegan ones.'

I turn away, so Angelica doesn't see me smile. That was *not* vegan bacon we had.

'OK, well, have a shower to get rid of the hospital.'

'Do I *have* to?'

Casey pulls a face at me behind her mother's back and I'm about to pull one back. But Angelica looks so weary.

These small battles must be tough when you always have to face them alone.

'Your mum's right, Casey.'

She tuts. 'You two are ganging up on me now?' But she trudges off towards the shower room anyway.

Angelica's eyes meet mine. 'Wow. Coming over the responsible parent? Whatever next.'

I don't respond. 'Listen, I've got some work to do tonight, so I'll go in my room so you can watch TV, hang out together. I'll see you tomorrow.'

'Exhausting, is it? Spending time with Casey.'

Don't rise to the bait. 'She wanted me to go to the hospital, which means I had to leave work early. I just need to do some catching up.'

'Yes, Dan, you picked her up from the hospital – once. But imagine doing it day in, day out. Or plaiting her hair before brain surgery, so it won't be in the way of the incision, and trying not to let her feel your hands are shaking,' she says. 'Or comforting her when she gets a message to say her friend from the unit has died. Or going to the scans and crossing everything that nothing will have changed, and then seeing in their faces when it's bad news. Or—'

'OK, Angelica, I understand what you've been through.'

'No, you don't. No one does.'

I hear a plea in her voice: to be comforted? To have someone else sharing the burden? Despite all my doubts about the future, I desperately want her to feel less alone. 'Angelica . . .' But her expression could still sour milk. 'Like I said, I've got work to do.'

It's hot in the bedroom, and a dozen emails appear when I start up my laptop.

I'm almost too tired to deal with them. I guess it's been

a full-on day. Deciding to go to the hospital to surprise Casey. Freaking out. Meeting that random woman.

Gemma.

When I close my eyes, I can see her face: the yellow-green eyes, like the sun on the sea. The thick, dark hair curling where it touches her shoulders. Her voice, kind but determined, a soft Somerset burr just audible. The shape of her, a proper hourglass.

Huh. Can't believe that when I was meant to be making the most minimal effort as a dad, I was checking out some pretty stranger in an alleyway.

Except . . .

That's not the whole story. I *did* make it to the hospital in time – or nearly, anyway. And I hugged Casey, and even told her the truth about the hospital scaring me, because hourglass woman had suggested it.

I replay it in my mind. The cloud of rose perfume, the smile, the incomprehensible jokes about crocodiles.

Hang on. Did she do a number on me? It didn't matter that I failed to get her croc joke. She was trying to chill me out, to distract me. Dad used that technique all the time, and I use it too sometimes. *I'm* the charmer, never the 'mark'. The reversal unsettles me, big time.

I turn back to the emails, motoring through them, until I get to an invitation from one of our trade contacts to a barbecue on Saturday. Angelica and Casey are going home for the weekend, so it's my chance to be selfish for a couple of days again, have a few beers and come home to a place that isn't filled with Angelica's simmering resentment.

Exactly what I need after this endless week of playing nice.

Chapter 9: Gemma

Thursday 5 July

I wake in a filthy mood and try to get out of today's game, but Dad's having none of it.

Bear stays at home because last time he stole all the balls. I drive towards my home town with the Mini's roof down, but even the wind in my hair fails to blow away my terrible mood. When a lorry driver cuts me up, I give him both barrels and almost cause a road-rage incident.

Dad's waiting, with the putters ready, and he pulls me into a massive hug when I get out of the car.

'Never seen the place this empty,' I say.

'I reckon they're all at the new pirate-ship course they've built on the front,' my father says. 'People are so disloyal these days.'

We've been coming here to play crazy golf since the putters were taller than I was, and we're both *terrible*. Mum and Laura can't understand why Dad and I love it so much, but our incompetence means we're usually laughing within seconds of reaching the second hole, marked by a windmill with real sails that creak whenever a breeze catches them.

But today our easy banter is beyond me.

'You seem out of sorts, Little Gemster?' Dad asks, deliberately focusing on the ball and his next stroke, rather than making eye contact with me.

'It's the treatment, that's all. The idea of going through it again, with no guarantees.'

It's a half-truth. Because the treatment *is* getting me down. But I've been fed up with the entire world since leaving the oncology unit yesterday. Whatever I do – housework, sketches, throwing the ball for Bear – my mind keeps drifting back to that girl and her terrible dad.

'Ah.' Dad strikes the ball and it goes off at a strange angle. He tuts to himself. 'So how about you start planning for things *after* the waiting is over? A nice holiday with Bear in a dog-friendly B&B? Or a spa day?'

'Since when have I been into spa days?'

He shrugs. 'Only a suggestion.'

'How can I plan anything when I don't know if I'll be – well, you know, if the treatment's going to work? If it doesn't, I might want to go bungee jumping or abseiling or something.'

'Since when have you been into adventure sports?'

I do smile now. 'Fair point.' I line up the ball, but the wind blows it along the perishing green felt.

'Gem, if you're not sure the timing's right, you could wait a month or two,' Dad says. 'No harm postponing for a bit.'

'Did Mum tell you to say that?' She's never been completely onside with the embryo transfer. Andrew's mother, Isabel, is the only person who supported the idea 100 per cent.

'No.' But he won't look at me.

'Tell the truth, Dad.'

'Perhaps she *was* hoping you might meet someone while you were taking a break from the treatment.'

From nowhere, the blood rushes to my head again. 'Oh yeah, and get knocked up the normal way? She'd rather I had a baby from a one-night stand than with someone I love?'

'Loved,' my dad says gently.

'Love,' I insist. 'Just because he's not here any more doesn't mean I love him any less.'

We move to the next hole: a rusty barrel. We never, ever get the ball inside and always run out of patience and end up cheating.

'It's hard for her to understand, I guess. I'm the same. I think – *we* think – that Andrew would have wanted you to meet someone else.'

'No. What Andrew wanted was to stay healthy and to have a family with me. Do you and Mum think I *want* this? Knowing that, if I beat the odds and it works, our kid won't meet the man who would have been the best dad ever?' The little flame that's been burning since I met Casey on Monday, and learned how she'd been ignored by her father, erupts into a full-blown inferno, and letting it out is like breathing fire. 'And yet the world's full of stupid, selfish men – and women too, but mainly men – who have children without giving a toss. Who don't realize what an incredible thing it is to make a new human, to be *with* them as they grow up.'

I am not thinking of men, I am thinking of *one* man. Of Dan, the man with the beautiful face and the hypnotic eyes, and the morals of a shitbag. The man I thought I recognized because I'd remembered the sad eyes of his daughter on the first day of cancer treatment. The man I went out of my way to help.

The man who kept me awake last night as I worked out what I'd have said to him if I had guessed who he was and what he'd done.

'Sweetheart—' Dad says, but I don't want to hear it.

I whack the ball with my putter and, by some fluke, it goes right into the hole in the barrel.

'Storming shot, Gemma. You need to let rip more often,

it's good for your game.' He tries the shot and misses spectacularly. As he picks up the ball to try again, he speaks softly. 'Not all men are terrible. And we want you to meet one of the good ones, whatever happens with the treatment.'

'I can't face all of that drama, to end up with someone who'll always be second best to Andrew.'

'Not second best. Different.'

'Right. Different,' I say bluntly. 'Let's see. Andrew was kind and open-hearted and trustworthy, so I should try someone mean and cynical and scheming?'

'Now you're being awkward, Gem – that's obviously not what I mean.'

He tries the shot again and, when he misses, he picks the ball up and pops it into the hole in the barrel and we hear the roll before it appears on the other side. Am I being awkward? I understand what Dad was trying to say – but the idea of meeting someone who isn't Andrew doesn't appeal to me in the slightest; I only want my husband, and how he made me feel.

But as I walk with Dad to the next hole, the thought morphs into something unexpected: into how I felt yesterday when I saw Dan. Now I understand: his *face* wasn't familiar, but the feelings were. Excitement. Possibility. And something much more basic. *Desire.*

Even as the shock of it hits me, my body is tingling, remembering. I hadn't met Dan before, but the connection was real. *Lust at first sight.*

What kind of craziness is this? I'd come from the fertility clinic where, in two weeks, they'll try everything to make me pregnant. Why now? I haven't been ambushed by my hormones since I was a teenager.

Unless it's not *my* hormones that are causing the trouble, but the ones I've been taking to prepare my body for the transfer. I could ask Laura if that happened to her.

'. . . and the one thing I know about you, Gemma, is you're a survivor,' my dad is saying. 'Whatever happens this time, you'll come through it.'

'Maybe I don't want to *have* to be a survivor. Maybe I'm allowed to want everything to go OK – for people to be what they seem, for everyone to leave me alone.' I stop because I'm starting to sound like a child on the verge of an *it's not fair* tantrum.

He sniffs and I realize I've hurt him.

'Sorry, Dad. It's nobody's fault. I need to get through July and then at least we'll know what's what.'

When I get home – I won by a whisker, though Dad might have let that happen – Bear gives me an extra-enthusiastic greeting. Maybe I'm projecting my own emotions onto him, but his dark eyes seem worried.

'It's OK, Bear. I'm OK.'

I make myself a herbal tea and go back to working on the samples, which I've got to send to my agent by Monday. The commission would pay well: the client is a bank launching savings products for young families, and they want ink-and-wash images that portray different children as they grow and learn.

I couldn't sleep last night, so I got up and started a new sketch, loosely based on Kyle, the naughty boy at the back of the queue of swimmers. Often when I work to combat insomnia the results are pretty crap, but this sketch captures the dynamism of his personality, his energy and his boldness.

But it's not Kyle's face.

It's Dan's.

What the hell is *that* about? I tear off the page – that is not going in the portfolio.

Right now I could easily rest my head on the drawing

board and fall asleep. If an easy day like this exhausts me, how would I manage with a baby?

When I sit down on the sofa, Bear follows straight away, jumping up and arranging himself so his head rests on the velvet cushion.

The Amazing Book of Us is on the coffee table shelf, where I left it on Monday. I'm not in the mood for reading, but I pick it up and let my fingers trace the cover image: a rough charcoal-and-pastel drawing of two parents, one child and a dog, all facing away. Of course we wanted a bigger family, but had agreed that showing more than one child felt like tempting fate.

Andrew worked on it for ages before showing it to me – 'There's a bloody good reason I haven't drawn anything since primary school.'

It's true that the kid seems taller than the adults, and the animal trotting next to our future family has the proportions of a hairy mammoth. But when I saw Bear at the rescue centre, he was Andrew's drawing brought to life: the chaos of his tangled coat, the pent-up energy of his chunky limbs. I'd actually gone there to adopt Kardashian, a fluffy Persian cat I'd seen online. She needed a home, I needed another soul in my flat. Mission accomplished.

Except that on the walk back to the office to finish the paperwork I saw one of the kennel staff chasing a young dog across the rainy pebbles and it was love at first sight. The rescue staff warned me he'd already been returned by two families, that he wasn't suitable for an inexperienced owner, that he'd been nicknamed Teddy Bear the Terrible and the Border Terrorist.

I *did* talk them into letting me adopt him – and for the first three months after he came to me, I wished I hadn't. He destroyed four skirting boards, nipped my feet with sharp teeth and picked fights with dogs twenty times his size. Everyone told me I should send him back, but I refused. I believed that, despite his 'difficult' past, he had the capacity to love. It'd just take time for him to trust me.

And now I wouldn't be without him.

If I can cope alone with an adolescent Bear, I am pretty sure I can cope with a baby.

I hug the book to me: it always gives me what I need, the closest thing I have to Andrew being at my side. We sprayed his drawing with fixative, to protect it from tiny fingers and thumbs we hoped might handle it hundreds of times.

So far, I'm the only reader. And if I want that to change, I *have* to keep going.

MUMMY AND DADDY WERE LITTLE ONCE, TOO: THE BEGINNING . . .

You'll find this hard to believe, but once upon a time Daddy and Mummy were littler than you are now. They grew up only twenty miles apart, but it took them a really long time to meet: almost thirty years. Even for grown-ups, thirty years is slow – but while we were waiting we made friends, went to school and learned to read, write, ride a bike, make toast, sing, dance and do jigsaws. The right person came along at the right time – even though sometimes we worried it might never happen! But it did, when we least expected it.

DADDY SAYS: One day you'll meet someone who'll change everything. So do your best to meet new people and travel to many different cities and lands. And do something daring every day. Because you never know what kind of enormous adventures are waiting for you around the next corner . . .

Chapter 10: Dan

Saturday 7 July

The barbecue starts at four, but I won't rock up till at least six. I'm never in the mood to make sober conversation over catering-sized vats of coleslaw.

Plus I'm enjoying lounging around the penthouse alone. Casey and Angelica left yesterday afternoon and, boy, does it feel good to be able to relax a bit and not worry that I'm about to make yet another stupid parenting mistake. The minute they were gone I opened all the doors and windows. Pollution? UV radiation? Bring it on!

Last night I played music, smoked weed, ordered pizza at 2 a.m. and only went to bed after the sun came up.

And yeah, if I'm delicate this morning, it's nothing coffee won't sort. Two double espressos fuel a quick tidy-up, getting rid of any signs that I don't live alone. I'm not *planning* to bring someone back, but you never know.

Everyone's mellow by the time I get to the party, in the garden of a Victorian semi south of the river. The host is the boss of a building company that often takes on our trainees, and I recognize one of my more recent 'graduates' hanging out at the end of the garden, flirting with friends of the boss's daughter. Good luck to him.

As I get myself a beer, someone taps me on the shoulder.

'This is *Dan the Man*!'

It takes me a few seconds to recognize the guy standing there, clutching a tiny baby to his chest.

'Arnie? Mate, it's good to see you,' I say, grinning. 'Is that yours or have you kidnapped it?'

Arnie is a nickname, earned from the impressive muscles sculpted in the prison gym. He laughs. 'A hundred per cent mine.' He beckons over a girl who looks so tired I'm surprised she's still standing. 'Ems, come over, this is Danny. From the workshop. Danny, meet my fiancée!'

Her smile transforms her face. 'Hello. So I've got *you* to thank.'

'What for?'

'I knew Craig before he went inside, and back then I wouldn't have trusted him with a house plant, never mind a baby.' She touches the baby's head and his eyes open wide.

Craig – yep, that's his real name, I remember now – nods goofily. 'Danny did a total number on me. God, I hated you at the time, but now I am all grown-up. An actual dad.'

'Suits you,' I say. It does; he's the proudest of new fathers. 'How old is he?'

'Two weeks and three days. And guess what his middle name is?'

'Arnie?' I say, and his fiancée looks puzzled.

Arnie – *Craig* – is blushing. 'It's Daniel.'

'You're kidding?'

'We registered his birth last week – he's Sammy Daniel Flanagan. I was planning to drop into the workshop to tell you and show him off. My dad's been all *Who the hell is Danny?* because we didn't use *his* name, but you were more use to me than he's ever been. Plus, who wants a kid's middle name to be *Wayne*?'

I'm bowled over. 'Wow. Mate, that's such an honour. I don't deserve it.'

'Er, you *so* do. Wanna take him?' Craig suggests and I take a step back.

'He seems happy where he is.'

'You got kids?' Ems asks.

I'm about to come out with my standard *No, I'm still a big kid myself*, but these two are ten years younger than I am. Plus, it feels like a bigger lie than it did a month ago. 'A daughter. Casey. She's twelve.'

Arnie raises his eyebrows. 'You kept *that* quiet. Got a picture?'

I should have, obviously. Every dad has a picture in his wallet or on his phone. 'No. New phone. Plus, me and her mum aren't together.'

'Bet that makes it extra special when she gets to spend time with her dad,' Ems says. 'The way Craig tells it, you're a natural, especially with *big* kids.'

The baby starts to grizzle and they both look panic-stricken and decide to go home. I slap Craig on the back and touch baby Sammy's head. It's warm and smooth, like a freshly laid egg.

All the children have gone now and I'm more relaxed, from the heat or the beer. Do I spot her first, or has she already been scoping me out? One minute the girl is on the other side of the garden and the next she's walking towards me.

She's my age, which I like. I used to go for the student types, because those girls had the same 'here for a good time, not a long time' attitude as me, but now I'm out of my twenties, that feels grubby.

'I'm Tegan and I'm so bored,' she announces.

'I'm Dan and I'm definitely not boring.'

Her laugh is sexy and her figure suits the vest top and boyfriend jeans she's wearing. She points over at a tight group of couples gathered around the bucket of iced beers. 'I'm escaping from the Bristol branch of the Smug Couples' Collective. You're not about to introduce me to your pregnant wife, are you?'

'No. You're safe with me. Where's your accent from?'

'Manchester. Well, Stockport, but you southerners have piss-poor geography, so let's keep it simple.'

'You're a long way from home. What do you make of Bristol?'

'Too many hills, too many vegans.'

I laugh. 'Harsh, but fair. Where have you been so far?'

'My cousin's back garden, here, one off-licence and the station. Which had a nice roof, but I'm not into trains.'

'Where I live – just over the river – it's a different world. Might even give Stockport a run for its money.'

'You offering to show me the bright lights?'

I hesitate. There's something so familiar – almost wearying – about this banter, like reliving a moment I've experienced a hundred times before.

What am I doing? This week has done my head in and I deserve some fun. 'We could walk it from here in twenty minutes.'

'Ah, but can I trust you, Dan?'

'Trust me to do what?'

She laughs again and reaches over to give me the briefest flirty but promising kiss. 'Let me check with my cousin that you're not *too* dangerous. If you pass the test, I may be back.'

'Tell her one of the other guests named his *baby* after me. Doesn't get much more respectable than that.'

* * *

Tegan agrees that the harbour is much more what she hoped Bristol might be like: we sit out on the terrace, and it's hard to imagine a sexier view.

'I mean, it's not a patch on Manchester, but this penthouse is impressive. How much did this set you back, moneybags?'

'It's not even mine. I'm borrowing it from a mate.'

'If you say so. He must be a *very* generous mate. Yeah. I can't afford to buy anything, either – I'm going to have to get help from the Bank of Mum and Dad.'

'Lucky you. I never even knew my mum, and I wish I'd never known my dad at all.'

What made me say that? Such a downer. I must be more drunk than I realize.

Tegan doesn't respond for a minute. 'Where's your loo?'

When she comes back she's all shiny and perky and I suspect she's done a line or two. Isn't it etiquette to offer to share? Not that I would have said yes.

She's talking faster about her plans to start her own consultancy business, but I've already forgotten what she consults in. Abruptly she realizes I haven't spoken for at least ten minutes, so she asks me what I do, and when I tell her she's even more excited, pumping me for festival stories – gossipy ones about artists she's heard of that she'll share with her mates back home.

Except I want to tell her *my* stories instead. The one about the lonely kid who started sneaking into gigs because the music drowned out the feelings of never belonging. Or the one about meeting a girl who was even lonelier than me and getting her pregnant during a storm at the rainiest Glastonbury in history . . .

When did I turn into a moody old bastard?

I change the music to my party playlist, upbeat sounds to shake myself out of my weird mood. Fatboy Slim comes on

70

and that works, because I need to be *RIGHT HERE, RIGHT NOW*.

And we're dancing and I'm trying to think myself back into this moment, this amazing flat and this smart woman, and the escape we're both after.

Tegan pulls away, dances on her own.

'You're married, aren't you? No way you live here on your own.'

'Not married.'

'Kids then?' Tegan has this sly look, as though she's got one over on me.

Did she sneak into Casey's room when she went to the bathroom? The thought of her gawping at my daughter's things makes me nauseous.

'It doesn't bother me. I've got a boyfriend at home: on–off, you know the score. What happens in Bristol stays in Bristol.'

'Her name's Casey.'

'Your wife?'

'My daughter. She's twelve and I hardly know her, but I want to know her better.'

Tegan seems startled by the change of tone, but not as startled as I am.

'Cute,' she says. 'Good for you. But, uh, not doing much to get me in the mood. More of a mood-*killer*, TBH.'

She's right: this wasn't the deal. My dad would be tearing his hair out at the missed opportunity. Tegan has stopped dancing and I lean in, wanting to kiss her, to make it up to her, to get the sexiness back, but she shakes her head.

'Let's not bother, eh?'

'I'm sorry. In a strange place right now. Nothing to do with you. Can I get you an Uber?'

Tegan shakes her head. 'I'm an independent woman, with an iPhone and a credit card. I'll get my own.'

After she leaves I can't quite believe I let her. She was my ideal woman: easy come, easy go, no bull.

So how come I'm thinking instead about the woman from the hospital? Gemma. Her figure. Her eyes. The way she listened *and* breathed with me *and* encouraged me to be honest.

I should blame *her* for what just happened because honesty is doing me no favours.

It's past midnight: I'm both wide awake *and* bone-tired. Casey and Angelica are coming back by four o'clock tomorrow afternoon.

No, they're back *today*.

So in fifteen or sixteen hours this bloody enormous flat won't seem so huge. Angelica will be here, shutting out all the danger, reminding me what a failure I am. And Casey will be back too, being herself.

I walk onto the terrace and the night finally feels cool. So how come I feel warm?

That's weird. It's because I'm looking forward to seeing them both.

Chapter 11: Casey

Monday 9 July

How come Saturdays take years to arrive, but Mondays come around super-fast?

'How was your weekend, Casey?' Fern asks, her voice coming from the control room where she's protected from the protons being fired into my brain.

'It was OK.'

The huge gantry moves into the exact position to send bolts of radioactive lightning through my skull to nuke Bob out of existence. My mask fits so tightly that I always end up with waffle marks all over my face when I take it off.

'Brilliant weather, wasn't it? What did you get up to?'

'Went home to Worcestershire. Saw my best friend. Came back again.'

'Oh, that's nice. I've never been to Worcestershire. Is that where the sauce comes from?'

Would Fern hate me if I asked her to give the small talk a rest? Not like I'm in the hairdresser, is it? I wish I *was* in the hairdresser. New tufts seem to be sprouting all over my head, even around my scars, while the greyish strands that survived radiotherapy are stringy, like an old man's comb-over. Molly reckons I'm a double for the duckling – and when I'm wearing my wig I can almost feel the tufts pushing through, like daffodils in spring.

Lights roll over my nose. I want to sneeze but I can't.

'OK, hold lovely and still for me now, Casey.'

You're not meant to know when the protons are firing out of the nozzle and penetrating your skull, but I think I do. It's like a hum or a vibration, deep, deep down, where Bob is hiding.

I try to picture the beams doing their work. *Zap! Bam! Take that, tumour!*

'All done, my love.' She reappears and helps me to sit up. 'Be careful stepping down.'

On the way out she gives me a new glass bead for today's PBT: six done, fourteen to go. I told Mum not to wait earlier, as she's in a weird mood, so I go straight up to hospital school, not meeting my waffle face reflection in the lift mirror. This weekend Molly was telling me about the end-of-year tests she's had in chemistry and Spanish and drama, and I'm worried I won't ever be able to catch up. That's if Mum even lets me go back to normal school when this is all over.

Will it ever be all over?

When Mr Porter loads up an algebra lesson onto my iPad I'm so focused that it's only when the little kids start getting fidgety and excited that I realize a whole hour's gone by.

'Casey, if you want, you can go and work in the art room while Bear is here,' Mr Porter says.

'Bear?'

'The therapy dog. Remember, from last week? He comes every Monday.'

Last week seems like *years* ago. I cringe, remembering my pathetic reaction to that little dog.

'I freaked out because I didn't expect to see an animal here. Usually I quite like dogs, so I don't have to hide or anything.'

The teacher nods. 'Well, if you're sure. He's a very good-natured animal. Hey, tell you what: your English project this week is to write an article, so you could write about therapy dogs? His owner, Gemma, has done lots of research.'

I shrug. Mum would still hate the whole idea of a dog here, but if the doctors are cool with it, I can try to be, too.

Because I'm ready this time, I don't panic when the dog comes in. My classmates go so crazy over Bear that I'm a bit sorry for him. Mr Porter explains about the article.

'Sure,' Gemma says. She's the same sort of age as my mum, nowhere near as pretty, and quite a lot plumper. Though these days *everyone* is plumper than Mum. But Gemma does have amazingly glossy, dark hair. I touch my own head, hating the falseness of somebody else's hair. 'Do you want to chat to me here? Or we can take Bear down to the garden and you can interview him too?'

'He's a *dog*!' I say.

'Sorry, that was patronizing of me, wasn't it?' she says.

'It's OK. Let's go.' In the garden it'll be easier to keep our distance so I don't get exposed to too many germs.

'So what do you want to know?' Gemma asks as we walk along the corridor. The dog trots happily into the lift and wags his tail when the door opens again.

I think about what Mum would ask. 'How can you be sure it's safe for people like me? Aren't dogs home to, like, *billions* of bacteria?'

The staff wave at Bear as we pass reception and, in the courtyard, a patient comes to fuss over Bear before Gemma can even answer me.

'We're all home to billions of bacteria,' she says. 'Most of them we get along with fine. And sure, Bear walks on dirty pavements, but so do we, and we don't make everyone wash the bottom of their shoes before they come into the hospital.'

'That's different. We don't touch our shoes very often. But people stroke dogs all the time.'

Gemma nods. 'You're very smart, aren't you? I use antibacterial wipes before *and* after Bear comes here. Because it works the other way too. Bear might pick up something on his paws while he's *inside* the hospital?'

I get out the exercise book where I'm going to write notes. 'OK, *normal* people might be safe around dogs. But my immune system is rubbish, and I catch colds all the time. I could catch something worse from him.'

The dog's lying on a paving slab now, but with his head on her sandal, like it's a pillow. He doesn't *look* dangerous. He looks cute enough to be on Instagram.

'I always check in with Mr Porter or the doctors, in case there's a patient who might be at risk. So the fact that I'm allowed contact with you means the medical teams don't think you're vulnerable right now.'

'My mum says I am.'

Gemma nods. 'It's natural for mums to worry. But there's evidence that people who spend time around dogs may have stronger immune systems.'

'How come?'

'I'm not a scientist, I'm an artist, but I think it's because our bodies get small doses of different germs which makes us better at spotting and fighting the dodgy ones.'

Of course she's totally an artist! The dress she's wearing has bright flowers on it, and her toenails are painted different colours, like a rainbow. 'What kind of art? Are you like Banksy?'

'Not quite. I draw things for websites and magazines.'

'So why do you come here? Do you get paid?'

'No. But Bear likes people and he likes to be busy. He's

a terrier. They were bred to work and if he gets bored, he's a monster. So volunteering is good for him.'

'I don't think I'd come to a hospital every week if I didn't have to.'

Gemma gazes past me, up at the atom sculpture above our heads. 'My husband was a patient here and I know how much it helps to have normal things to distract you, whether that's a nice cup of coffee or the chance to stroke a dog.'

I should write that down for my article, but instead I ask, 'Your husband. Does he come sometimes as well?'

Gemma smiles, but in a sad way. 'Unfortunately, my husband died. Almost two years ago now.'

My scalp starts to tingle and I get that horrible sensation like my skull's too small for my brain. 'Did he have a brain tumour, like me?'

'No. It was a blood cancer. And they tried everything. The medical teams here are amazing. I wouldn't come back if I didn't believe that.'

That's the thing. The doctors can be amazing, but you can still die. A year ago, when the specialists found my tumour, they said mine was treatable. So I wasn't that scared then. I even called it Bob, to make it less horrible. But since Bob started growing again, the consultants talk about reducing its effects: stopping cysts forming, battling the damage he can do to my eyesight, my hearing, my growth.

They never say the word *death*, but they don't *not* say it, either.

'Are you OK, Casey?'

'I'm sorry about your husband.'

'Thank you. What else do you want to know about Bear? Or you can ask me anything about the hospital. I'll answer you as honestly as I can.'

I'm thinking about Ram, my friend from the hospital in

Birmingham, who was funny and brave and much, much stronger than me, but died two days after Christmas. And I'm remembering the Aussie vlogger whose videos taught me how to tie the scarves. She survived till her sixteenth birthday but 'lost her battle' three days later.

'Oh, another thing for your article, Casey,' Gemma says. 'Bear is a very good listener. And he never tells.'

'Obviously. He's a dog. He can't speak.'

She smiles. 'Good point. But, Casey, there are play therapists here if you feel sad. Or your mum could book to see a counsellor, if she's worried about anything.'

I know all about the counsellors. But loads of people have talked to Mum about her worries and it's only made them worse.

'We should go back to the classroom now,' I say.

'You're right. But . . . I'll be here next week, if there's anything you want to chat about. And I do mean anything.'

What happens when someone dies in front of you? If I die, who will make sure Mum is OK? Do you believe in ghosts, and do you think I could come back as one?

My scalp itches and I go to scratch through the horrible dead texture of my wig. I can't take it off till I leave Bristol, but I could get my real hair done for when I go home. 'Um, I do have a question. Not for the article, but . . . I love your hair – who is your hairdresser?'

'Oh.' She reaches up to touch the waves that sit on her shoulders. 'His name's Pepe and he works at a salon near where I live, close to the suspension bridge. He's the best.'

'My hair – not the wig, but my *real* hair – is finally growing longer and I'd quite like to get a haircut in a fancy salon while I'm here.'

'Sure. I've got his number on my phone upstairs.'

'Can you WhatsApp it to me?' I ask, writing my number

on a corner of my exercise book and tearing it off. 'That way I won't lose it.'

Gemma hesitates. Perhaps she's one of those women who keeps her hairdresser a secret because she doesn't want other people to have nice hair, but then she takes the paper and slips it into her bag. 'Do you want to take Bear's lead on the way back to the classroom?'

The lead must be very germy, but I can use hand gel afterwards. She loops it round my wrist and Bear trots at my side, and people smile at me and I pretend that he's *my* dog, that I could take him home with me, into my bedroom, and we'd lie next to each other, staring out of the porthole at the harbour, like we're on a little boat; and I would whisper all the scary things in his velvety ears, and even though obviously he wouldn't understand them, it might feel better to say them out loud.

In the lift I lean down to touch his head, and Bear glances up at me. His eyes are so different from human eyes, there's no white bit, only black-brown like the colour of DL's espresso.

I slow down in the corridor because I'd like to keep hold of the lead for longer, but I guess the other kids are missing out on Bear-time. As we go round the corner, I hear a door open and a shriek that makes his ears twitch, then flatten with fear.

'What the hell is that filthy animal doing in a hospital?'

She's not meant to be here for another hour, but that's definitely my mum racing towards us.

I drop the lead.

Chapter 12: Gemma

She's so much like Casey that I almost do a double-take.

Younger than me, but the weariness in her face reminds me how it felt to have to *cope*, day in, day out, watching someone you love suffering. The effort it takes to be simultaneously optimistic and pessimistic: bigging up the latest treatments, while staying alert for hidden dangers.

'Casey, come here, right this minute. I hope you haven't touched that . . . thing.'

Casey moves nervously towards her mum.

'Actually, no, don't touch me,' her mother says. 'Go into the toilets straight away and wash your hands at least three times before coming out, please,' she orders.

Casey does as she's told.

I don't know how to react, but before I can, the woman turns on me. 'Are you *mental*?'

'That's a bit harsh,' I say, wanting to cover Bear's floppy ears. He's cowering, even though he can't understand the words.

'This is a *hospital*,' she speaks slowly, 'full of vulnerable patients. You're endangering them by bringing an animal and its germs into this place.'

I step back – she's too close to me and Bear, considering how dangerous she thinks we are. 'I'm sorry you feel that way, but the hospital trust is happy with its risk assessment—'

'Happy?'

'The risk of infection is incredibly low, with the precautions we take.'

'Low isn't zero, is it? Nothing ever is, with our bodies. We'll never be certain what caused my daughter's tumour, and I won't have her put at even more risk.'

Behind the anger, it's obvious how scared she is, so instead of arguing with her, I'm backing away, towards the lifts.

'Miss Parr? Angelica?' Jed has stepped out of the classroom now. His stance is open, his tone soft. 'I'm sure we can resolve this without raised voices. My students deserve a calm environment, and conflict isn't helpful.'

Casey's mum suddenly looks ashamed and I'm glad I kept my cool. 'I'll head off a bit early – it's fine,' I say.

Jed shakes his head. 'No. That wouldn't be fair to the children who are waiting for their turn with Bear.'

Casey emerges from the bathroom and smiles brightly. 'Mum, why don't we get a cappuccino downstairs? Is that OK, Mr Porter?'

Already she's taking her mother's hand and leading her away, going the long way round, so neither of them has to pass by me. She looks back only once and her face seems so sad, old before her time. Is her whole life like this – steering her mum around obstacles and avoiding fake danger?

As the other children gather around Bear again, I'm thinking about Casey. None of these kids have it easy, but it seems so wrong that she has to deal with so much on her own.

Bear's jumpy after our session and being shouted at, so I let him sniff every plant and lamp post on the walk home. During his wild adolescent phase I got desperate enough to see a dog trainer, and she told me that sniffing is basically canine aromatherapy, helping to chill them out after stressful experiences.

As we potter along, I pass the entrance to the alleyway where I ran into the school group last week. And where I saw Casey's dad, before I knew who he was.

A wave of heat passes through me. I try to distract myself by thinking about Angelica instead. They must have made a stunning couple. Even in the middle of her rage she was beautiful, with fair hair and the bone structure you see on supermodels.

He would never look twice at someone like me. On a scale of one to ten, I consider myself a seven and, though I thought Andrew was perfect, objectively he was a seven too. Relationships with a big difference seem high-risk to me.

How long did *their* relationship last? Fiery Angelica can't be an easy person to be around. Dan might have tried to make it work before Casey came along. And he's spending time with his daughter now, which most absent dads never do.

Why am I making excuses for him?

Bear cocks his leg for approximately the four hundredth time as we turn onto my road. Back in the flat, he goes straight to his bed and scratches wildly for a bit, before collapsing with a deep sigh.

I take off his coat as he sleeps, then unpack my bag. At the bottom I find the slip of paper with Casey's number on it. It's against the rules to get involved, so I should throw it away.

Except . . . really, what harm would it do to pass on my stylist's details? When everything else in her life is so hard, the least she deserves is a bloody good haircut. Before I change my mind, I text her the number:

Ask for Pepe and mention my name; he's the best hairdresser
I've ever had.

Within ten seconds she's trying to add me on WhatsApp.
I shouldn't accept, but now I'm remembering the sadness in
her small, round face. I want to know she's all right, and
for her to know that someone cares.

A minute later a message pops up:

Thanx am going to see if I can get Mum to make me an
appointment before I leave Bristol at the end of the month
when my treatment is over Sorry about before she worries
a lot about me

I send a reply:

It's fine. A lot of people do worry about dogs in hospitals
but, honestly, the risk is incredibly low. Have a lovely night.

She's typing a reply already. As soon as she's sent it, I'll
end this conversation, firmly but kindly.

Can I send you the article Mr Porter asked me to interview
you for, when I finish writing it

I shouldn't encourage her.
The second half of the message appears:

It's kind of important for my education to check I've got all
the facts totally right.

Did she guess I'm having doubts? Casey's had a lot of
practice reading adults. And I guess if I do proofread her

piece, I can also send her some science-based links that prove the world isn't swarming with hidden carcinogens and silent dangers. She needs someone logical and reassuring in her life.

Sure. I'd be happy to.

She sends me a row of heart emojis back. I can already imagine my dad shaking his head at me. *You're as bad as your mum.* And it's true: I never can resist other people's dramas.

Especially ones that distract me from my own.

Chapter 13: Dan

Tuesday 10 July

I wake up early and decide to treat Casey to breakfast in bed. She needs cheering up – there was a *massive* atmosphere between her and Angelica last night, but I was too chicken to ask what had happened.

'Toast incoming!' I say, knocking on the door and opening it at the same time, trying not to spill the orange juice or upend the tray.

She's lying on top of the duvet – you can't escape the heat, even this early in the morning – and for a few seconds I'm confused. It's like a different girl has crept into her room during the night. Her younger sister? No, she's an only child . . .

Casey opens her eyes. Yawns sleepily.

And just when I clock what's different about her, she squeals.

'GET OUT! Get out of my room – get out, get out!'

I back away, trying to turn, but there's not enough space to move fast in this tiny single room, and her mum's right behind me.

'What have you done to her?'

'Nothing, I—'

I saw my daughter without her wig.

Angelica bustles me out into the hallway and the bedroom door slams shut. I can hear her say soothing things to Casey, but it doesn't seem to be helping: the sobs are *horrible*.

I go back into the kitchen and wipe down the tray, putting the toast to one side in case she fancies it when she's calmed down. *If she calms down.* She looked much better without the wig, but she'd never believe me if I said so. I remember how shitty it felt to be different: the stares and the sympathy from adults. The whispers and teasing from the other kids.

Enough already. I can't compare what happened to me to what Casey is going through.

After twenty minutes of silence I start worrying about being late. It's my turn to walk her to the hospital, though she may not want me to now.

Seconds before I knock on the door, Angelica comes into the room. She holds her fingers up to her lips and I get the message that we won't mention this again. Right behind her, Casey walks into the kitchen, the wig back on her head, the blonde hairs brushed dead straight. She won't meet my eye.

'I'm going to walk to the unit on my own today,' Casey says.

'No!'

'I don't think—'

Angelica and I speak at the same time. This is a first: we agree on something.

Casey tuts. 'It's fine. I know the way now.'

'You're only twelve,' her mum says.

'Sometimes I'm a lot more of a grown-up than you are,' Casey snaps back and, though I see her point, I try to keep my face neutral.

86

'No. The traffic here is insane,' Angelica says. 'We haven't gone through all this for you to be run over by an articulated lorry or a deranged cyclist.'

'I've been crossing roads on my own since I was six.'

'Not in a city centre!'

Is this bickering just about whatever happened yesterday? Casey's treatment could be making her tetchy, but Angelica seems edgier too.

'If you don't get off my case, I'm not going in. You can't *make* me.'

There's a heaviness in the air, like you get before a massive storm.

'Let's stick to the original plan,' I say, after a bit. 'I'll walk you in, but we don't have to talk. Angelica, you deserve the day to yourself.'

Mother and daughter stare murderously at each other, but it's obvious they don't have any better suggestions.

'Whatever,' Casey says. 'I'll get my bag.'

I pick up the plate. 'I saved your toast.'

'Not hungry.'

When Casey stomps out, her mother gives me a rueful shrug. Being in the doghouse with our daughter makes us, briefly, united. Angelica must be stronger than she looks to cope with this day after day, year after year, with no one to back her up.

We don't speak as we leave the building, but it's good to be in the open air after the suffocating vibe in the penthouse.

But once we've got past the basin and are going up Christmas Steps, I decide I do want to say something, and it's so steep here she won't be able to run off.

'Casey, can I mention the elephant in the room?'

'We're not in a room, and I can't see any elephants.'

'The elephant in the room is the thing that people don't mention, even though it's so huge everyone knows it's there.'

'What are you even talking about?'

I'm about to give up when I notice beads of sweat where the fake hairline meets her forehead. She's only wearing the bloody thing because she believes I'll like her less if I see the real person underneath. I know how that feels.

'Your wig's great, Casey. But you're every bit as lovely without it.'

She turns away to glance through a shop window. I think I hear her say the word *lovely* in a mocking way, but I can't be sure. I wish I could pause the action, like we're in a video game, and call Vijay for advice. Should I back off? We only have a few weeks together, so why make things difficult?

Except it's not just about the wig, is it?

I stand next to her, facing the shop window, and my reflection meets hers. She looks a little like I did when I was a kid, but so much sweeter.

'Casey, you must see how pretty you are.'

She shakes her head, scowling at herself. 'My face is fat, from the steroids. And my hair is horrible. I *used* to be pretty. I didn't even think I cared how I looked, but now I'm not pretty any more, I realize I'm vain as well as ugly.'

'Oh, Casey. No. You are completely lovely. Inside and out.'

'You're only saying that to make me feel better.'

'I *do* want you to feel better, yes. But I wouldn't lie to you about this. You're gorgeous. What could me and your mum do to help you see that?'

She breaks the gaze between our reflections. 'It doesn't matter. None of it matters.'

She stomps up the remaining steps, towards the hospital. Defeated, I follow her. At the very top, she turns and stares at me. And now she wrenches her wig off her head, her face defiant, almost angry, like she's expecting me to be disgusted or to turn away.

She's stunning. Her violet-grey eyes blaze and her lips are dark pink and pursed with contempt, like her mother's. Her cheeks are a tiny bit puffy, but if I didn't know about the steroids, I wouldn't notice.

'See?' she says and now I *hear* the defiance.

I see a kid who needs honesty, but also love and reassurance. Who – despite my failures – is asking for that from me. 'Shall I tell you what I see, Casey? I see beautiful eyes and clear skin and a heart-shaped face.'

She huffs. 'But what about my hair?'

The strands on her scalp are damp with sweat. *Honesty.* I try to channel Gemma. 'It's a bit flat where it was squashed by the wig, but with a blow-dry, it'd be fab again.'

'You're wrong! It used to be blonde and soft, like Mum's. Now it's coarse and uneven and *bleurgh.*'

Casey turns away and I can see the back of her head. The regrowth *is* patchy in a few places, but most of the ageing rockers I've met would be over the moon if their hair transplants were half as lush.

'It'll be great. Hair is easy to fix.'

'A hairdresser would laugh at me!'

'No one would laugh, Casey. There are thousands of hairdressers in Bristol. We can find one who will transform your look.'

She gives me a sideways glance as I catch her up.

'Mum says we can't afford it.'

'I'll pay.'

'Good hairdressers are expensive.'

'It can't be that bad.'

'Like, a hundred quid or something.' The way she looks at me now is different: like she's testing me.

Another hundred quid is nothing on my over-extended credit card. What matters most is that she trusts me enough to believe I could help.

'A total bargain, if it makes you happy.'

'Plus colour on top. It costs less if it's not all over. My friend had a blue streak put in and it is *so* cool.'

I'm being played. But, weirdly, I don't care. 'Hmm. What would your mum say?'

Casey sighs. 'She's so weird right now, she'd probably think shampoo would kill me. Or a hairdryer.'

'Weird how?'

She shakes her head. 'Nothing like as weird as you.'

'Fair comment.'

But as we walk, I wonder what she meant. Angelica *does* seem stressed, and when she's in a bad place, who cares for *Casey*? The hospital's close, so if I don't try again to get at the truth now, I might not get another chance. 'Is your mum finding it hard, being here?'

Casey stares at the pavement as we walk. 'A bit.'

'How?'

There's a long pause. 'Like, yesterday . . . there was a dog in the hospital school.'

'A guide dog?'

'No, a therapy dog, we're meant to stroke them or whatever, to chill out. But Mum saw the dog and she *totally* freaked out. And . . .' She shakes her head.

'You can tell me.'

'No. She's doing her best.' Casey's voice shuts me down.

But when we get to the hospital, she asks me if I'll wait until her treatment is over. 'After I'm finished, would you have time to take me to the classroom and say hi to my teacher?'

'No sweat,' I say, though the buzzing in my ears starts the second we arrive in the hospital lobby.

'You could wait out in the garden while they zap me; it's less medical out there, remember?'

Her automatic kindness makes my heart break a bit. 'Brilliant idea.'

She nods, then looks down: she's still carrying her wig. I wait for her to put it back on, but she takes out a cotton bag and rolls the wig up, before stowing it away.

'Let me talk to your mum about a haircut. See if I can persuade her it's safe.'

Casey nods. 'Good luck with that. I should be back in fifteen minutes.'

I buy a coffee and take it into the courtyard, as my wise daughter suggested, but the humming is louder now she's gone. Tinnitus is an occupational hazard when you work the festivals. Nowadays they take it seriously, but the damage was done when I was fifteen, working on food stalls for free burgers and cash in hand.

The droning always gets louder when everything else is still. Now it's vibrating like . . . a ship's engine or a big amp.

No. It's the buzz of clippers. And I understand instantly what the memory is and why it's been triggered.

But I don't have to give in to it. I try to think about my life now, not my life then. Lazy weekends with my friends. Great days when the lads at work are listening to me. But the noise keeps intensifying. Fucking hell.

I close my eyes. All right then, bring it on.

'Turn and face the camera, Daz, that's it. No, don't smile. Think about when Mufasa dies in The Lion King. *That's right. Hold it – OK. You can smile again.'*

Buzz.

The clippers vibrate in his hand and the blades dart up and down like rat's teeth. Nadia holds up the camera, but doesn't look at me.

'Dad, it's going to cut me.'

'I promise it won't – that's what the guard is for. Look, I'm doing mine first.'

He locks eyes with his own reflection in the mirror. The vibration deepens when the machine touches the hair above his forehead and tiny black shavings rain down, settling on the chequerboard kitchen floor.

We'll be finding hair in our sandwiches for weeks; it goes everywhere.

There's no blood and he's still grinning. It almost suits him, but he doesn't have much hair anyway. I've got loads.

'Your turn, Dazzler.'

He moves the clippers towards the back of my neck and, with his other hand, pushes my head gently forward. Now I feel the noise in my skull. But it doesn't hurt, it tickles and his hand is warm against my head, pushing back the hair in lines, like he's mowing a lawn.

'You'll be bang on trend. All the tough guys have shaved heads. Bruce Willis. Grant Mitchell. And now we're done.'

I see in his eyes how bad I must look. Then he grins. 'You've been very brave, Daz. Take another piccy, Nadia.'

'Can I smile this time, Dad?'

'Let's do two, shall we? One sad, one happy.'

Somewhere I've still got a newspaper clipping featuring the 'sad' photo. I'll never forget how shocking it was when I didn't recognize the strange boy in the mirror.

The buzzing in my ears fades and I'm back, here in this sunny courtyard. My coffee's gone cold. I check my watch. Casey should be back soon, and then we'll go to her classroom. This morning has been a rollercoaster but, somehow, we've turned it around, together.

Except it's not just about today. I've no idea how *real* families are meant to work, because my dad's version was so warped. Yes, I can pretend for a few days, a few weeks, but I can only keep it up for so long. How am I meant to be there for her, when no one was there for me?

Chapter 14: Gemma

Wednesday 11 July

'Your endometrium is lush, Gemma,' the senior radiographer says, watching on her screen. 'Dani, can we see the ovaries now, please?'

Her colleague pushes harder with the wand, as if she's trying to tunnel her way up and out through my belly button. What would Andrew have made of this? He was a valiant patient, but when he went into remission and we decided to try IVF, I went to the hospital alone. He'd spent too long around doctors already; and I didn't want him to see me like *this*.

The physical side of our relationship had changed by then. When we first met there was an instant spark, but it took time to catch fire, fuelled by weeks of gentle flirtation and clever banter. Which meant that when we did get it on, we were *so* ready, as curious and unashamed about each other's bodies as horny teens.

But then illness imposed a different intimacy on our marriage, the patient–nurse kind. Our touches became gentler, beautiful in a new way. Oh, I miss that.

'Right, we're all done; pop your things back on and I'll show you the inside story!'

As the examination ends, I exhale. It's been so long since

I was touched by someone who *wanted* me. I pull on my skirt, before peering over the radiographer's shoulder at the screen.

'How am I doing?'

'*Very* well. Three lovely layers. The ideal home for a blastocyst.'

A flutter of excitement in my belly, or perhaps my endometrium basking in its duvet-like glory. I imagine it welcoming the embryo: *settle in, make yourself comfy. Hopefully you'll want to stick around.*

And, without warning, I burst into tears, and they take it in their stride, because everyone they see is stuffed full of hormones and hope, and *happy* tears are the best kind.

I try to call Isabel on the way home, but there's no answer. I haven't told her that I'm trying this month. In December her support became so intense that I felt smothered, but at least she's on my side. She's desperate for a grandchild.

When I get home, Bear goes crazy for five minutes, and I surrender to his excitement before checking my email.

Yes! There's one from my agent:

You got the bank commission, so it's full steam ahead to get it done by the end of the month!

This is huge progress, my first significant piece of work in months. The deadline is insane, but at least it'll distract me from my treatment.

I fetch the folder of prep work I did, so I can start right away. I'm researching details for the first character – a preschool girl playing football with her mum – when my phone pings with a WhatsApp message from Casey:

Guess where I am

She's sent a picture of a chrome wheel on a polished concrete floor and it looks familiar, but I can't quite place it.

Send me another clue.

I shouldn't encourage her, but she's been messaging me since Monday and each one is so much fun – the emojis that replace punctuation, her relentless expression of *all the feels* that veer wildly from breathless joy to deepest despair. I try to be a steadying influence with my replies.

Within a few seconds, another photo pops up: a muscular arm covered in wild cactus tattoos.

My hairdresser's arm. So the wheel was from his snazzy chair.

You're with Pepe! Hooray! How is it going?

He is amazing and he has nearly finished and I am scared to see it

I know he'll have done the best job. Send me a picture of the final result!

I hope, for Casey's sake, that her mum approves – and for Pepe's sake too. I wouldn't want anyone else to be on the receiving end of that woman's wrath.

Come and see it yourself if you want

I told Casey that I live round the corner from the salon.

After what happened with your mum on Monday it's better that I don't do that.

Mum is having a bad day so she hasn't come and I'm here with my dad and we are getting pastries afterwards at the cafe you love and I can get him to buy you one to say thank you

I stare at the screen.

Her dad.

Dan.

Here it comes again: that wave of warmth that spreads from my face all the way down to between my legs. Proper lust.

My theory about the fertility hormones causing it is *possible*, except this feels like the real thing. I start composing a polite *no* message in my head, but before I finish typing, she's sent another one:

PLEASE PLEASE PLEASE PLEASE PLEASE I want you to see it because Mum will freak even if it is actually nice and my dad will say it is nice even if it isn't and I cant trust anyone to tell me the truth except you

No one could say no to that. And I reckon Casey knows it.

OK but I can't stay long. Shall I bring Bear?

She sends me a row of dog emojis back.

I need time to work out where my head's at, and the cafe is around the corner from me, so I take Bear in the opposite direction. Walking has always helped me to think more clearly.

So . . . that chance encounter with Dan rattled me because I am hormonal and he looks like a film star. And yes, after I realized he was Casey's father I was consumed by rage. I'm not usually an angry person, so I could put that down to hormones too.

But today I'm calmer and the chances are Dan won't even remember me, so all I have to do is say hello to Casey, admire her hair, ignore him and go straight back home. Do not pass Go, do not collect a cheese and mushroom croissant.

Sorted.

I walk briskly back to the cafe, pulling along a reluctant Bear, who wants to wee on all the weeds that have sprouted in the hot weather. But the minute he spots Casey, he drags me towards her, his tail blurring as it wags.

'Hey!' I call out, focusing on Casey and not even acknowledging her dad.

As we get closer, I can see Pepe has worked his magic. With her wig on, Casey seemed like she was hiding. But her real hair is now perfect: shaped into soft waves around her sweet face, and cropped into the nape of her long neck at the back. It's sophisticated enough for a girl who will soon be a teenager, but still fresh and sweet.

'Oh, that is gorgeous,' I say. 'It really suits you. A brand-new Casey.'

She blushes. A haircut from Pepe never, ever fails.

'Oh, this is my dad,' Casey says, and there's pride in her voice. 'DL, this is Gemma and her amazing dog, Bear.'

I look at him as briefly as I can get away with, but it's enough to throw me. Those bloody eyes. I see recognition in them, and surprise. Of course he hadn't known it'd be *me*.

'We've met,' Dan says and Casey frowns.

'Yes. We have,' I say, trying to sound matter-of-fact.

'Where? When?' Casey asks, and I am so curious to hear how *he* remembers our very brief encounter.

'Outside the hospital. The first morning I came to meet you. I was nervous, and Gemma was very kind and calmed me down.'

Casey stares at me. 'How come you never mentioned it, Gemma?'

'I didn't even make the connection till now.' I'm a bloody awful liar, but it's not the fib that's making me dizzy.

It's him.

Every cell in my body responds to his presence. I can hear the familiarity of his breathing and smell a resinous, summery scent on his skin. In my peripheral vision, Dan is crouching down. 'So you're the therapy dog?' he says, and I catch a tremor of nervousness in his voice.

Bear's rolling onto his back to be scratched. It shouldn't matter what my dog thinks, but I trust his instincts about people way more than I trust my own.

'We were going to eat inside the cafe, but as it's so hot we thought we'd have a picnic. Would you like to come with us?' Dan asks.

Casey holds up a bag. 'I got my dad to buy you a cheese and mushroom croissant because you said they're your favourite.'

It'd be rude *not* to go. Plus, those are the best croissants this side of Paris. 'OK, but I can't stay long.' But as we head towards the Downs I've forgotten how to walk normally and it's a relief when we can sit down on the yellow grass.

Except now I have to eat without showering golden pastry flakes all over myself. Bear watches me, ready to hoover them up.

'When Casey told me about the volunteer she'd met at hospital school, I did wonder if it might be you, but I thought

99

it'd be too much of a coincidence,' Dan is saying. 'I'm glad it is you, because I wanted to thank you.'

I'm mid-mouthful, so I make an *mmm, it's nothing* noise.

'She volunteers because her husband died,' Casey says.

'Ah,' Dan says, and it's such a deep, sympathetic sound that everything goes swimmy. I'm in a far worse state than I was when we met before. 'I mean, you told me you'd supported somebody having treatment, but I am sorry it didn't save him.'

My throat closes up for a second and it's hard to swallow the last piece. 'Thank you. Volunteering makes a positive out of something sad. And it's lovely to see how Bear helps kids like Casey settle in.'

He nods. 'She is amazing. So smart and brave.'

Casey rolls her eyes and stands up. 'Spare me the brave tumour-kid stuff, OK? I'm like this because I don't have a choice. Gemma, can I take Bear for a walk?'

The idea of anyone else looking after him makes me nervous, but she was careful with him in the hospital. 'If you promise not to let him off the lead,' I say.

'And stay on this part of the Downs, where I can see you,' Dan adds.

Casey rolls her eyes again, but grabs the lead and sets off, Bear delighted to trot alongside her.

'I keep second-guessing what her mother would let her do, which is tricky.'

If you'd been there while she was growing up, it would be way easier.

'I met her mum when I went into the hospital on Monday. She was quite, um, forthright with me, and with Bear.'

'Not everyone likes dogs, even ones as cute as Bear. My father was always very jittery around them. Said they could see right into your soul.'

100

'Is that a bad thing?'

'My dad definitely thought so!' He laughs before I can ask more. 'I'm just saying that perhaps Angelica – that's Casey's mum – was on edge when she saw Bear.'

I grimace. 'It was a bit more dramatic than that.'

Dan frowns. 'Shit. Did she go off on one about germs? I had this sense that there'd been a problem when they got back from treatment, but Casey's too loyal to say anything bad about her mum. They've both been under so much pressure.'

'I guess it's difficult being a single parent at the best of times, never mind when your child is sick.'

'I haven't been much help.'

'Why haven't you?' I notice how he flinches and I add, 'Sorry, I didn't mean to say that out loud. None of my business.'

'Don't apologize. It's a fair question. Me and Angelica were never *together* together. We met at a festival and we hooked up for a couple of nights, that's all. We were kids ourselves.'

That fits with how young Casey's mum looked. 'And she got pregnant?'

Dan nods. 'I haven't been in the picture until now.'

This much I knew from what Jed told me. I dare to meet Dan's eyes again. They seem full of sincerity and kindness, but how does that square with him choosing not to be in his kid's life?

'How's it going?'

He shakes his head. 'I'm out of my depth. You saw the state I was in last week. If I hadn't seen you, I'd have let her down.'

There's something so dark in his voice that I want to reassure him. 'You wanted to be there for her. I didn't do much.'

'That's not true. You helped me do the right thing, just by believing I could.'

'I do try to see the best in people. Although my sister would say that's my biggest character flaw.'

'I always think people are as shallow as I am – that way I'm never disappointed.'

'You don't seem shallow to me, Dan.'

He laughs. 'I really am. I have no hidden depths. What you see is what you get.'

What I see is a man I want to kiss.

I try to gloss over that. 'Well, when we met before, you seemed open and honest, and I like that in a person.'

He shakes his head. 'Being with you feels like someone's given me a truth drug, and I get this urge to tell you *everything*. Which is not cool.'

'Openness can be really attractive.' *Did I really just say that?*

'Well, I promise I'm not trying to chat you up, obviously.'

Oh. It's *obvious*, is it? I know he's out of my league, but he doesn't have to spell it out. 'Right.'

'Because of the late husband thing, I mean. Not because you're unattractive. Because you're not. You are *very* attractive.' He stops, groans. 'Shit. What is happening to me, Gemma?'

He thinks I'm attractive. I gaze at him, and a shiver travels down my spine: a good shiver. I never even knew there was such a thing.

'Sorry. I've lost my thread,' he says after – what – ten seconds? A minute? It's like time doesn't have any meaning any more.

'You were talking about wanting to tell the truth?'

'Yeah. Mostly it takes me years to trust someone, and even then the closest I get to opening up is telling them what

102

music I like, or why I never have milk in my coffee.' He smiles and that sends my core temperature another degree closer to boiling point. 'So it makes zero sense.'

'Sometimes it's easier to talk openly to a stranger because you'll never see them again.'

'Except here you are. Again. And I am doing the same thing.'

'Yes. I am. And you are.' I want to say: *I felt it too. That connection.* But I won't, because it's pointless. What I have to do next week, I can only do alone.

'I should probably confess something else,' he says, gouging at the dry earth with his fingers, no longer looking at me. 'I keep thinking about you. Out of the blue, I'll remember your face or your voice.'

'Me too.' I whisper it, half hoping he won't hear. But he does. Because he is so close I can smell the citrus on his breath from the lemon tartlet he just ate. 'And this . . . this doesn't happen to me, either.'

We stare at each other. I *want* to kiss him, but I *should* run. Indecision paralyses me.

Dan's focused gaze feels like a searchlight. 'I'm trying to work out why you, Gemma? What's *your* story?'

I laugh instead of answering, because where would I begin?

'No, I want to know,' he insists. 'I want to understand what's happening to us.'

I think about what Andrew used to say about the puzzle of love. How nothing is random, but it can take time for the clues to add up.

Guilt follows immediately, because I loved Andrew so much. But when we first met I *never* felt this intensity. This *desire*.

To distract myself, I begin my potted life story, sounding like a TV dating contestant. 'OK, I'm Gemma, I'm thirty-four,

I was brought up in Weston-super-Mare by a very cool dad and a very nosy mother. I take more after her than him.

'What else? Um, I have one sister and one niece and one nephew.' I realize I am avoiding talking about Andrew, which seems disloyal. 'And I've been widowed now for almost two years and I still can't quite believe *that* word applies to me.'

'You don't look like a widow, to be fair.'

'What does a widow look like?'

'Grey-haired. A shawl. Or riding a horse along a deserted beach, wearing a long black cape.'

I smile. 'I did ride the donkeys on Weston beach when I was little.'

'I don't even think I've met a widow before. Though my dad was a widower.'

'Your mum died?'

'When I was a baby. Huh. Truth drug strikes again – I don't usually tell people about that, but it's no big tragedy.' Dan sounds defensive.

'It sounds like quite a big tragedy to me. Did your father remarry?'

'No, there were girlfriends – a *lot* of girlfriends – but he always said my mum was a one-off.' Dan peers past me, towards the Observatory. 'No one else could live up to her.'

I close my eyes. *I know how that feels.*

'Sorry,' Dan says, 'I bet that's still raw, for you.'

'Ah, it's OK. I did ask.'

But it's not OK. The intensity of this conversation feels like too much now.

Before I can say anything else, he's standing up, breaking the connection. 'Where's Casey got to?'

He heads off to search, and emptiness blasts through me like a gust of icy wind. What's wrong with me? Moments ago I *wanted* him to go. Now I can't bear that he has.

But already they're running back towards me – Dan, Casey, my little Bear. I don't want this afternoon to end yet.

'Anyone fancy a game of catch with Bear?' I suggest. 'He loves being piggy-in-the-middle, waiting for us to drop the ball, and that's hard to play on my own.'

When Bear hears the word *ball*, his body tenses in anticipation of his favourite thing in the world. I should try to be more like him: focus on being in the moment.

And as we all walk across the grass to find a space to play, I realize this connection with Dan might not be deep or meaningful. It could simply be about meeting new people who don't remind me of the past; people who have their own troubles and stories, but are still able to enjoy a ball game on a sunny Wednesday afternoon.

Chapter 15: Dan

'Stop hogging the ball, DL,' Casey calls out. 'It's my turn!'

We're sweating and Bear is panting after twenty minutes of this game. But I'd like to keep going till sundown.

'Strictly speaking, it's Bear's turn,' Gemma says. 'You two don't drop the ball enough to keep him happy.' Her cheeks are pink from the game and her body flows with a grace I never expected.

My dad believed every man has a type, and my type is pure cliché: blonde, fairly tall, slim, big eyes, button nose, full lips with a Bardot pout. Angelica, basically. Her face looks best when she's sulking, which is all she ever does.

But Gemma's face is always changing: smiles and frowns and scowls and grins, and about a hundred other expressions that don't even have names. She's not conventionally beautiful, but her face gets prettier every time I look at it, which I guess has something to do with how I am liking her more and more.

How does *she* feel about *me*?

She's stopped for a moment, to fill a water bowl for the dog, and he lollops over to her and drinks and drinks and drinks. He's a cute little fella, and whatever his owner thinks, Bear has taken to me. Which must mean Dad was wrong about dogs being good judges of character.

Perhaps Gemma is scouting for a fling. I'm the ideal

candidate, always happy to offer good sex, no strings attached, until she finds someone permanent.

In normal times I wouldn't think twice. But these are not normal times, because Casey's around.

'I should get back to work,' Gemma says once Bear's finished, his beard darkened by the water.

'Gemma's an artist.' Casey sounds proud of knowing someone with such a cool job.

'A commercial illustrator. It's not as glamorous as it sounds.'

'We don't have any artists or musicians in our village, so I think it's *very* glamorous indeed.' Casey picks up the lead. 'Can I walk Bear back to your house?'

'He'd like that.'

We keep throwing the ball as we walk. This feels so easy, like it was easy to say that stuff to her before. Despite my dad's voice in my head telling me to *shut up, Daz, you moron,* I wanted to tell her the truth. Honesty felt . . . good.

'That's me over there,' Gemma says, pointing up at the golden terrace of Bath-stone houses facing Observatory Road.

'Wow,' says Casey.

Wow! Gemma is rich. I didn't see that coming, and she didn't hint at it when she was telling me about her life. Shouldn't 'I live in a three-million-quid Clifton Village landmark' have been near the top of her list?

Dad would have wormed it out of her PDQ. Or he'd have known already. And aren't I behaving exactly like him now, instantly working out what Gemma is worth? My father's comparison-itis was contagious, but I've tried so hard to turn my back on the resentment that came with it, the *poor me* bullshit that he used to justify all his scams and betrayals.

No. I'm not like him. Gemma's not a 'mark', she's . . . well, I don't know yet, but I'd like to find out.

'I don't own the whole house,' she says. 'But my husband did get very lucky. He bought the balcony flat when the whole building was falling down. There were squatters and he had to wait almost two years before they left. It was worth the wait.'

Not *quite* a multi-million-pound pad then, but I don't think you'd get any change from £600k in this location. What would she think if she saw where I live? Or found out that, more than once, me and my dad would have been the squatters her hubby was trying to get shot of.

'Anyway, thanks for the croissant, and for giving Bear the best runaround he's had in ages.'

'Will you both be back at hospital school on Monday?' Casey asks.

'Bear and I never miss our visits.'

Gemma reaches out to hug Casey. I imagine how her body would feel if I got as close to her as Casey is now. If there'd still be a trace of the rose perfume I smelled when we met before. How soft she'd be, as I wrapped my arms around her waist and leaned in for a kiss . . .

When Casey lets go, I want to say something, do something, that delays the moment Gemma goes inside. Because despite – or maybe because of – our differences, I want to see her again.

You've been poison ever since you took your first breath.

The last thing Gemma needs is someone like me.

So I wave goodbye and slip my hand into Casey's, making sure I do not glance back at this woman who has given me what my daughter would call *all the feels*.

* * *

108

Even Angelica can't deny that Casey's haircut is fantastic.

'You look very grown-up,' she says, but there's a hint of disapproval.

'Pepe was amazing. He had an accident years ago, so now he's got this cool turbo-wheelchair that goes up and down, and he's covered in tattoos. And he thinks my hair would look even better with some organic colour on it; it's vegan and semi-permanent, so it wouldn't be a problem when I go back to school in September and—'

'No. No way.'

'*Please,* Mum.'

'If it's about the money,' I say, 'then that's not a problem – it'll be my treat.' I want to spend every penny of the income I'm getting from letting my place on Airbnb on spoiling my daughter.

'It is *not* about the money. It's about Casey's well-being.'

Casey predicted this, so I go into the spiel we rehearsed during the walk back. 'I talked to the hairdresser about it, and the colours are safe. He even did an allergy patch test to make sure it'd be safe.'

'*What?*'

Casey lifts the lock of hair curled behind her ear to show where the stylist applied a dot of colour with a cotton bud. 'I don't think you can even see it any more.'

'You let him poison her?' Angelica spits out the words at me, and I flinch.

Casey looks stricken. 'It's not poison. And it's not DL's fault. I said I wanted the patch test. Even though I knew you'd spoil it!'

'Casey, leave us alone, please.'

'But Mum—'

'No arguments. Go to your room. Now.'

Casey shakes her head, but does as she's told.

When the door shuts behind her, I prepare to take the flak. 'Angelica, I'm sorry if I did the wrong thing, but you weren't there and Casey wanted—'

All the blood has left her face, so she's ominously pale. 'What gives you the right to let some stranger damage my daughter's body?'

'It was the tiniest bit of dye. It won't have done her any harm.'

'Really? Did you qualify in chemistry or medicine in the years when you were missing in action?'

'Of course not. But those dyes are used on millions of people every day. You can even use them at home.'

'You're also allowed to *smoke*, Dan, even though it gives you lung cancer. You're allowed to drink alcohol, which screws your liver; and to eat crappy burgers full of antibiotics and trans fats; and drive cars that chuck out pollution. Because governments don't care about the little people, all that matters is big business and shareholders and—'

I raise my hands. 'Hold on. We're talking about a laid-back hairdresser at a vegan salon, not a plot by Big Pharma.'

She scoffs. 'Don't patronize me. You have no bloody idea what it's been like fighting to get a diagnosis, fighting to get the right treatment. Do you know she'd had headaches for *six months* and had to collapse in class before anyone took her seriously?'

'I didn't know that, no.'

'I failed her; she might have had treatment sooner if I'd pushed harder for a diagnosis. I can't let that happen again.'

'You didn't fail her, you're a brilliant mum—'

'How would you know? You have no idea what being a parent involves. I don't even understand why you've let us stay with you. Is it because Glastonbury isn't running this

110

year and you thought playing at being a daddy would pass the time?'

'No. I've never claimed to be any good at families. But Casey asked for help.'

'I should have stopped this. I *knew* you'd put her in danger.'

As Angelica rants and rages, it's becoming clearer that her response is way out of proportion.

'Have you talked to anyone about your worries?'

'Oh piss off, Dan. Don't make out this is *my* problem.' She shakes her head and stomps into the kitchen area, grabbing a Bag for Life and starting to fill it with food from the fridge.

'What are you doing?'

'I've had enough of your bullshit. We'll move into hospital accommodation. We should have done that from the beginning.'

Except the last thing Casey needs is to be cooped up alone with her mum while she's this wound up. 'No. Wait. Do you even know if they've still got space?'

As I follow her into the hall, it occurs to me that last week I would have been helping her pack. Yet now I'm fighting to keep them with me.

'If they haven't, we'll check into a hotel. Anything rather than having to spend one more minute cluttering up your perfect bachelor pad.' She bends down to take more food out of the cupboards: all gluten- and enjoyment-free. Poor Casey.

I know Angelica's doing her best, and that I've got no idea what it's like to fear your kid is sick but not be able to find help. So I make another decision. 'Listen, if anyone needs to go, it should be me. It's more important that you and Casey have somewhere safe during her treatment.'

'Oh, how magnanimous of you. You think you're better

111

than us, but you couldn't be more wrong. My dad warned me not to come here, because you're a man-child who hasn't grown up at all in the last twelve years.'

My hands shake. My ears ring. It sickens me that Vaughn still thinks he can pass judgement on me. *I have changed.*

Angelica pushes past me to go into her room and I hear the wheels of her suitcase turning as she pulls it out from under the bed.

I want to follow her, tell her the truth. It might be a relief to be honest about the penthouse, and about how much Casey has started to mean to me and how I can now see the damage I caused. I could even tell Angelica what her father did—

No. I can't risk it, because I don't know what will happen when July ends, when I no longer have the penthouse to offer them. All I can do right now is ensure Casey stays here, because this is the best place for her during her treatment.

The bangs and crashes from Angelica's room stop abruptly. I hear Casey's door opening and her feet tiptoeing across the hall. When she opens the door to Angelica's room, Casey's voice sounds soothing as she tries to calm her mother down.

I go out onto the terrace and peer out towards the suspension bridge, so close to where we were only an hour ago. Can Gemma see the bridge from her Clifton balcony? What would she advise me to do now?

She'd expect me to be kind.

'DL?'

Casey is behind me. 'Mum says she'd like to stay after all, if that's still OK?'

'Of course it is. That's what I want too.'

'She just . . . got a bit hyper. Sorry.'

I want to hug Casey, but it'd be almost like asking her to take sides. She needs her mum right now, and her mum needs her. 'There's nothing to apologize for. Tell you what: I know a knockout vegan place that does delivery. Shall I order you both a takeaway?'

'What about you?'

'I've got somewhere I need to be tonight. You two can have a girls' night in.'

After I've ordered the food, I leave. I was lying. I've got nowhere to go, nothing to do. I mooch about, buy a slice of pizza and sit on the amphitheatre steps, watching the skateboarders, then peer up at the penthouse, hoping everything has calmed down.

Turns out I don't have an appetite, so I drink beer instead. Only one. I don't want Angelica to smell it on my breath when I get back. Though she couldn't disapprove of me any more than she already does.

I did the right thing, leaving Casey and Angelica alone for the evening. I don't know if I'd have thought of that, if I hadn't channelled Gemma and the kindness she showed me that day on the way to the hospital . . .

Gemma. It's like I become a better version of myself when she's around, or even when I imagine her watching me.

Shall I call her? I could do it right now: Casey took a group selfie, including Bear, and sent it to us on WhatsApp. So I have Gemma's number.

No. I shouldn't use it. That's creepy. And she's a widow, and even if she *did* want something to happen between us, it'd end up complicated; and complicated is what I've spent most of my life trying to avoid.

But when I zoom in on the image so her face fills the screen, I have no doubt: *I want to see her again. Soon.*

Before I can change my mind, I begin to type a message into my notes app. I want the spelling and punctuation to be correct, to be my funniest Dan the Man version of myself.

Except . . . Gemma doesn't need fake charm or a sassy chat-up line. She needs honesty. So I start typing directly into WhatsApp and press Enter before I can edit:

I loved spending time with you today. I don't know what's happening between us, but I know it feels good. Would you like to see what happens next?

Chapter 16: Gemma

'There's no polite way of asking this, but did the hormones you took to conceive Zach make you horny?'

My sister laughs so loudly that people in the cafe look round to see what's wrong. When they realize it's Laura, they shrug. This place serves as an unofficial police canteen, so it's mostly her colleagues, and they know what she's like.

'I was *not* expecting that.' She stirs her tea with its three fortifying sugars. 'It seems like a lifetime ago, but I don't think so. What's the deal? Have you turned into a nymphomaniac?'

The server delivers a plate of egg, chips and beans to Laura and a toasted teacake to me: with its meagre dried-fruit content, it's the healthiest thing I could find on the menu. But I've zero appetite because . . .

'I've been asked out. On a date. Kind of.'

And it's tonight. In five hours and thirty-six minutes.

I have *no idea* why I said yes.

'You are *shitting me*.' Laura looks up from sprinkling way too much salt over her pre-shift brunch. 'That is the best news, Gem. Who? No, don't tell me, it's Lycra Puzzle Teacher Boy, isn't it?'

We've both seen Jed in his cycling gear. The thought of his genitals squished under neon-green cycling shorts and his

115

nipples wrinkled like the currants in my teacake dials down my excitement levels.

Until I picture Dan again, and my personal heatwave returns. 'Never. No. No. It's someone I met by total chance.'

Is it, though? Andrew always insisted that nothing is random: there's always a pattern or a reason why things happen, if you search hard enough.

'Tell me more! But quickly,' she orders me, between mouthfuls. 'I'm on duty at two.'

'OK, I know this is going to sound weird but I was on my way back from a clinic appointment when I saw this guy.' *This guy.* The oily smell and soft-rock soundtrack of the cafe fade away.

'So what was he like?'

'Cute. But also . . . familiar. Have you ever had that? Where you're like: *hello, I know you*? Even though you don't.'

Laura looks thoughtful as she squeezes more ketchup onto her plate. 'Nope. I fancied Mel more than I've ever fancied anyone, but it was a hell of a lot less spiritual than what you're describing. You've got it *bad.*'

I laugh awkwardly. It doesn't feel natural to have this kind of conversation with my sister. There are four years between us, but she was always *so* grown-up and sure of herself that it seems like a much bigger gap. Over the years I've taken her advice on career and money and DIY. Even on IVF.

But *never* love.

Love? Get over yourself, Gemma. You mean *lust.*

'Quite bad. Yes. Which is why I've been thinking it must be the hormones.'

'You're only on the pills, though, right?'

'I've started my injections now, but I hadn't when I met Dan.'

'Dan. Hmm. Solid name. Tell me more.'

116

'It turns out – and this isn't a huge coincidence, when you think of where I saw him – that he was on his way to Oncology to be with his daughter. Who I'd already met, when I took Bear to the hospital school.'

'Whoa! He's got a kid? Is he divorced? Widowed?' She's straight into interrogation mode.

'No. He and his ex were never really together.'

'You've got his entire life story now?'

I'd been planning to tell Laura everything, including the bad bits, and ask for a hefty dose of sisterly common sense. But now I'm not sure if I want my bubble bursting quite yet. 'Some of it.'

'Must be the oestrogen, because this is not your normal MO. You've never been one for grand love affairs.'

I give her a dark stare: Andrew and I definitely count – counted – as a grand love affair, though our attraction developed slowly. There's nothing slow about this.

'It's only a date. But it's . . . well, it's tonight.' In five hours and twenty-four minutes.

'Fuck me, Gem, talk about making me wait for the punchline.'

'I'm wondering if I should cancel.' But the thought of doing that makes the cafe – and this bright Thursday – seem instantly dingier.

'Who else have you talked to about this?'

'No one but you. I've lost touch with most of the old crowd. Even if I hadn't, they don't know about the embryos. So they wouldn't have the full picture.'

Laura pushes her plate away: she's polished off the lot while I've been baring my soul. 'Got to admit, your timing is insane. But life's like that sometimes, right? Everything happens at once.' She takes a giant slurp of tea. 'And why *shouldn't* you meet your next husband in the street?'

117

'Next husband? Now who's jumping the gun?' I sigh. 'I don't want to get married again, you know that.'

Laura stops eating, drinking or moving. My sister sitting still is unsettling. Is this how she scares suspects into confessions?

'But I want you to. We all do,' she says quietly. 'You deserve somebody to love.'

'If the treatment works, I *will* have someone to love.'

'Whatever happens with the embryo,' she reaches over to squeeze my hand, 'I won't let you stay a lonely widow for the rest of your life. Andrew would haunt me if I did.'

He threatened to do the same to me, when he started a conversation about life after he died. But I shut him down, because I couldn't admit that he might not make it.

'So what should I do? This is a guy I've met twice. It's probably nothing.'

'Probably,' Laura agrees. 'And you are a bit vulnerable and hormonal, so be careful. But there will be other guys, sooner or later. You've been focused on the treatment, but whether that works or doesn't, you've got too much love to waste.' She frowns. 'God, I hope no one overheard what I just said. That'd blow my reputation as the hard nut of Trinity cop shop.'

'I won't tell,' I say, glossing over how touched I am. 'So should I cancel?' I check my watch. Five hours and nineteen minutes to go.

'I will be very cross if you cancel. Treat it like a rehearsal for future dates. But don't shag him, eh? Your eggs are so ripe they'd explode if you have so much as a cheeky snog.'

'No kissing. I promise.'

But I can't pretend kissing hasn't crossed my mind.

* * *

118

I've not been on a date in five years, and everything's changed. There's a tonne of advice online, but dating now sounds like such hard work. I hope Dan isn't planning to take me axe-throwing or sushi-making 'to break the ice and #make-memories to ensure your date stands out in an ocean of dull dinners and drinks'.

Do real people behave like this? I have no one to ask and it's all my fault. When I got married, my single friends drifted away; and when I became a widow, I let the married ones go too. And even if there was someone around to explain dress codes or bill-splitting etiquette, they couldn't advise how to explain to someone you fancy that you're trying to become a mother with your late husband's baby.

My problems are pretty niche.

'Time to go, lazy dog.'

At least Dan asked Bear along. Online, dogs are recommended as an excellent dating 'accessory': funny, distracting and great at sussing out human beings. I already know Bear approves. We're meeting by the bridge, which I'm glad about. The flat was Andrew's space, our home, and it's all wrong to have another man come there.

As I step outside, the sultry evening wraps itself around me and the grass crackles with dryness, but the air is heavy with the hint of a storm.

I see him from a distance and everything else blurs: all I can focus on is his long, slim body, the angle of his neck, the taut muscles of his calves, revealed by the shorts he's wearing.

I don't move while I'm taking it all in. Why isn't everyone around me hypnotized by this man too?

'Gemma,' he says, when we're close enough to hear a whisper.

Close enough to kiss.

119

'Dan.'

Bear's yelps of joy break the spell. 'Yes, hello, Bear, we know you're here too,' Dan says, squatting down to scratch between his ears and rub Bear's belly, seeming to understand what makes my dog quiver with pleasure.

Would he know how to do the same to me? The thought makes me unsteady on my feet.

'I thought we could go for a walk in Leigh Woods? I've brought some bits to eat and drink.' He points at the messenger bag at his feet.

'Fabulous!' I say.

'Don't get too excited. We're not talking about a posh picnic.'

'I'm not a posh picnic kind of person.'

He raises an eyebrow, as though he doesn't believe me. 'After you.' He lets me go onto the bridge first. I'm wearing shorts, too, though now I wish I'd chosen a dress because I'm nowhere near as slim as Casey's mum. He must be able to see how my flesh dimples and wobbles as I move.

But when the pavement widens again, he's next to me and that smile he gives me . . . I don't think he's found me wanting at all.

Oh, I'd forgotten how it feels to be desired.

'Does Casey know we're out tonight?' His answer to that question might give me a sense of what he thinks is happening between us.

Dan shakes his head. 'Things are difficult right now with her mum. So I didn't want to make them even *more* complicated. I wasn't even sure I should meet you at all, but . . .' He shakes his head again. 'I *wanted* to.'

I think of his WhatsApp message and how I couldn't resist that. 'It might simply be to see what happens next?'

Dan nods and then smiles, and it's as if the earth has tilted so that the sun shines directly onto him and me.

We keep walking, towards Ashton Court, and a big, sensible part of me is thinking: *this is insane*, being here with him, when everything could be about to change for me.

'I guess it's not the most exciting date anyone's ever taken you on.'

'When the weather's like this, I can't think of anything nicer,' I reply. 'And Bear is at his happiest when he's walking.'

'How about you? What makes you happy?'

The question rattles me. Happy has seemed absurdly ambitious for so long, after Andrew's death sucked the colour out of everything. But that's not something you mention five minutes into a date.

'Um. OK. Happy? Bear makes me happy. Spending time with my niece and nephew. My parents, even though they annoy me. And making art, too. I take the piss out of my job, because I mostly draw stuff to sell other people's products, which isn't quite what I dreamed of when I was a student. But I've got a new commission that I'm working on and there've been times when I've been so absorbed in it that time totally flies.'

'I get that, sometimes. When I'm setting up for a festival. Or at an incredible gig. It's a good feeling.'

'Yeah, I'd forgotten *how* good. I didn't have it for a long time after my husband died.' It might be dating suicide to bring Andrew into it, yet I don't feel awkward. When I'm with Dan, I don't want to pretend.

'I'm sorry, Gemma. Had you been together a long time?'

'No. Less than four years. So we never had time to annoy each other, or to turn into one of those joined-at-the-hip couples. But still, losing him made me lose bits of myself. It's only very recently that I've started to remember who I am – what I like about life.'

Very recently. Only in the last eight days, since I ran into you.

121

Dan gazes at me intensely. 'I've known people who've fallen apart when they lost their partner. You must be a very strong person.'

Bear barks at a boxer dog on the other side of the road. 'Having him around really helped. When you've got someone – or something – in your life that depends on you, falling apart doesn't seem like an option.' I've had enough of talking about myself now. 'How about you? Have you had your heart broken or are you usually the one who does the breaking?'

'A bit of both. Though mostly I try to avoid either. Keep things light.'

Right. Like I've just been doing, telling him about my grief. The problem is, now I can't think of *any* topic that doesn't involve death or heartbreak.

He notices my silence. 'But it's different with you.'

'Sorry.'

'No. It's *good* different. You make me want to tell you what's going on up here.' Dan taps his head.

'Happens to me *all the time*. I've got one of those faces.'

'It's a beautiful face.'

I catch my breath. 'A kind one, people say. Whereas *your* face stops traffic. You do know you're very good-looking?'

Dan frowns, like he's going to disagree. Then he laughs. 'It's the luck of the draw, isn't it? Sperm meets egg. The ultimate lottery.'

Now. *Tell him now.* You're lying to him, and to yourself, by not telling him about the embryos.

But we're already at the castellated entrance to Ashton Court and Bear is pulling so hard at the lead I almost topple over. When I let him go, he rolls in the grass, making high-pitched squeals of pleasure.

'OK, Dan. Your turn now. Casey says you work in music. Is that what makes *you* happy?'

'For sure. The first time I ever got close to a band playing live – oh, I thought nothing else would ever be that good.'

'How old were you?'

'Fourteen. I spent some time in foster care when I was a teenager, and the family lived close to Reading Festival. Me and a school mate, we snuck in. That was me. Hooked for life. I can't even tell you how it felt.'

I'm curious about the foster-care part, but even more curious about his passion for music. 'Try. For me.'

He stops, closes his eyes, swaying as though he's back there. 'The way the sound travels through you. I'm not a music snob. It could be almost any genre, because when an artist puts everything they've got into their act, it transmits to everyone around. You can't resist, even if you try your hardest, and it's like we're all joined up, connected—' He stops. 'I sound deranged, don't I?'

'No. I like it. I hate small talk. This is real. Passionate.'

He stares at me and I almost regret using that word out loud.

Almost.

Bear has come back to me now, and he's doing his impatient dance, stepping backwards and forwards, waiting for me to throw the ball. I lob it as far as I can and he races after it.

'The downer is: it's a passion that's left me with tinnitus. So I get ringing and buzzing in my ears and I'll lose more of my hearing as I get older.' He laughs. 'Not exactly selling myself, am I?'

It wouldn't stop me wanting to get old with you.

Whoa! Stop this right now, Gemma Boxer. 'So what is it you do at festivals?'

'A good friend of mine runs one of the big staging companies. Setting up for the artists – lighting, sound systems, even pyrotechnics. I manage the project overall. But that's seasonal, so I also help run a carpentry training workshop. We take kids who've had a rough start and give them skills so they can apply for an apprenticeship.'

'Sounds rewarding.'

He nods. 'Yeah. I – I try to give them what I would have needed, when I was a teenager.'

'Needed but didn't get?'

Dan doesn't reply. Bear is back and has dropped the ball at our feet, so now Dan picks it up and throws it.

He watches the dog tear through the grass before speaking again. 'It's no biggie. When I was around Casey's age, my real dad stopped being in my life.' He's speaking slowly now, and I can see the effort that's going into deciding what words to use, and how much to tell me. 'My foster parents were great, but I'd just hit that adolescent stage when I wouldn't listen to anyone. It took me till I was well into my twenties to get my shit together.'

Is this why he let Casey down, and her mother too? The timing fits. 'Did you have your shit together when you met Angelica?' I watch his face, to see if I might be pushing too far, too fast.

He narrows his eyes. 'No way. Like I said before, Angelica and I got together at a festival. The soggiest Glastonbury there's ever been in fact. But the most memorable too.' He stops walking. 'I don't think I've ever talked to anyone about this. So how come I want to tell you?'

'That face of mine again.' The intensity of this moment makes me blush.

'Yes. That face. So Angelica got pregnant and it took her a while to track me down, but she turned up on the doorstep a couple of weeks before Christmas, out here' – he gestures a swollen belly – 'and wanted to play Happy Families.'

'I thought it was the child maintenance people that found you, after Casey had been born?' I remember too late that it was Jed who told me this, and hope Dan doesn't realize.

'That's what I told my friends. And what Angelica told Casey. Because the alternative makes me sound like such a bastard. Which is true, but it'd hurt Casey if she found out.'

'So you knew you were going to be a father, but you never gave it a chance?'

He looks ashamed. 'I am a coward unfortunately.'

Except I don't believe him. There's no logic, but deep inside, I *know* he's better than the man he thinks he is. 'Are you sure it was that simple? Because I don't see a coward.'

The air turns heavier. His answer *matters* to both of us.

Dan walks slowly, not acknowledging me. 'Once the shock wore off, a part of me believed that Angelica being pregnant – me becoming a dad – could be the best thing ever. I wanted to make everything all right.'

'So what went wrong?'

'After she was born, I freaked out. I knew nothing about how a family works, how to be a parent. I had nothing to offer a baby except maintenance, which I paid of course. I thought it would be better for her if I wasn't involved, so I couldn't let her down, the way my dad let *me* down.'

'So what changed?'

'Three weeks ago I got a Facebook message. From Casey. She told me she'd got a brain tumour . . .' His voice tails off and I can see on his face the shock he felt, even now. 'The message was so calm. She said she knew I hadn't wanted to be in her life, but she needed treatment in Bristol, and did I know of a place to stay?'

'Bloody hell.'

'Yeah. Nothing for years, then everything. Plus, there was something else about the message. I could tell she needed more than an address. I messaged her back to offer her my place. There was a bit of . . . negotiation with her mum, but it's worked out so far.'

'Letting her into your life must have taken guts.'

He shakes his head. 'She's the brave one, and I'm never gonna be Dad of the Year. But I'm not the basket case I was at twenty, thanks to my friends. They've stood in for family many times. They *get* me so much more than anyone I'm related to by blood.'

Each sentence seems to have a whole other story underneath, and I want to understand what shaped this man. Even solve the puzzle of our connection.

Before I can think of another question, he kicks at the grass. 'Sorry. This is way too heavy for a first date.'

He's right. We're breaking all the rules.

'It's the truth spell, remember?' I say. 'But it's good that your friends are there for you. I've been very lucky. My family isn't perfect, but they've always been ready to support me.' I think about Laura at lunch. 'Or, more often, to tell me what to do.'

Right now she'd be telling me to lighten up. So as Dan lays out a blanket and offers me a choice of a veggie or a chicken burrito, beer or juice, I joke about how limited my knowledge of music is, and he says he'll do me a playlist, so long as I take him to a gallery, teach him what to look for in a painting.

And even though we both seem to be making a big leap, assuming there will be a next date, or *multiple* next dates, I don't want to shut the idea down yet. Because it's such a lovely daydream, like my parents planning the itinerary of their round-the-world retirement cruise when, deep down, they know they'll never be able to afford it.

Bear lies on his back on the grass, enjoying the peachy

126

evening sun on his belly. We fall silent, but now complications rush into my head to fill the gap. Everything in my life is loaded and mission-critical.

Whereas this is a mirage and it must be the same for Dan, with his unstable ex and his sick daughter. We should finish our burritos, thank each other for a nice evening, make vague excuses about being too busy to meet for a while. Run as fast as we can back to our too-full lives. Except . . .

'This is perfect,' he says softly.

The intensity in his eyes mirrors my own desires. If this is a daydream and none of it is real, then whatever we do next doesn't matter. This is an evening out of time. Inconsequential. A balloon rising and disappearing.

I want to kiss him so much more than I want to run.

Chapter 17: Dan

Gemma shuts her eyes. This is when I should move in for the kiss we both want.

I don't *only* want to kiss her. She's the sexiest woman I've ever met. She has her own place. Angelica would be super-happy if I stayed out all night.

All I can hear is Gemma's breathing. She wants me as much as I want her. And I am Dan the Man, the people-pleaser, *here for a good time*, *not a long time*, living the dream. What is stopping me?

I want more.

The answer comes with more questions. *More what? Why her? Why me?*

I move back, out of range, breaking the spell.

'Are you OK?' Gemma asks, still leaning forward. I get this picture in my head – as clear as an actual memory – of her, in my bed, under a crisp white sheet, beckoning me back.

Am I OK?

Yeah. More than OK. I want to stay in this moment and not have anything change.

Because what's better than the time when you know you're going to sleep with someone, and your body *is* about to take over, and your brain bursts with hope.

The kicker is that nothing ever lives up to those hopes. After the sex, I am always hollow and desperate to get

128

away from whoever it was I wanted so badly only minutes or hours before.

I don't want that to happen with Gemma yet. I want this – the hope – to last a bit longer.

The sun's gone, like a director's clicked his fingers on our movie. *CUT. Kill the lights.* You missed your cue.

Gemma moves back now too, a hurt expression on her open face. I want to say: *It's not because I don't want you, it's because I really, really do.* But that would make no sense.

'It goes chilly so quickly, doesn't it, when the sun sets?' she says. Matter-of-fact, like the weather presenter on local TV. *Make sure you take a cardigan or jacket, because despite the heatwave, you'll feel the chill at dusk.*

I don't have a jacket, so I move the bottles off the smaller blanket and wrap it around her. As the rough wool touches the soft curve of her shoulders and the tanned flesh of her arms, I wish *I* was touching her instead.

'They shut the gates soon,' she says. 'We don't want to get locked in.'

The moment for honesty has passed; she's folding the burrito wrappers into tiny squares and replacing bottle caps. I help her up from the ground, even though I want to draw her down with me and undress her under that blanket and—

'That was nice,' she says. Like you'd say to the colleague who brought in value-range supermarket cupcakes for their birthday.

Gemma's fussing with her dog: busy, busy, busy with the lead. 'Bear won't want to go home now, so I have to put it back on to get him to come with us, it's the only way.' I can tell she's embarrassed – humiliated – by what didn't happen between us.

As we walk out of the park I search for the right thing

to say. All my usual lines sound wrong. *Not you, it's me* makes me sound like I'd struggle to get it up. *I want to take this slowly* is something I've never said before and it's not the whole truth.

So we cross the road towards Clifton.

And my arm bumps against hers and, without thinking, I'm reaching for her hand and hers is hot as mine closes gently around it, and she smiles at me and we stay like that, even though it's awkward over the bridge when we're going single file, but we don't let go.

We walk diagonally across the grass towards the terrace where her fancy flat is, and Bear pulls on the lead to go home. But he must read something in her body language because the lead goes slack and he lies down with a happy sigh.

Now? Is this my second chance? To kiss her.

But before I can act, she sighs and it's less of a happy sigh than Bear's. 'That was fun. Thank you. I hope you have a great weekend.'

And she moves in and I think, *Yes, kiss her now,* but she's giving me a firm, friendly hug – over almost before it's begun – and she drops my hand and walks away.

I half wake to what sounds like a knock on my door. Check the time. Too early for anyone else to be up.

Why do I feel like shit? It's not a hangover – I only had one beer. When I remember, I groan. Why didn't I kiss Gemma? I should have tried to explain. I pick up my phone to message her, but what would I say? *Sorry, I wanted you too much to kiss you.* Or: *Next time I promise I will?*

Ugh!

I turn over. What's happened to me? Two weeks ago I was living my best life. Uncomplicated, spontaneous, shallow. On the plus side, it's Friday and after Angelica takes Gemma to the hospital they're going back to the Midlands. I have the penthouse to myself again for the weekend, though it doesn't seem anywhere near as big a thrill as it did this time last week.

Another knock.

'DL? Sorry. It's me. Casey.'

She sounds worried. I jump out of bed, pulling on my boxers, opening the door. 'What's wrong?' Her appearance startles me: I'd forgotten about her cute new haircut. 'Are you sick?'

She shakes her head, but her frown deepens. 'I'm OK, but Mum's not good. We're meant to be up by now, packing and getting organized. But she . . .'

The door to Angelica's room is ajar. No way am I going in there to get my head bitten off. 'Is she ill?'

'Not in the way you mean.'

'Angelica?' I call out, trying to sound upbeat. 'Is everything all right?'

Nothing comes back: no sharp put-down or complaint.

'She won't get up,' Casey whispers.

I stand on the threshold. 'Angelica, can I get you a coffee? Anything else I can do to help?'

This time I do hear a sound, like a kitten's mew. Finally: 'Go away.'

Casey beckons me into the living room and onto the terrace. 'Usually, when she's like this, it doesn't last more than a day. But it seems worse this time.'

'Usually? This has happened before?'

My daughter scratches her head, even though the wig's gone. 'She's been through a lot. She gets tired sometimes.'

There's a catch in her voice on the last couple of words. Casey is trying not to cry. I want to hug her, but she'd

131

definitely cry then, which is the last thing either of us wants.

Except . . .

I do step towards her and I do wrap my arms around her, and after a second's tense hesitation, she lets herself sink into me and her chest begins to heave, but she stays silent. Even now, this brave girl can't quite let herself go.

'Oh, Casey,' I whisper into the top of her head. I smell the floral tang of hairspray from the salon yesterday and I feel her tears rolling down my chest. 'It's OK,' I say, the words sounding stagey to me. But they don't to her, because she grips me tighter. 'I'm here now. You're not on your own.'

I'm good at logistics. I cancel work meetings, get Casey to the hospital for treatment at ten, then we race back here, where I ask her to pack a bag for her and for her mum.

'How long shall I pack for?'

'Just the weekend,' I say. Because even if Angelica's struggling, she must understand that Casey can't have her treatment interrupted. Hopefully, a couple of nights in her own place where she can relax will sort Angelica out.

What if it doesn't?

I expect her to bawl me out when I go into her room. I hope she doesn't sleep naked. I've never seen her naked – not even when Casey was conceived. The still air makes the space oppressive, but when I sit on the edge of the bed there's no fire in her eyes and I think she's slept in yesterday's clothes.

'Go away,' she says.

'I can't do that. I am going to drive you and Casey back home,' I tell her. 'This isn't the right place for you to be while you're not . . . yourself. OK?'

It's like she's not hearing me or processing the words, but she doesn't argue. Is this what a nervous breakdown looks like? The only thing stopping me from calling a doctor is what Casey said about Angelica getting better before, with no treatment. How scary it must have been for Casey to face this on her own.

Together we get Angelica out of bed: she's like a sleep-walker, her eyes open, but not seeing the same reality as we are. When the lift moves, she jumps, but that deadness in her eyes stays the same.

I reach out to steady her and she grasps my wrists. For a moment I'm back at the first-aid tent, thirteen years ago. She was more out of it then, but at least there was an obvious reason. I sat with her, so she'd be less afraid of whatever the E was doing to her brain. I kept repeating her name, telling her she was safe, and after a few minutes she settled enough to close her eyes and doze. And when she woke again, she was smiling, and I felt proud, because it proved I could do something selfless for someone else. *That I wasn't like my dad*.

The lift jolts as it stops. *Basement floor. Mind the doors*.

Angelica heads for the driver's side, but we steer her into the passenger seat instead.

'It's OK, Mummy,' Casey says, and it's the first time I've heard her use that babyish name, 'you can sleep for the journey. And I'll be behind you, in the back. I'll be holding your hand.'

The Friday afternoon traffic means the journey takes for ever, and I daren't turn on the radio or even talk to Casey, in case it disturbs her mum. Angelica dozes most of the way, her neck bent, half waking when we go over bumps, but never enough to ask why I'm there, or where we're going.

The Ka is tinny, and although the interior is spotless, the strange noises the car makes suggest it hasn't been serviced or well maintained. Which, knowing Angelica's usual attitude to danger, must be because she's short of money.

I follow the satnav off the motorway and round the fringes of a couple of big towns before we get into proper countryside. It reminds me of Somerset, but lusher and greener, with dark hills hemming us in.

I catch Casey's eye in the rear-view mirror. She looks expectant and I wonder why, until I realize it matters to her what I think of where she lives.

'Lovely,' I mouth back, though the truth is that the empty terrain scares me. I need people around me. Noise.

The centre of the village is no more than a church, a pub and a general store, with the bus shelter that must be the only point of escape. The buildings are sturdy rather than charming. The maps app directs me instead.

'Here, on the left.' She points towards a row of buildings, then touches her mother gently on the shoulder. 'You can wake up now, Mum, we're home.'

I get out. There are three brick cottages and I try to guess which is theirs. The one with the murky net curtains shielding each pane from non-existent passers-by? Or the neater one on the end, with pretty window boxes?

But when I get the bags out, Casey is guiding her mum past the houses, towards a single-storey chalet-style building I hadn't even noticed. From a distance it's cute, like something from a cartoon. But the overgrown front garden has a path of slimy flagstones that leads to a scuffed front door. The whole building looks uncared for.

Is it about money? I don't pay a fortune in support, but surely there's enough for the basics? And Angelica's family is well off. Why isn't her father stepping up to help maintain the place?

Casey glances back at me, her eyes narrowed, almost like she's daring me to judge her – judge *them*.

I slap on a cheerful smile as she takes the keys out of her mum's handbag and unlocks the door.

Chapter 18: Gemma

Saturday 14 July

Whenever I'm wavering about the future, Isabel always gets me back on track.

As I search for an elusive parking space on the crowded streets near her house, I know I need a dose of her positivity. It's still hot, but the air in Bath seems more refined than in Bristol. I thought a change of scene might give me a break from *all the thoughts about Dan.*

All the thoughts about Dan that are counter-productive, as he hasn't called me since our date and the almost-kiss. I might be out of practice at dating, but I definitely know what that means.

Bear starts barking when we're still half a dozen houses away. Isabel must have been waiting for us, because she appears instantly at her Farrow & Balled front door.

I let go of the dog's lead and he runs towards her, his tail wagging so hard it could power the entire street.

Before I met my mother-in-law I had an image in my head of a well-upholstered farmer's widow, all dimples and cuddles and floury hands. Instead she was wiry, with toned arms and scarlet shellac nails. We had nothing in common except Andrew, and it was only when he got sick that we started to bond.

'Someone is about to explode with excitement!' Isabel says. She's immaculate, as ever, her petite frame draped in an expensively cut peach jersey jumpsuit. She'll be sixty later this month, but she could be mistaken for at least ten years younger.

I close the gate behind me and Isabel lets Bear jump up and down. 'Yes, I adore you too!' It's good to see her laughing. When we met at Christmas, even her expensive serums couldn't disguise the devastation my latest failure had wreaked.

Bear gallops onto the patio. The Moroccan table in the conservatory is laid for lunch, including wine glasses and a jug of iced water with mint. On the other table lies a half-finished jigsaw, a complex Klimt painting in shades of blue and gold. Andrew got his love of puzzles from his mother.

Isabel brings through a quiche on a marble platter. 'From the deli – I swear he uses unicorn tears to make this pastry.'

When she returns with a bowl of spiky coleslaw and a bottle of chilled Chablis, I let her pour me a small glass that I won't drink. But I don't feel like telling her my news until after lunch. Must keep to safe topics.

'That one looks hard going?' I say, nodding at the jigsaw.

'I've been neglecting it a little.' When she smiles, there's a hint of secrecy on her pink-frosted lips. 'I take it there's still no sign of Andrew's puzzle?'

For a while after he died, Isabel became obsessed with the idea that her son had hidden some kind of jigsaw or riddle in the flat for us. Apparently he told her he had when she sat with him one night, near the end. I've turned the place upside down, but there's no sign, so it must be wishful thinking on her part: a lot of what he said in those last few days made no sense.

'No. But I always keep an eye out for it.' I cut into the quiche. 'You're right, this smells heavenly.'

'Are you eating enough? You look weary, Gemma.' She scrutinizes me with those light-blue eyes and they're so much like Andrew's that I have to look away.

'I've got a new commission that I'm drawing preliminary sketches for, and I can't focus when it's this hot, so I work at night.'

Before she can ask any follow-ups, I try the quiche. The eggs are soft and the Brie melts in the mouth. She clearly doesn't suspect I'm trying embryo transfer again or she'd never risk serving me a listeria time bomb.

'You don't need to be working all hours, Gemma. Creatives are surely allowed to miss deadlines, be a little flaky?'

Flaky. She has no idea how bad things got. Only Bear knows how lost I've been, and I worry it's traumatized him for life. I peer through the doors: he doesn't appear too traumatized now as he whizzes around the garden, barking at the goldfinches pecking at Isabel's stained-glass feeder.

'Well, I need all the work I can get right now, especially as I can't be sure what the situation will be—'

So much for waiting till after lunch.

Her left eyebrow rises. 'What situation?'

I exhale. Let's get this over with. 'I'm . . . giving it another go. The frozen embryo transfer.'

Her body straightens up. 'Right now?'

We both glance down at my plate and I brace myself to have the remains of the killer quiche snatched away. Instead she smiles, but it doesn't reach her eyes. She felt my two failures almost as keenly as I did.

'Yeah. Summer seemed as good a time as any . . .'

Isabel lets her gaze fall onto my tummy, before checking herself. 'How far into the cycle are you?'

Previously I've given her exact dates and she tracked my progress as precisely as I imagine she used to track cattle being inseminated on the farm. 'It's very early on, and I'm superstitious. I am trying not to raise anyone's hopes.'

'But you haven't had the transfer yet?'

'No.'

Isabel puts down her fork. 'The thing is, Gemma, I was starting to hope that you'd decided to let it go.'

I gawp at her. 'I don't understand.'

'Don't you?'

'You don't think I should use the last two embryos?'

She stands up, walks towards the window. *Anything but tell me to my face that she's betraying me.*

'You know, when I lost my husband, the only reason I kept going was for Andrew. If it hadn't been for him, I think I'd have gone to bed and never got up again. The loss was so *physical*. As though when the stroke took him, it took away this vast chunk of me, too. My instinct for survival. My history. My future.'

She's lost in the memory and I should empathize, but all I'm thinking is: *This isn't about you.*

'But of course I *did* have Andrew – not to mention the farm – so fading away wasn't a possibility. When Andrew left for college five years later, and I sold up to move here, it came back. That *pointlessness* . . .' She turns back towards me and takes an inelegant gulp of wine.

'It must have been very tough, but I'm not you, Isabel,' I say. 'And I can't believe you've changed sides.'

Isabel finally glances up at me, her eyes bluer even than her son's. 'I am on *your* side, Gemma. If anything, more than before. Losing my son made me a little *unhinged*, and the idea of a grandchild gave me hope when I needed it.'

'Yes. Hope is the whole point!'

'But now . . . the grief has finally started to fade and I can see the other legacies that Andrew left. His business has helped dozens of food producers, even preserved some of our landscape. And for those of us who loved him, he's left memories. Words. There doesn't have to be a baby.'

'You're betraying your son.' Bear lifts his head, alarmed by the change in my voice.

'No, I'm not. I'm saying what he'd say. He wanted you to be happy, and you still have time to meet someone else – have a family with them.'

Or even meet someone who already has a family.

Thinking of Dan now is ridiculous. I haven't even kissed the man – though only because *he* backed off. And his silence since Thursday night says it all.

'I don't want someone else's child. I want Andrew's.'

Isabel sighs and takes another slug of wine, as though she's steeling herself. 'Are you sure you're doing this for the right reasons, Gemma?'

'What's that supposed to mean?'

'I know you and Andrew disagreed about timing. When you first married.'

No. Not this.

'That's not true.'

It *is* true. I wanted kids, but I also wanted a year or two enjoying being a couple before parenthood forced us to share each other. When I had a pregnancy scare, a few weeks after we got home from our honeymoon, the relief when my period came was huge.

And now that memory taunts me every time I get a negative result. Because if we *had* tried straight away, Andrew might have been a dad before he got sick. The thought of him with our baby in his arms makes my eyes sting.

SPLASH!

We both look up.

Bear has jumped into the pond. He thrashes about noisily until his movements turn into a chaotic doggy-paddle, and he's yelping in delight.

'Bloody hell!' Isabel appears at my side. Bear's flat head bobs up and down, covered in bright-green pondweed, like a miniature Loch Ness monster. His brow is furrowed and his dark eyes seem to say: *not my bad. It was the fish.*

Isabel clambers over the rockery, reaching for a large pond net, like she's the Child Catcher. 'Bear!' Her voice is stern but not angry. His ears swivel in her direction, followed by his entire upper body, creating ripples around him.

'Out, NOW!' she says, gesturing with her hand towards the patio. Bear swim-waddles towards her, a large lily pad resting on his head, like a designer hat.

'Isabel, he's going to—'

The moment Bear's paws hit the patio, he shakes, with my mother-in-law at the epicentre of the mini-tornado. Her peach jumpsuit is speckled green and black, her face freckled with algae and mud.

What would Andrew do now? Offer a towel, a hug, a burst of laughter?

Probably all three. God, I miss him.

Isabel has Bear in her arms, his filthy, wriggling bulk pressed against her chest, and his pink tongue pokes out as he tries to lick her.

'Let me take him,' I say.

'No. I can't get any filthier than I already am, and *you*—' She hesitates. 'Well, given your plans, you need to take care of yourself. Let's get him in the bath – sorry, Bear, but there's always a price to be paid for fun.'

* * *

I drive home with Bear snoring next to me on the passenger seat, his seatbelt harness tight against his damp chest.

'Did you do that on purpose?' I stroke between his ears as I wait at traffic lights.

After Isabel cleaned him up, we didn't go back to talking about the FET. But now my anger at Isabel has expanded to fury at the entire world. *Why can't anyone accept this is what we wanted?*

When we'd made our decision, we tried to get the whole family onside: we invited my parents and Isabel over in early January, shortly after Andrew relapsed. Things were moving much faster than we'd hoped.

I baked a banana cake and bought deli sandwiches and laid the food out on the table we previously used for jigsaws. (Our dining table had gone into storage to make room for Andrew's new hospital bed.)

Andrew did most of the talking, though words that had always come so easily were more halting now, from the cancer or the treatment, or both.

'We want a family so much, and it could still happen for Gemma. I haven't put any pressure on her, and of course she can change her mind at any time. But we got four embryos from the IVF. That's four chances.'

My mum couldn't contain her rage. We were *selfish and stupid and, what was more, we were giving up the battle against cancer too easily.* We should focus on drug trials, not distract ourselves by planning a baby in this morbid way.

As my mother's tsunami of anger crashed over us, I caught Isabel's eye and I knew she understood why we needed to believe in a future. But even my dad couldn't bring himself to say he approved, and after he bundled Mum off home, Isabel and I tried to force party food down our dry throats.

'Do you think we're mad, Mum?' Andrew asked her.

She shook her head. 'No. You're trying to make the best of a bad hand.'

'But is it unfair to Gemma, or our future children?'

'You might still get to be the brilliant dad we know you can be,' Isabel said, though I don't see how she could have believed that. 'But you lost your dad and still turned out all right.'

'I had Dad in my life for fourteen good years. It's different to bring a child into the world knowing they'll only ever have one parent.'

'If it comes to it, Gemma won't be alone, and neither will your child.' Her throat caught on *child*. She turned to smile at me. 'And, Gemma, your mum will come round, I'm sure of that. No one can resist a baby.'

She was meant to be my rock. But as I approach the flat, I'm wondering if her change of heart means I need to think again. I can postpone the treatment right up until the last moment, until they thaw an embryo to prepare it for transfer. Should I? Whenever I think about Andrew, I want our child so badly.

But when I was with Dan in Ashton Court I wanted *him* more than anything else.

Logic tells me you can't compare the two: one comes from love and a deep, human desire to reproduce. We wouldn't be here without that need.

But you could argue that we wouldn't be here without lust, either. The way I felt with Dan on Thursday night, nothing else mattered but the need for his body next to mine. For him to kiss me, touch me, *fuck* me.

The memory makes me horny again, before shame hits me hard. It was one-sided anyway. It *didn't* feel like that at the time, but something stopped him and he hasn't bothered to get in touch since.

I'm nowhere near as desirable to him as he is to me. Plus,

this might not be about Dan as a person. He could be my brain's way of checking I am doing the right thing.

That's one of the many downsides to trying to conceive this way. There's no passion involved in pills and jabs to the tummy, probes and scans of the uterus. Instead of letting yourself get carried along by a short wave of desire, conception becomes a major project, each step a new test of commitment.

I felt so lonely when I left this morning. After seeing Isabel, it's even worse.

As we approach home, Bear lets out a deep sigh, and his paws tremble as he runs in his dreams. He loves sleeping almost as much as Andrew did. I turn off the engine, pick him up and carry him up the stairs. His coat smells of biscuit and Isabel's Aveda shampoo.

I plonk him on the sofa and fill the kettle for yet another mug of bloody camomile tea. With his hair all fluffed up from his emergency bath, Bear looks even more like the dog on the front of our book.

It's not Isabel's advice I need, but Andrew's sweet, comforting memories. His words never fail me.

IT WAS MEANT TO BE: HOW MUMMY AND DADDY MET

The day we met seemed ordinary. Daddy needed some pictures done, and
Mummy was the best at drawing animals. We were both extremely shy at first, but
everything began to change when we spent very long hours working together.

After a few weeks Daddy asked Mummy to go on a date to the cinema, and the
next thing we knew we were falling in love. Mummy loved Daddy's brilliant
sense of humour, and Daddy loved Mummy's kindness and incredible smile.
The more time we spent together, the more we began to realize
how much we missed each other whenever we were apart –
and so Daddy asked Mummy to marry him, and she said YES!

Two years after we met, Mummy and Daddy got married in June 2015.
It was the best day of our lives. Weddings can be a bit boring, but ours was
terrific. We had a 'cake' made of cheese, and another cake with four tiers in the
shape of the cow Mummy drew that impressed Daddy when they met. Watch
the video and you'll see it really was an amazing day, full of love and happiness.
I think we look like movie stars! For our party we hired the pier, which is a
magic building that floats on top of the sea. Our dressed-up guests went on all the rides,
even the dodgems and the helter-skelter. One day you'll go there too with
friends and family, it's the perfect place for birthdays and celebrations.
Of course you can go on ordinary days too – to cheer you up if you're sad.

Ready for another (DADDY SAYS)? After the wedding we decided something big!
You came into the world because we had so much love that we had to share it!

Chapter 19: Dan

For once the buzzing isn't all in my head. It's real insects, waking me up. I bat them away as I remember where I am: the back porch of Angelica's chalet, in a sleeping bag.

I crept out here last night when the smell of bleach in the house made my eyes water and I longed for fresh air.

My bladder's full and my bones ache from lying on the decking planks. I used to be fine with sleeping rough, but I guess it's a young man's game. There are voices coming from inside – Casey's and two others. I don't want to face strangers in my dishevelled state, but there's nowhere in this scruffy garden where I can safely pee without being seen. I can imagine what Angelica would make of *that*.

I shed the sticky sleeping bag like snakeskin, heading straight for the bathroom, with its beige suite and corn-dolly tiles. The toilet flushes with the feeblest dribble: another little DIY task that needs sorting. I wrap a towel around my waist to cover my boxers and go into the main room to fetch the rest of my clothes. I'm guessing there will be an inquisition.

A sturdy woman with dark curly hair sits next to Casey on the sofa. In the armchair opposite is a girl with the same dramatic hair. The kid must be Casey's age, but she's longer, broader, wearing a cropped T-shirt and very short shorts.

'So this is the infamous Dan Lennon?' the woman says.

I nod. 'That's me.'

'You're exactly how I pictured you.' Her tone tells me this is not a good thing. She stands up and for a second I think she's about to slap my face. At the last minute she shakes my hand instead. 'I'm Harriet, Angelica's best friend, and this is my daughter, Molly. Casey's been filling us in.'

'Angelica's still in bed?' I ask, unnecessarily, because the chalet is so small there's nowhere else she *could* be.

'The car journey tired her out,' Casey says, and we all stare down at the warped laminate, because we know it goes a lot deeper than that.

'Girls, why don't you go for a walk?'

Molly tuts, but unravels herself from the armchair. 'Can I have money for a Coke at the shop? And a Magnum?'

Harriet reaches into her huge designer bag – I wonder what she does for work here in this backwater. Perhaps she commutes to run a private school or a big bank: she's used to getting her own way. Except, I reckon, where her daughter is concerned. She hands Molly a five-pound note and, when Molly doesn't budge, swaps it for a tenner.

Molly is almost out of the door, but Casey hesitates.

'Don't worry, sweetheart,' Harriet says. 'We'll be here if your mum needs us.'

A floorboard creaks when the front door shuts behind the girls. I wish I'd brought my tools with me, so I could leave the chalet in slightly better shape. 'This place needs a bit of TLC,' I say.

Harriet's sour face is back. 'It hasn't exactly been top priority since Casey got sick. My husband has offered to do some jobs, but Angelica said no. Her dad got so frustrated he even sent round a van full of builders, but she sent them packing too.'

147

I shiver. That sounds like Vaughn – if someone won't do what you want, try to bully them into it.

But this isn't about him. 'It's not just the house,' I say, speaking quietly because the door to the bedroom is ajar. 'I'm worried about Angelica. She seems to be very anxious all the time.'

'Not your concern, Dan. Thanks for bringing her home. We'll take it from here.'

Her rudeness lets me off the hook. If I get the train now, I can be home by lunchtime. Casey and Angelica managed fine without me for twelve years. Except it doesn't *feel* fine.

'Well, Casey is only halfway through her treatment, so we need to make arrangements for how that carries on.'

Harriet picks up the glass of water on the rickety table, puts it down again. 'They can do the other half when Angelica's stronger.'

'No. The doctors say Casey can only go through the process once.'

She raises her hands to massage her temples. 'We'll fix it somehow. You don't need to worry about it.' Her smile is fake, and she's clearly trying to get me out of the door as quickly as possible.

Perhaps this bossy woman *will* get everything sorted out. I should be pleased that Angelica has a friend who cares enough to dislike me this much on sight.

But what about Casey? Who is sticking up for her?

'It's my job to worry about it. I won't let my daughter's medical care suffer because of this.'

Harriet scoffs. '*Your* daughter. Now isn't that *sweet*? Born-again dad mansplaining parenting to a woman. You couldn't make it up.'

I hate her. For her lazy cliché, for her mocking voice.

For the fact that she's speaking the truth.

148

The easiest thing is to go with what this Harriet woman wants. And I could call Gemma on the way home, pick up where we left off. Except the first thing she'll ask me will be: *How is Casey?* And I'll have to admit I left her alone with a sick mother and neighbours who are in denial about how serious this is.

'Listen, Harriet, if you want to spend your Saturday morning slagging me off, go ahead. But it won't help Angelica or Casey, will it?'

'The best way you can help them is by leaving us to sort this out.'

'I can't wait to get the hell out of this Village of the Damned, OK? But your help isn't enough. Has a doctor ever seen Angelica?'

'She's not into conventional medicine. I downloaded a meditation app on her phone for stress and I thought she'd stopped getting herself into these . . . states.' For the first time, doubt crosses Harriet's face. 'Though I haven't seen her this bad before.'

'Casey has got pretty good at hiding the signs from outsiders, it seems.'

Harriet bristles. 'What's that supposed to mean?'

'Only that she wants to protect her mum.'

'No shit, Sherlock. But there are limits to how much you can interfere in someone else's family.'

Except, when a kid is suffering, surely you have to step in. If someone had done that with me—

This isn't about me.

My leg muscles twitch with the urge to scram, so I don't make things worse. But the instinct to protect Casey is stronger. She can't fight this alone. 'From where I'm sitting, Angelica needs her daughter to get well, so everything can go back to normal.'

Harriet sniffs. 'I suppose that's a valid point.'

'Which means Casey can't have her proton beam therapy interrupted. It's only another fortnight.'

She sighs grudgingly, takes out her phone. 'All right. I guess I could get a rota together to drive Casey up and down – it'd be tiring, but doable. Except it's the end of term and . . .' She shakes her head. 'Oh, this couldn't have happened at a worse time for me.'

This isn't about you. But for all Harriet's self-righteousness, I have to get her onside, because I've realized there's only one way of making this work.

'I have a solution.'

She raises her eyebrows, as though there's no way that could be true. 'Go on.'

'I take Casey back with me, on the train. Look after her this week. Drop her back next weekend. If Angelica's better, they can both come back to Bristol. If not, I'll take Casey again for the last week of therapy.'

Even as I am speaking, I'm wondering, *Can I do this? Can I be what Casey needs without anyone there to guide me, or to step in if I make a hash of it?*

I have to. It's the only way it can work.

Harriet pulls a face. 'You think you can be relied upon to take care of her by yourself? Mr Rock 'n' Roll?'

The noisy rush of blood in my ears is a warning sign. I am *this* close to losing my temper with the woman.

But that'd mean I lose everything.

The first thing to do is breathe.

I tune into the memory of Gemma's calm voice when we met for the first time. There. Her words rise above the hum and buzz of my anger. I imagine her in the room, expecting the best of me.

'Yes.' I look Harriet in the eye. '*Me.* I've spent two weeks with Casey now. I know it's not a lot, but I understand her routines. She's comfortable at the flat. I've met some of the hospital staff. I won't win any prizes for fatherhood, but I can keep her safe.'

'Wouldn't it cramp your style way too much to have your daughter on your own for a week or two?'

'I can handle it.'

Harriet breaks eye contact first. She stares at her phone, swipes, as though she still hopes she can find an app to make me – and the problem – disappear. With a final tut, she puts the phone away. 'Angelica won't like it.'

'No. But you're her best friend. You can make her see it's the least-worst option. *Please*.' I give Harriet a good old-fashioned Dan the Man smile, like my father taught me, and her sternness melts, just a fraction.

'Let me talk to her. But you'd better not let me down.'

And even though I never make promises, because I am terrible at keeping them, I find myself saying, 'I won't let Casey down. I promise you that.'

Harriet gives us a lift to Cheltenham station, which means I have to keep my mouth shut during ten miles' worth of snarky reminders.

'. . . and if her sleeping pattern is disrupted, it can affect her immune system, so it's very important you don't let her stay up too late.'

I catch Casey's eye in the rear-view mirror and she's moving her mouth up and down, imitating Harriet. Her supposed best friend, Molly, had to be press-ganged into taking the journey with us and has been staring at her phone the whole way.

'Also, remember to use the antibac gel whenever you touch any surfaces that other people might have touched too.'

When we finally board the train, I sigh with relief and Casey laughs. 'Molly's mum is a bit full-on, right? But she's always kind to mine. And to me.'

I want to hug Casey for her fairness and generosity. 'Fancy sitting in first class?'

'Won't they throw us out?'

'Not if I pay for the upgrade.'

It's the best twenty quid I've ever spent. We get a big table to ourselves, and Casey keeps reclining the seat and straightening it up again, like it's a fairground ride. The conductor brings us drinks and snack boxes – it surprises me when Casey asks for the kids' one.

Am I up to this? For all her smart talk and her teasing, she is still a kid: a kid who needs me.

'I've never been in first class before, DL – I love it!' Casey says.

'My dad and I always went first-class – until the guard arrived . . .'

'Did you get caught?'

'Never,' I say. *Not for that.*

Casey and I chat about everything *but* what has happened with her mum. Whisper about the other passengers in the carriage. Pick the houses we'd buy as the train speeds through the parched countryside.

When the snack boxes are empty, we fall silent. Her eyes dart back and forth as she watches the world whizz by. My eyes. My mum's eyes. I wonder what kind of a mother she'd have been, how my life would have been different if she'd lived.

'What was she like?'

Casey's question startles me. For a second I think she's talking about *my* mother, but then I understand she means Angelica.

152

'When you met her? What made you like her?'

I close my eyes, trying not to see the bony, exhausted woman we left behind. Taking myself back in time, to a filthy, sodden field and a different me.

'Well, the first time I saw her, everything stopped. I couldn't even hear the music.' I open my eyes and Casey is watching me intently. She needs to know her mum was special. 'Angelica was dancing in the coffee queue with her friend, wearing a bikini top and denim shorts under a big see-through poncho and flip-flops, mud all up her legs. She was knockout.'

'Did you talk to her straight away?'

'Yeah. I was fearless in those days. I bought her coffee, offered to warm her up by . . .' I realize that's not something to share with our daughter. 'You don't need to know what I said – it was very cheesy. She laughed at me, right in my face. But she said she was looking forward to seeing The Killers. It was a hint about where she'd be later, except it's almost impossible to find anyone at Glastonbury.'

'But you did?'

'I did. Almost straight away. I told her it was fate and I kissed her when they were playing "Mr Brightside". Because she made everything seem brighter to me.'

'That sounds . . . romantic.' She tuts. 'I mean, I know it didn't end up being a happy ever after, but when you talk about it, it sounds *sweet*.'

Sweet. 'I guess it was, in a way.' And mysterious: I've never felt such a draw to someone before. *Until Gemma*.

Casey takes the clown napkin that came with her snack box, folding it into a concertina shape. I don't think she's finished.

'Can I ask you something else?'

I pull a face. 'Fire away.'

'That weekend. You didn't meet her for all that long, but

back then was she worried about the stuff she worries about now?'

This is a chance to push a little deeper, but I have to be careful not to scare Casey off. 'What kind of stuff?'

'Dirt. Germs. And chemicals.'

'Like the ones in hair dye?' I wince, remembering how Angelica freaked out after Casey had the patch test.

'Chemicals are in *everything*. Food, drink, even *paint*. Did you know there's stuff in paint that can trigger allergies and even cancer—' Casey stops abruptly, maybe aware of how much she's sounding like her mum. No wonder the house hasn't been maintained, if Angelica thinks paint could have caused her daughter's tumour.

How can I reassure Casey without trivializing her fears? 'Well, the weekend we met, you couldn't be too fussy about dirt because we had the worst weather there's ever been at Glastonbury. You must have seen the pictures.'

'Mum told me a bit about that.'

'It was grim until you accepted it was a mudbath, and then it was fun.' I can feel my lips turning up into a smile. 'Your mum was on board with that. She laughed the whole time.'

It's a half-truth. Because even when she was laughing, there was something lost about Angelica: the element that drove her to go wild, to sleep with me, to take drugs for the first time. Did I recognize that because I was the same: desperate to escape from reality?

Casey nods. 'She still does. When she's well, she's so much more fun than all my friends' mums.' The love in her face makes her light up brighter than a field full of glow sticks after dark.

'She'll be herself again soon, Casey. When your treatment's over there'll be less to worry about and . . .' I tail off because we can't be certain.

'And will *you* still want to see me?'

The question takes us both by surprise. I want to say yes – to do my usual thing of saying what makes someone happy, even if I don't mean it. *But is that the truth?* I don't want to promise what I can't deliver, not this time.

'Forget it,' she says when I don't answer.

'Let's see if you want to see *me*, eh?'

She falls silent and I know I've screwed up. The right thing to do is to reassure Casey that I'll be in her life and I'll make it up with Angelica, and we'll all support each other and be like the Hugh Grant movie she mocked the other day. Because I wasn't fooled; I know it's what she wants.

Gemma would expect me to stick around too. The Dan she's met is at peak goodness, stepping up to the plate. But that's not the real me – I hardly recognize myself these days. If she even knew a fraction of what I've done in the past, she'd loathe me *so* much.

Casey's given up on her napkin origami and is tearing her snack box into confetti. Tonight I'll be taking total responsibility for the first time. And tomorrow we have an entire unfilled day ahead.

I WhatsApp Veej, asking for advice on where I could take her:

I'm back from Berlin, so why don't you come meet me and Harrison in the yurt, I bet she'd love it! Or we could get the whole gang together. We're pissed off you haven't introduced her already.

I type back my reply:

Possibly next week.

155

He answers:

Don't keep putting it off or we'll turn up and stage an intervention. But if you want to give Casey a treat, why not ASK her what she wants to do?

Why is what seems so hard to me so obvious to everyone else? I guess I can't remember my dad ever asking me what I wanted. *Poor little me.*

I put the phone face down on the table. 'So, we've got tomorrow to ourselves now. What do you fancy doing? There are loads of attractions – the SS *Great Britain*, the M Shed museum. Or stuff outdoors? The forecast is good. Your choice.'

Casey continues her shredding and I wonder if she's heard me. Then she looks up and I might be imagining it, but there's a cunning look in her eye. 'I quite fancy a balloon ride.'

'I don't think your mum would approve of that. Plus, they get very booked up in the summer.'

'Can't think of anything else.' She sighs and lays her head on the table, and I am glad Angelica isn't here to see *that*, as I haven't wiped it down.

'Come on, Casey. Bristol is full of cool things.'

She sits up. 'Thought of something. Could we have Bear over to the penthouse?'

'Bear?' I feel a brief flutter inside my belly. Imagine Gemma's smiling face, her eyebrow raised in a challenge. Her lips. A third chance to kiss them.

'And Gemma, obviously. I like them.'

'They might have other plans,' I say. *Please don't let them have other plans.*

Casey gives me a long stare, more adult than child-like. 'Oh, I bet they can make time to see *us*.'

Has she guessed I went on a date with Gemma? Seen the spark between us?

'I'll message her now,' Casey says and starts tapping on her phone before I have the chance to say no. Not that I want to.

It's been taken out of my hands.

Chapter 20: Gemma

Sunday 15 July

Was it boredom that made me say yes?

Right now, as Bear and I stand on the crowded Harbourside, this is like putting my hand into the fire, even though I know it'll burn me. Or even *because I know* it'll burn, and I want to feel something real.

I should turn back now, before I do something I regret.

'Gemma!'

Too late. I spin round to see Casey zigzagging through clumps of tourists queuing for the SS *Great Britain*. But it's Dan's presence that makes heat pump around my body faster than Brunel's steam engines. I'm remembering Leigh Woods and the almost-kiss that made me forget everything but the present.

Could an *actual-kiss* happen this time?

No. There are a hundred reasons why it's a bad idea, and the biggest is what I'm doing in less than forty-eight hours. I've got to stay focused.

'Hey, you two.' I wave, without daring to look properly into Dan's face.

He mumbles a half-hearted greeting. *Shit.* He doesn't want to be here. He's only agreed to it for his daughter's sake. But it's fine. Better that way. I smile at Casey, who is adorable in a floaty pink dress with a ditsy rose pattern.

'I love your dress. Is it new?'

'No, I brought it back from home.'

Studying her more closely, it isn't the dress that lights her up from inside. When Dan catches her up, he puts his hand in hers and the ease of it shows how close they're getting. It makes me melt, but there's a sadness too because . . .

Stop.

'When did you get back?'

'Last night,' Dan says, and I've missed that rich voice. 'Casey's mum was—'

'She was tired,' Casey says firmly. 'And had things to sort out, so we left her there. It was no big deal for me to be here on my own with DL for a week.'

Dan smiles – oh, that smile – and I see it is a *huge* deal, for both of them. What a difference a fortnight can make.

Bear starts pulling towards more life, more people.

'He's keen,' Dan says.

'He's a born extrovert.'

As he pulls us through the throngs of people – there's a maritime festival making the harbour even busier than usual – Casey asks if she can take Bear's lead. 'Be careful by the water,' I say, and she gives me this look that says, *I'm twelve, not stupid*.

Dan and I aren't quite in touching range. Which is A Good Thing. We keep our eyes on Casey and Bear, again A Good Thing, because I am *so* close to begging him to tell me the truth: why he stopped feeling that *connection*, whether he thinks he might be able to feel it again . . .

'Is Angelica just tired or is there something else to it?' I ask instead.

At the edge of my vision I see him shrugging, that delicious languor in the way he moves his long, toned limbs. Are his shoulder muscles precisely defined underneath that

T-shirt? Is his skin the same tan shade? What if he has a tattoo, something that would reveal more about him and—

'I'm worried about her. On Friday morning she wouldn't even get out of bed. I had to drive us all back to their village in the middle of nowhere and then get the train back here, so Casey wouldn't miss her next treatment.'

On Friday morning. Could that drama be the reason he hasn't called since our date on Thursday?

'So she's still not great?'

'No. Apparently it's happened before, but nobody's telling me the full story. Her best friend treated me like a mass murderer.' He looks at me directly, and this time I can't resist gazing back.

Oh. *You again.*

'Seems harsh.'

He stops walking. 'I *wanted* to call you before all this happened. But I also didn't know what I'd say.'

I gulp. 'I get it. We are both in the middle of stuff, and perhaps this is one complication too far.'

Except that's not how I'm feeling right now, as the world blurs around us and nothing else matters. This desire is the simplest thing I have experienced in months.

'I usually run a mile from complicated, Gemma. But . . .'

And he is leaning down, his head tilted, and I think, *Now. It's going to happen.*

But I step back, because Casey doesn't need to see her dad snogging the woman who volunteers at her hospital. Or, in fact, snogging any woman. Today should be all about her. I should chat with Casey, fuss over Bear – anything to distract me. But I can't see either of them.

'Where have they gone?' A second or two ago I was warm honey, sweet and liquid. Now red-hot panic surges through me, readying my muscles to take action.

160

Dan scans the crowd. His frown deepens and his pale eyes turn dark. 'Casey? CASEY, where are you?'

I push past carefree people clutching their ice creams and souvenirs, towards the quay, where an excited girl and an even more excitable dog could easily fail to notice that the walkway suddenly turns into a steep drop into the harbour . . .

Water laps calmly against mossy stone: no splashing or screaming. Are they underwater already? I don't have any sense of how long I was distracted by Dan, and he by me.

I'm too short to see above the crowd and I want to jostle and kick my way through the bodies. Something awful could be happening to Casey or Bear. If they're not in the water, has someone led them away? You read about kidnappings, dognappings, predators who come to events like this because they offer easy pickings.

'They've gone!' I call out to Dan.

The fear in his face mirrors my own.

I can't lose anyone else.

'Casey!' He's calling out and people are noticing now, asking questions. *Who have you lost? Is it your daughter? She won't have gone far. What was she wearing?*

When they use the past tense, it sounds like an omen.

'Casey?' he shouts, with so much pain in that voice, which floors me every time. 'Casey? CASEY!'

But his tone changes on that last *Casey*. From panic to relief. He's elbowing curious families out of the way and I know he's found her.

Please, please let Bear be with her.

And a path clears through the bodies and there they both are: Casey crouching down, letting Bear lick ice cream off an overflowing cone.

When she finally hears her name being called, she glances up and her surprised smile is so full of joy that I know neither of us will be able to stay cross with her. Bear ignores me, lapping more furiously at the ice cream, knowing he's got seconds before I stop him enjoying this illicit treat.

Dan bounds over to Casey and throws his arms around her. She pulls an embarrassed face at me as he holds on, but her body nestles into his. She's no idea how frightened we both were.

I decide to let Bear keep licking as I lean down to touch his warm back, as breath moves in and out of his broad ribcage.

I really, really can't lose anyone else.

What am I doing here, letting myself care about Casey and Dan, and perhaps letting them care about me? It's too soon, too dangerous. All the strength and the heat drain out of me and I'm starting to shiver.

Dan glances down at me and he seems to understand. 'These crowds are pretty full-on. Shall we go to the apartment to cool down?'

I wasn't expecting *this*.

The apartment is an enormous penthouse, a proper rock-star pad that *really* doesn't match my image of where Dan would live. As Casey gives me the tour, I'm waiting for the moment when they both collapse into giggles and tell me they don't live here at all – it was a wind-up.

I am confused. Sure, Jed told me Casey's estranged father was wealthy. But I struggle to see why he would have bought something that manages to be showy *and* bland.

'And the espresso maker cost about three thousand pounds, and the water cooler in the fridge gives you a choice of five different temperatures and it'll even remember your personalized selection,' Casey is saying.

Dan shuffles on the spot. It's almost as if he's ashamed of this conspicuous display of wealth.

162

She takes me onto the terrace – after checking Bear will be safe – and shows me the view. Now this I *could* live with. You'd never get bored watching the water.

'It's the best terrace on the harbour,' Casey says.

'Have you thought you might be an estate agent when you grow up?' I say.

'Ugh! My grandad's one of those lawyers who does house sales, and that's boring enough.' It's the first time she's mentioned anyone else in her family.

'Your mum's dad?'

'Yep.' She steps towards me and speaks in a whisper: 'My dad hasn't got any family left. But don't let that put you off – it's not his fault and he's a good guy, honestly.'

Is she trying to 'sell' her father to me as a boyfriend? Before I can find out more, Dan's bringing out a tray. There's a jug of water, a carton of juice and a bottle of rosé.

The thought of taking a sip makes me feel dizzy. His arm muscles tense as he puts a corkscrew on the top. There is something *so* desirable about a hot man opening a cold bottle of wine.

But I say, 'Don't open it unless you want some. I'll stick to water.'

He puts the corkscrew down again. 'Good idea. I shouldn't have anything while I'm in charge of a twelve-year-old.'

'Ha, more like this twelve-year-old is in charge of *you*,' Casey says, and we're all laughing because it's funny and true.

'Have you got a big family, Gemma?' Casey asks.

'Not huge, but close. My grandparents all live a long way away, so mostly it's me, my parents, my sister, her wife and two kids. They drive me mad – my mum and sister are *so* nosy and bossy, and my dad is always telling the same stories. But that's families for you.'

Casey sighs. 'My grandparents are all I've got, except Mum, and they are rubbish. I've tried to be funny and interesting, but they hate me because I ruined my mum's chances of going to university and having a proper career.'

'Oh. I'm sure they don't *hate* you.'

She thinks it over. 'My grandad might not, I guess. He makes a bit more effort. Gramps will pay the bills if we're running short, and Mum drives their old car. And they did help out a bit when I got my tumour, but I think that's so they feel less guilty about me.'

Dan pours Casey a mix of juice and water; his knuckles are white. I guess he's never met the grandparents. I can't imagine they'd approve of him deserting their daughter.

'Some people don't know how to talk to younger children.' I'm not sure why I am trying to make excuses for them. 'So it might improve, now you're older.'

She shakes her head. 'Doubt it. My grandma has literally nothing to say to me. She doesn't have a clue what I'm into, what I'm like.'

I can't bear the sadness that's settling on us like drizzle. 'So what *are* you into?' I ask, desperate to change the subject.

'YouTube. Me and Molly – that's my best friend – we like watching the makeovers and tutorials. I like meerkat videos too.' She stops and her deep frown is so like her father's. 'I know that sounds lame. But where I live is the most boring place on the planet. There is literally *nothing* to do. You have to drive for miles to get a Starbucks.'

'All the more reason to make the most of your time in Bristol,' I say cheerily. 'You could do *anything* here. What have you always wanted to try? I'm sure we can organize anything you fancy.'

But Casey's eyes have blurred with tears. Before I can backtrack, she says, 'I don't want to talk about it, I can't—'

She rushes past me, off the terrace, through the living room. A door slams and Bear's ears twitch with stress.

'Sorry,' I say to Dan. 'I didn't think that would upset her.'

He shakes his head. 'It's not you. She's dealing with a lot of stuff. Her mum. The treatment. Maybe she's a bit homesick for the "most boring place on the planet".' But even as he draws speech marks in the air, his eyes are heavy. 'I'd better try and talk to her. Would you come too? Please? I'm lost when she's like this, and you really seem to have a way with her.'

Should I go? She's already been let down by the adults in her life so it might be a terrible idea to let her trust me, only to leave too.

Except I can't turn my back on someone who is hurting this much.

I follow him and he knocks softly on her door. 'Casey, are you OK?'

'I'm fine.' Her voice sounds muffled.

'Do you want to talk about what upset you?'

After a few seconds the door opens. 'I'm fine.' Casey's skin is blotchy, but she's not crying any more. 'I'm tired, that's all.'

The room behind her is tiny and bland, with a childish woodland cover on the duvet. I stand next to Dan. 'Was it something I said? I'd like to help.'

She hesitates before nodding. 'You can come in. On your own.'

Dan smiles tightly.

I step into the room, sit down on the bed next to her. There's a porthole window in the wall looking out onto the harbour, and I change my mind about the room. *This* makes it special.

Bear follows me and jumps onto the duvet, which makes Casey smile: at least she's not scared of him now. 'Are you missing your mum?'

'No!' she says. 'OK. A bit. But that's not why . . .'

'Why you got upset? What was it then?'

'All that stuff about a wish list. I don't want to do *anything*. I want to get this over with and be *normal*.'

I nod. 'I know, sweetheart. But normal includes having fun.'

Casey shakes her head and I realize she's trying not to cry again.

'Whatever it is that's hurting, you can tell me. It might make you feel better. And I promise I won't tell anyone else, unless you want me to.'

She shakes her head again.

'OK. Well, like I mentioned at the hospital, the other thing you can do is tell Bear. He always listens.' At the sound of his name, my dog nuzzles his body into Casey's leg. 'I can leave, if you want,' I suggest.

But Casey reaches for my hand to stop me. 'Talking about doing stuff reminded me of my friends,' she says hesitantly. 'From hospital. Two of them got their wishes granted by charities. Ram got to be a VIP at his favourite team's match and to meet the players. And Liza got to walk on top of a volcano – her whole family got to fly out with her to Lanzarote and spend a whole week on holiday.' Her other hand is stroking Bear's tummy and he's gazing up at her. 'But then they both died like *really* soon afterwards.'

Shit.

'Oh, Casey.'

She's sobbing now. 'I'm not stupid, I get that it didn't . . . that they'd have died anyway, but what if . . . what if the same happens to me?'

I lean over Bear to hug Casey, feeling her chest heave as she cries. I rub her back and wait, because I know from my own bouts of crying that this can't last for ever. Gradually the rate of the sobbing starts to slow and, after a couple of minutes, she releases herself from the hug.

'Sorry, Gemma.'

'Don't be sorry. I'm so sorry you lost your friends. I know what it's like to lose someone you care about. But you said it yourself: it's probably chance that they died then. Or perhaps they got priority for having their wishes granted because they were so ill.'

Casey sniffs. 'Maybe.'

'Your dreams don't have to be big things. You could try lots of little treats that you've missed out on, like when Pepe did your hair.'

Bear's started snoring and I take this as a sign that he believes Casey is better, that his therapy work is done. 'I guess. I've always wanted to be a regular at a fancy cafe where everyone knows your name. And to go to a gig and . . .' She sniffs. 'Is that – did Bear just *fart*?'

I sniff too. 'Yup. That's what happens when you give a dog ice cream.'

'But . . . he's so small and that smell is so—'

'Overwhelming? He has farting superpowers.'

Casey starts to giggle. Has it helped her, to speak her fears out loud?

'Shall we go back to your dad? We could make a list of the small things and work out how to make them happen.'

'Would you come and do the things with us?'

'Casey, I can't promise that. I have a job – things to do.'

'*Please*. You can make time for me. For my dad too. He always seems happier when you're around.'

'Does he?'

Casey nods knowingly. 'Oh yes. He can be ultra-moody, but when he's with you, he can't stop smiling.'

* * *

The list we make together covers a page of A4 and fills me with joy *and* pathos. So many of the things are ordinary activities that I took for granted, growing up somewhere busy: shopping for vintage clothes with Laura in a second-hand market, a day at the beach playing crazy golf with Dad, a cinema trip with both parents and a giant bucket of popcorn.

I can't tell if it's the tumour treatment or lack of money that have made Casey's life so limited. And if it's because she's broke, then how come Dan has been living like *this* while his daughter struggles?

But he seems so determined to put things right that I can't believe it's been deliberate. As we add to the list, he keeps throwing in ideas. I see a new side to him, an imaginative guy who loves to problem-solve and make people happy.

Didn't think I could fancy him any more than I did, but turns out I can.

'Oh, I've thought of a big one,' Casey says. 'I am *desperate* to go up in a balloon.'

'I went up in a balloon once with my husband,' I say. 'It was a treat when he finished a course of treatment. We felt like birds, free from everything that was stressing us out down on the ground.'

Dan frowns. 'I can't see Angelica saying yes to that, Casey. Not now, anyway. We could try to do it later in the year, when you come back.'

Casey grins like he's promised to take her to the moon. And I don't think it's the balloon ride that's thrilled her; it's the idea that Bristol, and her dad, are part of her future.

We get a delivery of the most stunningly presented sushi – another thing on Casey's list – and she snaps a photo of their jewellery-box colours to send to her friend, even though she spits out the sashimi and sticks to spring rolls and bubble tea after that.

As the sky fades from blue to purple to soft pink, the lights on the harbour fade up to compensate and Casey can't stop yawning.

'Mum would say that's a sign I need my beauty sleep.' She gives me and Bear a hug each before she goes to bed, and hesitates when she passes her dad.

At the last second she turns and hugs him too. His delighted smile lasts long after she's left the room.

We're alone, except for Bear, who lies on the fluffy rug on the floor. Alone, together, facing each other on the two giant leather sofas. When he stands up, I hold my breath, in case he's coming closer. Instead he walks to the fridge. 'Sure I can't tempt you with a glass of rosé?'

I open my mouth to say no. 'You know what . . . yes. A very small one.'

He nods and the glasses chink against each other when he brings the tray over. 'My friends with kids always say this is the best part of the day. Casey's way easier than having a toddler tearing around the place. But still, every day she doesn't come to any harm feels like a reason to get the wine out.'

'That was scary, when we thought we'd lost them.'

He shivers. 'Terrifying. But that feeling when we found them . . . if you could bottle that high, I'd never bother with booze again.'

I watch as he uncorks the wine. His movements are fluid and relaxed, and time slows, fractionally, as though we're astronauts floating in altered gravity.

'Casey's such a special girl.'

He nods. 'She is. I hate it when she's upset. If you hadn't been here, she'd still be in her room and I'd be googling *how to talk to your daughter.*'

I haven't told him why Casey was so scared of her dreams

169

coming true: it's her decision whether to confide in him. 'You should trust yourself more. The two of you are getting closer, you just need to be patient.'

He hands me my glass and raises his. As we toast, our fingers brush against each other and now I wish time would stop altogether.

'To Gemma, who came into my life at precisely the right time,' he says.

I smile. 'To Dan *and* to Casey, who came into my life at precisely the wrong one.'

We sip our wine – oh, it's every bit as delicious as I hoped it would be. Although everything's heightened after the brief touch we just shared.

He's frowning. 'About the bad timing . . . So I know this – us – whatever it is has come out of the blue, but is it really such terrible timing? You're still grieving and I'm learning to be a dad, but what if that makes this the *best* time? When I'm with you, I feel . . . how can I explain it? Full of possibilities.'

I want to say: *Yes. That is how it is for me too.* But he's still talking.

'And it's more than that. Before Casey came down here, I thought I had nothing to offer her except a place to stay. But that started to change from the very first time we bumped into each other.'

'How?' I want more, greedy to discover what we share, and why.

'I've been trying to work it out. I reckon it's because you give off this intense kindness. I do know lots of good people. My mates, my colleagues. But most of us have learned to be wary. You're different. You're open, despite all the sadness you've been through. Maybe because of it. And whether it's the kids you volunteer with, or some random, ratty stranger who's got lost, you don't hesitate to do what you can.'

170

His intensity embarrasses me. 'That makes me sound like an insufferable do-gooder.'

'Not at all. You've got this *glow* about you. And it's made *me* want to try harder, to be better myself. I've never felt like this before,' Dan whispers. 'When I'm not with you, I can be rational about the reasons not to get involved. But as soon as I see you, that flies out of the window and I start coming out with all this stuff I've *never* told anyone before.'

Shouldn't I trust him too? Do it now. Cards on the table. And this – 'us' – might still work. Tonight I've seen Dan embracing being a father to a child he's never met before. What if that same laid-back approach means he's willing to welcome a baby too?

Madness. Two sips of wine and I am dreaming of a future that can't exist.

But the way he's gazing at me, the *present* seems pretty exciting. Shouldn't luck go *both* ways? I've had my share of shitty luck, so aren't I due something – someone – incredible?

Dan takes a deep breath. 'OK. This might be nuts, but I've got a suggestion that could help clear things up. When we're together I can't think straight, because there's this voice in my head saying, *Kiss her. Go on, kiss her.*'

I laugh to cover up how much I want that too.

'That must be distracting,' I say.

'Massively. So – before we do anything else – we *could* try out the kiss we almost had in Leigh Woods. I mean, it might be rubbish, which means problem solved, we can get on with our lives. As friends or something.'

'That's very logical. A small price to pay for peace of mind.' The jokiness is all that's stopping me from jumping over the coffee table and kissing him first.

'Your place or mine?' His voice sounds husky.

'Mine.'

Screw the past, and the future. Dan is here, now, and I want him.

He moves so slowly: he must be able to hear the thump of my heart as he stands up, crosses the room, sits next to me on the very edge of the sofa, and I can smell the sweet-sour wine he was drinking seconds ago, and my head moves towards his, and the sensation when our lips finally touch is . . .

Beyond words.

Chapter 21: Dan

I didn't really believe kissing Gemma would be rubbish. But I never thought it'd be *this incredible*, either . . .

When we finally move a few centimetres apart to breathe, I see it in her wild green eyes: she's as knocked out by what just happened as I am.

'So,' she whispers, 'what's the verdict?'

'I, er . . . I don't think that has simplified things.' My voice sounds different, like that kiss – one single kiss – has changed me completely.

She smiles the sexiest smile I've ever seen. 'Yeah, no. Neither do I.'

We kiss again. The kiss is *everything*. I want it to go on for ever. To stop time.

A huge sigh interrupts us: the dog. I like that dog, but right now he can do one. Because Gemma – beautiful Gemma with that soft smile and even softer lips – is pulling away . . .

Other stuff gets louder again: the hum of people and boats and life out on the waterside. The high-pitched buzz of tinnitus that rarely lets me be.

'Bear's waking up,' she says. 'I think he needs a walk.'

He's not waking up: he's settling back down again and already starting to snore. Gemma is making an excuse to get away. Is she scared? Am I?

No. I'm . . . happy. Happier than I've felt in so long.

Gemma waits for me to say something. It'd be so easy to switch on the charm, keep her here. It's my superpower. But I mustn't scare her off. She needs space on her own, so she can understand how right this is.

'OK,' I say. 'But you'll come right back here after walking him?'

She's standing up now, but her body still faces mine, like she can't decide what to do next.

'No. I need to go home,' she says quietly. 'To think. There's stuff happening in my life that makes this even more complicated than it seems.'

She's still so close that I can't help myself. I lean in, and this time we're closer than before, her body a perfect fit for mine, and *fucking hell, she is everything*.

I make myself pull away this time because in another ten seconds I won't be able to. And although my body wants her so much, my brain is telling me to go slow. To savour every bloody moment. 'Does that simplify things?'

'The opposite,' she says. 'That's why I have to go. I can't think straight when I'm near you.' Gemma turns away and nudges Bear awake. He stands up and shakes, the metal tag ringing against his collar.

'Can I call you?' I ask.

'No, I'll call you. I need some time,' she says, and I want to ask, *How soon will you call me?* even though I have never been the one staring at my phone, waiting for a message, my life on hold.

As she steps into the lift, I want to follow her. But I mustn't leave Casey on her own and I know I must let Gemma do the running. This is so new. So terrifying.

I stare at the lift doors long after they've closed. Anything to stop myself running down the fire-escape stairs to meet her at the bottom and kiss her again. I head back into the living space to tidy up.

Music is the only thing that might distract me. I stick on my headphones, scroll through Spotify, searching for random songs with a heavy beat to jolt me out of moping over Gemma.

'Another Brick in the Wall': that'll do. I crank up the volume, even though it's bad for my tinnitus.

As I finish loading the dishwasher, the song changes to 'Owner of a Lonely Heart'. Dad loved speeding on the motorway to this one, usually when we were driving away from trouble.

I shuffle forward before it ends, but Spotify must have it in for me, because I keep getting more songs that my father said reminded him of my mum: 'Up Where We Belong', 'Uptown Girl', 'I Just Called to Say I Love You'. His love of easy listening made me suspicious of sentimental lyrics.

Except right now they make sense for the first time in my life.

I take off the headphones and step onto the terrace. What's happening to me? I've kissed a lot of girls and never felt anything like this.

But it wasn't only the kisses – it was the whole afternoon. When I've seen other families out and about on a Sunday afternoon I've thought *how bloody tedious*. To my surprise, today wasn't tedious at all. It was . . . easy in all the right ways. After spending my whole life avoiding that kind of everyday closeness, now I can imagine days and weeks and months with Casey and Gemma at my side.

Out here, the sky turns crimson. *Red sky at night, hustler's delight*, Dad used to say. He *hated* the idea of normal life, told me over and over again that we deserved more than that. But everything else he told me was a lie, so why wouldn't that be too?

Maybe the ordinary can be extraordinary, if it's something you've never tried before.

I sleep better than I have in years and the moment I wake up, I check my phone for a message from Gemma and, even though there isn't one, the certainty that she *will* be in touch soon makes me leap out of bed.

Hello, Monday!

Everyone's friendly at the hospital when I take Casey in. She even shows me the proton beam therapy room itself and although my tinnitus makes its presence felt, I stay calm by imagining that Gemma is talking me through it, breath by breath.

'Don't forget Bear visits my school this afternoon,' Casey says. 'If you come in early to pick me up, you might get to see Gemma again.'

Did Casey see us kissing? We were pretty preoccupied . . .

Back at the workshop, I keep a close eye on the time. Vijay's back from Germany and we're interviewing trainees for internships on three August festivals: in between, I have to stop myself telling him about Gemma. He'd only laugh: *since when has 'Dan the Man kisses a girl' counted as breaking news?*

After we've finished the interviews, we grab a coffee in my office, the thrum of the workshop quieter after we close the blinds.

'Now that's sorted, I've got another mission,' Vijay says. 'We're getting very impatient about meeting Casey. Idoia especially. She thinks you're ashamed of us.'

'I do *want* to have you round, but things are tricky.' I explain what I found at Angelica's on Friday: how unloved the house was, and how isolated the two of them seem. 'Now it's just me and Casey at the flat, we're getting closer, but I don't know if she's ready. It's complicated.'

'Not *that* complicated. We're your family, and so is Casey. She's going to be a part of your life, so she'll be a part of ours too.'

Which is, of course, why I've avoided a meet-up. My friends have been banking on a happy ending, the kind I never thought I deserved. My original plan was to keep them away from Casey, so it'd be easier to tell them things hadn't worked out when July ends.

But that plan seems stupid now. I want it all: Casey, Gemma, this new life. Except how can I make *that* work when I have told so many lies?

'Danny-boy, you look like a wet weekend in Weston-super-Mud? Let Uncle Veej solve your problems for you.'

'I still haven't told her.'

'Told her what?'

'I haven't told Casey that it's not my apartment. Or any of the stuff before that. None of it. She thinks I'm this super-cool, super-rich music mogul.'

Vijay frowns. 'Mate. When were you planning to drop the bombshells?'

'I should have done it on day one, but Angelica was being petty, which made things tense, so I thought, all right, I'll do it tomorrow.'

'But tomorrow never comes.' Vijay sighs impatiently. 'OK, so you need to organize a get-together, to give yourself an unavoidable deadline for telling the truth.'

I shake my head. 'No, Casey will hate me.'

'Listen. She won't hate you. No one can hate you for long.'

'Angelica has hated me for twelve years.'

'That doesn't count. You're one of the good guys, Dan. And you've gone from nought to sixty on the parenting front, so you're bound to make the odd mistake. You need to fess up to Casey. Yes, she'll be disappointed, perhaps a bit hurt. But kids move on fast if you grovel. Trust me on this. If I had a pound for every time I've screwed up with Harrison, I'd be—'

'A millionaire? Oh no, you're one of those already.'

He laughs. 'I walked into that, didn't I? My point is, Harrison doesn't think any less of me because I admit to my mistakes.'

It is true. Despite his parents' divorce, Harrison adores his dad. 'Where would I begin?'

'Don't overload her. Start with the flat. You don't need to go way back – it's ancient history for someone Casey's age. Tell her you made a mistake; show her you won't do it again.'

He makes it sound so easy. And maybe he's right, not just about Casey, but also about Gemma. She's connected with this new me, the hands-on dad, the guy in touch with his feelings. What counts is the person I am now, not the things I got wrong years ago.

'So when could we come over? No need to prep. Delivery pizzas, a crate of beer and a chance to get to know each other.'

My eyes close as I imagine it. And even though it's way too soon, I picture Gemma in the room too. Crazy or what? Except that the idea of her not being there seems even crazier.

My fingers twitch because I want to check my phone, see if she's messaged me or tried to call. I pick it up, pretending to load my calendar app. No message. I don't let the disappointment last. She'll be having a busy day, that's all.

'OK, you're right. I'll organize it. This week.'

'You'd better,' Vijay says, standing up, rubbing his hands together, as he always does when he's excited about A Big Plan. 'Or we will turn up en masse and refuse to go away.'

I get to the hospital early and check myself in the jeep's mirror, straightening my hair and flicking sawdust off my shirt. For once, the buzz as I go into the lobby isn't fear: it's excitement.

I take the stairs up to the hospital school two at a time. *Gemma should be there already.* I could suggest a coffee, and Casey will take Bear for a walk, and I might even sneak another brief, earth-shattering kiss . . .

The door to the school is closed, but I peep in through the glazed part, holding my breath. I see Casey immediately, though she doesn't notice me. She's reading, her head bent over a book, her body still. *My girl.* My amazing girl.

But there's no Bear and no Gemma. The teacher, Jed, spots me and walks towards the door. 'You've come for Casey? It's still a bit early.'

She looks up and the smile on her face is so glorious it *almost* hurts.

'Yes, sorry, I can wait.'

'It's fine, we're nearly done anyway. We usually have an animal-therapy session today, but unfortunately the volunteer has had to call in sick, so you're welcome to head off now.'

Sick?

As Casey packs up her bag, I replay yesterday. Gemma seemed fine then. What if she's stayed away not because she's ill, but because she knew I'd be here and wants to avoid me?

No. We have *a connection*. She deserves happiness. And, maybe, so do I.

Casey says goodbye to the teacher and the other kids and follows me into the corridor, towards the lift.

'What's the matter with Gemma?' I ask, trying to sound as casual as possible.

Casey shrugs. 'Not sure. I tried WhatsApping her and she's seen the messages, but she hasn't replied. You didn't say anything to upset her last night, did you?'

I fake a laugh. 'Er, no. I was my usual, very charming self.'

She pulls a face. 'I hope she's OK. Or what if it's Bear?'

'I'm sure everything's fine.'

It has to be. As soon as Gemma's better, I know she'll be in touch, because she felt it too. Whatever the complications, we could have an extraordinary, ordinary future ahead of us, if we can both be brave.

Chapter 22: Gemma

I'm not ill. Unless this state of paralysing confusion counts as a mental-health crisis.

I half expected Jed to see through my lie when I phoned him to say I had a tummy bug. Instead he was *hugely* sympathetic, offering to drop in anything I needed on his way home from school. So now I can add a layer of guilt to the uncertainty that's already weighing me down.

I came so close to doing the wrong thing last night. I wanted Dan more than I have ever wanted anyone before and—

Do not *think* about him. Not even his name.

After Bear and I got home, and the kiss-induced madness faded, I realized I couldn't risk seeing him or Casey today. She's messaged me a few times, but how am I meant to reply? *Sorry, but I am discombobulated by kissing your father and have gone into hiding?* Or: *Tomorrow I'm hoping to persuade an embryo to implant in my body, and I'm worried that lust for your dad might be counter-productive.*

And then there's the whole issue of whether I should even be messaging a vulnerable child, however sad her situation.

I only leave the flat to walk Bear, who hugs the tiny strips of shade created by the buildings, to avoid the pavement that is so hot under his paws. He doesn't protest when I bring him home again.

What next? I need to be busy, busy, busy. The bank commission. Housework. Accounts. DIY. Anything to distract me from Lustful Thoughts. Once the transfer has happened, and my future is firmly in the lap of the fertility gods, I will let myself think about Dan, but until then it's too much.

Too late.

Because I'm already thinking of him: his face. His voice. That kiss.

Nothing about the connection makes any sense from this distance – but that all changes as soon as I am close to him again, breathing the same air, sensing the beat of his heart.

The only thing I've ever wanted with the same intensity is Andrew's child. How can those two desires coexist? One started years ago, but only built to this pitch because it was fed by love and sadness and hope. The other began with a single glance.

I *know* logically that you can't compare a silly crush with the monumental choice Andrew and I made together. But *everything* changed when Dan walked into my life.

My WhatsApp buzzes. It's Casey:

We missed you today, especially my dad. Would croissants make you feel better? We could do a special delivery for you and Bear.

She's added at least thirty crying emojis underneath. I desperately want to message her back, but instead I dial Dad's number. It rings for so long I almost end the call, but then he answers.

'Hey, Little Gem.' He's out of breath.

'What are you up to?'

'Been trying to fix the garden awning. The mechanism's

182

seizing up, and your mother can't bear the noise the hydraulics are making.'

I picture my mum watching through the kitchen window while Dad stands on the stepladder, the sun and sweat making his eyes water, as he oils and twists and tweaks. He's a perfectionist, for her. Nothing in the house is allowed to be bodged: every problem solved, every challenge faced is an act of love.

'I don't want to interrupt.'

'Ah no, no, Gem. I need a breather anyhow.' I hear the clack as he unfolds a garden chair, the slight sigh as he sits. 'Hot enough for you?'

'Even Bear doesn't want to be out in this.' Now I've called, I'm scared to speak my doubts out loud.

'Is this about tomorrow?'

'Yes.' My voice is small. 'I don't think I can do this on my own.' That wasn't what I expected to say.

'Except you won't be, sweetheart. You won't ever be on your own, because you've got us. Me and Mum, and Laura and Mel. And Isabel too. We'll be there, all lined up, ready to help care for the baby. And for you.'

I imagine them lined up, my ragtag army of helpers, and it's comforting. Except that Isabel's already declared herself out.

And now I think about Angelica, her fearful face as she shouted at me and Bear, and I try to imagine myself coping if the worst happened, as it has to her and Casey. Yes, people will give you supportive hugs and run errands, but single parenting still means it ultimately comes down to you. 'I don't think I'll sleep tonight.'

'I could come over and stay with you, if you like?'

'What about the awning?' We laugh. 'No, I'm all right.'

'But if you change your mind and *don't* want it to happen tomorrow, that's all right too.'

What if I don't know what I want? If I want all of it and none of it, at the same time?

I wish we could run our many possible lives through a computer before picking the right one. The life where Andrew *had* gone to the doctor sooner. The life where his treatment had worked. The life where the first embryo had settled in for the ride, before I had time to develop doubts.

The life where I hadn't taken the shortcut after the clinic and got stuck behind those schoolchildren, with the man with movie-star looks . . .

But you don't get the simulations. You make your choice and you try not to look back.

'I'll be there, Dad.'

'Well, Little Gem, so will I.'

The night before, I always reread *The Amazing Book of Us*, though never the last page.

When we first started work on it, we honestly believed that Andrew's brush with cancer had earned us a happy ending. We hadn't lost our faith in things working out for the best. So as I began hormone treatment to harvest my eggs, Andrew researched how best to explain the process to young children. Together we gathered photos that documented our joint history: how we met, how we fell in love, our wedding and all the tiny landmarks that would only ever matter to us, and to the child or children we longed for.

I even found the original sketches I'd drawn for Andrew's company, the pen-and-wash vegetables and fruits and farm-yard scenes that helped to relaunch his delivery business.

Our book project kept growing. It would be an archive of us, stored in a wooden box full of brilliant things. We imagined exploring the contents on rainy afternoons, every item with a memory or story attached.

Andrew and I might not have had the furious passion that's knocked me off course this last week, but he *was* the love of my life. And our children would have been loved as fiercely as we loved each other.

They still could be. Gingerly I touch my belly, avoiding the tender spots of bruising where I've injected myself to help prepare the womb lining. As I close my eyes, I try to picture my body as a welcoming home for the baby we wanted so much for so long. I imagine the two embryos on ice, waiting for their chance.

You are loved, even before you have a safe place to grow.

In less than twenty-four hours the transfer will have been done and I can start considering what else to say yes to. I just have to stay focused until then.

OUR BODIES ARE AMAZING THINGS

Unique, beautiful and incredibly strong, they're the most complex machines in
the world, and probably in the entire universe.

Our bodies do so much. You can see, hear, feel, walk, talk. But having so many moving part
means sometimes stuff goes wrong. You can get a horrid sore throat or a runny nos
or even break a bone (when I was six years old I broke my wrist
very badly falling out of an apple tree. That hurt. But it mended very fast and I was
ever so careful next time I climbed that tree).
Of course, most of the time doctors will give you medicine to make you as good as
new. When Daddy's body went wrong, the experts tried lots of treatments and
life got back to normal. Mummy and Daddy still wanted a family, so they tried
IVF, which is a special way to make babies. With eggs from Mummy and sperm
from Daddy, and love from both of us, doctors made tiny embryos.
Everyone starts as an embryo, but these ones are amazing because they wait till
it's the perfect time to come to life. But then Daddy got ill again and very
sadly this time he didn't get better. When he died everyone was upset for a long
time. But Daddy wanted Mummy to have the family they'd wanted so much. So
one day the doctors took out the embryo and put it back into Mummy, and
our dreams came true and you were born. It means you are extra-special, and I'm s
sorry I can't be there. My own dad died when I was fourteen and I
have missed him every day.

Of course, it's even harder for you, but whenever you're sad or angry, please
remember the most important (DADDY SAYS:) You and your mum mean
the world to me, even if I'm not here to say it to your beautiful faces.

186

Chapter 23: Gemma

Tuesday 17 July

The clinic car park is almost empty when Dad and I arrive. I prefer my appointments early, so I don't have to face the couples in the waiting room.

I'm not a jealous person and I don't crave what they have. I crave what I used to have with Andrew. Which is why I'm here, kicking back against what death took away.

'This could be it, Little Gem,' my father says as I buzz the intercom.

But if it's not, then what?

The fertility counsellor talked it through with me: I could make an active choice to leave the last embryo unused. Except then I'd always wonder if that would have been the one that made me a mum. Deep down, I think I've known I would see it through to the end.

But Dan's made everything as clear as mud. Why am I thinking of him again here, of all places?

My father takes hold of my hand and squeezes it. 'Let's try to think positive, Gemma. It might help.'

Andrew was the biggest positive thinker I'd ever met, right to the end, and it didn't help him.

But I smile at my dad. 'I am positivity personified.'

The second we walk into the consultation room I can tell

something is wrong. The doctor – one I haven't met before – has adopted the guarded facial expression they must teach at medical school, the one that subliminally prepares patients for shitty news. He's younger than I like my doctors to be, late thirties. I prefer greying consultants with a reassuring aura of wisdom.

He shakes our hands, waits for us to sit down, blinks. 'I'm afraid that the blastocyst we'd earmarked for the transfer today has not survived the thawing process.'

Not survived. He means *dead*.

Our embryo is *dead*.

I'm shivering uncontrollably.

'Oh, Gemma.' Dad stands up and holds me, and after a minute or so I manage to stop shaking. He sits back down, his face closed in, as he tries to disguise how upset he is.

'We have the option of trying the last blastocyst we have in storage. Your endometrium is in the ideal state for transfer.'

What the doctor said makes perfect sense, practically, medically and financially. But it'd also mean today is the end of the line. I haven't realized until now how much I've been relying on having a final roll of the dice, if this month fails.

'You're welcome to take a few minutes to think it through. It's bad luck, this morning's failure. There's no reason why the last one shouldn't survive thawing.'

I wish he wouldn't keep saying 'the last one'.

He leaves the room quietly.

'So?' Dad asks. 'You thought this might be your last try anyway, didn't you?'

Last, last, last.

Tears start trickling down my face, because this isn't how today was meant to go.

'Oh, my poor Gem.' Dad embraces me. 'It's not fair, is it? None of this is fair. But you're never on your own.'

Despite his arms around me, I do feel alone, in this chilly clinic, with my body plump and primed for the baby I want so much, with a person I will never see again.

The door opens again and the doctor shifts from foot to foot. 'So what would you like to do?'

I close my eyes and try to summon Andrew's hope and his pragmatism. An image comes to me: not of him sick, but of us when we first moved in together. He had thrown out loads of his things to make space for me, but he wanted to explain his system. There was a place for *everything*, as painstakingly worked out as any jigsaw puzzle, and everything had to be back in its proper home before bed. I teased him about it and he laughed. But he never relaxed his standards, not even when medical supplies threatened to turn our living room into a hospital storeroom.

I'm a fusspot, but I can't sleep unless I know that in the morning everything is ready to begin again. Fresh starts are the best.

Fresh start.

'I'm going to say yes.'

Because of what the doctor calls the 'mishap' with the first thawing, we have to wait for longer than usual and soon the clinic gets busy. Dad and I go out for a walk, speculating on the other couples and which stage of their 'fertility journey' they might be at, without acknowledging that mine could be about to hit the buffers.

I could call Isabel. I texted her last night to tell her I was going ahead, and she texted back, wishing me luck. But knowing this is my final embryo – my final *chance* – changes everything.

Before I can work out how to break the news, an alarm sounds on my phone, making me jump. Without a word, Dad and I turn back towards the clinic.

'What if this one hasn't survived thawing, either?' I say to him.

'You'll be sad and angry. But you'll survive, because you're my Little Gem, and Andrew's, and you're made of strong stuff.'

But when we walk into the consultation room, the baby-faced doctor is smiling.

I go in alone. Dad might have delivered me, but he's got no business seeing *this*.

They check my name and date of birth, before getting me into position. 'OK now, Gemma, let me explain what's going to happen.'

It's my third transfer, so I know the ropes. Except this time I sense even more care and precision as they insert the catheter and wait for the flash of white on the ultrasound. When it happens, I close my eyes and wish and wish and wish.

Dad drives me home, and hands over the almond croissant he bought for me to eat later. The grease has made the paper bag transparent and it looks disgusting, but after I've waved him off, I sit on the front doorstep and tear into it and wish he'd bought two.

Bear goes mad when I get in, and not only because of the smell of the almond croissant on my hands. I give in to his doggy devotion for a few minutes, and everything seems better.

I turn on my laptop and check the time. Just two hours have passed since the transfer. Ten endless days to go. At least I don't have to wait a full fortnight, because our lonesome embryo spent four days developing outside my body.

Please stick around.

What happened at the clinic has changed the direction of

my life. Or changed nothing at all. And if the treatment hasn't worked, could that open up a future with Dan?

He hasn't messaged me, but then I promised I would be the one to get in touch. Is he pissed off, hurt, worried?

Bear's desperate to go out, so I take him round the block. Gentle exercise is allowed, but nothing strenuous. Beats me how a baby is ever conceived the natural way but, like every other woman who has had IVF failures, I now follow the rules.

As we head onto the grass, my phone vibrates with a new WhatsApp and even before I check the screen, my intuition says it's him. My body hums when I see his name and I open the message:

Everything OK? Casey said you've been ill.

I don't even know what OK is any more. But I do know I want to see him so much.

Yes, fine, a 24-hour thing.

Or possibly a nine-*month* thing. I stare at the message, working out what else to say.

Sorry, I did plan to message you, but didn't feel up to it.

He types back instantly:

That's cool.

I wait for him to say more and then realize he's waiting for me. Before I can change my mind, I tap on the phone icon and he picks up after the first ring.

191

'Hey.'

That one syllable sounds like a love song: it sends a familiar wave of heat through me. I try to bring it under control by replaying the grim part of my morning I spent in stirrups.

'Hey, Dan. Sorry. Again. How are you? How's Casey?'

'Good, though she was disappointed not to see you yesterday. So was I.' He sounds unsure of himself. 'Were you really ill?'

'No.'

'Right. That's what I thought.'

'Sorry.'

'Listen, Gemma. It's OK if you wish Sunday hadn't happened. I mean, I've been hoping to sweet-talk you into another date. But hearing you now, I don't want to be that guy who can't take no for an answer. If you're not interested, tell me now.'

Plenty more fish in the sea for him to catch.

Except that's unfair. It must seem to him that I'm the one playing games. 'I don't wish Sunday hadn't happened. I can't stop *thinking* about Sunday.'

He sighs. 'Me neither.'

'But . . . what I said then is still true. There's a lot going on for me, and that kiss doesn't make things any simpler.'

Silence. I picture him in his swanky penthouse, living his rock-'n'-roll life. Why would he bother with me?

'I want to understand all your complications,' he says. 'I want to understand why it's you I've connected with. Why you feel something for me. It's driving me crazy, but so is not seeing you.'

'Me too.'

'So when can I see you again, Gemma? Tonight?'

The sound of his voice makes me want to head over there this minute, but it'd be wrong to do that today. 'No. But soon.'

'How about tomorrow?' he suggests. 'I'm planning to do something from Casey's list and I know she'd love you to be there.'

Still too soon. I am improvising an excuse when Bear spots a squirrel and pulls me so hard that I stumble and drop the phone.

When I pick it up again, he's still talking: '. . . having some mates round to meet Casey. Remember she said she wanted to go to a gig? Some of my friends are musicians, so there might be some jamming, or we'll hang out, eat pizza, drink beer. Like we're ten years younger than we *actually* are.'

The difference in our lives hits me all over again. 'I don't know, Dan. I'm not much of a party person these days, and I'm not very knowledgeable about music, so I can't see me fitting in.'

'It's not going to be a *party*-party like that, I'd never put Casey at risk. But if I could talk you into coming, I need a decoy so it's a surprise for her. Someone to take her to a cafe with Bear, so I can get ready and she'll come back to this mini festival in the living room.'

Bear trots alongside me, now he's given up on the squirrel. I can picture Casey's delight at the surprise, and Dan's too, when he sees her face. I don't want to miss it, but I also don't know how I'll feel tomorrow.

'Can I think about it?'

'Why not say yes? Please. Now that I've started imagining you there, it won't be the same if you're not.'

I said yes to the transfer earlier. Could I say yes to this too? My other options are to spend tomorrow sitting at home, bent over my sketches, or go to my sister's, where she'll keep me under close surveillance the entire evening, watching for signs the transfer has worked this time.

There's no competition. And I'm curious about his friends and what they might reveal about Dan. 'OK. I'll come. So much for not sweet-talking me.'

'It's a hard habit to break,' he says, and I can hear the delight in his voice and I think, *I did that. I made him feel that way.*

'What do I bring?'

'Just Bear and yourself. I want it to be an easy, laid-back night, but one Casey will remember for a long time. And maybe we will too.'

Chapter 24: Casey

How dumb is my so-called father?

It's obvious even to Bear the dog how ultra-perfect Gemma is for him. When she turns up and offers to take me to BayCaff, she's put on make-up and a swirly dress that brings out the different greens in her eyes, and she isn't doing that for *my* benefit.

But DL hardly looked up from his laptop and didn't suggest coming out with us. I haven't been so frustrated since Mum refused to let me have my ears pierced in Worcester on my tenth birthday.

'Hey, Gemma. Hey, Casey,' the barista says when we walk into the lower part of the BayCaff boat to order. 'Mocha, right, with almond syrup?'

Wow! How cool is that? He knows what I want. I am a regular . . .

Except Gemma's smiling at me in a weird way and I realize it's a set-up; she must have called in advance, because this is on my wish list of nice things that I wanted to happen in Bristol.

To go to a cafe where they know your name, like Central Perk in Friends.

I've only been here twice, so Gemma must have played

the tumour card when she rang, and this barista will go home tonight to his girlfriend or boyfriend and tell them how he made the sick kid's day.

My head throbs, right between the eyebrows. It's been doing this all week, on and off, so it could be Bob – or the treatment to get rid of Bob – that's making me so tired and grumpy.

On Monday I was so disappointed that Gemma and Bear didn't come into the hospital, then I argued with Molly on WhatsApp because she never replies to my photos, and then she *blocked me*.

On Tuesday I argued with Mum on FaceTime because she kept sniping at DL about stuff that doesn't matter. And I'm *always* angry with him, because he's stopped talking about what's going to happen after this month is over, so that must mean he can't *wait* for me to be gone.

'I'll bring these to you on the roof,' the barista says. 'Your usual table by the funnel?'

We climb the steps and 'my' table is free. The sunlight lands on the big chunk of timber like a bright-orange table-cloth and it's hard to stay angry because it is amazing here. Bear does that funny thing where he scratches at the deck and circles three times before resting his head on my feet with a giant sigh. His hair prickles against my skin, but I don't want him to move. I wish I could stay *for ever*.

No going home to a dead village where even my best friend doesn't want to know me. No worrying about Mum. No going in for the final appointment with the consultant, where he shakes his head and says, *I'm so sorry, but this hasn't worked and there's nothing else we can do . . .*

'Penny for your thoughts?' Gemma says.

'Huh?'

'You're miles away.'

I shrug. 'Just happy here. Can we stay till it closes?'

Gemma frowns. 'It gets more like a bar later. Lots of annoying drunk people.'

'I've never been drunk.'

'I should hope not. You're twelve!'

'Molly is twelve and she got drunk on Baileys at Christmas. She says it's like being in a dream, but also like being seasick.'

Gemma weighs it up. 'Personally, I think alcohol is like holding a magnifying glass to whatever mood you're in. If you were happy, you get happier, but if you were sad or pissed off, it becomes even harder to hide.'

'We shouldn't hide how we feel anyway.'

'True. How do *you* feel right now, Casey?' she asks.

'Scared.' *I didn't mean to say that.* 'And angry.' *Or that.*

Gemma leaves space to let me go on. I don't even think I want to, but when I open my mouth, the words start pouring out.

'I'm not meant to be scared and angry. I'm meant to be brave and *wise*. They give you beads at the hospital whenever they do anything horrible to you. They call them beads of courage and they come in different colours, depending on what you've had, like a scan or a cannula or radiotherapy. My chain is three times as long as I am tall, but I'm not *really* courageous. Whenever I'm tired or headachy, I think, *I'm never even going to live long enough to get drunk or kiss a boy, or learn to drive or fly in a balloon at sunrise, because Bob is going to finish me off.*'

I *won't* cry. I *won't*.

Gemma shakes her head. 'Oh, Casey. You're one of the bravest people I've ever met.'

'You don't even know me.'

'I haven't known you for long, that's true. But every time we meet up, I think what an impressive person you are.

Which doesn't mean you can't tell your mum, or dad, or me, when you don't feel brave.'

'Nobody wants to hear it, though. Not really.'

'I do,' she says and opens her green eyes even wider than she does when she's flirting with my dad. She reaches out and takes both my hands and, when I don't pull away, she stands up and moves close enough to hug me, and I don't want to let her go because it's so lush.

Lush. That's a Bristol word, for when something is amazing. I'll miss Gemma, and Bristol, when this is over.

We leave when the barista replaces the coffee menus with a cocktail list. We walk past the pancake stall on the way back to the flat, and I ask Gemma if I can have one with Nutella and banana because *it's on my list*.

It's not, but I've worked out the list can be very useful when I want something to happen and adults don't.

'Sorry, no. I lost track of time. Next time, though.'

I could change her mind if I reminded her that time might be the one thing I don't have. But I like her too much to do that.

'Bob?' she says, as we cross the bridge.

I didn't mean to say his name out loud. 'Don't laugh at me. Bob's my tumour. I gave it a name because other people at the hospital named theirs.'

'Right. Why Bob?'

'It just came to me. But it's weird. You know they do a list of the most popular baby names? I know four people with tumours called Bob. It must be a good name for something small but deadly.'

The lift to the penthouse smells different when we get into it, of perfume and baby powder. Before I can work out where it's come from, the doors are opening and—

'Welcome to the Harbourside Music Festival!' DL says. He's wearing a tie-dye T-shirt and cut-off jeans and there's Billie Eilish playing in the background and loads of strangers behind him, and he's grinning like he's expecting me to be pleased.

But I've got no make-up on and am wearing the dungarees that make me look fat, so instead of taking the glass he's holding out for me, I'm pushing past him, and the juice spills all over him and me, but I don't stop until I am back in my room and I slam the door.

After a few seconds the music stops. My head throbs and my face in the mirror is beetroot-red and the juice on my hands smells sickly sweet and I'm dizzy and breathless. So I do a visualization of a paradise island, like the vloggers suggest for when you're in the MRI scanner, and very slowly the panic subsides and now I feel like a total idiot. Why did I react that way in front of those people?

There's a soft knock that must be Gemma.

'Go away, I want to be on my own.'

'I only want to talk for a minute,' she says. 'Dan is about to send everyone home, but I want to make sure that's what you want. Can I come in?'

'Everyone' must be DL's friends. He'd talked about having them over. And I wanted to meet them. But not like *this*. I've messed up.

'OK.'

Gemma pushes the door open and Bear trots in behind her. 'This is cute,' she says, stroking the babyish woodland duvet cover.

'None of this is my stuff. I don't even *like* rabbits. They're vicious.'

'You could swap it for one you like. Paint the walls, put up some pictures.'

'What's the point? I'm only here till the end of next week.'

'Casey, I'm sure your dad will want you to be here as often as you like.'

I don't want to tell Gemma that DL never talks about August. Bear jumps onto the bed next to me, and I rest my hand on his body and feel his ribs moving up and down.

'Who is out there?' I ask her.

She shrugs. 'Friends of your dad. They seem nice. But he says they'll go if you're not in the mood. They won't mind.'

'Is it a party?'

'Sort of. He wanted to give you the closest thing to a gig, without the crowds and the disgusting toilets. I think some of the people are in the music business.' Gemma sounds as wowed by this as I am.

'Seriously?' What would I say to them? Literally the only interesting thing about me is my tumour, and no one wants to talk about *that* at a party.

'You don't have to hang out with them,' Gemma says. 'I'm a bit nervous myself, as they're so cool. How about you and I go onto the terrace together with Bear and eat the pizza your dad ordered? He won't mind.'

He will mind; I know how important it was for me to like them, and for them to like me.

What bead of courage would I get for talking to strangers? I take my chain down from the shelf, touching the gems, remembering how scared I was the first time they did the things each colour represents. How hard it was not to freak out, but how much easier it got. This party might be the same. If I'm going to be part of DL's life, I can't let Bob, or fear, beat me. Not tonight.

'I can do this,' I say to myself as much as Gemma. 'If my dad likes them, so will I.'

'You *go*, girl.' Gemma reaches for my hand and squeezes it. 'Let's do this!'

When I get off the bed my legs wobble a bit. Mostly all I do is meet nurses and doctors and other sick kids. Tonight will be different. It's what I wanted, right?

I catch sight of myself in the mirror.

Yuk. My hair looks good – thank you, Pepe – but my face is pale and bloated.

'Gemma, before we go out there, could you help me with my make-up?'

This might be the best night of my life. I am feeling literally *all the feels*.

My father has the coolest friends in the entire *world*. There's Vijay, who runs the staging and fireworks company that DL works for during the summer. Plus Eddie, a real-life guitarist, and his Spanish wife, who is a music agent – whatever that is – and so ultra-beautiful I can't even speak to her without blushing, plus their baby daughter, as cute as a doll.

Hanging out on the terrace are a couple of guitarists who've played with bands I've never heard of, but Gemma has.

And there's a boy . . .

I can't speak to the boy without blushing either, but he doesn't seem interested in talking to me. He's sitting in the hanging egg chair on the balcony, watching the harbour, swigging from a bottle of Diet Coke.

He has thick, dark hair and eyelashes like Molly's after she's put on four coats of Wonder'Lash, and he wears shorts that show off his legs, which are so buff and dark they could be varnished.

DL doesn't make a big song and dance when I come out of the bedroom. He smiles and gets me a drink – fruit punch ladled from a big bowl, with ice and sliced strawberries.

Vijay is sharing his dream playlist and every track goes on *for ever*, and he's telling stories about the raves he helped organize when he was a teenager.

'That's how he earned enough to play with fireworks and light shows for the rest of his life,' my dad says, and everyone smiles.

DL's different with his friends. He's relaxed and funny, and the way they tease him, it's obvious that they're all so happy together.

Gemma's seeing it too. I want to tell him to say something to her, to show he likes her as much as she likes him. Not kissing – they're way too old. But he mustn't let her go. She needs to be here whenever I come back to Bristol.

Because he wants me to come back, doesn't he? That's why he's done this. He is going to let me be be a part of his life. I won him round. I was cute enough and funny enough. I even brought Gemma into his life.

I fixed it. How amazing is that? *But what about Mum?* I haven't fixed her.

DL could, though. If he can afford all this, then he could pay for Mum to talk to someone who'll help her get better, the way that Gemma helped me. Even though Mum doesn't have a Bob, she has stuff in her head that stops her being happy. She needs help getting rid of it.

'I love this song,' Gemma says as the music changes.

And I recognize it: the curtains song, 'One Day Like This'.

Eddie picks up his guitar to play along. The words are weird, but the melody sounds like tonight feels: bright and happy. Soon they're all joining in: the pretty agent and her husband are harmonizing. Vijay taps out the rhythm on the floor. Wow! I can tell by watching them that evenings like this aren't even a big deal, because music is in their blood.

I always thought I was like Mum – she isn't bothered

about dancing or music, has only ever been to one festival, and that's the one that made me.

But what if music is in my blood too, because of DL?

Everything about being here is magic. I can *almost* forget Bob and tomorrow's treatment and what the consultant might say next week.

These people are what I want to be when I grow up.

If I get to grow up.

Chapter 25: Dan

I feel high, even though I haven't taken anything.

It's this night. It's perfection: the music. The sky. The *people*.

After fetching another beer from the fridge, I pause for a second, taking it in. Idoia sits with her tiny daughter snuggled in her lap. Eddie's fingers strum his guitar. I've missed my friends this month. But mostly I keep going back to looking at Casey and Gemma. Eighteen days ago they were strangers. Now I never want to let them go.

Vijay walks into my eyeline and gives me a thumbs up. He knows how much this matters to me.

'You seem happy,' he whispers. 'No wonder. Casey is adorable.'

They both are. I nod. 'Right? I'm bloody lucky. Angelica did all the hard work and I got this incredible daughter.'

'How is her mum?'

'Not sure. But I heard her and Casey bickering on a video call, and I don't think Casey would do that unless she thought her mum was getting better.'

Together we watch her. 'She moves like you. Looks like you.'

'Does she? Let's hope it's only skin-deep, for her sake.'

Vijay groans. 'Why do you keep doing that?'

'What?'

204

'Putting yourself down. Sure, you've made mistakes, but show me one person in this room who hasn't, except Idoia's baby. The important thing is, you're trying to make up for lost time.'

'I guess. Though I still haven't told her about this place.'

Vijay pulls a face. 'Bloody hell. The longer you leave it, the more painful it'll be.'

'I'll do it at the weekend,' I say, sounding more determined than I feel.

He pulls a sceptical face. 'When do you find out if it's worked? The treatment?'

'There's a final scan a week today, before the last consultant appointment on Friday. If the tumour's shrunk, that's good, but it could still cause problems for her. Plus, the treatment itself might cause long-term side effects.'

'Shit. You wouldn't guess she's got that hanging over her. She's so full of life.'

The kitchen island is piled high with pizza boxes, and Gemma comes in from the terrace to grab one. Her green silk dress shimmers like leaves in a breeze.

'Your new friend is interesting too,' Vijay whispers. 'Not your usual type.'

'What's that meant to mean?'

He laughs. 'Nothing bad. It's nice to see you dating someone who eats pizza rather than push a lettuce leaf around a plate.'

'We're not dating.'

'Don't be defensive, Danny-boy. All I'm saying is, I've been taking soundings and the gang approves. How did you meet her?'

'Bumped into her on the way to the hospital.'

'Old-school! Is it time to shut down our Get Dan Coupled Up WhatsApp group?'

Tonight is so special that I don't feel irritated by how much my friends interfere in my life. 'Ha ha ha.'

He laughs. 'Seriously, mate, I'm thrilled for you. Everything sorted, in three weeks?'

'Don't tempt fate.'

'It's not fate. It's overdue. Now all you need to do is believe it's what you deserve.'

The track changes to 'Umbrella' and I watch as Casey comes in from the terrace, pulling Bear with her, looking for Gemma. Casey persuades Gemma onto the part of the floor with space to dance. Casey moves so naturally, and Vijay's right – she's inherited my dancing genes, not her mother's.

A couple of my friends join her, following her moves, and she grins, enjoying being the centre of attention for the right reasons.

When you're sick, you're sidelined. I lost count of the times I was supposedly the reason everyone was at some charity soccer game or fun run. I would get the best seat and the pick of the cakes, and a blanket to keep me warm. But what I wanted was to be on the field, muddy and breathless, like everyone else. I wanted to be seen for who I was, not what I was suffering from.

I blink. When I open my eyes, Gemma's lost her self-consciousness and I can't look away. She's so sexy it hurts.

She must sense me watching. She glances at me and keeps dancing, her hips swaying and her dress clinging to her breasts, and *bloody hell, how much do I want her now?* More than I've ever wanted anyone. The question is: can I be the man Casey and Gemma deserve?

Later.

Most people are leaving. Eddie punches me on the arm. 'Cheers, Danny. Awesome party, great gaff.' He winks.

And then there were five. Four really, because Vijay is out for the count, snoring on the sun lounger, his lips trembling under the moonlight. At his feet, Bear snores to the same rhythm.

Casey is at the far end of the terrace, sitting in the woven egg chair, talking to Vijay's son, Harrison. They're leaning in and she's laughing, and her posture makes her seem so much older than twelve.

What is he saying to her?

I step towards them, trying to eavesdrop. Harrison has just turned thirteen, and I've always thought he was geeky, like his dad, and young for his age. Now my hackles are up. I know what teenage boys can be like.

Gemma steps onto the terrace next to me and everything else fades away.

'So that's another thing to tick off Casey's wish list,' she says. Her skin shines in the soft light from the solar bulbs. 'She's made a friend too.'

'He'd better not get any ideas.'

Gemma chuckles. 'Harrison seems like a nice lad. I chatted to him earlier. Before they decided they only had eyes for each other.'

'She's too young.'

She touches my arm. My skin hums and she springs back slightly. 'Let her be. Perhaps having a friend who happens to be a cute boy is on her secret list, the one she'd never share with her dad.'

That idea makes me want to go right over and throw Harrison off the side of the terrace. 'That makes it worse!'

'He's young too. It looks sweet to me.'

I see them through her eyes now and, yes, they do look innocent and kind of . . . *new*. 'I guess.'

'You can't stop Casey getting hurt unless you lock her

207

away. I think a parent's job is to make her feel so safe that she can cope when things *do* challenge her. Because she knows she's loved.'

No one did that for me. But right now I believe I could learn to do it for Casey. Whenever I'm with Gemma, the impossible feels not just possible, but *easy*.

'Let's go inside, give them some space.' She touches my arm again to guide me, but doesn't let go this time.

It's greenhouse-hot indoors. Gemma and I are standing thrillingly, dangerously close to each other.

'Would you like to see the view from the mezzanine?' I suggest.

She laughs. 'Is that a line?'

'No. Unless you want it to be?'

Without answering, Gemma begins to climb the ladder. I wait for a few seconds so that I am not creepily close, but when I get near the top, she holds out her hand to pull me up the last two rungs.

'This *is* amazing,' she says. 'We can see everything . . .'

'But no one can see us,' I reply. The air between us has its own pulse, and it's racing.

Last time, before I kissed her, I wanted to prolong the moment *before*, in case it didn't live up to expectations.

This time I don't want to waste a second, because I know it will.

Chapter 26: Gemma

Dan's lips part. He's either about to say something or he's about to—

Kiss me.

Yes. *Kiss me*.

Except *kissing* is the gateway drug to the other things that I want, but can't allow to happen.

I shouldn't have come up here with him. I should have kept my distance for ten days. Ten days is nothing.

No. Ten days is for ever. It's only three nights since I remembered what it's like to give in to desire, and I'm seconds away from doing that again.

Must focus on something else. Something logical and sensation-free, like . . . numbers. Cost of my embryo transfer: three thousand, nine hundred and eighty-two pounds. Hours since the transfer: thirty-six. No, *thirty-seven*.

The first time I had an embryo transferred I printed out a timeline that told me, hour by hour, what might be happening. I checked as compulsively as I checked my own body for signs. *There were none*.

After the second transfer I tried to pretend nothing was happening. And I was right, of course. But the timeline from transfer one has lodged in my brain, so I know without thinking that, right now, the embryo should be hatching.

Hatching.

Could the joy I've been experiencing tonight be the blasto-cyst doing its thing? That tiny bundle of cells can trigger thousands of changes inside my body, readying it for a journey that seems both everyday and impossible. Who's to say that euphoria isn't one of those changes?

'Gemma . . .'

Has anyone spoken my name like that before? The lips that made that sound are *almost on mine*.

Yes.

Soft and sweet and summery.

No thoughts.

Only sensations.

His fingers in my hair. My hands against his back. Our bodies arching, closer, closer, *closer*.

But also: startling spikes of achy tenderness in my belly. Each one a dotted bruise caused by the jabs I've been giving myself. Count them: one, two, three . . .

I rear back so fast my neck hurts, like whiplash.

'I can't do this,' I say, even though my body is saying the opposite. 'Not now. Not tonight.'

His eyes bore into me: shock or anger or loss—

'It's OK,' he says, stepping back.

'We shouldn't have . . . *I* shouldn't have let that happen. Not because I don't want it to. You must know that, but I need more time.'

Before I can mess up further, I climb down the ladder, though my hands and feet still tingle so much I can barely feel the rungs. On the terrace, Bear stirs and I lift him into my arms, his body warm and loose. We brush against the potted night jasmine and that releases a scent so sweet it makes me dizzier still.

'Bye, Casey. See you soon.' I wave towards her and Harrison, but don't wait for the reply because I am back inside the flat, grabbing my bag – *hurry, hurry, hurry*, calling the lift. Come on. *Come on.*

I sense Dan behind me, but not close.

Follow me.

Keep away.

The lift doors open and I step into the lift. He's on the other side of the gap and—

Mind the doors, lift going down.

I don't know how, but he's in the lift moments before the doors close and we're kissing again, my body arching against the cool metal walls as the lift travels down, so we're suspended between one reality and another.

Dan sets every nerve ending on fire. My hands explore his shoulders, his spine, his waist – his body even more powerful and muscular than I'd have guessed.

And his hands, touching me, make the heat spread every-where, orange and red and molten gold.

Ground floor, doors opening.

We stop, move a few millimetres apart. The doors open. Beyond the frosted glass of the entrance door, blurred people crowd the dark waterside.

The doors close. We kiss again.

But I can't. I *mustn't*. Because every time we do this, my resolve weakens. And if I give in, it will threaten *everything* I have planned for.

The doors open again.

'Dan, I think – I must go. Now.'

He leans in to kiss me again and his hands touch my waist and I think, *Hatching*.

I shrug him off properly, revolted at myself. I push past, pulling a sleepy Bear with me, backing out of the glass doors onto the quay, staggering towards the next warehouse, resting against the brick.

It takes me a few seconds for the shock to go and for my breath to slow. I'm safe. I stopped myself going further. Even though this night – and Dan – made me want to go all the way.

All the way? I smile to myself. That's what a teenager would say. But I don't just mean sexually. It hits me now: *I could fall in love with this man.*

What if I already have?

It sounds like insanity, but change is coming, whether I like it or not. Soon the waiting will be over and I'll be ready to start the next phase of my life.

Will Dan be part of it? After our first kiss I went into hiding, and now I've run out on him. No one could blame him if he thinks I'm a flake.

That scares me. I get my phone out, type a new message, tweaking and deleting until I think I've been as honest as I can without sounding insane:

Sorry. Again. I don't make a habit of running away but I need a little more time. I won't blame you if you've lost patience, but please don't. That connection gets stronger every time I see you and I promise I will be in touch soon.

As soon as I've sent it, I regret the intensity. Dan has his pick of women, and who wouldn't walk away from someone as messed up as me?

It's not only that. I am keeping this huge part of myself hidden by not telling him about the transfer.

Though that will resolve itself soon enough.

Bear and I walk towards Clifton, my feet more solid on the ground. But the humid air still smells of jasmine, and every time I close my eyes I see Dan's face and it's all I can manage not to change direction and run back to him as fast as my legs, and Bear's, can manage.

Morning, and the disgust has kicked in, worse than any hangover.

What the hell was I thinking?

I phone Laura in such a state I can barely talk and she invites me over to Weston. I drive like I'm doing my test because I don't quite trust myself.

'Uh-oh,' she says when she answers the door. 'You have the look of a very guilty woman.'

She makes tea and we drink it in her garden, where Charlotte grizzles and Felix pats Bear with firm toddler fists. Bear puts up with it, an expression of stoicism on his face.

'I need tough love, please. No holds barred.'

'You've come to the right place for that. Charlotte had me up all night, teething.'

I might come to regret this. 'I am a mess, Laura.'

'The hormones again?'

'Could be.' She gives me the death stare and I sigh. 'Actually, no. Not the ones you mean.'

'What else would it be?' Her eyes narrow. 'Holy shit. It's that bloke, isn't it?'

'I kissed him last night. I *kissed* Dan. And it wasn't the first time. I kissed him on Sunday too, but last night was the worst because . . . because I've had the transfer now.'

The *transfer* of the precious embryo I created with Andrew, to help our love live on. His final chance of passing on what made him wonderful is somewhere inside me, yet *I kissed another man*.

Could the blastocyst know, somehow?

Laura touches my hand and I think it's a gesture of comfort,

213

until I see the frown on her face. 'Am I allowed to ask supplementary questions?'

I nod, almost relishing the chance to confess, so I can move on.

'How long did you kiss him for?'

'Um. Cumulatively? The first kiss was a few seconds. The second one . . .' My brain replays the lift journey, the doors opening and shutting, the urgency of his lips and his hips against mine. 'Longer.'

She raises her eyebrows. 'Were they good kisses?'

Pleasure spreads through me, like I'm lowering myself into a hot bath. 'Yes.'

Laura swigs her tea. She brews it too strong for me on purpose, so she gets the entire pot. Plus, caffeine is a no-no right now. Like kissing *should* be.

'Cards on the table, Gems. How long since you've kissed someone properly?'

'Well, not since Andrew obviously.' Even then, we hadn't kissed *properly* – passionately, sexily – for at least a year before that.

'There's no obviously about it, Gem. I've been telling you to date again. If only to prove that a kiss is just a kiss, et cetera. Ah well, better late than never. At least you don't have to see this bloke again, do you?'

The clouds seem to darken overhead. 'No.'

Laura stares at me. She's always been able to read me better than anyone else. 'Unless you *want* to see him again?'

I don't want to answer.

'You could. There's no law against it, so I won't be arresting you. As long as you don't do anything below the waist before you get your result.'

I shake my head. 'Don't be disgusting. Anyway I won't do anything to risk the transfer.'

'Is that the only reason you didn't sleep with him?'

'I think I'd prefer to change the subject now.'

She sips her tea. 'You really like him, don't you?'

'I think I do, Laura. Shit.'

'So tell me what he's like.'

'He's . . . very different from Andrew.' I can't imagine them having anything to say to each other: Andrew proper and quietly confident and clever with words; Dan laid-back and savvy and charming in a completely different way.

'That's a good thing. You don't want the next person you fall for to be a poor imitation of your dead husband, for either of your sakes.'

Ouch. 'I asked for tough love, not police brutality.'

She snorts her tea. 'Sorry. So tell me what you like about him.'

'He's funny and sociable and a bit of a charmer. But not sleazy. And I told you about his daughter. She's *so* sweet and brave. I'm getting close to her, too. Which is another massive dilemma, because I really don't want to let her down.'

'What does he do?'

'A mixture. He helps build stage sets at music events, but also runs some kind of social enterprise.'

'Are you sure social enterprise isn't code for a weed farm? Music people are usually broke and stoned most of the time.'

'There wasn't even a whiff of weed when I went to his *penthouse* last night. And all of his friends are down to earth.'

'He's introduced you to his *friends*? So it's not just you who's got it bad.'

'I don't think it was a big deal for him. Not like I've been summoned to meet his family, is it?' Except, as I say it, I remember he told me that his friends *were* his substitute family.

Laura laughs. 'Mates are a big deal for men. Bigger than family. Except for their mums, that is.'

'His mum died when he was young.'

She raises her eyebrows. Years in the police have given her a dim view of human beings and sob stories.

'Come on, Laura,' I say. 'Normal people don't lie about stuff like that.'

'You'd be surprised.' She takes a slurp of tea. 'OK. If you want to cut through all the crap and find out if Dan is The One, I've got an idea.'

I'm already shaking my head. 'I can't tell him about the embryo transfer yet.'

'I don't mean that. Has he met any of your friends?'

'Only Jed, because he teaches Casey, but that doesn't count. It's not like I'm overburdened with social engagements right now.'

'You need a second opinion. Which is why I think it'd be a good idea to haul him over the Coles.'

'No. No way, I don't want to scare him off completely.'

Laura's eyes glitter with excited steeliness. 'Gems, I worry about you. You're hormonal. Grieving. Easy prey for someone who could take advantage. So it's maybe a good idea to get a second opinion, right? We're meeting for Charlotte's birthday on Saturday anyway, so why not ask him along? Bring the daughter too.'

Casey *did* have a day at the seaside on her wish list. And I suppose Laura's right: if this was no more than a fling, it wouldn't matter what my family thought.

But this feels like more.

'Let me think about it—'

'Mummy! The doggy is doing a stinky poo!'

We both look up. Felix is giggling delightedly as he watches

216

poor Bear at the far end of the garden, trying to find some privacy.

I stand up, hand already in my pocket, getting out a poo bag.

'You know it makes sense, Gems,' my sister says, averting her eyes from Bear's squat. 'It's the fastest possible way to find out if he's a keeper.'

Chapter 27: Dan

Thursday 19 July

It's hard work getting Casey to hospital this morning. She's dreamy and keeps asking about Harrison. And I'm grumpier with her than I should be, because I keep thinking about Gemma.

Have I messed it up again somehow? At least walking into the deafening workshop forces me to get my head out of my arse and focus on real life.

'Boss, we missed you yesterday!'

'Oi, Mr Lennon, were you bunking off?'

'You got a new girlfriend, sir? You look like you been up all night.'

I walk in between the benches, chatting and checking in, because I'm in no hurry to face today's biggest challenge.

'Are you ready for him?' Sue, our education officer, asks when I go into the office. 'I'm worried he might leg it – or break something – if he has to wait much longer.'

'OK. Bad cop or good cop?'

Sue shrugs her skinny shoulders. 'Search me. He's not in a good place.'

Finn Mackenzie takes up a lot of physical space in my small office, and his dark mood makes the room seem even more claustrophobic.

'Take a seat, Finn.'

I half expect him to pick up the chair and throw it at the wall – wouldn't be the first time that's happened – but he nods without making eye contact with me. As he sits down, the chair metal groans. I don't have the heart to be bad cop today.

'How are things going?'

'You know already.'

Finn arrived drunk and stinking of weed yesterday and almost punched one of the other lads, before taking off again. 'Tell me your side of the story.'

He scoffs. 'If you're gonna boot me off, get on with it, OK?'

'I don't want to kick you out without understanding what's happening. Here, I've got your reports for June – everything was brilliant. So what's changed?'

He gives me a half-glance from under hooded eyelids. 'He's back.'

'Your stepdad?'

Finn shrugs. 'Doesn't want me there. So I go out.'

'And when you go out . . .'

'I drink, yeah.'

'Is that all?'

'Smoke a bit too. No more than that.'

'Because yesterday you were out of order, you know that?' He shrugs again and I smell stale sweat. 'Where are you sleeping, Finn?'

'With mates. He bolts the door so I can't get in. No biggie, I don't wanna be there and hear how he talks to Mum. I might lose it, shut him up for good.'

Usually Finn lumbers around the workshop like Shrek, and I can't imagine him being violent. 'Sounds tough.'

Silence.

'You've come on a long way here, Finn. You're bright. Picked up machine work way faster than most of the lads. Plus, you're creative. So many ideas.'

He scoffs, finding praise way harder to take than criticism.

'I mean it. There'll be no problem finding something permanent for you, if you can get your shit together. But that needs to happen fast.'

He doesn't respond.

'See the photos on the wall?' Finn's head doesn't move, but his eyes follow to where I'm pointing. 'This is my rogues' gallery. The lads who made the biggest progress. Take this guy, Arnie? He was in worse shape than you, but I bumped into him a few days ago and now he's sorted: job, house, girlfriend, even a new baby. I believe you could be on this wall one day.'

'That ain't the way I'm made.'

'No, that's bull. You *can* change. But we can't do that for you. Think about it. If you come back tomorrow – on time, tidied up – we can start over.'

'I got nowhere to go,' he mutters after a pause, then kicks his backpack. 'My last mate kicked me out last night and I kipped in the park. How am I gonna tidy up there?'

Oh, mate, I've been there. Should I tell him that now? No. This isn't about me – it's about him.

'What if I call the Foyer, see if they've got space? It's basic, but it's five stars compared to a cell. Or the park. And no stepdad hassle.'

I hold my breath. *Make the right choice, Finn. Please.*

'OK.'

Bingo! I try not to let him see how relieved I am. 'I'll do it now.'

As Finn stands up, the chair sighs again. 'Why bother with me, boss?'

I could say it's about protecting the project's success rates, so he doesn't feel under pressure. Or go the opposite way: turn up the volume on my hopes for him, on how I *know* he can change.

'You're one of us, Finn. We look after our own.'

The half-smile he gives me means I got it right. I stand up and open the door, miming giving him a kick up the arse as he walks back into the workshop, and the others shout and jeer, asking if he's been thrown out, but cheer when he says he's staying.

I bloody love those lads.

Sue pops her head in. 'Sorted?'

'Sorted myself a load of extra work,' I say, but I'm smiling as I grab the paperwork and get ready to plead his case with the Foyer.

I'm holding on the line when it hits me: I've been telling the lads for years that they can change, without ever believing that it applies to me. Sure, I'm in a better place than I was when I was their age, but that wouldn't be hard. And despite my job and my flat, and even my new name, deep down I've always felt like Darryl Lennox, who betrays everyone, is *nothing* underneath the charm.

But these last weeks I have felt more like the Dan that Vijay and Gemma and Casey see.

The thought is so shocking I almost drop the phone. I am changing because they believe in me – same as I believe in lads like Finn. And sure, they don't know the ins and outs of my shoddy past. But if I want Finn to be judged on who he is today and tomorrow, not who he was yesterday, don't I deserve the same?

'Sorry to keep you hanging on. So you've got someone you want to refer?'

For a second I forget I'm on the line to the Foyer. 'Yes.

Finn Mackenzie. He's had a rough time, but I reckon, with your support, he can turn everything round.'

By the time I pick Casey up, I've decided I'm going to tell her about the penthouse this afternoon. We go to BayCaff and I buy her a slice of banoffee pie, to soften the blow. Though when the pie arrives, covered in clouds of whipped cream, I wonder if it'll be too tempting for her to throw it back in my face.

All she wants to talk about is *Harrison*. What he's like. What he likes.

'Do you know what star sign he is? I'm a Taurus, so my best match would be Aquarius.'

'I think he was born in October. Or February. One of those.'

She tuts, annoyed by the sketchiness of my answers. Already she knows more about him than I do, as they've been WhatsApping since they swapped numbers last night.

'He says he lives mostly with his mum, up near where Gemma lives. Have you ever been there? Is the house massive?'

My jaw tightens and the tinnitus turns shriller. 'Yes, before his mum and dad split up I used to go to their house, and it is pretty massive.'

'So they are as rich as Harrison says they are?'

I laugh. 'He told you they were loaded, did he?'

'He wasn't showing off. He's not that kind of boy,' she says, and I try not to smile, because if he *wasn't* showing off, how did she know?

'They're pretty well off.'

'So how come his dad lives in a tent in his mum's back garden? Is he a hippie?'

'It's not really a tent. It's a deluxe Mongolian yurt, with

222

its own rainfall shower. But it's temporary.' Now is my chance to explain why. But her lilac eyes fix onto mine with such trust that I can't bring myself to do it yet – I'm too much of a coward. 'He used to live on the Harbourside too, but he's had to move out for a bit.'

Not a lie, not the whole truth.

'Cool.' Casey puts her spoon down and begins to run her finger along the plate to get the very last of the banana caramel cream.

'You're definitely too young to have a boyfriend,' I say.

She laughs. 'Harrison's not my *boyfriend*.' But she blushes and I think, *She wishes he was*. 'He's a boy who I'd like to be my friend.'

'I work with lads and I know what they can be like, that's all.'

Casey works her way around the plate until it's cleaner than it would be after dishwashing. 'Could I come in? To your work, I mean.'

The idea of my daughter among all those loud men terrifies me. 'I don't think so, it's pretty rough and ready.'

She frowns. 'Molly's always going into *her* parents' offices on Take Your Daughter to Work days. I've missed out. And I liked meeting your friends.'

I can tell from her *oh-so-innocent* face that she's piling on the guilt on purpose. And it would be satisfying to show her what I do. I'm proud of it, and of her.

'Let me think about it.'

'Hospital school finishes early on Fridays,' she says, 'so tomorrow would be the ideal time.'

'I said I'll think about it.'

As we walk back to the penthouse I *do* think about it. I saw *my* dad at work all the time when I was growing up, but I'd forgotten how proud I was of him. I was only five or six when I first realized that other dads weren't like mine. It was the mums who picked up my classmates. Dads were invisible. Except for *my* dad. He'd be there, parking his brilliant black Mazda on double yellows, 'so we can make a quick getaway'. The bug-eyed headlights would wink at the women as we roared away.

Of course I didn't understand then what he did, but I knew he was great at talking to people and changing their minds, like Derren Brown or Paul Daniels. It was only later that I realized how he abused his talents. But just because my father didn't deserve my admiration doesn't mean Casey shouldn't see my work, and how important it is.

I don't often give myself credit, but the lads are desperate to prove themselves, underneath the swagger – and the reason I do this job is because there's nothing quite like seeing them slowly beginning to believe in themselves. I want my daughter to believe in *herself*, too.

Chapter 28: Casey

Friday 20 July

As the proton beam fires more invisible lightning bolts at Bob, I'm planning my next message to Harrison.

'Earth to Casey!' Fern's voice comes through my headphones. 'Treatment's all done, you can come out now.'

DL is waiting with my backpack, ready to take me to his work. I grab my phone. Hooray! Harrison is on his break and has sent a TikTok video of meerkats, because I told him they were my favourite animal. It makes me laugh out loud, which is excellent because the same sense of humour is important – everyone says so.

Oh. *Wow!* He's forwarded photos of him at Glastonbury last year. He is *so* good-looking. Too good-looking for me. Except if he didn't *like* me, he wouldn't bother sending all these messages.

That thought makes me feel sunny inside, so I send him a flurry of sunshine emojis.

'. . . they're good lads, but you might hear them swearing,' DL is saying.

'Don't worry, Dad,' I say, 'I have heard people swear before.'

He doesn't reply and eventually I look up from my phone to see he's grinning wider than a YouTuber who's just gone viral.

'What?'

'You called me Dad.'

'Oh.' I stop. Weird. 'Yeah. Well, you are my dad. It's no big deal, is it?'

That's not true. It *is* a huge deal. But what's even more amazing is that it felt so natural I didn't even notice I'd said it.

As I follow my father out of the hospital, the sun shines even brighter.

'We're here, Casey. You're about to see that my life isn't all penthouses and jam sessions.'

I put my phone away. Whoa, this is ultra-*real*. Dad told me he was a lecturer, but I can't see a college. We're surrounded by brick buildings covered in graffiti tags, and the only one with lights on has a big sign: *SOUTH BRISTOL CAN-DO TRADE AND CRAFT WORKSHOP.*

Inside smells of wood and varnish and . . . ugh, sweat. The warehouse is huge: each workbench has its own halo of light, where men are working. It's like Santa's workshop, except the elves are wearing hoodies instead of pointy hats.

'It's full-on at first, but you'll get used to it,' Dad says.

Dad. I like how that sounds in my head. 'I'm tougher than you think.'

He smiles at me. 'You're tougher than any of this lot.' He reaches for something on a shelf. 'But your ears aren't. Put these ear defenders on.'

They're like the world's ugliest headphones and they're tight, but at least they muffle the sounds.

'. . . can't you, Finn? Casey, meet Finn. He'll look after you while I do a bit of catching up in the office.'

Dad's talking to this big lad wearing a Tupac T-shirt. A cherry blush spreads in big blotches up his throat to the top of his shaved head.

'Hi,' I say and I wave, but he stares down at his trainers.

Dad smiles at him. 'Show her what you're working on. But don't let her touch anything dangerous. She's my girl and she's precious to me.'

Finn looks scared now, even though he must be eighteen or nineteen and weighs three times as much as me.

'What are you making?' I ask.

'Eh?'

'WHAT ARE YOU MAKING?' I shout.

'BIRD BOX,' he shouts back.

'DO YOU LIKE BIRDS?'

Around us, I see the guys laughing. The ear defenders squash my skull, which is not good when you've got a brain tumour.

'Fuck off!' Finn snaps at them, but then glances apologetically at me. 'Sorry,' he says. 'LET'S GO TO THE SHOP.'

I follow him again, through a door marked *SHOWROOM*. If outside was like Santa's workshop, this could be his outlet store. The chunky shelves are crammed with beautiful things: a farmyard jigsaw, a miniature doll's house, a sailing boat with stamp-sized fabric sails and a bearded captain figure at the helm. 'Did you make any of these things?'

He hands me a bowl: the grain of the wood is smooth and warm under my fingers, the same colour as Harrison's skin.

'It's amazing. Have you always been good at woodwork?'

Finn blushes. 'No way. Probation officer got me a placement. I – well, I was inside. This is meant to be my fresh start.'

I stare at him. 'I've never met anyone who's been to prison before.'

Finn gives me a weird look: he must think I'm a bit rude. 'How do you know? People don't wear a sign round their necks.' He pulls down the sleeve of his hoodie, but not before I have time to see thick lines inked on his wrist.

The tattoo: did he get that 'inside'? 'Was it horrible? Being in prison?'

'Not as hard as being at home when your stepdad hates you. But jail changes you. When you get out, the people you left are the same. But you'll never be the same again.'

And I want to say, *Yes! I know how that feels*, but I guess he'd be freaked out if I told him about my brain tumour and the hospital.

'So how long have you been coming here?' I ask. Get me, Queen of Small Talk.

'I'm three months in. It's good here because we've all been through the same shit.' He blushes deeper. 'The same *stuff.*'

Like hospital school, except there the kids are younger than me, and it's not like I can chat to a Year Four kid about why I still have a chest as flat as when I was eight.

Finn is waiting for me to say something.

'What happens after you leave here?'

'Dan and Sue help us find apprenticeships. Hardly anyone who gets to the end goes back inside, thanks to your dad.'

'Wow. That's amazing.'

'None of us knew he had a daughter, but it makes sense.' Finn is still talking. 'He's patient. And he gets us. I guess because he's been there.'

'Been where?'

Finn shakes his head. 'I . . . um, because he's a dad. Used to dealing with big kids.'

I smile, but it doesn't totally make sense. Because my father hasn't been a father to me – or anyone – until the last three weeks.

*   *   *

228

Dad drives me back. The jeep's high up, so I see loads of places I'd like to go to. Four weeks in Bristol isn't long enough. Four years wouldn't be.

Even if my dad wants me around after next week, I think Mum will try to stop that happening. But will he stand up to her? *I need to know.*

'So what's left on your wish list, Casey?'

'There is something I forgot to put on there, but it's the most important.'

'Anything you like. Except balloons.'

'OK. I want to get my hair coloured.'

He sighs. 'But your mum was dead against it . . .'

'It's not dangerous. It's only that Mum thinks *everything* is dangerous. *Please.*'

His jaw goes tight as we turn into the basement car park. 'Is this because you want to impress Harrison?'

'Doh! Obviously not. I want to look nice for myself.'

Dad frowns as he gets his bag out of the car. 'She'd be angry with us both if the next time she sees you you've got pink hair.'

'She's angry with you most of the time anyway.'

'Ha, you're not wrong.' We take the lift and I'm watching him for clues about what he's going to decide.

The lift jolts into place on the penthouse floor.

My scalp prickles.

Something's not right.

'Dad, do you think somebody has broken . . .'

The doors open.

'What the fuck—' Dad shouts as we both see the shadow of a man standing at the window. He jumps towards the intruder, fists tight – a different dad from the one I know. One who can fight.

But I'm not scared, because my body recognizes the intruder before my brain does.

229

'Harrison!'

He turns round, his face as shocked as my dad's. Oh, Harrison is so cute. Even cuter than I'd remembered.

'Surprise!'

Now the fear's worn off, I'm embarrassed. My hair's messy and I don't have any make-up on. He stares at the floor and I notice a rucksack at his feet.

'How did you get in?'

Harrison stares up at Dad. Neither of them says anything.

'We've got a key,' Harrison says eventually. 'My dad does. A *spare* key, because your dad is forgetful and has locked himself out loads of times. I borrowed it because I left something behind last night. Sorry, Mr Lennon, I didn't mean to freak you out.'

'Call ahead next time,' Dad says, 'because I was *this* close to knocking you halfway to Hotwells with the baseball bat I keep under the sofa.'

They stare at each other. 'No sweat.'

And now I get it: this is Dad's way of warning him not to hurt me.

Dad cares.

Harrison cares.

And there's this tension between them, but that's the way it should be. Dads and daughters are meant to be close. Boyfriends are supposed to be nervous around fathers.

This is everything I've ever wanted.

And it keeps getting better. I'm set up for the most fantastic weekend ever. Gemma called Dad an hour ago to ask if we want to go to the seaside tomorrow afternoon, because her family is having a first birthday party for her sister's baby.

My dad couldn't stop smiling, and straight after that he said I can have my hair coloured, so long as it washes out before the end of next week. And when I called the salon – *me*, calling a salon to ask for *my* stylist – Pepe had had a cancellation for the morning, before we go to Weston-super-Mare.

My iPhone's ringing: Mum. Before I answer, I remind myself that I can't mention *any* of this, so I don't stress her out.

'Hey, gorgeous girl. Guess what! I'm so much better. I thought I could drive down first thing and bring you home.'

I hold the phone further away, so she can't see I feel like bursting into tears. *I don't want her to spoil everything, like she always does.* 'What does Harriet say about you coming down?'

'She's not sure about the idea, but you know what she's like – always fussing.'

'I think she's right, Mum. You should save your energy for next week, for my final scans and when I ring the end-of-treatment bell.'

She blinks at the screen. 'I thought you'd be missing me.'

Dad stands behind me. 'Angelica, I promise I'm looking after her. Wouldn't you rather have the chance to chill out some more before you come down? You haven't had any time to yourself in twelve years.'

'Mum, he's right. Da—' I stop myself just in time. 'DL is keeping me safe and I'm quite tired; we're going to take it easy this weekend, so it'd make me happy if you got the chance to do some stuff for yourself instead.'

'Hmm. Well, I guess I could think of something.' It's hard to be sure with the blurry camera, but her voice sounds excited. The way she used to sound before I got ill and she got worried. 'Harriet's always trying to get me to go to the wine bar in Ledbury. Or the multiplex in Worcester – I haven't seen a good rom-com in years.'

'Perfect!'

But after the call ends, I feel guilty. I did want Mum to have fun, but mostly I didn't want her to stop *me* having fun. This weekend is all about getting the final bit of my plan in place: Dad has to meet Gemma, I have to meet her family, and everyone has to see that I'm a mega-fun person to have around.

Chapter 29: Gemma

Saturday 21 July

Charlotte's first birthday won't be one she'll remember, but that doesn't stop us giving it the full Cole family treatment.

It starts, as always, with lunch at Patti's Diner, where Mum and Dad went on their first dates in the eighties. We squeeze into the torn leatherette banquettes and order monster milkshakes and burgers, cooked and served by Patti's three strong-armed daughters.

Laura loathes the place, so she's 'accidentally' been rostered on this morning and won't join us till we get to the pier. Which I'm relieved about, because at least Dan won't have to face her till later. He has *no* idea what he's in for. If he did, I don't think he'd show.

He still might not.

'Not hungry?' Mum spots that I've left most of the fries and my bun untouched. Her question is more loaded than one of Patti's quarter-pounders.

'That's right. I don't have an appetite. I'm not pining for anyone or feeling sick because of unexpected events in the baby-making area.'

'No need to be so touchy, sweetie.'

Mel, Laura's partner, raises her eyebrows at me over Charlotte's straw sunhat. She survived her own 'hauling over

233

the Coles' because she gives as good as she gets. Andrew got through his because I prepared him in advance, telling him to gossip with Mum, talk engines with Dad, and keep his fingers crossed with my unpredictable sister.

Dan is *so* different. More charming, which should make it easier. But my family came to love Andrew completely, and they may be as baffled as I am by what I'm feeling now . . .

Bear begins to bark, and I look up to see Casey walking into the diner.

I do a double-take. Is that Casey?

Because her hair is *pink*.

Not bright pink, but soft apricot and rose tones that make her style seem fuller and her skin glow.

'You've been back to Pepe,' I say, jumping up from the booth and giving her a hug before inspecting again. 'That's so beautiful. Are you happy?'

'It's the best my hair has *ever* been,' she says.

'And the most I have ever paid a hairdresser,' Dan says, wincing.

Look at him.

It was already a warm afternoon, but my body's turned *tropical* now. When Casey crouches down to get the full-blown Bear love-bombing, Dan inches closer.

'You're beautiful,' he whispers.

I *have* made an effort, something Mum noticed straight away. I ended up rifling through the suitcase of ancient clothes under the bed, because nothing in my wardrobe felt quite right. On a whim, I pulled out the sunset maxi dress from my art-student days and smiled as I tried it on, remembering.

Am I being daft? Hankering after the person I was seventeen years ago? Or, even worse, trying to compete with Angelica? That's a competition I'll always lose.

234

Except now I see the hungriness in Dan's eyes, I don't want to be her. Being me is enough.

'Is *that* your family?' Casey nods nervously at my gaggle. They're waving like shipwrecked people who've spotted a lifeboat. She scratches her head and I want to move her hand away gently – tell her they can't fail to love her.

'Yes. They might seem eccentric, but I promise they are nice in their own way. They can't wait to meet you.' I look up at Dan. 'And you.'

If anything, he looks more nervous than his daughter. But despite my earlier doubts, I am suddenly convinced it *will* be OK. Casey and Dan deserve to be loved. I think about her beads of courage, and his decision to take the risk of getting to know his daughter after so long.

I *do* take Casey's hand now, to walk her towards our booth. 'Meet Mum, Dad, Mel, Felix and baby Charlotte. Guys, this is Casey. Currently the smartest twelve-year-old in Bristol. This is her first time in Weston and we are going to show her *all* the highlights.'

As my dad shuffles up and pats the space he's made to welcome Casey, Mum gives Dan an up-and-down leer that would get a man branded a sex pest. 'And you can come and talk to me.'

Poor Dan.

Still, as my sister said, this is the best way to find out if we have a future.

I try to chat to Mel, but it's hard not to tune into the conversations around us. My left ear picks up Dad extolling the many virtues of crazy golf to Casey, and my right hears my mother interrogating Dan.

So far, he's surviving. More than that. He's telling her nuggets about himself I've never heard before: the bands he's worked with, the places he's visited. I try to focus on Mel's stories about potty-training Felix . . .

'Right, Casey has *never* been on the pier, or in fact *any* pier,' Dad announces, 'and it's high time we corrected that very sad state of affairs.'

I haven't been to the pier since Andrew died, though we came on our one and only wedding anniversary.

A lifetime ago.

Being here with new people helps take away the sting. Mel stays with Charlotte and Bear down on the beach, and Dad buys wristbands for us, so we can go on all the rides. I take Casey into the Hall of Mirrors, and even though the first one gives a true reflection, she jumps as soon as she sees herself.

'I'd forgotten about my hair.'

'It looks incredible.'

I start to walk towards the first of the distorting mirrors, but Casey hasn't moved. 'It's semi-permanent, but Mum hates chemicals so she'll go mental if I don't manage to wash it all out.'

Yup. From my one encounter with Angelica, that's the most likely outcome.

But I smile at Casey. 'She might be surprised at first, but I'm sure she'll be so delighted to see you that she'll get over the shock pretty fast.'

'Maybe.'

We turn the corner and the vast mirror in front of us turns our bodies into huge round balls with tiny marble heads, and we both giggle.

'This is *so* retro. It's like Snapchat from the olden days.'

I laugh. 'I can't believe you've never been on a pier.'

'Where we live there's no sea, remember.'

'But you go on holiday?'

Casey shrugs. 'Sometimes. Mostly to other boring bits of countryside, though. Mum doesn't like crowds. Or noise.' The next mirror elongates us, and she points. 'I used to be almost that skinny. Before the steroids.'

'I like you exactly how you are now,' I say. 'You can tell me to mind my own business if you want, but has your mum always been quite *anxious*?'

In the mirror, Casey's pencil-thin head nods. 'A bit, but a lot more now. It took ages for the doctors to believe anything was wrong with me, and she blames herself, so now she's extra-cautious. That coin waterfall in the arcade would have made her freak out. *Think of all the thousands of people who've handled those coins. Think of the bacteria, the viruses, the sweat.*'

She stops abruptly. When I turn to glance at her, she looks ashamed that she imitated her mum.

Round the next corner, the mirrors turn us into tiny boxes of humanity, and then into narrow discs. 'It's OK to get angry with someone. It doesn't mean you love them any less. I love my parents to bits, but I can still see that my dad's nerdy. And my mum gossips about people, which isn't the best quality.'

'I'd give anything for a family like yours,' Casey says quietly.

And I want to say to her: *Yes, yes, you'd be made so welcome.* But I don't want to give her false hope that anything might happen after today. Maybe I've already let her get too close.

The final mirror merges the two of us into one, and I link arms with her as we step out of the hall, back into the sunshine.

'Where next?' I ask as we scan the attractions: the ghost train, the helter-skelter. I notice her eyes widen as she sees something and follow her gaze: FORTUNES TOLD: PALM, TAROT, CRYSTAL BALL.

'I've *always* wanted to have my cards read.'

Casey does *not* need some fake mystic giving her even more reasons to be worried about the future. 'You know it's not real, don't you? Plus, it won't be included in the wristband.'

'Obviously no one can tell the future,' she says, but she sounds so dejected that I wonder if a fortune teller might cheer her up with some vague chat about tall, handsome strangers.

'Let's talk to your dad and see how much they charge. But if you go, you must promise to take it no more seriously than the spooks on the ghost train.'

Dan seems as doubtful as me, but my mum's on the case now. She knows Mystic Debs – apparently she's a regular at the surgery because of her tennis elbow, and as a thank-you to the doctors, she did a turn telling everyone's fortunes at last year's Christmas party.

'It was a riot, and there's no way she'd say anything upsetting. Go on, Casey, my treat.'

While Casey has her reading, I fetch ice creams for everyone. Casey comes out smiling, but refuses to reveal what Debs said. We go down onto the shore, where Mel and Charlotte have been waiting with Bear. He tears across the sand as soon as he sees me, and it's almost enough to make me forget this is the same stretch where Andrew and I posed for our last official wedding photo, as the sky turned crimson and the silvery sand rippled like fish scales beneath our bare feet. When I close my eyes, I almost feel the weight of damp silk around my ankles.

So don't close your eyes.

I open them. Casey, Bear and Dan are chasing each other up and down the beach and I can hear laughter and barking. They're not thinking about the past, so why am I?

The scene is so perfect I have to take a photo. I WhatsApp it to Dan, and then zoom in on Casey. She has colour in her cheeks, and there's no hint of the nervy girl I first saw in the classroom at the hospital, flinching when she saw Bear.

I turn towards my family: Dad fusses over baby Charlotte while Mum chats to Mel. I lower myself into a deckchair and try to focus on them, not Dan. On the magic that happens when people you care about come together: the crazy alchemy of it.

But it's no good. He is all I can think about.

He's close by again. I can tell. I open my eyes, shielding them against the sun with my hand. He's rolled up his shorts so high that I can see the shape of his thighs.

'I wouldn't kick him out of bed,' my mum whispers and I tut.

Neither would I.

My lips tingle with the memory of our kisses and the sensation spreads through my entire body.

Casey flops down onto the waterproof blanket and Mum offers her a drink.

'I am so tired, but *so* happy,' Casey says.

For a moment I consider suggesting they leave before my sister shows up: I don't want her judgemental tendencies to spoil the mood. But that's daft. There's no rational reason why Laura wouldn't approve of Dan, when everyone else does . . . It's gone so well, I could hug the world.

'Bear's not tired yet. Fancy a game of catch?' Dan suggests, and when I struggle to climb out of the deckchair, he reaches down to help me up. I take his hand without thinking, but the sudden movement makes the chair collapse underneath me with a clatter and I brace myself to hit the hard sand.

But Dan jumps forward and pulls me upright. His strength sends a wave of something primal through me.

Not pure lust this time. It's . . . the knowledge that he would not have let me fall. *I am so tired of handling everything alone.*

Bear is jumping up as if to say, *You're not alone. I'm here. You'll never be on your own with me.* And I laugh at his sand-speckled muzzle face and his skinny-wet paws. Bear has helped me to *feel* so many things again.

But a dog – even this one-of-a-kind dog – is not enough.

'I always forget how far out the tide goes here,' Dan says when we're out of Mum's earshot.

'It's not nicknamed Weston-super-Mud for nothing. When the tide's out, it's hard work swimming. Or skinny-dipping. Though every teenager here gives it a go at least once.'

Why did I say that?

His expression makes me realize why. Back in lust mode.

'Including you?'

I nod as his eyes travel from my face down the length of my body, the silky dress clinging to my shape where the water wicks up the fabric. 'We were kids. Well, seventeen. I seem to remember scrumpy was involved. What about you?'

'Yeah, in the Caribbean. Rum punch was involved. Back when my life was more rock 'n' roll.' He winks at me.

'I skinny-dipped in Ibiza too, on my first holiday without my parents. I was nineteen. But I think it's the kind of behaviour you outgrow.'

'Only if you decide to,' he says. Is he imagining us taking off our clothes and running into the sea? I picture it too.

Bloody hell. Bloody hormones.

'So what do you think of my folks?' I want to pivot the conversation into safer territory.

'Your dad is fun and your mum's hilarious. Though she kept asking me about how much I earn. I got the impression she's worried I'm after your money.'

240

'Yeah. There's a lot less than she thinks, before you get too excited.'

He frowns. 'I've never taken anything from a woman, and I never will.'

I shrug. 'I was kidding.'

'Good. Anyway, me and your mum have bonded over a love of 1980s heavy metal. I've bought her affections with the promise of an old Motörhead tour T-shirt. And your dad's a legend. Your sister-in-law too. You were right when you said you'd lucked out on the family front.'

'Other people's families always seem so much nicer than your own.'

Dan laughs. 'Tell me about it.'

'Why don't *you* tell me about it? I'd like to know about your family.'

He arches the ball-thrower back from his shoulder and chucks the ball with such force that Bear almost disappears as he thunders after it, paws scarcely touching the wet sand. 'It's boring. Like I said, my mum died when I was born and my dad wasn't around after I hit my teens.'

'That's a big thing. Having no one, when you're the same age Casey is now?'

Dan shakes his head. 'Listen, Gemma, like most men, I can talk about myself for hours. But I prefer to talk about now – not mistakes people made twenty years ago.'

Maybe I should just enjoy this glorious afternoon. Except the balance between us feels off now. I'm revealing so much about myself by introducing him to my family, and I might soon reveal even more. *If I can trust him.*

'I can't help being curious,' I say. 'But the more you change the subject, the more I wonder if you're keeping something hidden.'

241

Chapter 30: Dan

Keeping something hidden.

You could say that. As I throw Bear's ball again to buy myself time, I try to work out which of my lies is the least damaging: the penthouse, my criminal record, the reason I walked away from fatherhood, what I did to my own dad . . .

Perhaps someone like Gemma could forgive *one* of these. But together they're way too much.

I could kiss her instead of answering. I've wanted to all day, and it would make her forget her question. But her mother is watching.

OK then. Let's roll.

'I've never told anybody this, but my dad went to prison,' I say. 'That's why I lost him.'

Gemma stops. 'Bloody hell, Dan. What happened?'

Her mother's pointed questions about money still ring in my ears, so already I need to lie about what he did. 'Petty theft. Nothing violent. He couldn't do regular work, because of looking after me, and sometimes he did the wrong thing to stay afloat.'

'That's awful. So your dad was trying to care for you and they sent him to jail for *that*. Even though you'd lost your mum, too.'

Of course Gemma automatically thinks the best of him, because she does of everyone. 'He wasn't an angel,' I say.

'No, but under those circumstances . . . it's cruel.' Somehow Gemma looks even lovelier when she frowns. 'How long did he go to prison for?'

'He got six years, but he would have played the system to get out early, knowing my dad. But I'd cut off contact. I was angry with him.'

'Six years. That's a travesty.' She's shaking her head. 'And you've had nothing to do with him since then?'

'He didn't search for me, either. Even when I was growing up, I always felt Dad would have been so much happier if Mum had never got pregnant with me.'

Why did I say that? It's raw, as well as true. Perhaps I want to make up for the lies I just told.

'You could have been a reminder of how special she'd been.' But Gemma sounds doubtful. 'Sorry, I like to think everyone behaves well, but if he made you feel crap and never bothered to find you after prison, well, perhaps it's for the best.'

We walk and I kick the ball in and out of the shallow surf, as Bear weaves around my feet, making little gruff sounds of excitement. Gemma's silence makes me think out loud. 'When he was sent down, I thought I didn't need him, that I was all grown-up. But it's like you said before: I wasn't far off Casey's age. A kid.'

She nods. 'If you hadn't had the best parenting, I guess it's no wonder you didn't know how to respond when Angelica got pregnant.'

'I'm not trying to make excuses, but part of it was fear.' I can picture myself in the filthy kitchen of my flat, the terror spreading through me, the blood rushing in my ears.

There *is* such tenderness in Gemma's eyes. 'I guess the choice of whether to be a dad yourself was taken out of your hands. But now you have chosen to be in Casey's life, you shouldn't feel guilty about it any more.'

'Maybe not.'

'Definitely not. Even in the couple of weeks since I met you both, I've been able to see you're changing.'

'Yeah? Well, some of that is down to you, Gemma.'

She blushes. And even though we know the Cole family are on red alert for any signs of closeness, she still reaches out to take my hand, squeezes it once and lets go.

'Risky,' I say, wanting to pull her towards me, to touch her everywhere.

'Today I feel like taking risks,' she says.

'I *could* kiss you, if you want to live really dangerously.'

'So tempted. But Casey would find it excruciating. Let's wait till we're alone again. It'll be worth it.' Her eyes shine.

'How soon?'

'Tomorrow, after I come to the hospital with Bear? We could take Casey out for supper and then' – she hesitates – 'we could be on our own.'

'I can't wait.'

'Nor me. Although . . .' Her face turns serious and she nods, deciding something.

'What?'

'Now that you've been honest with me, I need to do the same. Tell you some stuff before we get more involved. It's about time.'

And before I can ask what she means, she's walking back towards her family.

The afternoon drags. The kids are getting fractious and I'm struggling with being so close to Gemma but not being allowed to touch her. I'd like to leave now, but apparently we have to wait for Gemma's sister to give me the once-over.

I'm building a sandcastle with Felix, even though he lost interest some time ago, when Mel starts waving.

244

'Here comes Mummy!'

Laura is striding towards us: taller and stronger than her sister, like a Hall of Mirrors version of Gemma. Her hair is dead straight, and her posture straighter still. It unsettles me, seeing a stranger who looks just like the woman I love.

Love? No, I don't love Gemma. Do I?

Felix runs towards his mum, and she scoops him up as they both laugh with delight. But now she's staring back at me and her smile drops.

'So *you're* the mystery man,' she says, holding out the hand that isn't supporting her son's chunky body.

The force of her handshake tells me she means business. A chill goes through me.

'I've heard a lot about you too. I'm Dan.'

'Go easy on him, Laura,' Gemma says, laughing.

One moment all I can hear is weekend voices, and the next moment the squealing tone of my tinnitus kicks in. An alarm going off, telling me something is wrong.

Laura's greeting the rest of her family now, and Casey steps shyly forward to meet her. I can't explain why I have this urge to snatch my daughter away.

'Where are you living while you're staying down here?' Laura asks Casey.

'On the Harbourside. It's amazing.'

Laura nods. 'It is. I work really close by, at the police station.'

'Wow, are you an actual cop?'

When Laura nods, it all makes horrible sense.

The buzzing in my head's like being ambushed by a swarm of wasps as my daughter asks how many people she arrests on an average day, and Laura tells her that most of what she does is about keeping people safe, and she's glad, because chasing people is a bit of a nuisance in a heatwave, but luckily most criminals are even slower at running than she is.

I want to run so badly.

Except I've done nothing illegal. *Not this time.* But I feel so guilty, just like I always did when Dad and I saw a police car or a glimpse of a dark-blue uniform. *Never hang around any longer than you need to, when the filth are lurking*, he said. *They'll always find an excuse to feel your collar.*

Laura looks up at me and her eyes are questioning: I flinch, then turn away. She can't have guessed.

Can she?

The longer I spend in this state of panic, the more likely I am to screw up.

As Laura sits down next to her wife and baby daughter, her son still in her arms, I approach Gemma. 'Look, I'm really sorry, but I've messed up. Ages ago one of my friends asked me to a barbie this afternoon and just sent a message asking where I've got to. I ought to put in an appearance before they pack up.'

'Oh. That's a shame.'

'I'd completely forgotten. Sorry. But it's been fantastic to have a chance to meet everyone.'

She grins. 'My sister will say you're doing a runner to avoid interrogation.'

'Ha. She might be right.'

Gemma leans in closer. I hear her breath above the humming in my head. 'But I'll see you tomorrow, right?'

Laura's freaked me out so badly that it takes me a moment to remember my next date with Gemma. 'Of course.'

When I tell Casey it's time to go, I expect her to argue, but she's so tired that she's happy to leave. As we pack up our stuff, I try to avoid being in Laura's eyeline.

Gemma's mum gives me a hug, and her dad reaches into

his pocket and gives Casey a ten-pound note, and she beams, as much at the gesture as the cash.

She kisses Gemma's niece and nephew, and Mel, but holds back from doing the same to Laura. Even kids can tell when something – or someone – feels wrong.

Casey turns back towards Gemma. 'Best day ever,' she says, her voice sleepy.

'Thanks for letting us come,' I say. Immediately I start walking away so fast that Casey struggles to keep up.

'Oi! Hang on.'

It's Laura calling after us. Has she seen through me?

As I turn, I promise myself that *if* I get a reprieve now, I will tell Gemma everything when I see her again tomorrow. It's what she deserves.

But it's not Laura shouting after me. It's her mum. 'Don't forget you've promised me a vintage Motörhead T-shirt the next time we see you.'

They all laugh, except for Laura, who stares at me as though she is trying to piece together the case for the prosecution.

Casey stumbles and I catch her before she falls, lifting her into my arms. She's heavier than I expected, but the effort of it means I have something to focus on other than Laura.

But my tinnitus continues for the whole drive home.

Chapter 31: Gemma

Everyone else blurs as they move away. Casey falters, tired out, and she's about to stumble and—

Before I can call out, Dan's instinct to protect his daughter kicks in and he scoops her up, as he did when he stopped me from falling. Casey's body relaxes in his arms, as though she's a much younger child.

How often has she felt properly protected? Her life revolves around keeping her mum safe and happy, when it should be the other way round. She deserves to be held.

We all do.

Dan more than any of us, perhaps. What he told me made sense: he was completely alone by the time he was Casey's age. No wonder he couldn't process the idea of being a young dad. His behaviour had consequences, but what matters now is that he's making amends.

So how would he feel about having another child in his life?

And how do I feel about having Casey in mine? I have been wanting a baby, *Andrew's* baby, not a girl her age. I know nothing about looking after teenagers.

But I *do* know about people – Casey is amazing, and I know we'd have the *best* times together if—

'Well, *you* never do things by halves.'

I turn to see my big sister in full earth-mother mode, with

248

Charlotte cocooned against her chest, the baby's eyelids flickering as she dreams.

'What's *that* supposed to mean?'

She tuts. 'Dan. Some serious rebound action going on there.'

I try not to let her see how crushed she's made me feel. 'You don't like him?'

'Oh, he's very cute. I can see why you picked him.'

That's better. 'Can you see why *he* picked me?'

Charlotte mumbles in her sleep and my sister sways from side to side, matching her baby's sounds until the threat of waking is past. Where did she learn that? Will I ever learn to do it too?

'How much does he know about you?' Laura asks. 'About your circumstances?'

'Not this again. Mum's already given him the third degree. He has money of his own – a flat that's worth twice as much as ours.' I correct myself. 'Mine.'

'And did he know I'm police before I arrived?'

'I hadn't mentioned it.'

'Because did you notice how soon he cleared off when I mentioned it to his daughter?'

'He had a clash,' I tell her. 'A commitment he'd forgotten.'

'If you say so. He didn't want to hang about. Seemed shifty to me.'

I don't say the obvious: that my sister makes *everyone* feel like a criminal. 'I like him, Laura.'

'I can tell. But what do you know about him? His background, his prospects.'

I sigh. 'Sorry, the credit check and criminal records aren't in yet – my private detective has been on holiday.'

'Don't be touchy, Gem. I'm just trying to look out for you; you have so much going on, without starting a hot and heavy new relationship with a total stranger.'

249

'I've not had much luck in the happy-ever-after department, so can't it be my turn? Can't this be the universe offering me a gift, to make up for all it's taken away?'

'I got your share of good fortune, I guess. Sorry, Gems.'

We laugh, but the unfairness lingers. Laura has sailed through everything: revealing her sexuality, building her career in the police, succeeding straight away with the IVF that's helped her and Mel make their family.

'How are you feeling about the transfer? Mum told me they'd had to use the final embryo.'

'Yeah. The last chance saloon.'

'I'm rooting for you, Gems. You deserve it.'

'Since when did deserving something make it more likely to happen?'

Charlotte's eyes pop open, full of panic until she recognizes her mother and her little fingers reach up to touch her face. 'Are you going to tell Dan?' Laura asks.

'I want to. It doesn't seem fair to keep this bloody great secret from him.'

'When?'

'Tomorrow, possibly. We're seeing each other at his place. His *very, very expensive place*.'

'You could wait,' Laura says. 'Honesty is the best policy, et cetera, but you'll know for sure in a week if it's even relevant. We hope everything's going to work out, but if things don't, perhaps having someone to take your mind off it wouldn't be the worst thing. Something tells me he's much more fling material, anyway.'

I turn away, not wanting to think about the FET not working out. Or Dan being just a fling.

Behind Laura, our parents are tidying up the picnic rubbish. I check my watch: almost six o'clock already. By the time I get back it'll be time for my jab.

'We're heading off,' Dad says. 'Your mother can't miss *Pointless*. I don't know why I even bother trying to compete with Richard Osman.'

'It is a lost cause,' I agree. Although Mum wouldn't survive ten seconds without my dad. He is the glue that holds our family together.

'This new friend of yours . . .' he says, when we're close enough that no one else can hear.

'Don't, Dad. Laura has already warned me off.'

'What makes you think I'd be warning you off?'

I try to read his face. 'You're not?'

He winks. 'I think I could like him.'

'Wow, I didn't think you would. He's very different from Andrew.'

'Well, that's not the worst thing in the world. Losing him has changed you.'

'Aged me, more like.'

'Wait till you're past sixty before you talk about old age. We loved Andrew, but we'll also love anyone who makes you happy again.'

I exhale. 'The timing sucks, though, right?'

Dad doesn't break eye contact with me. 'Listen, Little Gem. How often do I impart words of fatherly wisdom?'

'Rarely. So don't start now.'

'There's no such thing as bad timing. We've seen you grieving for the last eighteen months. It was like . . . a frost in a lovely garden. In the middle of winter you can't believe that the earth will ever be warm, or that flowers will bloom again. But as soon as the sun starts to shine, life comes back. Grass, buds, flowers. All at once.'

'Huh?'

'You understand what I'm saying.'

'Something about gardening?'

251

Dad laughs. 'That's right. Something about gardening.'

'Steve, can we go? Alexander and Richard are waiting for me,' Mum says, with a wink.

'So the party's over already?' my sister says, pulling a face. Mel folds the picnic blanket, loads a squirming Felix into his buggy.

Bear drags his back paws as we begin the procession back towards the car park, making grooves in the sand. What did Casey say? *Best day ever.*

I don't think it was quite that. But it was better than any day I can remember since grief came into my life. Dad could be right. Winter is finally over.

As soon as I get home, my phone buzzes to remind me it's time.

I change out of my dress, then wash my hands and sit at the bar stool in the kitchen while I draw up the syringe. OK. Deep breath. I raise my T-shirt to expose my tummy and inject myself.

The jolt of pain always shocks me, but it's over quickly. I stare at my belly, which is polka-dotted from the progesterone I've already administered. I touch the skin. Is this working?

I want this so much. But it's not all I want, not any more.

Today was dreamy and soft-focus, yet as I think of Dan, lust hits so hard that I'm glad I'm sitting down or it'd knock me off my feet. How the hell can I be sweetly broody one second, recklessly horny the next? I apologize to Andrew in my head. *Not me – it's my hormones.*

No. It's more than hormones. When I'm with Dan I'm a woman, not a widow or a future mother. I'm about desire and connection and making new memories, not reliving old ones.

Laura is right. I should wait before I tell Dan about *this*, because it might not end up being a part of our story.

Bear looks up from where he's curled in his basket and raises his paw wearily.

'Oh, no prizes for guessing what *you* want.'

I take his liver-flavoured toothpaste off the shelf, squeeze some onto the long pink doggy toothbrush, and try to attack his back molars before he has a chance to lick all the paste away. I'm tired, but not yet sleepy.

When I close my eyes, I see Dan.

Is this OK, Andrew? For so long I've believed that my husband would forever be the man I saw when I shut my eyes. But maybe what I need is someone who can also be there when I open them.

The Amazing Book of Us still calls out to me, because I want to remember how it felt to be loved by Andrew. As I pick it up, a pang of nostalgia hits me. Of course I always knew in my head that he could never come back. But now I know it in my heart, too.

THE SECRETS OF A HAPPY LIFE, ACCORDING TO DADDY

Our story is in the past, but yours is just starting. Before I go, here's what I know:

Bed is one of the best places in the world, so enjoy every minute you spend there.
Energetic people are fun to be around. Be a busy bee & make your own energy.
Lemons taste sour but make amazing lemonade. Use whatever comes your way.
Older people can teach you so much — listen to their stories whenever you can.
Never say you're bored. That's what jigsaws, crosswords & sketchbooks are for.
Edinburgh, Bristol, Wookey Hole: find the places you love and visit them often.
Look after yourself — eat your veggies, brush your teeth, sleep when you're tired.
Yes is the most important word in the English language. Say it more.

Chapter 32: Dan

Sunday 22 July

'Dad?' Casey shouts through the bedroom door. 'Wake up, it's mega-sunny today, we need to be out doing Bristol things!'

As alarm calls go, being called 'Dad' takes some beating.

But now I'm remembering yesterday's encounter with Gemma's sister and the fear comes back. I grab my phone. Nothing from Gemma telling me I'm scum. That has to be good news, because she'd be in touch if Laura had suspected anything.

I know I have to find a way to tell the truth.

The door opens now: Casey's dressed and ready. 'Dad, get up. Can we go to BayCaff, please?'

We're the first customers. The barista greets her by name, and she grins. She's grinning at *everything* this morning. We settle in our favourite spot on the deck, and the chef brings us our brunches: Mexican eggs, the skillets sizzling and the peppers smoking.

'You look happy,' I say once he's gone.

'I am *so* happy my face hurts. I must have been smiling in my sleep.'

'What about?'

'Yesterday,' she says, blowing on the forkful of hot cheese

and egg, before putting it into her mouth and sighing with pleasure.

'Anything in particular?'

'The baby, and the diner, and Gemma's dad's awful jokes. And throwing the ball. Oh,' Casey gives me a slightly secretive glance, 'and the tarot too.'

I wasn't sure about letting her see Mystic Debs. 'You know it's trickery?'

'That's what everyone said. But, Dad, she *saw* so much about me.'

'About the future?'

'No. She was very strict about that, said she can't tell the future. Which I said was good, because I don't even know if I have one.' She stops, sees my shocked face, laughs. 'Joke! No, Debs said tarot is about making sense of the present, and where your head's at.'

Perhaps I should go and see Debs myself. 'OK. So what happened?'

'I got to choose a tarot deck – one with animals on it – and I had to think of a question to ask the cards as I shuffled them.'

'What question did you ask?'

She blushes. 'That's private. But I had loads. Debs got me to pick three cards. The first one was the Queen of Wands, this cat in a red-and-orange dress. Her face was like Gemma's – if Gemma was a cat. The second one had two hugging otters, and that was called The Lovers.'

'Please tell me you don't think that's you and Harrison?'

'Da-ad. He's a friend. The third one was creepy. It showed a rabbit in a bow tie hanging upside down and the caption read: The Hanged Man.'

'That's not on. A grown woman should know better than to show that kind of image to a child.'

Casey shakes her head. 'Well, a: I'm not a child; and b: Debs says that card's not about hanging or dying – it's about surviving something. Like my treatment? So what you do is put the cards together so they make a story, and mine is about inner strength and about Team Casey. The people who're getting me through.'

I'm pleased she wasn't freaked out, but this stuff sounds about as mystical as one of my father's cons.

'Then when I came out of the little booth, the first person I saw was Gemma. In her red-and-orange dress. And then a bit later I . . . I saw you two together, and I got all the feels and I thought: *you* could be the lovers.' She blushes. 'I mean, boyfriend and girlfriend. Maybe?'

Oh, Casey. I want that too.

But I can't raise her hopes, or explain why it might not happen. 'Let's see if I've understood this. The cat is Gemma, the otters *might* be Gemma and me. So who is the upside-down rabbit?'

'Me. Because they're always doing weird stuff to me, to get rid of Bob. But if I can just keep going till the end of the week, hopefully everything – and everyone – will be OK. Because I'll have earned a happy ending.'

I smile. She has earned it. But we don't always get what we deserve.

After brunch I have some paperwork to catch up on and Casey says it's cool, as she gets how important my work is, after meeting Finn. She settles down to watch make-up tutorials on YouTube.

I don't do much paperwork, though, because I'm trying to work out how to tell Gemma my secrets, without making her hate me. I've told her some of it already, and she's been very fair and understanding, especially about the mistakes I made with Casey and Angelica. I *know* Gemma likes me, but is it enough to make up for the worst things I've done?

I take some Post-its and try to rearrange my confessions in the least shocking order:

Mum

Dad

Vaughn

Jail

Penthouse

When I close my eyes, I try to picture Gemma's face as I reveal each one. After so long lost in my own lies, the idea of somebody seeing me completely – and loving me for it – seems outrageous, but also . . . wonderful. Hope is such an unfamiliar experience. But it's also good. Too good to be true?

When the intercom goes, it takes me a moment to realize what the sound is.

When I do, I know it has to be Gemma. Bloody hell. I'm not ready.

Except I'll never be 100 per cent ready. The most important thing is to tell her the truth. Unless her sister has already found out and that's why Gemma is here . . .

I come down the steps from the mezzanine, smoothing my hair with my fingers, checking my breath by puffing into my closed hands.

'You look good, Dad,' Casey says. 'And she likes you so much it doesn't matter, anyway.'

'That obvious?'

'*Totally.*'

I can't help grinning when I pick up the videophone and the screen comes to life.

And then I stop.

Shit.

It's not Gemma furiously eyeballing the intercom camera.

It's Angelica.

Chapter 33: Dan

'Angelica? How did you get here?'

'Magic carpet.' She tuts. 'I drove, obviously. Let me in before I melt, it's so hot down here.'

Casey is standing next to me and, as my finger hovers over the entry button, she points at her hair.

Shit.

We haven't worked out the best way to tell Angelica about Casey's pink streaks. I'd been hoping that by Friday she'd be too preoccupied with the scan – and, hopefully, good news – to worry about her daughter's hair colour. Or even that the dye might have started to fade.

'Seriously, Dan, let me in or I'll buzz all the flats in the building until someone else does.'

I press the button and pull an apologetic face at Casey. 'You could put your wig back on,' I suggest, once the camera shows Angelica is safely inside the lobby.

'She'll panic and think my hair's fallen out again.'

'Can you wash it out now?'

'I've already tried a few times and it looks exactly the same.'

'OK . . . How about we tell her you had booked in for some kind of deep-conditioning treatment and it went wrong?'

'That'd make her even more paranoid about chemicals and I'll never be allowed near a hairdresser again. Plus, I don't want to lie to my mum.'

'Then blame me. Say I encouraged you. It won't change how she feels about me.' Being the fall guy seems like the least-worst option.

'I want you to get on with each other, for *my* sake. So you're like *grown-ups* are meant to be. Grown up?' The hint of sarcasm in Casey's voice reassures me she will be OK, however bad a telling-off she gets from her mum.

Which is just as well, because the lift has arrived on our floor.

'Mummy!' Casey flies into her arms the second the doors slide apart. They hold each other so tightly and I get this brief, guilty flashback to kissing Gemma in that same space only three days ago.

'My lovely, lovely girl . . .' Angelica's eyes are shut as she rests her head on her daughter's shoulder. Taking time out has done her good. She's more like the young woman I met at Glastonbury thirteen years ago.

Her eyes snap open.

She clocks the pink colour and rears back so forcefully that I wonder if she's given herself whiplash.

'What the hell have you done to your hair?'

Casey cowers and I turn to Angelica, ready to tell her to calm down. But I can see the fear in her eyes now, and my own stupidity hits me. What was I thinking when I let Casey get her hair dyed? It's a slap in the face for Angelica, after she's tried so hard to keep our daughter safe.

Why was I too stubborn to see that before now?

'The colour is ninety-nine per cent organic,' Casey whispers. 'And I totally love it.'

'I don't care if it's made from unicorn horn and cockerpoo-puppy breath, I told you not to get your hair coloured and you disobeyed me.' Angelica's voice rises as she's winding herself up more and more. Her eyes lock onto me. 'As for you. How could you let her do this? You've been a parent

261

for all of three weeks and you think you know better than *I* do. You think it's OK to go behind my back, defy my wishes?'

'No, I don't. Look, Angelica, I should have—'

But Casey interrupts me. 'Mum! Stop being so mean all the time. Dad is trying his best.'

Angelica's eyes narrow, and I can see how much it must hurt her to hear Casey call me that. 'Dad? He's decided that *this* month he's going to pretend to be a daddy, because he's bored. But it won't last. He's incapable of committing to anything – he's proved that more than once.'

'At least he doesn't try and stop me from living *my* life. Why can't you stop being such a bitch?'

'That's not fair, Casey,' Angelica says, and the pain in her voice makes me wince. I can see on her face that she regrets her harsh words too – not because she thinks they're untrue, but because she cares too much about Casey to hurt her.

'Nothing's fair. It's not fair I'm sick. It's not fair that we don't have a proper family, like normal people. Yesterday I got to hang out with grandparents and babies and aunts. It was amazing. So it's not fair that I'm twelve and I've never even had that before.'

'Yesterday?' Angelica's eyes flick over at me. 'You always claimed not to have family. Unless that was another one of your lies.'

Before I can come up with an explanation that won't inflame things more, Casey stamps her foot, more like a toddler than a tweenager. 'Not *his* family – Gemma's.'

'Who the hell is Gemma?' Angelica speaks each word slowly, as though she's trying out an unfamiliar language.

'She owns Bear,' Casey says.

Angelica shakes her head, still not remembering. 'Who is Bear? Why are you both talking in riddles?'

'The dog? From the hospital? You went nuts when you

262

saw poor Bear in the corridor. Like you go nuts at everything that hasn't been dipped in bleach first.'

'Casey . . .' I say, a gentle warning in my voice. 'Your mum only wants what's best for you.'

They both glare at me now, their mouths set in identical uncompromising lines.

'You're friends with this dog-therapy woman?' Angelica asks me.

Whatever I say now is going to cause more trouble.

'I met her at the hospital.'

It seems impossible that I only met Gemma a few weeks ago. And that if I hadn't been lost on my way to the hospital, I might never have met her at all . . . The thought that I could have missed her makes my ears ring, as though I'm only feet away from a fire alarm.

Angelica laughs bitterly, a dry, snorting sound. 'Oh, I've heard it all now. You told me you were going to devote this month to Casey – but you've been using your daughter to chat up women? Is that why you left me at the chalet and brought Casey back alone?'

'No! That's not what happened.'

The look she gives me is so venomous I have to look away. But in her eyes I deserve it. Maybe she's right.

'Casey, I need to speak to your father alone.'

'Shout at him, you mean?'

Angelica shakes her head. 'If you had *any* idea what he's put us through, you wouldn't be sticking up for him.' Again I hear the exhaustion in her voice.

'I bet he couldn't stand being with you. Because you're horrible to everyone, the entire time. I wish you weren't here. I wish you weren't my mum!'

I see the shock on Casey's own face as the words leave her mouth. But it's too late. The damage is done.

No one speaks. Eventually I try. 'Casey, you need to apologize to your mum.'

'I won't . . . I can't . . . *Nothing* is fair. Nothing!' Casey turns round and stomps off to her room. I brace myself for the door slamming, but somehow it's worse when she closes it with extreme care.

Angelica's face is hard and expressionless. 'Should I go and talk to her, see if I can calm her down?' I suggest, though I don't know where I'd begin.

Now Angelica's mouth twists into a grimace. 'How will you do that? By taking her side against me again? Or maybe you can buy your way out of trouble.'

I shake my head. 'Look, I know I've got a lot of things wrong, but this isn't helping the situation. Did you really drive all the way back down here just to have a go at *me*?'

She scoffs. 'You are irrelevant. I drove here to see my girl, because I missed her. And I thought she might be missing—' She stops herself. I think Casey's cruel words are still bruising her.

'She *has* been missing you.'

Angelica's eyes mist over. If she can only let her guard down, maybe I can apologize and we can begin sharing the burden of worrying about Casey.

But when she blinks, I see the shutters closing again. 'I'm surprised that Gemma woman is your type.' She pulls a face.

'Why?'

'Always thought you aimed higher.'

I don't even know where to begin responding to that. But Angelica hasn't finished. 'I bet she's loving *you*, though. Has she come over to your *penthouse*?'

I could lie, it's not like Angelica is asking because she cares – she's only looking for more reasons to hate me. But there have been so many bloody lies. 'Once. Briefly. It's very early days.'

'And Casey was here at the same time?'

I shrug. 'Yes. Casey likes her a lot. And her dog.'

Angelica's lip curls up in disgust. 'Careful, Daniel. Women Gemma's age are only after one thing.'

'Angelica, please.'

'I'm trying to do you a favour. She must think she's hit the jackpot: a man with a fancy flat and a cute daughter to prove he won't shy away from commitment. I bet she thinks you're *daddy material*. Just wait till she finds out the truth.'

The bitterness seems to eat Angelica up, but I can't blame her for how she's feeling. 'Gemma's not like that. And you're right: I haven't gone for women like her in the past. But she's generous and kind, and perhaps she's come into my life at the right time. To teach me how to open up with Casey?'

Angelica is shaking, her face twisting with hurt and rage.

I don't blame her. I blame myself. Why couldn't I have learned these lessons before I damaged her and my daughter.

'How heart-warming,' Angelica says. 'But what about the effect on your daughter? Playing Happy Families with Gemma might make you feel great, but it's rubbing Casey's nose in it – offering this woman what you have refused to give us for the last twelve years. Besides, we both know you're not in this for keeps.'

'What if I *do* want to be?'

She stares at me. 'You're talking to *me* now, Dan. Don't bother pretending.'

'I'm not. This has changed me. Casey has.' *Gemma has.*

'Oh my God, you're for real.' Something in her tone chills me.

'I get why you're suspicious, you've every right to be. And it must be hard for you to see that Casey does want me around, after you've done all the work, but what if you did let me do my share? It might make your life easier.' My nerves mean this comes out in a rush.

Angelica pours herself a glass of water. She walks back towards me and I wonder for a moment if she's going to chuck it in my face.

'How *much* do you want to be in Casey's life?'

'What kind of question is that?'

'I'm trying to get it quantified. What you'd give up.'

'What do you want me to say? Money, a finger, a limb?'

As I speak, it hits me: I'd give up my own life for Casey. The knowledge is so deep, so certain, that despite the darkness of the thought, it also feels like a kind of happiness.

'You need to choose,' she says, and for a second I think, *She's lost it completely and actually does want a pound of my flesh.*

But then I understand.

'You want me to choose between Casey and Gemma?'

She nods. 'If you're really committed to Casey, you should be focusing all your attention on her, not on some ridiculous infatuation with a woman you just met. Besides, what a child needs is *stability*. Are you telling me that in the span of a few weeks you've gone from being a commitment-phobe to a guy who wants parenthood *and* cosy coupledom? Do you even believe that yourself?'

'Who says I can't do both? Just because you're on your own, you think I should be too?'

Angelica shakes her head now. 'No. It's not about me or you. Our priority has to be our sick daughter. You've had twelve years to play the field while I've stayed single to make sure Casey doesn't get close to men who could disappear. Like you did. So if you can't put Casey first now, you don't deserve her.'

Is she right? I know sod all about how this works. What if it is impossible to love both of them enough? Perhaps it is ridiculous to think I love Gemma when I've only met her half a dozen times. Except, right now, it's one of the only things I can trust. I *do* love her. And I think it's possible she *might* love me back.

But the other thing I know is that if I chose her over my daughter, it would prove I am not worthy of either of them.

'So what's it to be, Dan? Personally, Gemma seems the better choice to me, for quick thrills anyway. Better for Casey too.'

'This isn't a game to me, Angelica. I want to change. I *am* changing already.'

She finishes her water slowly. 'Well, it's your choice. But I bet you haven't told Gemma the details of how you screwed me over. And I know for sure that Casey doesn't have the full story.'

'You'd tell them, to stop me being happy? To stop me being there for both of them?'

Angelica shrugs. 'These things have a funny way of coming out when you least expect it.'

If only I'd told Gemma sooner, this wouldn't matter. I could laugh off Angelica's threats. But I've been a coward. And although I do now want to tell Gemma the truth, I can't bear the idea of my daughter knowing everything too.

'Even if it'd hurt Casey more than anyone?'

She snorts. 'It's about her happiness in the long term. I'm a she-cat where my daughter's concerned. I've had to be. At least you have a choice, which is more than I did.'

Except it isn't even a choice, is it? There are hundreds, even thousands, of men who could make Gemma happy – probably happier than I would. But Casey only has one dad. I'm flawed, but I'm it.

Angelica's eyes bore into mine and her usually expression-less face lights up with triumph. She's got me. The only way to prove to her that I deserve to be in our daughter's life, to stop her taking Casey away from me, is to sacrifice the possibility of a future with Gemma.

Chapter 34: Gemma

Monday 23 July

The heat wakes me at 4 a.m.

Not only the heat. It's also knowing that in ten hours I'll be seeing Dan again. Yesterday dragged so much without him.

I try to work on the bank commission, but the heel of my hand sticks to the paper. On the horizon, balloons puff up like ripening berries. It's going to be the hottest day yet. What am I going to wear?

I return to my suitcase of old clothes. Each garment triggers memories of carefree summers gone by, but the one I pick is a green batik skirt I wore all the time at art school. It still fits me perfectly: I've had the same curves since my teens. I add a white linen-mix top with a stretchy neckline that I could tease off my shoulders later, to look sexier . . . I haven't thought about trying to look sexy in *so* long.

In the bedroom mirror, the top billows out. I flatten it with my hand, but when I catch sight of my face in the mirror, there's *something* about the reflection that makes me wonder . . .

No. The transfer was only six days ago. Of course I wouldn't be showing yet. But my eyes have a strange glow, and the linen fabric feels almost abrasive against my skin. I can't remember a sensation quite like this before.

Snap out of it!

'What am I like, Bear?' I say. His ears jerk up and he gets off the bed and comes trotting in my direction. He stops abruptly, his nose twitching, and his doggy brows get closer together, as though he's trying to make sense of something. When I crouch down, he approaches me tentatively, as he would a stranger.

Do I smell different? Could Bear even be sensing changes that are too early to show up in a test? When I researched therapy dogs, there were stories about animals trained to detect seizures long before there were obvious signs, so could hormones show up too?

'This is no good, is it, mate?' I say. 'I'll know on Saturday. Until then I've simply got to wait.'

When I get to hospital school, Casey gives me a listless *hello* instead of her usual hug, and even Bear's yelps of delight don't make her smile. She keeps her distance as the other children fuss over the dog.

I walk over to the desk where she's pretending to read a book.

'Are you not well, sweetheart?'

'Just tired,' she says, but won't meet my eye.

My skin prickles with anxiety. But her mood probably has nothing to do with her tumour. She's almost a teenager, so maybe she's been taken hostage by her hormones too. They have a lot to answer for.

As the clock ticks towards the end of my session, I keep checking through the pane of glass in the school door, hoping to catch the first glimpse of Dan.

'What foods does Bear like?' the brown-eyed boy asks.

'He loves sausages and hamburgers and Cheddar cheese. But *these* are his favourite.' I reach into my pocket and pull out a new packet of sushi treats that are his Kryptonite. 'Would you like to give him one?'

As I tease open the foil, the fishy smell of the treats wafts out. *Ugh!* But Bear has already adopted his best sit-up-and-beg pose and all the kids are laughing now.

'Hold out your hand. He won't bite, but he will try to grab one. You must make him do a high five with his paw for each treat.'

I tip the pack and the smell gets stronger, as intense as an old-fashioned fishmonger's. My hand's trembling and the more I fight it, the more powerful the wave of nausea becomes, until—

'Jed. Um, Mr Porter, can you keep an eye on Bear . . .'

I drop the packet, wrench open the door and run down the corridor towards the loos, pushing into a cubicle and making it just in time to throw up my lunch.

Afterwards I splash my face with water, trying to calm down. *Don't jump to conclusions.* And yet, how can I *not?*

The blotches on my face won't settle. Will Jed guess something's up? He's already been asking me questions, knows that I spent Saturday with Casey and her dad, and I don't think he approves of my getting involved with a patient.

If only he knew how far it's gone.

OK. Time to go. As I turn the corner onto the corridor, I almost walk into someone rushing the other way.

'Sorry.'

The woman doesn't move out of my path. I look up. *Shit.*

'Oh. Hello.' I smile too broadly. 'You're Casey's mum, aren't you? I'm Gemma. We met before. Um. Here. Remember?'

She seems to be inspecting me, judging me – surely Dan hasn't told her what's going on?

'Casey is such a great kid. You must be very proud.'

Angela scoffs. 'You think you've lucked out, don't you?

The sexy rock-god. The harbour lifestyle. The ready-made family.'

'I'm sorry?'

'If it was only you and him, I wouldn't give a toss. But Casey is my daughter. Not Dan's – not really – and *definitely* not yours.'

'Hang on. You're saying Dan isn't her dad?'

She shrugs in a way that makes me want to shake her, and I've never been violent towards anyone in my life. 'Biologically he is. Technically. But when the novelty of this wears off, I am sure he'll dump her like he dumped me. And you won't last five minutes.'

I open my mouth to stick up for Dan by telling her what happened when he was a kid, but looking into her hard eyes, I realize there's no point. 'OK, well, that's my business, isn't it?'

'Not when you start muscling in on Casey. I heard about your weekend at the beach. It sounds *amazing*. But she's vulnerable, and I can't have her getting hurt by you as well as Dan. So stay away from her, before you do any more damage. Do you understand me?' Her fiery determination to protect her daughter isn't in doubt. But I think it's misguided: Casey wants more than a risk-free, smothered life.

'It wasn't a big thing, just a day out. But you're wrong about Dan – he wants to make up for lost time.'

She scoffs again. '*Bless*. Poor lost boy Dan, who tries his hardest, but everyone's got it in for him. I'll let you into a little secret: it's a giant *con* job. He can't help but manipulate people. It's in his blood.'

Con job? I won't give her the satisfaction of asking what she means. Angelica is bitter for good reason, but the guy she knew and the one I have got to know are different.

Aren't they?

'I understand why you're resentful but . . .'

She holds up her hand: it's trembling slightly. 'I don't need your understanding. But let me make this super-clear. You will stay away from Casey. I was *this* close to complaining about you and your filthy dog when we met before, and I won't hesitate next time. They must have a rule about volunteers meddling in patients' lives. Especially when the patient is a vulnerable child?'

It's not like I haven't worried about that myself. I *thought* I had it under control. But surely she wouldn't carry out her threat? 'You'd stop Bear's visits, even though the children love them, to get back at Dan?'

'No. To protect my girl. You don't have kids, do you?'

I shake my head, which is throbbing with stress.

'Thought not. Because if you did, you'd know how far I'd go to keep Casey safe.'

She's so self-righteous and I won't win this argument. But however much she threatens, she won't ruin what's developing between me and Dan. We might have to keep *us* quiet for a bit, until he can prove to Angelica that he's serious about his relationship with Casey. But things are bound to settle down.

'Fine. Can I get past now? My dog is in the classroom with the kids who look forward to a little respite when they're in the middle of their treatment.'

She rears back, as though Bear has appeared in my arms and wants to give her huge slobbery kisses. I walk ahead though my legs are weak after the confrontation.

'Gemma?'

I don't turn round because whatever she wants to say, it won't be nice.

'For your sake, don't believe a word that comes out of

his mouth. He'll just tell you what you want to hear, never the truth. Dan Lennon only ever thinks of number one.'

It's only when I'm in the classroom that I'm calm enough to realize: if Angelica is picking up Casey, then Dan isn't coming . . .

And when Casey slinks off without saying a proper goodbye, it's a struggle to make small talk with Jed. When I tell him I think I've eaten something that doesn't agree with me, he's advising me to see the GP as it's the second time it's happened, and saying he'll text me his mother's recipe for ginger tea.

Outdoors, Bear pulls me towards the shade to stay cool. I step towards the university gardens and call Dan's number, in case I've got it all wrong and he's waiting for me—

It rings once before diverting to voicemail.

'Hi, um, I think we're meant to be getting together. I'm at the hospital, but your ex was there. Does that mean you're not coming? Call me back, please?'

Bear does his customary roll on the grass, so the crisp blades massage his body. I won't let Angelica's words mess with my head. She's had a rough time, but that doesn't mean I should listen to her.

Except . . . I've only met Dan a handful of times; do I really know him better than she does?

With Andrew, our relationship was the way it should be, when you're a grown-up who has found the person you're going to marry: we were romantic and sweet and careful. We built foundations. *Trust.* As a result we were solid, even when the world threw the worst at us.

But my attraction to Dan is not an adult, rational thing. These last three weeks, emotions took over. I don't trust them, and perhaps I shouldn't trust him.

Although I haven't been honest with him, either. I've kept the most important thing in my life a secret. It's despicable, now I think it through: letting him care about me, when the transfer could be a deal-breaker. It would be, for most men.

I *have* to tell him. No more excuses. That's how we'll know if this – whatever *it* is – can outlast July.

When I check WhatsApp, he's online, so I type a message:

Where are you? Are we still meeting up?

The app tells me he's been typing for so long that he must be writing me a Dear John message. What the hell changed since Saturday?

Finally the reply appears, stupidly short:

Things have got tricky. I don't think it's a good idea tonight.

I type back:

Is it Angelica? She told me I shouldn't be with you or see Casey again.

He doesn't reply.

Dan. Don't ghost me, it's not fair. Please, we need to talk about this. Unless that connection was all in my head after all.

He goes offline and I want to throw the phone across the grass. *I don't need this crap now.* I need to be calm and well balanced and . . . the handset buzzes.

It wasn't in your head. You're right. 7 by the Observatory? I'll come alone.

Chapter 35: Dan

When I get home from work, Angelica has closed all the doors and windows again, so it's oppressively hot. She doesn't speak to me once, and Casey hides in her room, only coming out to raid the fridge in sulky silence.

It's a *massive* relief to leave the penthouse straight away. But that doesn't last, because I know I'm about to meet Gemma for the final time.

I don't do break-ups. One-night stands mean you never raise anyone's hopes, or promise more than you can deliver. So you never hurt anyone.

Until Casey and Gemma walked into my life, I couldn't see why I'd want to get in deeper, risk disappointing someone, or being disappointed myself. Now suddenly I have two people I *want* to commit to. But there's only room for one, and my daughter needs me more.

The Clifton Observatory sits in the middle of the grass, out of place with its lighthouse tower and grey-stone walls and flat roof with cafe tables. I haven't ever been inside, but I bet Gemma has. I can see her family doing Weekend Activities: zoos, play parks, stately homes. We only went to those if Dad thought there might be rich pickings.

I spot Gemma straight away, in a patterned green skirt with Woodstock vibes. I want to take a mental snapshot of her beauty now, before I tell her that this has to end.

She's walking faster. Already in kissing distance.

I back away.

'Oh,' she says. 'It's like that, is it?'

I don't know if I can do it.

'You look amazing,' I say. *What the hell?* 'I mean, different?'

'Do I?'

'The way you were walking.'

'It's because I'm alone. I left Bear at home, so we wouldn't be distracted. But walking without him makes me feel almost . . . naked.'

She blushes. *Naked.*

Fuck, I loathe Angelica so much right now for making me turn my back on this incredible woman. I must do this now before I change my mind.

'Gemma, listen—'

'Dan, look—'

I open my hands. 'You first.' It feels like the least I can do.

She inhales. It's not just Bear's absence that makes her different tonight. Or maybe I'd made myself forget how stunning she is, how *alive*.

'So . . . I don't understand what's going on between you and Angelica, but I saw her at the hospital. She hates you, doesn't she? Said some stuff about you being a liar. About how you can't help yourself.'

'Gemma, she's angry with me. But I can explain why.'

'Not yet. Let me say my bit. I've been planning it all afternoon. OK, you might not have told me everything. But I can't expect that of you until I tell *you* everything about my life. My . . . circumstances.'

What is she talking about? Debt? Addiction? Another man?

277

'I think we should sit down.' She heads for an empty bench overlooking the big white swoop of the suspension bridge. 'OK. There's no real way to prepare you for this, so . . . I might be having a baby.'

'You're *pregnant*?'

She blinks. 'I honestly don't know yet. I can't take a test till the weekend. And I don't want to tempt fate, but it's possible.'

The ringing in my ears starts up so loudly I can't think straight. I try to focus. 'OK. So you're seeing someone else? As well as me?'

It shouldn't be a shock. Gemma is normal and pretty and caring. She belongs with someone else normal and good-looking and caring. But I didn't think she'd be two-timing them. *Or me.*

Bloody hell. Is this what *jealousy* feels like? We never really defined our relationship, but I thought we'd had an understanding.

'I'm not seeing anyone, Dan. But I've been having treatment. Like IVF, except with frozen embryos. I started the latest cycle the week we met.'

Of course I know women go it alone, but Gemma still seems young to be doing that. 'So you're . . .' I nod at her belly, feeling like a total idiot. 'I mean, it might all be kicking off already. Inside?'

Gemma's eyes widen. *Kicking off inside?* What am I: six years old?

Maybe I am. Maybe deep down I am a small boy who killed his mum at birth and has been hurting other people ever since.

'Yes. It may already be happening. Or it may not.'

'Bloody hell.'

'You know what they say about meeting people when

you're not looking? I promise you I wasn't looking. I tried to convince myself this – our connection – was triggered by the hormones I've been taking, but it's not. The way I feel about you is real.'

Real.

She's sitting close enough for me to reach across and touch her. But I don't. Because my head's full of noise.

'Say something, please, Dan?'

'*Well, say something, Dan!*'

The pregnant, bedraggled girl on my doorstep tries to sound brave, but her voice has a crack down the middle, like the rest of her could fall apart at any moment.

'Are you sure it's mine?' It's the shittiest thing to say – Brad Pitt dumping Jennifer Aniston level of shittiness.

'Of course it's yours. That's mean; I've never been with anyone else. Can I come in? I'm bursting for a wee because there wasn't a loo on the train.'

I can't remember her name, but as she squeezes into the hall, I remember the rest: Glastonbury. How she danced so clumsily that she was impossible to miss; how we'd snogged to The Killers, then shagged in my tent. How I wondered if it was her first time, so I'd been cautious, which made everything even more intense: rain pinging against the polyester tent, the smell of weed, other people's voices so close, the dried mud on her skin and mine.

And now I'm remembering the second night, when she took something that freaked her out. I sat with her in the first-aid tent and missed all the acts and lost a night's money. I was more pissed off with myself than with her, because even though I knew she wasn't my responsibility, I couldn't let her deal with that shit alone.

But once I knew she would be OK, I didn't want to know. On the Sunday, I hid from her when she came back to the contractors' area to say goodbye. Never expected to see her again.

But here she is. No hiding from her, or from the round belly straining the buttons on her Santa-red winter coat.

I make tea while she uses the bathroom, hoping my filthy flatmates flushed the toilet, it's hit-or-miss here. What the hell is her name? Anneka? Andrea?

She reappears, her body still skinny, like she's got a bowling ball up her jumper.

'How did you find me?' I ask, handing over the least cracked tea mug I could find.

'Internet,' she says. What else did she find? 'So, before you say anything, I'm keeping it. Her.'

Her. Ten minutes ago all I had to worry about was the court case, and now I'm gonna be a dad. Have a daughter.

'How long have you known?'

'Since I went back to sixth form. When I put my school skirt on again and the button wouldn't do up, that was when I stopped pretending.'

School skirt. Fuck. At the festival there'd been no obvious difference between us, but now the four-year gap is a lifetime. She's too young. And me? I'll never be old enough for this.

'What do your parents say?'

She sighs. 'They're not over the moon. They keep saying I'm immature, mentally and physically. They think they know what's best for me, but they don't, they really don't.'

I think of my mum. She was only a few years older than this girl when she died having me. When I got stuck and they had to operate, and I made it and she didn't, and I took the life of the person who gave me mine.

Fucking hell.

The girl peers into her mug as though something could dive out of the brown liquid and bite her.

Angelica. It comes to me in a flash. Her name is Angelica.

'Angelica, why did you come and find me?'

She looks up, the wary expression intensifying. 'You're the father. It's not like I expect you to marry me or something Victorian like that, but . . .'

'This can't happen.'

She points at her belly and makes a face. 'Er. It is happening.'

'You don't get it. I'm probably going to prison.'

'What?' Her eyes open wide. In her world, I guess, no one goes to prison.

'I haven't killed anyone. Or hurt anyone.'

'What did you do?'

I did what I was raised to do: took money from the rich and the dumb, to give it to the disadvantaged – me, that is. Yeah, my dad used that line too. 'It's to do with money. When I'm not working the festivals, I can't pay my rent.'

'Did you steal?'

'Only technically. We did some work on houses. Overcharged here and there.' It's a version of the truth.

She takes in the squalor around us. At least she can see I haven't spent the proceeds of crime living the high life. 'So will you really be sent to prison?'

I shrug. 'I'm going to plead not guilty.'

'Are you not guilty, though?' she asks, like it's ever that simple.

'Listen, Angelica, what do you want from me? There's no happy ending here, you can see that, right?'

She stands up hurriedly and the tea splashes all over the floor. 'I don't want anything from you, wanker!' She's trying to get out, but the hallway's too narrow for two people, one of them pregnant, and as she struggles, I can see she's crying.

'Don't rush off while you're upset.'

'I just . . .' Her breathing's gone weird.

Mine too. What if I've triggered something disastrous with the baby? With my daughter. If I am going to be responsible for another death. Even two.

'Please calm down, Angelica.'

'I don't want to be on my own.'

Of all the things she could say . . . I put my arms out and around her body, familiar from that weekend but different too. My dad would comfort her, make promises, then immediately relocate somewhere he couldn't be found.

But as her tears soak my sweatshirt, I think, This could be my chance to make everything right. To change my future.

'You won't be alone.' *And she cries louder, and I tighten my hold on her, but not so tight it'd hurt the baby.* 'It's OK, Angelica, I'll be here.'

'Dan?' Gemma's voice comes as a shock.

'Sorry, I was thinking. I wasn't expecting you to say what you did about your . . . future plans.'

She takes a deep breath. 'There's one more thing,' she says, and I think, *What else could there be?* 'The IVF. The embryo? It's my husband's. My *late* husband's.'

I stare at her.

'When my husband got his diagnosis, we were advised to have his sperm frozen before his treatment started.' She speaks slowly, like a maths teacher trying to explain a complicated equation. 'When he went into remission, I had a cycle of IVF to create embryos to use when he was a hundred per cent better. We made four. But then, he didn't get better.'

I nod. 'I'm sorry.'

'But the embryos were still there, frozen. Andrew wanted me to have the choice of using them. So we saw a counsellor. And . . . after Andrew died, I waited to make sure it wasn't grief that made me want to do this. But those embryos were made out of love and so they deserved their chance. The one they put in this time,' she touches her tummy, 'it's the last one.'

I wait for the words to make sense to me, try to block out the buzzing and humming noises. I can't work out what I should think or feel.

Until suddenly I do. Now I'm not thinking as an adult, but as Darryl, the kid who never knew his mum. I always tell people you don't miss what you never had, but that's bullshit. I missed her every single sports day, Christmas, birthday. Especially every birthday, because Dad could never forget it was the day he lost her, too.

Wouldn't it be even worse to know your parent was dead years before you were even born?

Unless Gemma could be enough on her own. She has so much to give.

'Say something then.' Gemma looks at me and her eyes reflect the red evening sky.

'I don't want to say the wrong thing.'

'You disapprove?'

'No. Not that. I just – it's a lot.'

'I understand it wasn't what you thought you were getting. With me, I mean. I almost didn't tell you. By the weekend it might not even be an issue, if it doesn't work. But still, it's a big thing for me. I wanted to be honest.'

Honest. How would I feel now if I could be honest with her too? I've imagined my own big confession, followed by . . . what do priests call it? Absolution.

Huh. That's a fantasy. How much must she have loved this guy to want to do this alone? I've never dared to love anyone that much.

'Say something, please, Dan?' She twists the patterned fabric of her skirt into tiny knots.

'Sorry. I need a minute to get my head around it.' But my tinnitus drowns out everything. The noise is too big.

Gemma stands up. 'OK. Well, at least now you know.'

I want to hold her and tell her everything will be all right, as I did thirteen years ago to stop Angelica crying.

But if my betrayal taught me anything, it's that lying to make people feel better in the moment is the worst thing you can do. Whatever my bloody father said.

Chapter 36: Gemma

I wake up feeling completely drained.

I've wasted too much time on this stupid obsession with a man I barely know. How crazy was it to think Dan might embrace the idea of another man's baby? Not as crazy as convincing myself I was in love with him.

Dragging myself out of bed takes all my energy and, when I get to the loo, I want to go straight back to bed. Ideally until Saturday.

Then I look down and everything falls apart.

The dots of blood on the toilet roll are like tiny bullet holes.

I freeze.

No. Not this time. Because if it's over this time, there won't be a next time.

Every step I take back to the bedroom feels perilous. Bear snuggles into me, and I decide to stay horizontal for as long as I can. Even though I know, *logically*, it will make no difference.

I can't hold back the Bad Thoughts. Whatever the spotting means – that I am not pregnant, or that I was but am no longer – I realize that if I'd only kept my secret for a few more days I might have hung on to Dan.

And now, a worse thought: what if my confusion caused this, by sending a message to the embryo that I didn't want it to implant after all?

I could call the clinic about the bleed. Except they'll say, *You must wait; everyone is different, it doesn't mean anything. Unless there's something specific you're worried about?*

What would I say? *Funny you should mention it, but I'm worried my mental infidelity to my late husband has interfered with implantation.*

Oh shit, I'm so scared.

There's something in *The Amazing Book of Us* about fear, but I'm too scared even to go into the living room to fetch it. So I try to remember the gist of Andrew's message: that you have to embrace fear, because it's often a sign of good change. That fear and risk are worth it for the benefits they can bring.

But if he was here right now, I'd be arguing the opposite. That there is a limit to how much fear and pain we can take. That sometimes staying safe and hiding from the world is the only option.

When Bear begins to squirm, I know I need to take him out. Tentatively I get up again and, when I go to the loo, there's no more spotting. But I can't be sure if that means everything's OK.

'Let's brave the outside world, Bear.'

We go onto the patch of green outside the flat, and he has the longest wee I've ever seen, then does a Downward Dog stretch on the soft, warm grass. But he stays close to me, not pulling or showing any interest in the sun-drunk squirrels that run across his path.

A couple with a buggy walk past, the baby hidden by a cotton zebra-striped comforter. The stab of envy takes me by surprise.

I make myself keep going, one slow step after another. I have only four days left to wait. Four days till I get a glimpse of what my future holds. As I picture those binary possibilities – P/not P – I can't predict how I will feel.

Every gain comes with a loss. Every choice means choosing not to do the other thing.

I watch my dog as he sniffs delightedly, unable to resist following a new trail, totally lost in the moment. No worries for him about the road not taken. If there's one thing I could learn from Bear, it's that.

But not yet. Right now, the hollowness looms too large. I miss Dan. I miss Andrew. And I miss the illusion that my life – my destiny – is under my own control.

When I return to the sofa, I pick up *The Amazing Book of Us* and go to the page about fear, and this time I try to memorize it, holding every word inside because it is the closest I can get to being back, safe, in the arms of my husband.

YOU ARE ALWAYS BRAVER THAN YOU THINK YOU ARE

Occasionally, on horrible days, I wondered if I could take any more. I used to feel so sorry for myself and wonder why bad things happened to me.

During my illness, Mummy was always there and she gave me courage every single time. We're stronger when we share how we feel and when someone's got our back. But emotions can be confusing. Sometimes excitement or change feels like fear, because we're facing a challenge or a revolution that turns everything we believed upside down. So be very curious about what your body is telling you. When you're feeling emotional, look for someone you trust, who can help you make sense of what life throws at you: good and bad. Being lonely is the scariest experience of all, so always keep an eye out for amazing new friends who can help you visualize what things will look like after the storm is over. *DADDY SAYS:* Even the bravest people have low points – the highs will make up for it! Whatever you're feeling, tell someone who loves you. A hug makes everything better.

Chapter 37: Casey

Wednesday 25 July

I feel like the tarot rabbit: my world has turned upside down and nothing looks the same from this angle.

Mystic Debs said the cards are tools, not destiny, but already my best day ever seems like five months ago, not five days.

Everything's gone wrong since then: Gemma has stopped replying to my messages, probably because I was so grumpy on Monday. Dad looks miserable and Mum keeps snapping at him, and I'm scared he'll decide he doesn't want me in his life. Why couldn't Mum have stayed away?

But *I'm* the one who is really to blame for everything. Was it Bob that made me lash out, or have the proton beams hit the wrong part of my brain, frying the good bits I've got left?

The only person who knows how crappy I feel is Harrison, and even he's getting slower at replying to my messages. I've tried to mix it up, sending at least four funny memes or videos for every moan. I scroll through our messages, trying to work out when he went off me:

Saturday – Me: My head's all itchy. What if Bob has got so big he's about to pop out of my ears and spill all over the floor?

Harrison: Not scientifically possible. I googled it. It could be because of the colour you had put on your hair. Might have dried out your scalp. Worth it, though!

He has the best grammar and punctuation of anyone my age I've ever met. That's private school, I guess.

Sunday – Me: Do you think eating fatty food also makes Bob grow fatter? Because I just had a massive brunch at BayCaff?

Harrison: I don't think tumours work like that. The brunches at BayCaff are worth every calorie.

Monday – Me: I keep being horrible to people. Do you think my mum and dad and Gemma will forgive me if it turns out that my brain isn't right and that's why I'm being such a bitch?

Harrison: Everyone has bad days.

People get bored very quickly when you're sick. Molly was supportive when I first got diagnosed, like she was in a movie where she'd be the cool best friend and we'd meet cute boys with mysterious diseases. But the excitement wore off before I'd even had my surgery.

I don't want the same to happen with Harrison.

He'll be home from school now, at his mum's house. Maybe – like the Queen of Wands and the Hanged Rabbit – I should be super-brave and call him, instead of waiting for more messages. He liked me when we were face to face.

Before I change my mind, I call his number.

He doesn't answer.

Obviously. He thinks I am the most boring girl on the planet.

290

I stretch out on the woodland duvet cover that I used to hate and stare at the boats through the porthole and listen to the sounds of the Harbourside. Only two more nights of noise left, before I go home to the silence of the village.

My phone buzzes and my heart beats faster. *Harrison is calling me back*. I sit bolt upright, check my reflection, then swipe up to accept the video call.

'Hey,' he says.

'Hey, you.'

Harrison smiles at me, but crookedly, like he's nervous. 'Is everything OK?'

I shrug, keeping my chin tucked under, so my face looks as slim as possible. 'Kind of.' Is this where I've been going wrong? I should be all positive and kooky and upbeat. 'It's great. You? How was school?'

Harrison shrugs back at me. 'No one's doing any work, because it's the end of term. I don't get why they even bother to make us go in.'

I've lost track of when normal school finishes: hospital school runs all year round. 'Are you going on holiday after this?'

'France, but not till the middle of August. I'll be back with my dad for a bit, though.'

'In his yurt?'

'No. That's temporary.' Harrison sighs. 'Listen, Casey, they're not telling you the truth, and it's really not OK.'

'Who aren't?'

'Your dad. My dad. I don't agree with it.'

I'm trying to make sense of what he's saying. It'd be obvious, if Bob didn't slow my brain down. 'What are you talking about?'

'Ask your dad about the penthouse, Casey. And when you've asked him, call me, any time. I don't think it's fair that he's lying to you, and it can't go on for ever.'

I stare at Harrison on the screen.

He looks shocked at what he's said. 'I'm sorry. Maybe I shouldn't have said anything. But I like you, and I don't like having to be a liar too.' And he cuts off before I can ask anything more.

Ask your dad about the penthouse? I know he doesn't own the place – he's never pretended he could afford it. So what else could it be? He might usually live here with another woman. But he likes *Gemma*. He wouldn't cheat on her, would he?

My dad's still at work, and last night it was after midnight before he got in. But if there's any clue about what's going on, it'll be in Dad's bedroom, the one space I'm not allowed inside.

I tiptoe out of my room and peer through the living-room door: Mum's doing a *Yoga with Adriene* video on the floor. I creep backwards and try the door to my dad's bedroom, half expecting it to be locked, but the handle moves.

Should I do this? I don't think I'm going to like what I find. But I am *so* sick adults springing bad news on me and how then I have to pretend it doesn't matter. I want to be prepared.

I push inside. The space is *messy*: clothes all over the place, plus his precious trainers higgledy-piggledy on the carpet, like there's been a hurricane in a Sports Direct. But that's not a surprise – Dad's office is chaotic too.

At the far end there are two doors: one to a shower room. I open the cabinet, hunting for another toothbrush or women's perfume. The only strange thing is a box of dye for beards. Maybe Dad shaved off his facial hair, so he wouldn't break Mum's hygiene rules.

I go into the other room now. I think it's what they call a walk-in wardrobe, but the space is bigger than my bedroom at home and it's *stuffed* with clothes. Expensive suits and ironed shirts hang from rails on both walls. There are two freaky things about it. First, it's tidy. Second, I cannot imagine my dad *ever* wearing a suit, plus they're *way* too big for him.

At the bottom of the third wardrobe, someone's stacked shelves with blue polo shirts folded into perfect squares. A pull-out unit holds pairs of shiny shoes. Why doesn't he use this to store his favourite trainers?

Plus, where are the scrappy T-shirts that look like they've been round the world on tour, with the bands printed on the front? Where are the khaki shorts with multiple pockets for this tool or that? It's like my father has never lived here at all . . .

I hear a noise behind me. *Dad?* Or the real owner of these horrible clothes?

'What are you doing in here, Casey?'

It's Mum.

I can't find the words to tell her what I'm doing, or what I've seen. I wish I could run away, get as far as I can from the things that scare me: Bob, my mother's nerves, my father's lies, the strange suits in the wardrobe.

'I was looking for . . .' I shake my head. 'See for yourself, Mum. Can you imagine him wearing *any* of this stuff? And it's not even his size.'

As she comes in next to me, I smell the faint sweat that always defeats her mineral-salt deodorant. She touches the arms of the suits and opens drawers full of neckties and good-as-new socks.

Another drawer contains only small boxes, and she lifts one out. Inside is a shiny, blingy Rolex, and she removes the slip of paper that's tucked into the lid. A name has been written in deep-blue ink alongside the date of the guarantee.

'Who the hell is Vijay Pyne?'

293

And that's when it falls into place and I realize everyone has lied to me: my dad, his friends. Even Harrison.

If my dad has lied about this, has anything he's ever said been true?

Chapter 38: Dan

'You've been staring at that spreadsheet for the last three hours,' Sue says when she comes in to ask what I want from the sandwich van.

'It's the heat, it wrecks my concentration.'

She gives me a sympathetic smile. 'The storm's meant to break tomorrow. Why don't you take the afternoon off? You're owed it. Spend some time with your daughter, before she goes home.'

I don't argue, because *no one* argues with Sue. But when I get in the jeep I can't face going back to the penthouse early, as I don't think either Casey or Angelica will be pleased to see me. Out of habit, I head for the Wells Road, past my flat, but I don't stop to look. The villages pass by in a Bath-stone blur: Pensford, Clutton, Temple Cloud.

Suddenly I know where I'm headed.

If this had been a festival summer, they'd still be cleaning up, but the Glastonbury site has had a year off to recover. I park up on the main road and, when I get out, the terrain triggers dozens of memories: smells and sights and fragments of music.

None come from the year that matters, that flooded weekend when this mess kicked off. It's hard to believe I'm standing in the same place: then it was a sea of dark mud and multicoloured Gore-tex. Now everywhere has been bleached by the heatwave, like someone has applied a vintage-photo Instagram filter to the countryside.

I walk until the sweat soaks through my T-shirt, trying to make sense of everything. If Gemma were here, she'd help me find a way through – except she's part of the problem.

What would life be like with her, and a new baby, and Casey too? Dan the *Family* Man.

That makes me laugh. It's not me – never has been.

It's time to return to my old life, appreciate the freedoms I have spent the last fifteen years guarding. It won't be *exactly* the same, because I'll spend weekends with Casey—

Except what will she think when she sees my *real* place? Even if she can accept it, Angelica might not: the pollution on the main road is off the scale.

When I try to picture what relationship I'm going to have with my daughter, I draw a blank. And I realize something else. Angelica made me choose between Casey and Gemma, but in reality I don't believe she *does* want me to be in Casey's life, even if I play by the rules. She will do everything she can to scupper my chances – and there is nothing I can do to stop her.

I climb back into the jeep, disappointed that coming here hasn't helped. I imagine putting my foot down, driving away from the whole shitshow. My dad would have been long gone by now. His ultimate escape plan was always the Costa del Sol, and for all I know, that's where he's ended up. I'm not even sure whether he's dead or alive, though he has the survival instincts of a cockroach.

I turn on the stereo to drown out my thoughts, but turn it back off again straight away. I can't even face music, that's how bad things are.

But as I join the main road I spot a signpost to Weston-super-Mare and, without thinking, take the turning. No point walking back into the penthouse firing line before I have to.

The tide is out – is it ever really *in* on this beach? I close my eyes, trying to recapture those hours with Casey and Gemma and her family. Not only what I saw and heard, but how it felt. Why did this flat stretch of sand seem so spectacular then, but so ordinary now?

Then I was with people. Now I'm alone.

Alone. I think of all the songs people have written about this state. I'd laughed them off for years. Alone didn't have to mean lonely, I insisted. It meant you could choose to do what you wanted, be independent, spontaneous.

It meant you wouldn't be hurt, or hurt anyone else.

But now I've experienced togetherness, I realize I've been kidding myself. I was – I *am* – lonely.

And I don't want to be.

On Saturday I let myself be a part of a family. And despite my lack of experience, I didn't suck at it. I responded to them like they responded to me. I guess I've always seen families as mysterious entities, with rules I don't understand.

But they are just collections of people, good and bad.

As I walk, I make heavy footprints along the wet shore. Haven't I learned how to be good with people, through work and friends? Is it possible I might have what Sue at work calls *highly developed interpersonal skills?*

OK, I don't understand the first thing about babies, but neither does Gemma. What if we could learn together? If I love her – and I'm starting to believe I do – then it doesn't matter whether the baby has my genes or not.

I've walked further than I planned. The footprints behind me have disappeared, as the tide reclaims its territory. I take off my trainers, and the cool sea water feels so delicious on my soles that I break into a jog.

As my feet slap against the sand and my breathing speeds up, everything comes into sunlit focus. I have to try one last time with Casey and Gemma – and Angelica too. Admit to my flaws, and resolve to be better.

I've done things I am ashamed of, and even when I've tried *not* to hurt people by keeping my distance I've ended up causing damage.

But I don't have to be that way for ever.

It's only by facing up to my mistakes, and saying sorry, that I can take away the power the past has had over all of us.

The slow traffic driving back towards the city centre makes me thump the steering wheel in frustration. I want to get on with putting things right.

As I drive the jeep into the underground car park, I get this chilling premonition of driving straight out again. No. I've got to believe I can get them to listen, to prove I'm changing.

The penthouse lift purrs, and one of the geckos on the tropical wallpaper seems to stare me out: *you don't belong*. How could anyone have believed that *I* live *here*?

As the doors open, the intense heat of the apartment makes me flinch.

'Casey? Angelica?'

The silence creeps me out. They should both be at home by now. The words of explanation I've been planning are drowned out by the hum of panic in my ears.

'We're in here.'

I can hear *that*: Angelica's voice, sharp and threatening. Coming from the bedroom. *My* bedroom. Well, *Vijay's* bedroom. And as I step inside and see their faces, I realize instantly that I am too late.

Casey already knows that I've lied. Everything I've built in the last few weeks is lost. Worst of all, I have nobody to blame but myself.

Chapter 39: Gemma

Thursday 26 July

No balloons this morning: the sky's the colour of ashes, and any minute it'll be split in two by lightning. I hurry Bear out of the door, so we can be home again before the downpour begins.

There's been no more blood. And though my body keeps reporting new sensations – tenderness, dizziness, another bout of nausea when I serve Bear his corned-beef and kibble breakfast – I pretend it's not happening. This limbo ends on Saturday, but until then I am resolutely in denial about everything.

My phone buzzes. In the seconds it takes me to get it out of my bag I've imagined a dozen messages Dan might have written.

But it's my agent: I sent her my finished illustrations last night.

Back on form, G! I'll be sending more pitches your way next week!

I've always rewarded myself for finishing a job with a cheese and mushroom croissant. I buy one at the patisserie now, but it tastes wrong. The last one I had was on the Downs with Dan and Casey, so maybe that's why.

The first spits of rain hit as I'm opening the gate, and I'm fumbling for my key when I hear my name being called. I turn to see my sister getting out of her car.

'Laura! This is a surprise, I didn't think you were working today.'

But she doesn't smile back: her expression chills me. 'I'm not. I came to see you. I . . . have something I need to tell you.'

'What is it? Is it Dad? Mum?'

'No. Nobody's died or anything.'

'So what is it?'

'Can we go inside?'

As I let her in, I think of all the other times she must have stood on doorsteps, knowing that she was about to shatter someone's world.

She won't let me make tea, even though my hands twitch with nervous energy, desperate to do *something* to delay finding out whatever she's here to tell me.

'Have you seen that man again?' she asks when I finally sit down.

'Dan? No.' *So whatever it is you want to tell me, don't bother.*

'And do you plan to?' She's still standing, blocking the light from the window.

'OK, Laura, I know you don't like him. But you can let it go, because Dan and I are not going to be an item anyway now and—'

'He doesn't exist,' she says, interrupting me.

'Huh?'

'Daniel Lennon doesn't exist. Or, rather, he *didn't* exist, prior to 1997.'

'Sorry, what?' The room goes darker still and I grab the top of the sofa to steady myself.

'There's no trace of the guy being born. He doesn't show up till about twenty years ago. So he is not who he says he is. And there's something else—'

'Hold up,' I say, because something has occurred to me. 'How do *you* know this?'

'Um, well . . .'

'Because the last time Mum asked you to check someone out at work, you said you could be sacked for it.'

'I didn't do it myself. But I know a guy . . . an ex-colleague, who has ways and means. After I met "Dan" at the weekend' – she does air quotes as she speaks his name – 'I had this feeling. A bad feeling. So I asked my guy to do the absolute basic checks, and when those rang alarm bells, I got him to dig a bit deeper.'

I stand up so fast it makes me light-headed. 'You did that without talking to me first?'

'You'd have said no. Look, when you've dealt with as many dodgy characters as I have, you get a sixth sense. The moment he found out I was police, we didn't see him for dust. And, as it turns out, my instincts were right. He's been inside, Gems.'

And that's when I realize it's a case of mistaken identity. 'No. You've got the wrong guy. His dad has been to prison, but not Dan.'

'Gems, it's definitely him. I'm sorry, but it is. He went to prison for fraud, got fourteen months, though I bet he wormed his way out a lot sooner than that. I'll forward you the email, but I had to talk to you in person first. I didn't want to do this, Gems, but we've been so worried about you, I couldn't let it go.'

I want to shout and scream at her, but I can't kill the

302

messenger. It's not Laura, but Dan – or whoever he really is – who deserves my anger. He's the one who wormed his way into my life and my poor, bruised heart.

Laura makes me a tea with three sugars and tries to get me to talk about Dan-who-isn't-Dan, but I don't have the words.

I sink onto the sofa after she leaves. I need all my mental energy to find an alternative explanation. 'People change their names all the time, don't they, Bear? Yours kept changing when you were in and out of the rescue centre.'

If he didn't exist before 1997, Dan was only twelve or thirteen when he changed his name, the same age he was when his dad went to jail. Perhaps that's the reason: he wanted a fresh start, so he took his foster family's surname.

But still . . . fraud: that's not so easily explained away. Was I a 'mark' to him? Did he lie about our 'connection' and plan to exploit me further down the line? However hard I try to silence the questions, they nag at me, like a tooth with a hole that I can't stop probing.

I have to ask him myself.

I try calling his mobile, but it goes to voicemail. I look up the number for the carpentry workshop, but when I call, they tell me Dan's taken the day off.

I shouldn't go back to the penthouse, not after how he responded when I told him about the embryo transfer on Monday night. But I want to understand what's been going on, if only so I never make the same mistake again.

The rain's pummelling down now, so I bundle Bear out of the flat and into the car. The windscreen wipers can't keep up, so the city's blurred as I drive towards the floating harbour. I *should* turn back, but the rage and the hurt won't let me.

Despite my umbrella, Bear and I are soaked through,

seconds after leaving the car. I push the buzzer for the pent-house, but nobody answers. I step back to squint up at the top floor, but all the windows are closed.

Where is he?

I think I catch a glimpse of movement at the window, the slightest change in the light.

I press again. This time I don't let go, and the button vibrates under my finger. If he's in there, I hope the sound is unbearably loud.

What difference is confronting him going to make? If Dan is a con man, he'll only come out with more lies –

'Hello?' A woman's voice: tense, abrupt. *Familiar.* 'I can't work the video on this bloody thing, but if that's you, Dan, the lift access is turned off and it's staying that way. You've got no more right to be here than I have.'

Angelica. But why won't she let him in? Coming here was a mistake. The last thing I need is to get embroiled in *their* arguments.

But now a green light appears above the camera.

'Gemma?'

'Sorry, I shouldn't be here.'

'But you can't keep away, right? Dan Lennon, catnip to rich women everywhere.'

'He's not Dan Lennon.' I say it before thinking about the consequences.

'What are you on about? If this is a joke, I'm not in the mood.'

'It's not a joke. Someone just told me Dan changed his name when he was a teenager. It might not mean anything, or even be true, but that's why I came, because I want to understand what's going on.'

The silence from her end means she must have cut the call. Except the green light still blinks.

'You should come up.'

I hesitate. 'I've got my dog with me. And he's very wet.'

She laughs bitterly. 'Oh, I couldn't give a toss any more. Let him pee all over the bed, it'll serve them both right.'

Both?

And before I can work out if Angelica has lost it, the door buzzes, I push it open and Bear's pulling me inside, out of the rain.

Angelica looks different when the lift doors open. Before, she was glacially pretty, almost untouchable.

Now her hair's a mess and her eyes are wild. When I'm in a bad way, I'm a total sight. But Angelica is more gorgeous than ever.

'In here,' she says, ignoring Bear, who ignores her back. He shakes the rain off and settles on the doormat.

I follow Angelica into the living room. Smoke hangs in the air and the terrace doors are closed, so we can see the rain sheeting across the city, but can't hear a thing.

'I warned you on Monday that he lies the whole time. So what's this about?'

I'm light-headed from stress, so I sit down on the same bit of the sofa where Dan and I kissed. I clench my fist, driving my nails into my palm to stop myself remembering . . . 'I don't know if he is who he says he is.'

Angelica goes to the kitchen island and takes two slices of bread out of the toaster: they're burnt, but she doesn't seem to notice, slathering butter onto them and then jabbing the knife into a small tin of something black.

'He's a shit, is what he is,' she says, loading two more slices of bread into the toaster before sitting down opposite me. 'What have you found out?'

Does Angelica even know Dan has a criminal record and

305

went to prison? Despite everything, I don't want to ruin his relationship with his daughter, so I have to tread carefully. 'Dan Lennon didn't exist before 1997. So sometime before his thirteenth birthday he must have changed his name. That's around the time he went into care, but I wondered if there might be more to it.'

She shrugs her shoulders, which makes her top gape: she's so skinny she almost looks ill. 'More than him being an inveterate liar, you mean?'

I don't reply.

Angelica sniffs the toast. 'This is caviar from the cupboard. Ever tried it? It smells rank, but I googled it and it's fifty quid a tin. When I first met Dan, he had a shared fridge that should have been condemned by Environmental Health. But when I came here a month ago he was living like a king. I thought it meant he'd changed.'

'I guess we all lived in hovels when we were young.'

She stares at me for a very long time. Then she bursts out laughing. 'You're still making excuses for him. Sorry to tell you this, but the *real* reason he appears to be living like a king is that this isn't even his flat.'

'There's nothing wrong with renting—'

'He doesn't rent it. He's borrowed it from a mate, while Casey is here. Which would be OK. A nice gesture even, if he hadn't let us think it was his permanent place. It's such a pointless lie, but Casey had to find out by going through his wardrobe and finding it full of someone else's clothes. And finding the kitchen cabinets full of someone else's caviar.' She takes a bite of the toast, pulls a face.

'Seriously?' The shock of the lie makes me flinch and I look around me, reassessing the furniture and decor. I remember how surprised I was at how flash it seemed when

I first came here. 'What did Dan think would happen when his friend moved back in?'

'When we confronted him, he said he hadn't thought that far ahead. That Casey had got the wrong end of the stick and he didn't know how to set her straight without disappointing her. Almost like he was shifting the blame onto her. Pathetic, right?'

'Yes. Though it's also very *him*. He seems to want to keep everyone happy.'

She scoffs. 'For as long as it suits him. It means Dan only ever planned to play at fatherhood for four weeks. I lied to Casey for years about him not knowing I was pregnant, so she wouldn't realize he'd rejected her only days after she was born. Bad mistake on my part, because if she'd known all along that he was a pathological liar and a con man, she'd never have searched for him.'

A liar and a con man. 'Did he con *you*?'

She pauses. 'No. When we got together at Glastonbury he was really generous, and kind too. Took care of me when I took my first E and got spooked. Some guys would have taken advantage. Not Dan. He was . . . sweet.' Angelica frowns at the memory, as though she'd forgotten he could behave decently. She shakes her head. 'But that doesn't cancel out everything else. I bet the fake-name stuff is the tip of the iceberg.' She puts her plate down, the toast almost untouched.

I worry she's going to run out of patience with me soon, so I have to take a risk. 'Do you know anything about him going to prison?'

Angelica raises an eyebrow. 'Oh yes. It was one of the first things he told me when I tracked him down to tell him I was pregnant.'

'What had he done?'

'According to him, it was no big deal. He'd been working with some other lads doing odd jobs and they overcharged. Of course when it got to court, I heard the real story. He was in a gang conning elderly people. How low can you go?'

My head throbs. 'I can't imagine him doing that.'

'The guys he worked with had been doing it for years, knocking on doors telling people their roofs were about to fall in, taking enormous amounts of money for tiny repairs. Or even for doing the damage themselves. I sat in court as the poor victims gave evidence; it was heartbreaking.'

'But you stayed with him after that?'

Angelica glowers at me. 'Look, I was a kid who wanted to rebel against my parents, and Dan can be charming, as you well know. He convinced me that the best chance of him avoiding prison was if I played the supportive fiancée. His lawyer made a big thing of how Dan was turning over a new leaf, pointed to me, said he was determined to be a caring dad.

'But the judge didn't buy it. He announced the sentence and I realized I'd be giving birth alone. I sobbed for two days in the bedsit we'd rented here, but then I calmed down, made it cosy, buying things from charity shops, nesting. I'd write three times a week, and he always wrote straight back.

'Casey arrived early and her birth was really rough on me. She was a big baby and I was tiny. My parents rallied round for once, took me back home to recover. I kept trying to call the prison, but I was so out of it . . .'

She looks very young now, as she remembers. 'And when I finally got back to the bedsit in Bristol there was a letter waiting. The envelope was so thin, I didn't open it for hours, because I knew what it was. Dan had changed his mind.

Wasn't ready for a kid or commitment. I was so exhausted I didn't have enough spare energy to hate him.'

'That's terrible.'

'My parents said he must have been conning me too, stringing me along to reduce his sentence and ditching me when it didn't work.'

I picture Angelica as she realized there was no other explanation. Her bitterness makes much more sense. 'That's so cruel. To give you hope and then—'

She shrugs. 'I got over it. I don't regret Casey, and I'd have been bloody miserable following the path my parents wanted for me. She helped me escape. But this' – she gestures around the space – 'what he's done to Casey, I can't forgive. She's hurting so badly. I can't believe I let myself be fooled a second time.'

'Why do you think he chose to reply to her messages after so long?'

'Best case? He wanted to help because of the tumour. Maybe it's the same instinct that made him help me at Glastonbury, because he's a sucker for waifs and strays, but when he actually realizes that means commitment, he runs a mile. The worst case? A scam of some kind? Who even knows?' She stands up. 'I'm done with trying to psychoanalyse him. I need to go and pick Casey up soon: it's her last day at hospital school and they're having a little send-off for her.'

'Sure. Of course. I'll be keeping everything crossed for tomorrow. Will you tell her I'm thinking about her?'

Angelica smiles tightly and I think, *She's not going to mention me at all.* Perhaps that's best for Casey. 'I tried to warn you, Gemma. But we never listen till it happens to us. He should come with a health warning tattooed on his forehead. Or his dick.'

I want to tell her that we never slept together, but the truth is, if it hadn't been for the FET, we probably would have. 'Thanks for talking to me. It must be hard.'

She holds my gaze. 'No. It's easy. Casey comes first. Like I told you before, kids make life simple.'

And I see that even though some of her choices seem flawed to me, she *will* protect Casey, and Casey will be OK.

But what about me? As soon as I'm in the lift with Bear, my throat tightens and my eyes sting. I make it to the car before the first angry sob bursts out. I'm angry at Dan for lying and cheating. Angry at Andrew for leaving me at the mercy of con men.

Mostly I'm furious with myself for thinking I could trust anyone, let alone love anyone again. Andrew was a one-off. Most men aren't puzzles, they're booby traps.

Chapter 40: Dan

Heavy feet stumble towards my pitch. 'Oi, mate, you OK in there? We're hanging out in the ruins – it's drier.'

I poke my head through the tent flap. 'Might come out in a bit.'

He shrugs and trudges away. The faces of the rough sleepers are different from twelve years ago, but their desperation hasn't changed, and neither has the smell of weed and sour bodies.

Most are already wasted, even though it's not quite midday. The handful with more get-up-and-go will have been working their pitches around the city, but they'll be heading back, now the heavens have opened. You don't get much for begging or drawing pavement pictures when it's pissing it down.

I'm half-tempted to join them. Last night, after I left the penthouse, I knew I couldn't go back to my place and boot out my Airbnb guests. So I grabbed the tent from my jeep and came here, buying a six-pack of gut-rot cider on the way. I held off drinking any, but I couldn't face work today, and a few cans now might knock me out and stop the bad thoughts.

Except that's too much of a cop-out. The look on my daughter's face when I tried to explain my lies was the most shameful moment of my life. And God knows, there's been some stiff competition. Pretending the penthouse was mine isn't the worst thing I've done, and I did try to explain that it started as a misunderstanding. But then Angelica, calmer than I've seen her all month, pointed out how pathetic my excuse was, how I always go for the easy option, never face my mistakes until there's no choice. And she was right, of course.

Oh, Casey, I am so sorry.

They didn't try to stop me leaving the apartment. And now it hits me: that might have been the last time I'll ever see my daughter.

I crack open a can of cider. The cheaper the booze, the more intense the memories. As the alcohol hits my brain, *happy* snippets come to the surface. They're the bloody worst.

Eating chips at the seaside, the vinegar bleeding through the paper, stinging my fingers. 'Always tastes better when it's been paid for by punters,' he'd say, after a day ripping off holidaymakers with his favourite find the lady scam.

Shopping for child-sized Doc Martens lookalikes to match his own. 'We're the terrible twins. Always buy the best shoes you can afford, Daz. Shoes show what you're made of.' He could be bloody generous and liked me to look sharp, because it reflected on him.

Would he be proud of me, despite everything? I've got more than he had. The jeep, a flat – OK, no penthouse, but somewhere with an actual mortgage and bills that I pay by direct debit, instead of waiting for the cut-off notices and doing a runner.

Paying for stuff is for losers, kiddo. People like us, we play the system and we win.

He made it sound like a game. And the people he screwed – the bargain-hunters who bought at his mock auctions, the donors giving generously to causes that didn't exist, the grieving widows he'd scope out before sliding effortlessly into their lives – were paying the price for having more money than sense.

I'm doing them a favour, Dazzler, teaching them a lesson. Better they lose a few quid to me than thousands to an actual criminal.

And Pete Lennox had his own code of honour. Rule number one: look after your own. Rule number two: never grass.

Stop this now.

I leave the tent for a piss in the bushes. As I walk back, I take in the view across the water: shiny office windows, funky brewhouses, cranes promising more of the same. So different from how rough it was when I first camped here, after prison. But search hard enough and there's plenty of poverty and addiction underneath.

A couple walk past, so into each other that they don't notice me or my tent. As I squeeze back into my sleeping bag and zip out the rest of the world, thoughts of Gemma climb inside with me. If there's any justice, on Saturday she'll find out she's pregnant with her husband's child. A new adventure. I close my eyes. Did *my* parents see Mum getting pregnant as an adventure? My dad only talked about her when he'd been to the pub, and the sadder he was, the more likely he was to turn on me.

'If the doctors had given me the choice,' he said more than once, 'I wouldn't have hesitated. I'd have said: Save her, not the bloody baby. You wouldn't be here.'

Of course it wasn't fair to say that to a kid. But it wasn't fair either that my father, a man who'd have struggled to keep a fairground goldfish alive, was saddled with a baby and a bucketload of grief, when what he'd wanted was the life of Riley with his glamorous young wife on the Costa del Crime . . .

I know I've got it bad when I feel sorry for my father. I push the other cans of cider to the other end of the tent and gulp water instead, to sober me up.

I turn my phone on for the first time since leaving the penthouse last night: I told myself I was saving the battery, but I also wanted to avoid angry WhatsApps from Casey, or crowing from Angelica.

There's nothing. Hopefully they're moving on already. As my thumb hovers by the off button, the screen lights up:

ANGELICA CALLING

I let it go to voicemail. An alert pops up a few seconds later:

You have 4 new messages

As I dial my voicemail, the buzzing in my head begins. Angelica's first message was left an hour ago:

'Hi. It's me. Is Casey with you? We went for her scan this morning and I left her to go to hospital school on her own. But she never showed up and she's not answering her phone. So if you've picked her up on some bloody secret jaunt, you need to tell me now. I hope you did, because if she's not with you, then . . . Call me, OK?'

My hand tenses around the handset as her newer messages play out, and I keep hoping the next one will tell me that Casey's turned up.

But the most recent voicemail is the hardest to hear. Angelica's crying so much that I can't make out all the words:

'She's still . . . not . . . back. My baby girl has gone. Where is she, Dan? I need you to help me find her. Call me, please. I don't know what else to do.'

Chapter 41: Dan

Now I get it.

To experience real fear, you have to love someone. *That's* why I've never felt fear like this before.

I did feel something close to it for those three endless minutes on the Harbourside when Gemma and I thought we'd lost Casey and Bear. But this is another level of terror.

I throw my things into my backpack, rip the tent pegs out of the earth, roll it all up in a messy bundle that I can barely carry and take off along Welsh Back, the rain still pouring, drunk guys jeering and shouting after me.

As I half walk, half run, I call Angelica.

'Is she with you?' she asks, sounding breathless too.

'I'm so sorry. No.'

'Fucking hell, Dan. Where *is* she?'

'We'll find her,' I say, because we *have* to. 'Where are you now?'

'I've been walking round the hospital and the university. There's no sign. But she doesn't know Bristol at all, so where could she have gone?'

'You've tried calling her?'

'Oh, that's a good idea, why didn't I think of that? Of course I've bloody called her. In between trying to track *you* down, which wasted precious time.'

'I'm sorry,' I say, panting as I speed up, and almost slipping as the water floods the cobbles.

'This is down to you. She hardly spoke a word this morning. I think she's gone because she's so upset.'

'Angelica, I mean it. I *am* sorry. But I'm near the flat, I can pick up the jeep, go wherever you want me to.'

'I can't think straight. You know this city – you've taken her to different places. The only thing we can do is go where she's already been. And hope she's got some shelter.'

Has the walk sobered me up enough to get behind the wheel? I'm light-headed, but that's from losing Casey. It was only one can of cider, an hour or more ago. 'OK, I'll go to my work, in case she's tried there. And I'll call Vijay and Harrison, see if they have any ideas or suggestions about—'

'Do they know?' she interrupts.

'About the penthouse?'

Angelica scoffs. 'Obviously they know that you've been living in *their* home. I wondered how much you've told them about everything else you've done. Prison. Oh, and the fact you're not even Dan Lennon.'

My body keeps propelling me forward on the cobbles, but my brain seizes. 'What are you talking about?'

'Your girlfriend told me. She came round to confront you, but ended up filling me in on how you'd changed your identity. I thought I knew everything, but turns out there's always something new to discover about *Darryl Lennox*?'

'Gemma told you about my name? Was she very upset? She must hate me.'

'Why do you care?' Angelica is crying again now and, despite everything, I want to comfort her and, more than anything, I *need* to find Casey.

'We can talk about this later. After we find Casey.' There's silence at the other end. 'Angelica?'

She sobs. 'What if we don't find her?'

For the first time, that possibility fills my head, more appalling than the most deafening burst of tinnitus.

My city no longer seems like a friendly place. Instead the floodwater and the cobbles and the cyclists and the cars and the strangers – *all the strangers* – loom like threats, a million hazards that could take Casey from us.

'We are going to find her.'

I wait for Angelica to challenge me, because neither of us can know for sure.

'Yes. You're right. She's going to be OK. Call me once you're on the road,' she says.

I get hold of Vijay as I'm walking into the underground car park.

'Hi, Dan, what gives?' He sounds as cheerful as ever.

'Veej, I need your help. Harrison's help.'

'O-kay.' I can hear the question in his voice.

'It's Casey. She's . . . gone.' My voice cracks on the word.

'Gone where?'

'We've no idea. She left the hospital on her own, two hours ago now. Isn't answering her phone. And it's my fault. Why didn't I tell her the truth sooner?'

'Because you're a human being. Listen to me, Dan, what's done is done. You need to stay calm and focus on finding her. What can I do?'

I load my stuff into the back, peel off my sopping raincoat. 'Is Harrison there? He might have heard from her. Or have some ideas of where Casey could have gone?'

'He's out with friends. I'll see if I can get hold of him.'

'He wouldn't be with Casey, would he?' Hope makes my heart beat even faster.

'Didn't say so. I'll track him down and call you as soon

as I have. She's a smart cookie, Dan, she'll be somewhere sulking, and hoping you're all suffering. It's what they do sometimes. To prove to themselves how much you love them.'

'I hope you're right. I don't think I'd even realized till now how much I did.'

Vijay sighs. 'Mate. I hear you. Call me when you've got any news.'

I drive and I drive. St Nick's Market, the road next to BayCaff – everywhere I can think of. I leave the jeep on double yellows to dart into the spaces I can only explore on foot. When I return the third time, there's a warden writing out a ticket. I show him the photo of Casey I took on the beach and beg him to keep an eye out. Soon he's cancelling the ticket and posting her picture in the Bristol wardens' WhatsApp group.

WhatsApp. I should check when Casey was last online.

She hasn't been on the app since nine this morning. I can picture her around that time, going into the proton beam room alone – facing every new treatment with courage that awes me.

I put my foot down to get to the workshop, pulling up outside and racing around the space in case she's hiding, and asking Finn if she mentioned anywhere special when the two of them were chatting. No. I have *nothing else to go on.*

When I get back into the jeep, I force myself to slow down. Where else has Casey been? Weston? I guess she might have got a bus or a train to the coast . . .

Gemma might know.

Gemma must hate me now. But she could be the key to all this. Casey might have gone to see her, or to the Downs, or . . .

The spectre of the deadly steepness of Avon Gorge fills my head. No. Not that.

As I drive towards Clifton Village I dial Gemma's number – it rings twice, then goes to voicemail, and I take a deep breath before speaking:

'I know I shouldn't bother you. Especially not with what's going on for you. And I have no right to ask, but it's Casey. She's gone. She's upset and she's gone, and we don't have a clue where. So please call me back, because Casey talked to you more than anyone else.'

I ring off, hoping that she won't delete my voicemail without listening to it.

Before I've even got to the end of Regent Street, Gemma's calling me back.

'Where have you been so far?' she says, straight down to business.

'Everywhere I can think of,' I reply, 'except near you. I'm in the jeep, heading towards the bridge and the Downs.'

'Pick me up. Two are better than one.'

Chapter 42: Gemma

I must be resolute when he arrives. Daren't look him in the eye. Or even at his face. And when he speaks, I will not listen to that voice, but will focus purely on the information that could lead us to Casey.

It's the *only* way I can handle this.

But when I see him through my balcony window, parking up his jeep, my body betrays me. A wave of heat passes through me. Except, who am I trying to kid – it's lust, always has been, from that first meeting. But now a chill, too. This man is a liar and a con man.

Could the call about Casey be a way to get back into my life? He must be frustrated that the groundwork he's laid with me has been wasted. Makes more sense for him to try one final time, rather than find some other 'mark' to manipulate.

'Right, Bear. No jumping up, no licks, no—'

But Bear is already poking his nose through the balustrade, yelping. Dan sees him, and me, and the despair on his face seems utterly real.

'So much for you being a good judge of character, mate,' I say to the dog, before pushing my feet into my sandals. It takes more effort than usual, because the skin seems tender, swollen. Is that caused by the humidity that's lingering, despite the rain, or by something more?

Before I can let the thought grow, I pull on my waterproof jacket and march out of the flat and onto the street, holding Bear back when he tries to say hello. I can't let Dan think any of this is OK.

'Gemma, I'm so sorry you had to find out all the bad stuff about me. I planned to tell you, but I kept losing my nerve. Also, I'm sorry for how I reacted when you told me about your treatment, it's an amazing thing—'

I hold up my hand. 'Don't. We're doing this for Casey, and once she's back, I never want to see you again.'

He nods. 'I appreciate you saying you'll help at all.' His clothes are crumpled and his face is so bloody sad that I don't know if I can stay businesslike.

'The cafe first? And then the Downs? I can let Bear off.'

Dan stares into the jeep. 'I might have something of hers that he could sniff and then see if he can smell her nearby?'

'He's not a bloody police dog.'

'No. Sorry, I'm not thinking straight.'

'Have you called the police?'

'Angelica will have. She turned up at the hospital and realized Casey had done a runner. I'm not – I'm not living at the penthouse any more.'

'I know that.'

Dan looks away. At least he still feels shame.

We work through everywhere I can think of. I talk to Pepe in the salon, but he hasn't seen her. In the cafe I show them Casey's picture and give them Dan's phone number. No one remembers seeing a girl like her today – and she *is* distinctive, thanks to her pink-toned hair and her sweet, sweet face.

Not just distinctive. *Vulnerable*. A country girl lost in the city. I'm getting more worried: my sister was *always* running away when we were kids, but we were in a small town that we knew backwards, and we couldn't walk down the street without some busybody recognizing us.

Bristol is different. Casey is different.

The Downs are sodden from the storm and although the rain has stopped for now, the black clouds promise another downpour. We let Bear off the lead, but he rolls in the mud and gets frustrated when we don't throw the ball for him.

Dan's phone keeps ringing: his friend's son calls and swears he hasn't seen Casey, but tells him about the places she wanted to visit: the zoo, to see meerkats. A skateboard shop, to buy her own.

Dan thanks Harrison, but when he ends the call, his face goes grey. 'It's like a needle in a fucking haystack. And she's still not been on WhatsApp. She spends her whole *life* on WhatsApp.'

'She could be out of battery.'

'Or someone has taken her. Or she's had an accident. Or the tumour has made her lose consciousness and—' He stops. 'I promised Angelica we'd find her. But what if we don't, Gemma? What if she's really gone?'

And despite all the lies I know about, and the doubtless thousands more I don't, he's not pretending now. I can't *not* reach out to touch him. This time there is no erotic charge. Only my hand gripping his, the simplest reassurance one human being can give another. *I am with you while you face this. You are not alone.*

'She's only been missing a couple of hours.'

'Because of me. I've messed everything up. I need to put it right with her. I need to put everything right. Is it too late, Gemma? Do you think it's too late?'

Is he asking me if I can forgive him? Despite everything, now he's here, I can't promise I wouldn't let him back into my life if he said he genuinely wanted to be with me.

'Let's find her first.'

Bear sniffs the air. The atmosphere changes as the first lightning bolt crackles through the clouds, over the other side of the bridge, where the balloons would usually be starting to inflate.

And I remember something: a fragment of the conversation we had at the penthouse, about the balloon ride I took with Andrew, after he'd been sick but had got better.

'Do you remember, after Casey got upset, she wanted to go up in a balloon?'

He shakes his head. 'They don't do balloon flights in this weather.'

'But she doesn't know that,' I point out. 'If we've not got any better ideas, we could go over to Ashton Court?'

His jeep rattles and rumbles as he drives over the bridge. I can smell musty, sour fabric – there's a crumpled tent on the back seat, and I wonder where he spent last night, and where he lives when he's not borrowing his mate's penthouse.

We park up: usually there'd be rows of baskets and a buzz of tourists clutching tickets and champagne flutes, chattering with nerves. Instead there's a woman standing by a sign reading: *REBOOK YOUR CANCELLED FLIGHT HERE.* Dan runs over to her, and by the time I reach them both, she's examining the photo on his phone and nodding.

'. . . earlier. An hour or so ago? I told her all the flights were rained off today, so she begged me to sneak her onto one tomorrow. I explained it doesn't work like that – we book up months in advance for this time of year.'

'How did she seem?'

'She was upset there were no flights. And her words were, I dunno, a bit garbled? If I'd had more time, I would have tried to chat, but there was a guy stressing about his cancelled ride because he'd been planning to propose to his girlfriend . . .'

Her face lights up from a huge bolt of lightning and the thunder follows straight away. We're in the eye of the storm now.

'Did you see where she went?' I ask.

'Towards the woods? She's bound to be sheltering somewhere.'

Dan tries to call Angelica, leaving a message. 'She's been seen at Ashton Court,' he says, 'so we're getting closer.' Even though his voice sounds calm, his knuckles where he grips the phone are so white it's like the bones are showing through the skin.

'She can't be far,' I tell him when he ends the call. Except we both feel a new urgency, after what the woman said about Casey's manner. What if something has gone wrong with her brain?

'You don't know that,' Dan says. 'The estate is vast and she could have collapsed. Or there's someone here who targets children on their own—'

'Stop that. Come on. Between us, we can cover plenty of ground. Let's be logical, divide up the territory.'

We agree that Dan will go right and I'll go left. Bear comes with me, and when he realizes I'm not going to throw the ball for him, he keeps disappearing.

I start calling out Casey's name and Bear joins in by yelping. I follow him into a copse, trying not to get my hopes up. When he stops, I look down to see he's pawing the remains of a squirrel and that makes me think dark thoughts, however hard I try to fight them.

We keep walking, and the rain has soaked through my jacket and I can't stop shivering. Bear barks again as we get deeper into the woods and runs off, and I can see he's digging.

He heads back with the filthiest tennis ball in his mouth, pure delight in his eyes. I think I'm going to have to prise it away from him, because the more disgusting the find, the more determined he is to bring it home.

But now he drops it and tears off into the undergrowth again, running in excited circles. I follow him once more, convinced I am about to stumble into something putrid and rotting.

The tree cover means it's less damp here and heat rises from the earth. When I breathe in tentatively, I can only smell good things, moss and leaves, like someone's bottled the colour green. Bear keeps checking that I'm following, before bounding over more fallen branches, revelling in every obstacle. I'm not as nimble in my skirt and flat shoes, and my skin stings where I brush against nettles and brambles.

Could Casey be here? And if she is, what if she's sick or injured? Or worse . . .

No. She was OK an hour ago when she saw the balloon woman. Well, not completely OK. Distraught and betrayed by everyone. Including me. I *should* have called her. Should at least have sent a WhatsApp or two, checking she was all right after finding out about her father's lies, but I was too wrapped up in my own problems.

Up ahead, I see – or do I imagine? – the briefest flash of pale pink.

'Casey?' I call out.

Bear tears ahead, his dense, muscular body bred for rough terrain, for the hunt. He's fifty metres in front of me and there's no movement anywhere.

'Go!'

The voice is faint. I can't even tell if it's a woman or a child.

But my body – and Bear's reaction – tells me it *is* her.

'Go away!'

Bear is yelping, refusing to do as he's told.

'Casey? Is that you? It's Gemma.'

Bear yelps.

'Go away, I want to be on my own for once in my life!'

Yes! She sounds stroppy – which must be a good sign. I pull my phone out of my bag, ready to call Dan, but not wanting to scare Casey away.

'At least let me see you're all right? You haven't fallen or hurt yourself?'

'I'm totally fine. I wanted to get away from everyone, but I'm not even allowed to do that!'

I still can't see her, and if it hadn't been for Bear, I'd never have known she was here. He vaults back towards me, tail wagging so fast it makes his whole body move, mouth open in a wide, panting grin.

'You know I can't leave you here, Casey? Not in the middle of a storm. Your mum and dad are so worried, so I'm going to call Dan now—'

She steps out from behind a tree that's broader than she is. Her hair is soaked, her skin mottled, her skirt covered in wet leaves and sore-looking scratches on her bare legs.

But she's standing, and the defiance on her face tells me she's going to be OK, physically at least.

'Neither of us are dressed for a hike, are we?' I say, raising my leg so she can see the nettle rash. 'Do you want some water?' I reach into my bag again for the bottle.

Casey grabs it and drinks almost every drop before blinking. 'I'm so sick of it. Dad lying. Mum being bitchy. The treatment. Of feeling mega-tired the entire time and not knowing if it's because I'm getting worse. I want to smash my beads of courage into little pieces and be normal again.'

I hear the despair and remember Andrew one freezing winter day after his relapse. Standing outside Oncology, telling me he couldn't go through another round of treatment, that he was out of strength. I talked him back inside, but it was touch and go, and I felt guilty, because I was making him face more pain . . .

'I understand,' I say. 'My husband had moments like this.'

Bear has stopped jumping up, but has returned to Casey's side. He always knows what someone needs and, as she reaches down, he licks her fingers and she sinks back down onto the earth and he snuggles in closer.

Casey shakes her head. 'It's not the treatment. It's everything.'

I nod, aware that each second must feel like an eternity to her mum and Dan. 'Can I call your dad now, to let him know you're OK? He's got the jeep, so he can take you home to the penthouse.'

'That's not home. And he's not my dad. He's a liar. He cares more about his stupid trainers than he does about me.'

'Still,' I say, not disagreeing, 'you do need to get back to your mum.'

Her eyes fill with tears. 'I didn't mean to scare her.'

'I know, love, I know.' I reach down and Casey takes my hand so I can pull her up. 'And I'm sure your mother knows, too. She'll just be happy you're OK.'

Except I don't think Casey *is* OK. And how could she be, with everything she's had thrown at her?

'I'll go back in the jeep, I guess. But I won't talk to DL. I am never going to talk to him again.'

Chapter 43: Dan

I'm on the phone to Angelica as I run towards Gemma and Casey. I can't see her face yet, but she doesn't look injured.

My daughter is safe.

'She seems all right, Angelica,' I say. 'Not hurt or anything.'

'Oh God. Oh God, thank you. Bring her back now, please, as fast as you can.'

For a moment I wonder if this awful fear we've shared could make everything OK again – with Angelica, with Casey, with Gemma. But when I'm in touching distance, Casey recoils from me. I remember that first day, at the penthouse, how wary we were of each other, and how far we've come. But now she's even further away.

'Don't worry,' I say. 'I'm not going to hug you. But I've got your mum here on the phone and she needs to talk to you.'

And my hand brushes against Casey's as she takes the handset, and I wonder if it's going to be the last time we ever touch. Angelica will make sure Casey never trusts me again as a result of my stupid lie. And Gemma? Well, she's already told me she wants nothing more to do with me.

I turn back to my daughter, whose face crumples as soon as she hears Angelica's voice.

'Oh, Mum, I'm sorry. I am so, so sorry.'

* * *

Gemma's in the front, Casey's in the back, cuddling Bear. It's a version of what I wanted – us all together again – but the tense silence in the jeep shows how short-lived it's going to be.

I turn into the underground car park, but there's a BMW in the second penthouse space. I block it in. *You're going nowhere, sunshine.*

Gemma gets out and hugs Casey. 'You've scared us all, sweetheart. Please don't do that again. Call me, OK. Any time.'

Casey stays rigid in her arms. 'I'm fine.'

'I've got to say goodbye now, but good luck tomorrow. I hope your results are the best they can be.'

Casey's mouth purses. She says nothing. But just as Gemma begins to let her go, Casey grips tighter and I can see she's struggling to say goodbye.

'We should go up. Your mum needs to see you in one piece,' I whisper.

'Is she angry?' Casey asks.

'Not with you.'

When Gemma tries to pull away again, Casey resists, her eyes brimming with tears. 'I want Gemma to come up too – she found me.'

So we step into the lift and it's a squeeze, and Bear's body goes rigid with tension as we go up, and I think, *Yeah, me too, mate.*

'Shh, Bear, it's going to be OK,' Casey says.

Gemma's eyes meet mine and there's so much sadness. When we get to the floor below the penthouse, the lift stops, and I remember Angelica changed the settings, so my key card won't let me in. I press the intercom. 'It's us. We're here.'

The lift begins to move up to the top floor. *I can do this. Be gracious, smile and let my daughter go.*

The doors open.

My fists clench without my knowing why.

I'm looking up, expecting to see Angelica, but she's not alone.

Blood roars in my ears.

Him.

Older, but still instantly recognizable, from the arrogant way he stands to the cool cruelty in his eyes.

'Gramps!' Casey cries out, pushing past me. 'Why are you here?'

'Because *you're* a drama queen, young lady.' He leans down to kiss her, oddly formal for a grandfather. 'I came to be with your mother, she's been worried sick.'

Now Casey falls into her mum's arms, but I am staring at Vaughn Parr. Although his hair and skin are twelve years greyer, his sneering expression hasn't changed.

But I have. Twelve years. *Twelve fucking years* away from my daughter. Everything would have been so different, if it hadn't been for him.

'So you're Dan,' he says, as though we've never met, and my fists itch with the desire to knock him down.

Violence is for stupid people, Dazzler. A smart guy talks his way out of a situation.

Dad only lashed out if he was cornered and had no other means of escape. But I am not my dad.

It happens so fast, but in slow motion too somehow. My right arm jerks forward, and I love the panic in Vaughn's eyes as his elbow moves up to protect that loathsome face, and my hand misses by millimetres and I grunt, and someone's pulling me back, hands on my shoulders, and although they're not strong, it's enough of a shock to stop me going for a second punch.

The fear in Vaughn's eyes has changed to triumph. I peer beyond him to see Casey staring at me, horrified.

'What the hell are you doing?' Angelica says. 'That's my dad – don't you dare attack him.'

It's Gemma guiding me backwards into the lift. 'Come on, this won't help.'

Too late, I'm understanding the damage I've just done. 'Let me explain,' I say to Casey, but there *is* no explanation that makes it OK to throw a punch at your child's grandfather.

The lift doors are closing and I know I've made it a cast-iron certainty that *this* will be the very last time I see my girl.

'What the hell was that about?' Gemma hisses as soon as the lift is moving.

My breath is ragged as the rage ebbs away. 'He's Casey's grandfather.'

'I worked that out for myself. He's the spitting image of her, and Angelica. But what did he do to deserve that?'

He really is the spitting image. Even before he's shown to my table in the visiting hall, I can tell he's Angelica's dad, from the sharp chin and the haughty posture. The other visitors grin as soon as they see their partners or dads or sons. Vaughn Parr stands apart, and everything from his clothes to his pained expression screams: This is not my world.

We sit opposite each other, in seats bolted to the floor, so they can't be used as weapons. His letter asking for a visiting order had been polite, even caring. He wanted to talk about the future and what Angelica would need from me.

I said yes because I'm so bloody lonely. Angelica has begged to visit me too, but I said no, because she'll never be able to see me the same way again if I let her come here.

I pull my shoulders back, trying to match his posture. 'It's great that you want to help us—'

331

'She's had the baby.'

I stare at him. 'It's not supposed to be for another two weeks.'

'Well, the baby had other plans. She was born the day before yesterday, and it was very dangerous, because Angelica is petite and the baby is big. But you didn't think of that when you were taking advantage, did you?'

Dangerous? Panic makes the room fill with noise. Not like my mum. Not again. 'But they're alive?'

'Yes. You have a daughter.'

The word 'daughter' makes the dingy hall fill with light. 'And they're going to be OK?'

'For now, yes. But it's the future I'm worried about. That's why I'm here.'

Vaughn Parr is as relentless as my father. He starts off talking 'man to man' about how I won't want to be burdened by a kid once I leave 'the nick' – the word sounds ridiculous coming out of his mouth.

When I disagree, he switches seamlessly into flattery. 'You're a bright young man who has taken a wrong turn. I'd like to help you with money for training, or a flat deposit? You're not like the others here.'

He's right, but not in the way he means. Unlike most of these guys, I haven't been beaten or abused. I'm not an addict, or trapped in a cycle of repeat offending. Plus, knowing I'm going to be a dad has kept me out of trouble. Even the most violent lads see fatherhood as a badge of honour, showing off snaps of their kids, giving me advice.

'You'd pay for our flat deposit? That'd be fantastic until I can get a proper job lined up. I'm planning to apply for carpentry training and—'

'No. Angelica and the baby are going to stay with us, so Angelica can resume her studies in September. This mishap shouldn't stop her going to university.'

Finally I get what this is. Bribery. I can almost hear my dad's words: The rich think they can buy people like us, Daz, like we're worth less than them. The trick is to set your price as high as you can.

'*You came here to bribe me?*'

'*Don't be histrionic. You like an easy life, don't you, Daniel Lennon? Well, parenthood is not like that. Parenthood is about self-sacrifice and putting someone else first.*'

'*I'm ready—*'

'*No, you're not. I can see through you. You're a charmer, but there's nothing underneath. My daughter could have died because of you, and she's too precious to waste her life on a con man. You're poisonous.*'

The same word my dad always used about me: You've been poison ever since you took your first breath. You killed your mum; never forget that. You're a danger to yourself and others.

Vaughn Parr sees me more clearly than anyone since my dad. And he hasn't finished.

'*I appreciate that this isn't really your fault, Dan. Or should I say, Darryl?*'

I stare at him.

'*Oh yes, I know who you are and what you came from. Your own father was a little shit, so it's inevitable you're following in his footsteps But this is your chance to break the cycle. My daughter, and her daughter, will be so much happier if you're not in their lives. So the best way you can show you're better than your dad is to let your child go, for her sake. And yours.*'

I don't even question how he knows: money can buy anything, including information. What I do know is that he's right. This is the only thing I can do to keep my baby safe.

And now Parr sees that I've given in. He stands up, touching his smooth hands together like a priest. 'Good. That's sorted then. I'd like to recognize your . . . maturity financially, so please send your bank details via my office.' He hands me a business card.

I go back to my cell, too dazed to speak to anyone. But later, in the dinner queue, I get into my first and only prison fight. As the guy's fists power into my ribs and belly and the side of my face, pain spreads like heat and I welcome it. I don't fight back.

'*Dan?* I think the least I deserve is an explanation.'

The lift has stopped: I'm back with Gemma. She's shaking her head in frustration, and when the doors open, she steps out into the lobby. 'OK, suit yourself. Nice knowing you, Dan. Except, actually, it wasn't.'

I put my hand out to stop her. 'No. Don't go. I'm so sorry you saw that – I'm a lot of bad things but I'm not violent, I swear.'

'It's not me you should be apologizing to. It's your daughter, and your ex. And the guy you almost knocked out.'

'I'll never apologize to him. He's the reason I haven't been in Casey's life. The reason for this whole bloody mess.'

Gemma shakes her head as she pushes the door open, letting the heat and the noise of the harbour in. 'You're blaming someone else for your own screw-up? Nice. Like I needed even more proof that you're not the person I thought you were.'

I can't bear the idea that she'll always think of me as violent as well as a liar and a con man. I follow her out. 'Gemma, please? I understand it's too late to change things. But you're right. I do owe you an explanation for this whole bloody mess.'

'Don't bother. It'll only be more lies.'

'Not this time.'

Chapter 44: Gemma

We find a bench overlooking the grey water, brushing away the pools of rain before sitting down.

'OK, that guy was Vaughn Parr and I've met him once before, a long time ago. Though Angelica doesn't know that.'

I remind myself: *Don't fall for it – he lies for a living.*

'He came to the prison to tell me Angelica had given birth. She'd been meant to call me as soon as possible afterwards, but Vaughn said she'd had a very rough labour because the baby was too big for her, and that was down to me. And – well, I told you my mum died having me. I felt like it was history repeating itself. That I was to blame.'

It's such a cruel thing to say that already I am seeing the man Dan hit differently. *This is how it starts, with Dan getting my sympathy*. There's no proof that Angelica's dad said anything of the sort. I have to try to stay detached. 'Go on.'

'While I was trying to process the shock of that, he told me Angelica and Casey would be better off without me. That the best thing I could do for them would be to let them go.'

I shake my head. 'Yeah, well, I think you proved him right. You're a violent con man who can't even tell the truth about his own name.'

We stay silent for a while. The sun burns through the clouds, and the air smells fresher than it has in days.

He turns back towards me. 'I was born Darryl Lennox. I changed it when I was twelve, after I went into foster care. I was already into music, identified with rebels, Sid Vicious, David Bowie, John Lennon. So I went with Dan Lennon: close enough to be easy, different enough to forget who I was.'

'Not many kids change their name.'

'Are you still a kid at twelve? I felt grown-up at the time, but now I see how young Casey seems . . .' Dan's voice cracks. 'Do you think she's going to be OK?'

'It's pretty tough finding out you've been lied to by someone you trust.'

He nods. 'I always let people down in the end.'

I'm losing patience. 'You act as if it's out of your control. You're not twelve any more. You have choices, and you could make better ones. It's not that hard.'

Bear senses my irritation and pulls on his lead to get away, almost tripping up a jogger.

'Parenting *is* that hard, though.'

'Another excuse. Angelica didn't walk away, even though she must have had doubts, too. But she stuck at it because Casey needed her.'

'Trust me, Gemma, no kid needs someone like me in their life. I'm like my dad, and I was better off without him. So Casey will be better off without me, too.'

The more he comes out with this self-pitying BS, the angrier I feel. 'You've made mistakes. We all do. But the mistakes aren't the problem. It's running away, instead of facing up to what you've done.'

'So it wouldn't have bothered you if I'd told you I'd been in prison? That I'd conned people?'

I try to answer honestly. 'It would have shocked me, yes. But I'd have listened, if you'd explained why and how it changed you – how you're different now.'

He exhales, closing his eyes as he speaks. 'Who says I'm different now? My dad was a con man, I'm a con man.'

'No, Dan. Darryl. Whoever you are. You're not predestined to behave like your dad did. We all have baggage; take me, for God's sake. A widow trying to get' – I stop before I say it – 'you know. But I muddle along and try to bounce back.'

'And you deserve happiness, Gemma. But you had good foundations. Your family is normal. But my normal was about cheating and stealing.'

'You've moved on from that. Haven't you?'

'Yes, I'm an upstanding taxpayer now. But I had to betray my own dad to get there.'

The bitterness in his voice startles me. 'What do you mean, betray him?'

He shakes his head. 'Take no notice of me. It's in the past, like you said. You should go home, Gemma, look after yourself. I don't want to hurt you any more than I already have.'

Have I stumbled on a truth that might make sense of the other lies? I'm too stubborn to give up if there's a chance of understanding what this has all been about. 'I'm going nowhere. Not till you've told me what you mean.'

'I gave evidence against him, OK? When my father went to jail, it was because I put him there.' Dan's eyes are fixed on mine, daring me to judge him.

'How? You said he was convicted of theft?'

'He was sent down for charity fraud, but he'd done so many cons, they only charged him with the biggest.'

'Sorry, I don't understand what charity fraud means.'

Dan exhales. 'He pretended I had cancer and needed private treatment in America.'

I stare at him. 'Bloody hell. Why would he do that?'

'To raise money. He said it was a victimless crime. The

337

people who did sponsored walks and raffles and the rest felt proud that they were making a difference to a sick kid. And we got to keep the money and have a nice life. Everyone's a winner.'

'But you weren't actually ill?'

'No. Though the first time my dad tried out the scam, I thought I was. It started when I kept getting dizzy, and then I fainted and they took me into the children's ward for a night, to have tests done. That's what gave my dad the idea, I think. The tests must have come back clear, but he told me they'd found something bad and I was sick and I needed specialist treatment that you couldn't get in England. So for quite a long time I really convinced myself that I was dying.'

Despite the warmth here on the quay, the shock feels like I've plunged into the icy harbour. 'Jesus, Dan! How old were you?'

'Ten, when it started. I was small for ten, and skinny, which helped.'

The matter-of-fact way he says it chills me more: there's no self-pity at all. 'How many times did your dad do this?'

'Three. He told me after the first time, when we did a runner to a different part of the country. After that, it was less scary, because even when he was telling everyone I was really sick, I knew I would be OK. Though I hated him lying to all these people who were trying to be kind. I mostly kept quiet, but sometimes . . . well, sometimes I had to lie too, because Dad said he could go to prison otherwise.'

I can't quite believe what he's telling me. Yet at the same time it makes sense, in a warped way. 'How did he get caught?'

'We were packing up to move on again when they arrested him. A journalist on the local paper got suspicious. These days you'd be rumbled straight away, with the internet, but the nineties was a golden age for con men.' Dan's voice drips with irony, and his handsome face is almost defiant.

But I don't only see him as he is now; I also see a skinny boy whose father used him as a prop. What parent would tempt fate by pretending their child was dying?

And I remember that morning we met, when he was scared to go into the hospital. Now I understand.

'That's why you hate anything medical?'

He nods, shamefaced. 'Even though I've never had anything worse than a cold. Unlike poor Casey.'

'So when she got in touch and said she was sick . . .'

'Felt like karma. That she was being punished for what me and Dad did.'

'Except you were the one who stopped your father doing it again?'

'I grassed him up. The police and the social workers talked me into it. Made me think I had no choice but to betray him.' His voice is monotone, as though he can't let himself feel the emotions behind the memories.

'Dan, listen to me. You didn't betray your father. He betrayed *you*.'

Dan scoffs. 'You don't understand. In our world, grassing someone up is the worst thing you can do.'

'Worse than scaring your son into thinking he was going to die? I can't believe someone would do that to a child. It's incomprehensible.'

How do you recover from something like that? Everything I take for granted in my family – love, nurturing, loyalty – has been twisted in Dan's. Yet despite that, he's tried hard to make amends through his work with young offenders, and the way he's tried to get to know Casey.

'I promise I'm not lying now,' Dan says softly.

'I know you're not. But your dad's actions are unforgivable.'

'He didn't have it easy. He had to raise a kid alone, one who reminded him of the wife who'd died in labour. Then if that wasn't bad enough, I switched sides. No wonder he hated me.'

I let the words settle as we both stare out at the boats bobbing in the water. 'You were his son. He should have loved you, taken care of you.'

'Maybe he did, in his own way.'

From Dan's body language, I can tell I'll get nowhere in convincing him how badly his father behaved. 'So he went to prison, and you went into foster care?'

'Yes. But I never settled. I didn't know how to behave in a normal family. Still don't. I couldn't even manage four weeks with Casey without fucking up.'

'You didn't fuck up. Casey saw an important part of the real you – someone charming and fun who wants to make people happy.'

'I think you mean a laugh-a-minute chancer who let her down.'

'For what it's worth, *I* saw someone who was trying hard to give her a little joy in the middle of a difficult time. You were what she needed. And . . .' I hesitate.

'What?'

'Maybe what I needed too. With you I had fun, for the first time in so long.'

'Sure you did. I'm good at making people like me. I'm the "dazzler" my dad raised me to be. But it doesn't last.' He stands up.

'Don't go. You can still make this work.' I stand up too, and my mud-spotted legs are unsteady, the muscles tired from racing around Ashton Court, searching for Casey. I don't have the energy to follow him. But I do still have words. 'You've got a choice here, Dan. Do you want to be your father's son, or your daughter's father?'

He doesn't turn round, but he does stop.

'Your child rings the end-of-treatment bell tomorrow, and you should be there. Prove that you're not only here for the fun stuff, but for the serious stuff too.'

He scoffs. 'She just saw me take a swing at her grandfather. After I lied to her for weeks about the penthouse. Why would she want more of that crap in her life?'

'What Casey needs is people who love her. And you do, don't you? You didn't get love yourself growing up, but it was always inside you, and you've worked so hard to show you care.'

'Caring isn't enough.'

'That's where you're wrong. You can do this – I believe in you.' I hadn't expected to say that, but it is true. When he turns to face me, I catch a glimpse of the Dan I thought I'd got to know. The Dan I was falling in love with . . .

'Why would she trust me again? Maybe she could have got over the penthouse stuff, in time. But I can't expect her to forget seeing me fly into that horrible rage.'

'She might not forget, but if you apologize and try to explain, she might be able to forgive. Because she wants her father in her life, and she deserves far more than a holiday dad, with the treats and the penthouse and the grand gestures. I've seen it myself, how she's changed these last weeks. And part of that has to be down to you.'

'Really? Angelica is the one who raised her, made her who she is.'

I think about angry, anxious Angelica and shake my head. 'Stop putting yourself down. It's infuriating. You can be vulnerable without being pathetic. Tell Casey everything and then let her decide if she wants you around.'

'Everything? Including what her grandad did when she was only a couple of days old? No. I don't want to hurt her even more.'

'OK. Maybe not that. But you have to try to find a way.'

He closes his eyes. 'Even if I could work out how to explain it, Angelica won't let me anywhere near her.'

'Hmm.' Something occurs to me. 'You said Angelica doesn't know you met her dad in prison?'

'No.'

'What if you told her the truth, exactly as you told me just now: what happened when he came to visit you, and how much you regret going along with what he wanted? If you really *do* regret it, that is.'

'I really do.' Dan turns towards the apartment building, gazing up at the penthouse, the windows blazing orange as they reflect the sun. 'And you believe I can be a better dad this time around?'

I want to believe it. I want to make everything we've been through mean something.

'The more important question is: do *you* believe you can?'

He says nothing for so long that I think he's about to say no.

'Maybe.'

'It has to be yes,' I say. 'You have to be the one who believes it, if you're going to stand any chance of persuading them to let you back into their lives.'

Chapter 45: Dan

Do I believe I can do better? The stuff Gemma said has disorientated me and brought the buzzing back, louder than ever.

'I need to get going,' she says. 'I'm knackered and I ought to be taking better care of myself.'

Shit. I've been so wrapped up in my own drama for the last few minutes that I haven't even considered what effect if might be having on her.

'When do you find out if . . .' I remember she doesn't use the word 'pregnant', so I say, 'whether the treatment has worked?'

'Saturday. They do a blood test, because it's more reliable and shows how my hormones are behaving. Last time I got a positive result, but the changes were chemical. Not real.'

'Shit, Gemma, that's terrible.'

She shrugs. 'It was a low, that's for sure.'

'How are you feeling about having the test?'

'I don't care what the result is. I just want an end to this limbo.'

I don't believe her. 'Really?'

Gemma sighs. 'The thing is . . . I haven't told my family, but I've been feeling nauseous and my skin's been extra-sensitive.'

'So it might have worked?'

'It could be stress. The last few days have been intense.'

'I'm so sorry for causing all of it.'

'I know.' Her eyes focus on mine and the hum of the harbour fades away.

I should say something else. Something to show how much she's meant to me these last weeks. I can't expect her to forgive me for lying. But I wouldn't even be thinking about trying again with Casey and Angelica if Gemma hadn't been around, showing how kindness can make everything better.

'You've changed me, Gemma,' I say.

'I haven't done anything.'

'You did it by being you. Sorry, I sound like a cheesy song, but whatever happens next, you made me think I could be good. Better than I really am.'

She smiles and I want to kiss her *so* badly, but it's the wrong time. As she stands up, I realize there will never be a right time. 'Can I drop you and Bear back home?'

'I'll walk to College Green, get a cab from there. I need some air.'

'OK. If you're sure.'

'Yeah. So, say goodbye to Bear, otherwise he won't come with me.'

I crouch down and touch his hot, hairy shoulders and let him lick my chin. I'm as messy and dishevelled as he is. 'See you around, mate.'

When I straighten up there's a moment when we could embrace, Gemma and me, but we don't take it. Like everything between us, the timing is all wrong.

It's only after she goes that I remember I've got nowhere to sleep tonight.

I consider going back to camp in Castle Park – no. Or sneaking into the car park to kip in the jeep. No, I can't

344

risk seeing Angelica until I've worked out what I have to say.

If I have anything to say.

I cross the bridge and check into the Travellers Rest. It's your standard budget hotel, but at least it's clean, which is more than can be said for me. I undress in the shower, then turn on the water, scrubbing my body and my T-shirt and pants and shorts until all the mud has washed away. Finally, I try to dry my clothes with the feeble hotel hairdryer.

I think about the stuff I told Gemma this evening: stuff I've never told anyone before.

Back when Dad was first arrested and I went into foster care, plenty of grown-ups tried to talk to me. I resisted everything my foster parents stood for: Dad and I had never done 'normal', and I wasn't about to start. But eventually the doggedness of family life wore me down. No matter how much I played up, the adults caring for me stayed calm and kind. It wasn't just me: their own children's bad moods were forgiven swiftly too, and afterwards there'd be toast and TV to make you forget the fury.

Normal was so predictable, so boring. And so *nice*.

None of it is your fault, they'd say. *It's your father who exploited people, including you.* They told me my father wasn't Robin Hood, or Del Boy, he was a con man. But I couldn't – *wouldn't* – turn against the person I hero-worshipped. I said that if they wanted to lock him up, they should lock *me* up too, because we were united: the Lennoxes against the universe.

When they recognized the strength of my loyalty, they changed tack. Persuaded me that being honest would mean a fresh start. If Dad and I cooperated, we could put the past behind us.

In the lobby of the Crown Court I recognized some of

the people we'd conned, and the shame made my mouth dry. When I walked into Court 3 to give evidence, it was the first time I'd seen my dad in a month. He wore his only suit, the one he always kept dry-cleaned in case he spied a *merry widow with a generous heart and a bank balance to match*.

As I stood in the witness box, my foster mum close by for reassurance, Dad kept mouthing stuff at me that I couldn't hear, and the judge told him off. The lawyer in the wig asked me about the first time I got ill. I explained about going to hospital, and the big pills my father made me take, and the fundraising. Dad stared at the floor as I spoke.

'So you genuinely thought you were ill, Darryl?'

I nodded. 'Yes. I was quite scared.'

'Because when the police interviewed your father, he said you like to play-act. And that you'd cooperated willingly in the fundraising efforts because he'd promised you a trip to Disneyland?'

'No. That was later. The first time . . . I thought I was dying.'

One of the ladies in the jury gasped.

'Come on, Daz,' my father called out. 'Don't lie. I've owned up to what we did, but you're making me look like the bad guy here. We're a team, remember.'

My eyes met my dad's. *I'm not lying, and you know it.*

'Mr Lennox, do not address the witness or I will have to remove you from my court.' The judge sounded impatient.

The lawyer nodded, then turned back to me. 'Darryl. You need to tell the truth here. During the first period of fundraising did you know you were, in fact, perfectly healthy?'

I shook my head, not wanting to say anything that would harm my dad.

'Please answer yes or no.'

'No.'

'So when *did* you find out?'

I spoke fast, trying to get it over with. 'After we did a runner. We left Dad's girlfriend Nadia behind without saying goodbye. She thought we were going to London to see the American doctor, but we went to the seaside instead, and my dad told me I couldn't call her or write to her, because I wasn't really ill and she could never find out. He said it had been a perfect con – no one had suffered – but that it got too big too fast. So next time we'd be smarter.'

'How did you react when you knew you were well?'

'I was glad I wasn't dying and didn't need horrible treatments. But I felt bad about Nadia.' I spewed it all out, as this new fury took hold of me. 'And when we did it again, I hated having my head shaved and being paraded in front of people. And not being allowed to eat before events, so I'd look pale. I got so hungry I fainted once—'

'You liar! They've put words in your mouth.'

'Mr Lennox, final warning,' the judge said.

But Dad was too angry to stop. 'What have they promised you, Darryl? Whatever it is, once this is over, I'll give you double. Just stop telling lies.'

'Court adjourned while we remove the defendant.'

And as the guards manhandled my dad out, I knew I had to explain. 'We have to tell them the truth so we can start again, Dad. You might not go to prison if you do the same—'

My father stared at me like he'd look at a 'mark'. 'You're a fucking grass.'

'No, Dad, I'm helping us.'

'You've picked your side, Judas. You've been poison ever since you took your first breath: first your mum, now me. This is the last fucking time you'll ever see me.'

He was true to his word. For once. After he'd been taken

out, and the jury and judge left the courtroom, the space filled with the chatter of the lawyers and journalists left behind.

But above that chatter, suddenly I remember a high-pitched hum. Bloody hell! For years I've thought the tinnitus started after I went to a gig. Now I know it goes way, way back.

The hotel room's silence takes me by surprise: the dryer has overheated. I drop it, so it hangs like the tentacle of a beige octopus, and I lie down on the navy bedspread.

This is the first time in years I've allowed myself to think about that day. My social worker tried to get me to talk about what happened in court, but I couldn't bear the shame. I was a bad kid. No wonder I was alone. My foster parents were kind, but they weren't my flesh and blood.

I shake off the memory. This isn't about me. It's about another kid, on the other side of the harbour, whose heart is breaking right now.

What am I going to say to Casey if I'm allowed to see her? I dig deep to think about the right words. *None of it is your fault. It's your choice whether to let me in again. Whatever happens next, you have to remember that you're twelve years old and I'm the adult, your father, and I have a history of letting people down. You must never, ever blame yourself.*

Something shifts as I form the words in my head.

At twelve, *I* thought I knew it all. Except actually I knew nothing. I was less mature than Casey is now. *But every bit as scared.*

That's bullshit. How can I compare my situation to hers? She's facing her own mortality and I was facing . . .

Being alone. Casey has always had her mum, but I knew that the bond with my dad wasn't strong, that I could never count on my father.

If Casey is not to blame for her illness, couldn't the same apply to the boy who was Darryl Lennox? And if that's true, was any of the early stuff my fault: Mum dying, Dad being broke, then ending up in prison? He could have made different choices, but I had no choices at all.

Finally I get it. Gemma was right. I am not responsible for what happened when I was a kid. I never bloody have been.

Tears run down my cheeks. Now I can see the truth. It's like my whole world has been turned upside down.

It was my father who betrayed me, not the other way round.

Chapter 46: Gemma

The fresh air doesn't help clear my head, and all the cab drivers refuse to take Bear because he's muddy, so I have to walk the whole way home. The humidity is back already, so I get back to the flat a sweaty, dirty mess.

I am so cross: at cabbies, at the world, and especially at the shitty fathers who pass their misery on to the next generation.

What I really need is a *drink*.

The more I tell myself it's too risky, the more I crave one: a fridge-fresh glass of Sauvignon Blanc or Andrew's favourite Viognier, or the slightly fizzy Portuguese one I can never pronounce. Any one of them would take the edge off just enough to make me care less about all this crap.

Would one glass make any difference to Saturday's result? Logic tells me it wouldn't. But . . . I would never know for certain, and staying away from booze is the grown-up thing to do.

I walk to the fridge and the blast of cool air when I open the door is so delicious I could stand there for an hour.

Instead I peer into the polar-white interior and try to spot something to eat that might be *almost* as desirable as a glass of wine. There's some strong Cheddar in the drawer – can't even remember buying it, but it might be nice with some crackers and red-onion marmalade.

And a glass of red Bordeaux.

I take out the cheese. Not quite past its use-by date, but it's yellower than I'd like, slightly cracked, like dry heels.

I put the image out of my mind and cut it into near-identical slivers. Line them up on a plate. I'm usually a slapdash cook, but doing this might use up ten minutes of the hundreds that still lie ahead before my test.

The crackers in the cupboard are an artisan brand, one Andrew championed when it was a mother and daughter baking in their little Somerset kitchen. I haven't bought any since, so the pack must date back to before he died.

How? How can they still be here when he isn't? It makes no sense.

In the early days I used to go round the flat, picking up items that belonged to him – his hairbrush, his wallet, his sunglasses – unable to grasp that they existed when he no longer did. But I haven't ever felt that way about a box of bloody biscuits.

Am I going backwards?

The best-before date was six months ago, but no one ever died from stale crackers, so I rip open the cellophane and stack half a dozen next to the cheese.

At least the jar of onion marmalade is brand-new, with no spurious sentimental value.

But the lid won't budge. I wrap the tea towel around the top and twist until my palm hurts. I grunt, hoping that might give me an extra burst of Neanderthal strength, but it still doesn't bloody budge.

My hand moves before my brain registers what I'm doing.

The jar seems to fall in slow motion towards the centre of the kitchen floor, and I think it's not going to break at all.

Until it explodes everywhere.

Shards of glass shatter and the lid tinkles on the wood. Dollops of vinegary jam spread like long brown worms.

'Fuck YOU!'

I grab the pack of biscuits and tip the crackers onto the floor. Stamp up and down on the ones that have landed away from the glass.

'Why did you have to leave me, you bastard?'

STAMP!

'Why couldn't you have listened to me and gone to see a fucking doctor?'

Now I see Dan in my head. *STAMP!*

'Why couldn't you have got your shit together by now? I love you, you arsehole – you could have been the second love of my sodding life!'

I look up and see Bear cowering in the hallway. He must have heard and come to investigate. He's shaking.

'Good boy,' I say, trying to hide the tremble in my voice. 'Stay back, Bear. Everything's all right. Everything is fine.'

I wonder if not understanding the words means he can hear the lie more clearly.

He licks his nose and stares up at me, those brown eyes full of uncertainty. *What was that about?*

I wish I knew, Bear.

The floor is a horrible sticky mess. It'll stain the wood if I leave it, so I should get cracking, remove the glass, wipe up the marmalade, mop it all clean again.

But instead I step away, close the kitchen door to shut in the debris and lift my squirming dog into my arms. He usually fights, but instead Bear licks my nose, as though it's the best way he can think of to make me – and him – feel better.

And I start to cry. Rage? Loneliness? Hormones?

It doesn't matter. The tears know why they're here. I simply have to let them fall.

*　*　*

When I'm cried out and my body's stopped throbbing, I sit on my balcony and watch the early evening life: families picnicking on wet grass, groups of teenagers flirting and drinking and smoking illicit cigarettes.

Bear lies at my feet, snoring. As far as he's concerned, the crisis has passed.

I take my phone, check for messages. There's one from Isabel, the first since we argued a fortnight ago:

Dear Gemma, I wanted to check how you are. I'm here, if you want to talk.

Without weighing up the pros and cons, I call her number.

'Do you ever get angry, Isabel?'

She says nothing for a few seconds. 'Oh yes.'

'With Andrew, or with your husband?'

'Both. But especially my husband. Sometimes it was only the anger that got me up in the morning. The stroke wasn't his fault. But that didn't stop me hating him for leaving.' I hear her sigh. 'I'd forgotten about that. Grief makes no sense, so much of the time.'

I nod to myself. 'I'm sorry I got angry with you, Isabel. It wasn't even with you, exactly.'

'I knew that. And I'm sorry for being all over you and the treatment one minute, and appearing not to care the next. I was living *through* you for a good while, but now . . .' She tails off.

And I think I know what she's going to say. 'Have you met somebody?'

A laugh, almost a girlish giggle. 'Um. Yes. Actually. I joined a book group and he's the only male reader. Much sought after. We connected instantly over *Wuthering Heights*. It was quite a surprise.'

I understand how that feels.

'Wow, Isabel. That's wonderful.'

She giggles again. 'It is rather wonderful, yes. I keep remembering what Andrew said at your wedding, about the puzzle of love. And Robert has completed the jigsaw, for now at least. Sorry. Was it OK to mention Andrew?'

'Of course. He'd have been thrilled for you.'

'Yes, I rather think he would. May I ask you about the transfer? Do you know yet if it's worked?'

'On Saturday.'

'I hope you get the result you want.'

I don't even know what that is. 'I'll call you.'

I'm about to ring off when she asks, 'Have you found it yet?'

This again: she's like a dog with a bone. 'The puzzle? No. I'm sure it'll turn up one of these days.'

'I know you're dubious, Gemma, but he was *very* lucid when he mentioned it. And excited. Almost boyish again, you know. Like he always was when he'd thought of something clever.' Her voice sounds so tender, as she remembers him.

'Perhaps he really did believe he'd left something. At the end he found it hard to tell what was real, didn't he?'

Afterwards I search the flat half-heartedly, knowing that I would have found something by now. But I cherish the idea of him *wanting* to leave me a final surprise.

I'm not furious with Andrew any more. The opposite. I think about Isabel's news and imagine him meeting his mother's new boyfriend. A bookish man sounds perfect, and Andrew would have made him comfortable.

What would my husband have made of Dan? Before I understood his past, I was sure Andrew would have been suspicious of such easy charm. But my husband was a sucker for a story, for battles and cliff-hangers, followed by redemption.

I'm so sick of battles and cliff-hangers. Right now there is nothing I can do but wait.

I realize I'm hungry, and I can't face cleaning up the kitchen yet. So I order a pizza with *all the cheeses*.

Chapter 47: Dan

Friday 27 July

My head's too noisy for sleep. Today I need to be the most persuasive I've ever been, to reach past the obstacles that are stopping me getting what I want.

It's like being in a computer game where Level 1 is Angelica: I need to get past her defences so I can explain why I lashed out at her father, and how much I regret listening to him thirteen years ago. More than that, I have to convince her I want to be different now. If I get through that . . .

Level Two would be talking to Casey. Asking her to give me another chance at being her dad, and proving I can change.

And if that works, Level Three would be going back to Gemma, to thank her and ask her—

Mustn't get ahead of myself.

At 6 a.m. I message Angelica, asking if she'll meet me. She must be awake too, because she texts back immediately:

Give me one good reason why I should.

I reply:

I need to tell you what happened when I met your dad thirteen years ago.

She doesn't reply for a couple of minutes. Then:

Outside, 6:30. You've got 5 minutes. No more.

My clothes are still damp, and there's a crispness in the air when I walk along the deserted Harbourside. I'm early and I sit on the quay, my legs dangling over the side. I breathe in the tang of moss and fuel.

'Your five minutes start now.'

When I turn, she's silhouetted against the early light, and her uneven walk on the cobbles reminds me of the very first moment I saw her.

'I don't know why I'm even giving you that long,' she says, 'after that unprovoked attack on my dad.'

I scramble to my feet, almost slipping. She doesn't help. 'That's what he said, was it? That it was unprovoked?'

When she steps forward, the sun falls in her weary eyes. I think I see a flicker of doubt. 'You're down to four minutes now,' she says.

'Your dad and I have met before. Two days after you gave birth he came to visit me in prison.'

The doubt turns to disbelief. 'No, he didn't. He and Mum were there at the hospital, with me – unlike you. Do you ever stop lying or is it some kind of . . . sickness?'

'He *was* there. He came to tell me you'd had Casey. That you'd nearly died and Casey had too.'

'Now I know you're talking shit. I *did* feel like I'd been run over by a double-decker bus, but I was never in real danger.'

So Vaughn did exaggerate. Which must mean he'd found out what happened to my mum, and used that against me? That's more than cruel. It's *evil*.

'Well, that's not how your dad explained it. He sat in the visiting hall and said it had been touch and go. Which was terrifying, because you know that my mum *did* die giving birth to me.'

'I'm sorry you lost your mum. But you never mentioned this visit before. It's your word against his, and you are the expert at telling lies to get yourself out of trouble.'

'Ask him if he visited. If he exaggerated how poorly you were. Ask him if he remembers telling me I wasn't fit to be a father. That I'd do the same thing to Casey that my dad did to me.'

'I'm not going to ask him any of this. Even if he did show up and say those things, he was right, wasn't he? Especially if all it took was a quick suggestion from a total stranger to convince you to ditch me and Casey.'

I close my eyes. Until yesterday I thought the same: that I was 100 per cent to blame. But talking to Gemma has made me see it's not that simple.

'I was lost, Angelica. I've only just admitted that to myself, never mind anyone else. Stuff that happened when I was a kid made me think I was bad to the bone. Didn't deserve love and could only ever hurt the people I got close to. And I think your dad saw that and used it against me.'

'Spare me the psychobabble, Dan. My dad isn't exactly perfect, but I don't go on about it, do I? And you had a choice, whereas I didn't have the luxury of changing my mind about being a parent.'

'No. And you've done an amazing job, but—'

My dad isn't exactly perfect.

And that's when I get it. Why we found each other on a crowded, sodden festival site. It's made no sense to me for thirteen years, but now it totally does.

It's because her dad and my dad are the same.

OK, they didn't *seem* the same, outwardly. One is rich, entitled, a pillar of society. The other is – *was*, for all I know

358

– broke, with a giant chip on his shoulder, and contempt for anyone who tries to live an honest life.

But at heart, Pete Lennox and Vaughn Parr are both controlling bullies, imposing their dodgy values onto their kids. And they've taken too much – not only from Angelica and me, but from Casey too.

It has to end now.

'Angelica, I can't undo my mistakes. I regret all the years I've not been there. But your dad played us both. He even offered to pay me off, to stop me being involved in his granddaughter's life. What kind of person does that?'

Angelica stares at me. 'You took money from him?'

She still automatically believes the worst of me. I can't blame her. Until Gemma came into my life, I always thought the worst of me too.

'No. But he offered it. A bribe to stay out of your lives. When that didn't work, he told me I was poisonous – and because my own dad had been telling me that, in different ways, all the time I was growing up, I believed him. But I don't believe it now. I'm not perfect. But I want to be in Casey's life and prove to both of you that I deserve to be there.'

Angelica turns away, shaking her head. 'This is crazy.' But there's doubt in her voice and I *know* she can imagine her father doing that.

'There must be a record of visitors to prison I could ask for, or . . .' I remember something else. 'He gave me his business card. If I could find it, when I'm home, would you believe me then?'

Her eyes close, as though she's replaying the years and possibilities we've lost because of our bullying fathers.

'I don't know what to think or . . .' she says, but seems to have no idea how she's going to finish the sentence. She stares up at the penthouse, and I follow her gaze. Vaughn leans

359

against the railings in a T-shirt and pyjama bottoms, surveying the harbour like he owns it all.

I see the moment when Angelica decides I am telling the truth: her lips make a straight, hard line and she shakes her head.

'If this is true, what will it do to Casey?' she's saying. 'He's been there her whole life. He's not been great, but he's a better grandfather than he was a dad.'

She thinks I want Casey to know what Vaughn did. And yes, a big part of me does want to make her hate him. But I won't stoop to his level.

Because Casey is proof that Vaughn's bullying won't win: she's her own person. Smart. Brave. Independent. More grown-up than Angelica or I have been these last few weeks. But we're changing too. This has been the most adult conversation I've ever had with Angelica.

'I take responsibility for my bad choices,' I say. 'And I don't want to come between Casey and your dad. What matters is the future. The only thing I do want is for Vaughn to know that *you* understand what he did.'

'I think he already does,' Angelica says. We both gaze upwards and Vaughn's staring down at us, his mouth open.

I let myself feel triumphant when he scuttles back inside. Angelica steps away.

'What do you want to do now?' she asks, and I know I've passed the first level, that somehow I haven't screwed up the first of the three most important conversations of my life.

'Talk to Casey.'

'She might not want to talk to you.'

'I understand that. But, with your backing, I really, really want to try.'

360

Chapter 48: Casey

'Morning, Casey, my love. Can't believe today's your last day. How are you feeling?' Fern turns away from her screen to give me a hug.

'OK. Nervous.' It's not a lie, but not the whole truth, either. However much I've resented coming here day after day, the idea of *not* coming again scares me. Because what comes next?

Fern smiles at me. 'Ah, that's understandable. But the sooner you get in there, the sooner you can ring that bell!'

The idea of ringing it without Dad makes me feel empty. I *should* hate him for the lies and for the way he went for my poor grandad, for no reason. It'd be so much easier if I did.

I push open the doors, climb up and shuffle myself into position on the bed and pull the mask onto my face: it's almost like it's a part of me now. I've even decorated it to look a bit like Bear, after the play therapist said it'd make me feel better. And she was right. Every time I put it on, I think of his funny barks and his wagging tail.

My iPad is packed in the boot of Grandad's car, so there's no distracting music today and the noise of the giant gantry moving almost does my head in. I close my eyes, to shut it out . . .

Fern's voice comes through the speaker. 'All finished, Casey, my love. Well done!'

I glance back at the room before I leave it. Whatever happens, I'll never be back here. This has either worked or it hasn't: there will be no second round with the proton beam.

Mum's waiting in the changing room and gives me a hug. 'You're so amazing,' she says. 'I'll never understand how someone like me ever created someone as strong as you.'

Not just you, I want to say, *Dad too*.

'Listen, Casey, before we go to wait for the consultant and the bell, I need to talk to you about something.'

She has her serious face on, and I don't want to hear it. Have the doctors already warned her that Bob has grown?

Or is it Grandad? He wasn't there at breakfast, and Mum said he'd gone for a mooch around the harbour, but he *never* does that, he's all about being productive and focused.

'I don't want bad news. I can't handle bad news today,' I say. 'Can you brush my hair for me, Mum? So I look right in the photos?'

She looks surprised, but we sit next to each other on the changing bench, and she uses the soft brush to tease the waves at the back of my head. She's always been gentle, never pulling. It's the first time she's done it in so long; recently, I've not really had enough hair to brush through.

'Are you going to keep the pink?' she asks, like it's a possibility.

'I doubt Cheryl at Village Snips could do them like this.'

'Well, we could go to a funkier salon in Cheltenham or Worcester. An organic one, obviously. You could even go on your own, on the bus.'

I turn to face her. 'For real?'

'You're going to be a teenager soon. I swear you've grown up by about a year in a single month.'

'They won't let me have pink hair when I go back to school.'

'You'd get away with it, after what you've had to go

362

through. I could send a note, say the pink is a side effect of the proton beams.' Mum giggles.

I laugh too. 'I'm hoping no one at my new school will know about Bob. I don't want to be tumour girl. I want to be normal.'

I hadn't realized I felt that way till I said it out loud.

Mum narrows her eyes. 'So . . . about normal. I need to talk to you about something. Some*one*. Your father. And it's not bad news, by the way. Or good. It's whatever you want it to be.'

'You're not making sense, Mum.'

'Dan came to see me, first thing this morning.'

'When I was asleep?' Knowing I missed him makes my stomach clench like someone's punched me.

'He didn't come inside, but we talked and . . . It's your decision, Casey, but he wants to talk to you too.'

'What about?' The sharp pain in my belly has turned into a sick feeling, because I don't think I can survive being disappointed by him again.

'The future. And the past, too – why he lied about the flat and other stuff.'

'Won't he keep lying, though?'

She puts the brush down. 'I've been quite hard on him this month. You thought that, didn't you?'

I shrug. She's my mum and I am loyal to her first. 'He deserved it.'

'I think he's learned his lesson. He's waiting downstairs, in the lobby, if you want to see him. But it's down to you.'

'He's here now?'

Everything tingles, like I've dived into a swimming pool full of sherbet. I don't even think about it. I rush out of the changing room, along the corridors and down the stairs, and I can hear Mum's sandals slapping on the floor behind me;

and I'm in reception and there he is, under the sculpture, and I can't help myself: I run towards my dad because whatever he's done, he's the only dad I've got, and I was so scared I might never see him again.

But deep down, I think I knew he couldn't – wouldn't – let me down.

He lifts me up like I'm five years old.

'Casey, I'm so, so sorry. If you can forgive me, I will never lie to you ever again. You can ask me anything, and I promise to be honest.'

When he lets me go, I try to look stern. 'OK. Why did you pretend you lived in the penthouse? And what were you going to do after Vijay moved back in?'

His forehead crinkles and he already looks like he's about to make something up. 'Well, the thing is . . .'

'You literally promised not to lie, thirty seconds ago.'

He pulls a face. 'OK. I *honestly* thought you'd be fed up with me long before the four weeks were up. Plus, I wanted to give you all the things you'd missed out on over the years. Including the fancy city pad you thought was mine when you found me online.'

'You're saying you thought I was totally shallow?'

'My mistake. One of thousands of mistakes. But if you give me another chance, I'll make up for them. I don't want to be your movie dad. I want to be the real thing. I want to embarrass you with my clothes and music. I want to protect you from bad hairdressers and bad boyfriends like Harrison.'

'Harrison is just a friend.'

'Good. You're even smarter than I gave you credit for. I will do whatever it takes. Move closer to you, whatever you and your mum want. So we can be a real, flawed, messed-up family. Like you wanted.'

Mum tuts. 'You told him you wanted a messed-up family?'

'Yeah. They're much cooler than boring ones.'

My mum checks the clock. 'We're going to miss your appointment. Do you want your dad there, Casey? Forget what we'd prefer. This is about your future.'

It feels so simple. I reach out to both of them and, as Mum takes one hand and Dad takes the other, we walk towards the lifts. When we step inside and I see us reflected in the mirrored metal, I laugh.

'Mum, I look like Violet.'

Violet was the heroine of my favourite picture book when I was very small. In *Rainy Days and Rainbow Days*, Violet hated the rain and refused to go out in it. She had blonde hair, like mine used to be, so I identified with her *totally*. That stuff matters when you're a kid.

After days of wet weather, Violet's parents buy her red wellies and a bright-blue mackintosh. The best part comes in the park, at the end, where there's this puddle that she's got no chance of jumping over. You *expect* Violet will get soaked and hate the rain even more.

But the pictures show her *flying* across the water. At the last moment Violet's mum and dad lift their arms, still holding Violet's hands, so she soars over the puddle.

Today I get to be Violet. My parents can't protect me from what the consultant has to say, but despite that, I understand how Violet felt as she took on the puddle, knowing that even if she fell into the water, there'd be hugs and towels and a warm bath to make things better once they got home.

The door to the consulting room is open.

I look at my parents and, because the doorway is too narrow, I let go of their hands and walk in first.

Dr de Silva sits on the edge of his desk. He is smiling.

* * *

It's over.

For now.

Bob has shrunk by more than they hoped and, with luck, he'll carry on shrinking. There will still be scans and checks to keep an eye on him, and on any side effects from my treatment.

A voice in my head says, *You've been here before and it still came back*. I shut the thought out. Right now I've cleared the puddle and the sun is coming out.

I hug my mum. Then my dad. The nurse hugs me. The doctor hugs me. When we leave the room, my grandad is back and he hugs me as well, though he doesn't look at Mum or Dad. Fern comes from nowhere and she hugs me too. I am all hugged out, and now it's time to ring the bell.

It's brass and shiny, hanging on the wall, and I try not to think of the previous time, after normal radiotherapy in Birmingham, when I thought it was over for good. I stand next to it, as the people from my care team gather round.

There is one person missing, though. One person and a dog.

My eyes smart. *Don't cry*. This is the big moment for all of us.

'Gemma couldn't come?' I whisper to Dad.

'She didn't want to be in the way.' His voice catches on the last couple of words, which doesn't help my efforts not to cry. 'But I could call her, so you can say goodbye before you leave Bristol?'

I nod. Suddenly I want to get the ringing over with. Fern records on her phone as I grip the piece of rope underneath the bell. 'I'll never forget you guys, or the hospital, or Bristol. You've been mega. No, you've been *ultra*!'

I pull the cord towards me and the metal clapper rings against the side, and my fingers and ears vibrate at the same pitch.

The second time it's even louder and seems to last for ever. But now applause drowns it out, and I clap too, back at the people who helped me get to today. And Fern is crying and even Dr de Silva's eyes are bigger than usual.

The tears are falling down my cheeks too, and it feels like a relief to let out a month's worth of fear and hope.

Casey Parr is back and this time she will be *unstoppable*.

Chapter 49: Gemma

When my mobile rings, it's Dan, and I ignore the way my heart leaps when I hear his voice. 'Casey wants to say goodbye. But you'll have to hurry – she's about to leave Bristol.'

I bustle Bear into the Mini and break the speed limit driving towards the unit. *I don't want to miss her. Miss* them.

But when Bear and I race into the quad – ignoring the *NO DOGS* signs – Casey is nowhere to be seen. I'm too late. As I sink onto a bench, I hear children's voices: a gaggle of kids are emerging from the path leading to the university pool.

It's less than four weeks since another group stopped me and Dan in our tracks. In that time I've felt sexy and desirable again. Learned from Casey that there are other ways to have children in my life, if tomorrow's test comes back negative.

And, of course, I've fallen in and out of love.

Bear barks, but I can't see anybody. 'Shh, you're not even meant to be in the grounds.'

But as the last straggler of the crocodile comes out, Bear's pulling like crazy. And there, behind the school group, are Casey and Dan, walking hand in hand.

What about the tumour? I'm close enough now to Dan and Casey to see the same fierce happiness in their violet-grey eyes, and to see they've been crying.

Now I'm crying too.

'Bob's shrunk!' Casey calls out, and my tears blur everything. Bear jumps and she catches him in her arms. I remember how she pulled away from him the first time we met. What a month it's been for all of us . . .

'So you've been discharged?' I don't say *cured* because we both know it's never that simple.

'From the hospital down here, yes. I rang the end-of-treatment bell and everything. Fern is going to send me the video of it, so I can WhatsApp it to you . . .' Casey stops. 'I wish you'd been there.'

I smile. 'Me too. But what matters is that the treatment has done what your consultant wanted it to, right?'

Casey puts Bear down on the pavement, holding onto the lead as he sniffs the weeds growing around the legs of a bench. 'I guess.'

'You're leaving now?'

'Yeah. Mum wants to miss the Friday afternoon traffic.'

'How are you feeling about going home?'

'I won't miss the hospital, but I will miss Bristol. And you. If I come back,' she glances up at Dan, 'can I come and see you and Bear, too?'

'I'd love that.'

'Plus, Dad wants to show me his flat. His *real* flat. He's promised to always tell the truth, but . . .' Casey frowns. 'Have *you* forgiven him, Gemma? Because if *you* believe he won't let us down again, that's enough for me.'

I can hear in her voice how much she needs it to be true. 'I think your father is a decent person who made some bad choices, after even worse things happened to him. And I believe he'll keep his promises this time.'

Dan's face softens. 'Thank you.'

I have to force myself to turn back to Casey.

Casey smiles mischievously. 'Are you and Dad going to stay friends?' She puts air quotes around 'friends'.

I say nothing. Dan is squirming too.

Her mobile rings. 'On my way back now, Mum. Don't panic!' After Casey ends the call, she throws her arms around me. 'You and Bear are the *best*. I love you both so much. And I'll be back before you can say *cheese and mushroom croissants to go*.'

She gives me a kiss before half walking, half skipping along the path back to the main road.

Dan gestures towards her and says, 'This is all down to you, Gemma. I called Angelica first thing. Met her. Told her what happened with Vaughn, but also we talked to each other like adults for the first time. So thank you.'

'Don't be silly. I'm sure you'd have worked out a better way of communicating with her on your own.'

He shakes his head. 'I don't think that's true. I was too stuck in that headspace where I blamed myself for everything going tits up, but still felt like a victim. You made me see what I have to do to live in the present and—'

Casey calls out, 'Come on, Dad!' and he shrugs apologetically, then jogs across the grass to catch her up.

Bear pulls, wanting to walk with them, but it's time to let them go.

'Good boy, Teddy Bear,' I say when he stops pulling. I'm so tired I could lie down on the grass and fall asleep. He watches until they both disappear, then shakes himself off and begins to lead me back to the car to go home.

I have to park a couple of streets away, and I buy myself a bunch of sunflowers to cheer myself up. I'm ecstatic for Casey, but I can't help remembering appointments with Andrew that didn't end so well.

I ought to focus on the future, but there's nothing to focus on for twenty more hours. Back home, I'm cutting the stems and my phone rings: *Dan*. I answer without hesitating, hoping . . . What am I even hoping for?

'Hey,' I say.

'Hey, again,' he says.

'Did Casey get on the road OK?'

'Yes. We all got a bit tearful, but Angelica is going to let her come back down next month.'

I hear him breathing and it's so nice, knowing he's there.

'Listen, Gemma, I've been thinking about you. About tomorrow. Are you going to the clinic on your own?'

'Yes, it's only a blood test.' I always go alone, so I can process the result without Mum or Dad or my sister watching me for my reaction.

'So this might be a crap idea, but do you fancy coming to my place afterwards? I've been letting it out on Airbnb, but I have to get the keys back in the morning and it'll give me a deadline to get it cleaned up again.'

I know his suggestion has nothing to do with deadlines or housework. He's offering me a glimpse of who he is, and I want to take it. But when I get my result, I might want to go home and sob.

People say they want a simple life. But the simplest life is one where you cut yourself off from others. And that is not the life I want any more.

'Can I let you know, afterwards?'

He's silent for a moment, maybe weighing up what I mean.

'Dan, I *like* you. A lot.'

'Despite everything?'

I think about it. 'Maybe *because* of everything. But I've no idea how the test result will affect me. I need you to be patient with me, if you can.'

371

As I wait for his response, I hold my breath.

'I've never been much good at patience, Gemma. But perhaps it's another thing I've got to practise.'

'It's a life skill,' I say. 'I promise I'll call you afterwards. I can't say how soon, but it will be tomorrow.'

Tomorrow.

After the call ends, I sit and I watch Bear asleep on the sofa, the rise and fall of that sturdy ribcage, the twitch of black whiskers and the air-trotting of his front paws. He has the simplest life: sleeping and dreaming and waking and peeing and eating and pooing and playing and sleeping again.

But that's not all he does. Bear inhabits every emotion completely: worry, joy, fear, loss, love. I wish I could live in the moment, like him. But humans are cursed and blessed by knowing there's such a thing as the future.

Do I want Dan in mine?

I pick up *The Amazing Book of Us* and turn to the last page, to the illustration I did of Andrew and me peering up at an inky sky, the planets above bright in silver and gold paint – my most honest response to the last words he ever wrote.

Words I only ever dare to read when I won't be disturbed, because they're almost unbearably poignant.

Until I got ill, I didn't think much about time. Thirty-two won't sound young to you right now, but I hadn't done many of the things I dreamed of: trekking in a forest, watching tennis at Wimbledon, learning Italian and, most of all, growing old with Mummy while we watched our children grow up. But I will never regret the time I wasted driving a tractor with Dad or perfecting my javelin throw, even though I've never done either since. Mummy doesn't regret dyeing her hair violet or learning to sail, even though it made her seasick. The only things I'd ever change would be the days I sulked because someone beat my javelin record, or I stayed inside instead of helping Dad, because I said it was too wet to plough. The planet never stops turning, but we only have a short time here. So use every minute to enjoy all the wonders this world has to offer, from trips to the zoo to surfing the waves when it's icy; from quiet hugs with Mum to trying the zany ideas you have last thing at night, even if they seem bonkers by morning.

Let's end *The Amazing Book of Us* with my final (DADDY SAYS:)
I want you to be so happy you only think of me occasionally. On bad days, never forget that this too shall pass and there's always sunshine after rain. Go bravely and boldly — and always try to have a dog at your side.
Andrew/Daddy

But despite how emotional I'm feeling, I get to the end of the page without the tears coming. Instead, it strikes me for the first time how a child might not grasp what Andrew means until they grow up. What if he didn't only write this page for the children who might never exist? What if it's really written for me?

I laugh. Because it's a mad idea. But also because I suddenly understand that *The Amazing Book of Us* is *meant* to be two books in one: a message to the family he dreamed of, but also a love letter to our short life together. And now I'm flummoxed by how it could have taken me this long to realize.

I turn back to page one and reread it all. It still works as a storybook, yes. But even if I discover tomorrow that we're never going to be parents, it works as a celebration of Amazing Us.

My clever, clever husband.

Of course there are a few clumsy phrases. No wonder: he worked so hard to finish it, even when he was very sick. He typed and edited, often falling asleep over the keyboard. Each evening he'd read the latest part out loud. I never mentioned the odd awkward sentence, because I didn't want him to know I'd noticed the mental deterioration he was trying to hide.

And when he copied it with a fountain pen onto 225gsm cartridge paper, I also pretended not to have seen how randomly he spaced the words on the page.

Nothing is random.

I leaf backwards and forwards and spot something weird. The clumsy words are always at the very beginning of a line . . .

Could he have done it on purpose? I grab a notebook and jot down the words, feeling foolish, but too curious to stop:

This

Of

Me

You

Game
With
Happened
Excited
Not
OK, I was wrong. That makes no sense.
Until I run my eyes down the first letters of each word on the page: **TOMYGWHEN**
To my G. When . . .

It's the puzzle. The last puzzle Andrew told his mother he'd hidden for me to find. It has been here the whole time.

My eyes smart from staring at the page, but I keep going, writing down the first letter of each line:

TOMYGWHENYOUDECIPHERMYLASTRIDDLEIT
MEANSTHATITSTIMEFORYOUTOMOVEON
LIFEISTOOSHORTTOBELONELYYOUDESERVE
LOVEYOURFOREVERPUZZLING

The words appear as though he's writing the message in front of my eyes. I daren't take a breath.

To my G, when you decipher my last riddle, it means that it's time for you to move on. Life is too short to be lonely. You deserve love. Your forever-puzzling
Andrew

Oh God, I *am* crying now as I imagine him creating the puzzle, secretly, and smiling to himself as he pictured me deciphering it, on a day like today.
The new understanding breaks my heart *and* makes it soar.

Andrew's right. It *is* time to be free. To look forward. *Nothing is random.*

I put the book down and lie down next to Bear, shaping my body into a C around his back. I breathe along with him – one breath for every two of his, because his life runs much faster. He stretches his legs without opening his eyes and sighs his way closer to me.

Whatever the result tomorrow: **Life is too short to be lonely. You deserve love.**

Chapter 50: Dan

Saturday 28 July

The knock wakes me. 'Room service!'

The door opens and I blink. *Not a hotel* and not room service. Vijay looms over me, gangly but kind of heroic. My best mate.

'What time is it?'

'Caffeination time!' He sits on the bed and passes me an espresso. 'Also, eight a.m.'

In less than two hours, Gemma should know.

I check my phone: nothing from her, but there is a message from my Airbnb guests telling me they've checked out and are on the way to Temple Meads for the train ride home.

I stretch out, surprised by how rested I feel. 'Didn't think I'd sleep at all.' When I lay down on the sofa bed – the one Angelica has been sleeping on for the last month – my ears hummed and my brain did too. I told Vijay I was worried that my flat had been trashed.

But really I was worrying about Gemma.

'You look fresh as a baby. Or a daisy. Or both.'

'I'm scared, Veej.'

He nods. 'At least you know your beloved trainers are safe. Except for the pair your ex trashed.'

We packed up my collection last night: my most expensive

pair were sodden, full of something vinegary. A month ago I'd have been angry, but once we worked out what it was – organic kombucha, a very Angelica-specific revenge – I laughed my head off. I was just grateful she'd only ruined one pair.

'That's not what I'm scared about.'

'Yeah, I get you. It's the price of caring.'

Forty minutes later the city's already baking hot when I drive out of the underground car park, two cases on the back seat, plus my airtight box of trainers. As I leave the centre, the buildings get tattier and the cafes greasier, but they're as familiar as old friends. This is *my* manor, where I don't need to pretend.

A lorry ahead of me spews out exhaust fumes. Do they even allow lorries in Clifton? Yeah, if they run on recycled extra-virgin olive oil. Gemma lives in the fanciest part of Bristol, while I definitely don't. It's not only where we live that makes us so different: it's our backgrounds, our work, our history – but that's irrelevant. We have a connection, even though we've tried so bloody hard to ignore it. I don't know why I love her, but I know that I do. And if she comes to see me, I am going to tell her so.

I steer the jeep left, and there's my block, in unlovely 1980s brick. The window to my flat is open: to disguise a month's worth of skunk-smoking or to disperse evidence of a fire? I reverse the jeep into my parking space and let myself into the communal hallway: tidier than usual, if anything.

I'm used to seeing this place critically, through my father's eyes: *is this the best you can do?* It's time to leave his twisted world view behind. What I care about now is how this would look to Gemma if she shows up.

I climb the two flights of stairs with my first suitcase and hesitate before putting the key in the lock. OK. Moment of truth.

When the door opens, I smell nothing but disinfectant and . . . flowers? Walking inside, I can't quite believe it. All the surfaces are shiny and on the counter there's a bunch of yellow wild flowers in a jam jar, plus a bottle of wine and an envelope. Inside, there's a thank-you card: *We loved your place.*

I love it too. Because it's *home*. Not a penthouse, but it's mine and I bloody earned it.

The bottle of wine glints in the sunlight, but I'll settle for tea. Ah, they've used all my teabags. I can forgive them that. Plus, they've left some herbal teas: mint, camomile.

Perfect for Gemma.

If she turns up.

If she's pregnant.

I fill a glass with tap water instead and sit on the new sofa bed I bought so I could let the flat out to four people. How will it work if Casey comes to stay? She can have my room – I can paint it whatever colour she wants. Except pink.

Screw it, if she wants pink, she can have it. I'll paint myself pink, and the jeep too.

I can't settle. Something is different about the flat. Something seems to be missing, but I can't work out what.

It's half-past nine. I consider messaging Gemma, but I have to let her be. If the test is negative, it is easier. We could pick up where we left off.

But if it's positive?

I remember another flat, another day, another girl: Angelica on my doorstep, with news of a baby that resulted from a weekend when two lonely kids found each other in a muddy field. A baby neither of us wanted, but who, it turns out, was exactly what we both needed.

If Gemma has a kid, it'll happen because of love and science.

I can imagine her as a mum, and it makes me smile goofily because I can imagine myself as a dad, with her. Does it matter that any child would carry Andrew's genes, not mine?

Not to me. I could do this with Gemma. If she wants to do it with me.

As the flat is spotless, there's nothing I can do now except unpack, buy teabags, then wait to see if she calls.

The message appears as I'm putting my trainers back in their right places:

If you still want to see me, can you send me your address?
G

I send it. I wonder if she's gone on Google Maps to check the area out on Street View. I barely breathe till her reply comes back:

I'm getting an Uber now. If that's still OK?

I type:

I'll put the kettle on. PS: it's not the Ritz.

She doesn't reply to that.

The kettle boils and turns itself off. I work through the pile of post from my basket downstairs, wincing at my credit card bill that itemizes the treats I bought for Casey. But I can do extra hours to pay it off. Nothing seems impossible today.

My buzzer goes. Instead of picking up the entryphone, I walk onto the landing, down the stairs. Will I be able to tell right away if the result was positive or negative?

I want whatever will make her happiest.

When I open the door, I can't read her face. 'Welcome to my non-penthouse,' I say. 'No Bear?'

'I came straight from the clinic.'

Without thinking, I hold out my hand and she takes it and squeezes. 'Two flights up – sorry, no executive lift.'

'Stop apologizing, it's annoying,' she says.

We take each step together: her movements seem slow, dream-like. I get her to go in first and watch her closely until I realize I'm coming over a bit intensely, so I switch the kettle on again.

'Camomile tea? Or something stronger? I've got wine or—'

She turns to me and I can see she's trying not to cry.

Shit. It hasn't worked.

Usually when I'm near a crying woman I want to run. But Gemma needs someone and, right now, I need to be that someone.

'Gemma, I'm so sorry.' I step towards her, my arms open, and she leans against me and lets herself be held. And while there's a tiny part of me that might be relieved, I also feel her loss. 'I'm here.'

She's sobbing now.

'Dan, listen.' She moves back slightly and her eyes are bright. 'It *worked*. The treatment. I'm . . . I am pregnant.' Her lips stay open after she's said that word, as though it hasn't sunk in.

'For real?'

She nods. 'For real. My hormones are sky-high.'

'Is that bad?'

'No. It's brilliant.' She steps back further and touches her flat belly. 'I can't believe it, though. It doesn't seem possible.'

Now we're apart again, I don't know what to do with my hands. *Is this the end or the beginning?* 'Wow. Congratulations. Camomile tea then?'

But before I can turn away, she reaches for my hand and leads us both to the tiny sofa bed. When we sit, side by side, it's like we're on a train, setting out on a journey together. 'You seem shocked,' she says.

'No. Well, yes. But not *bad* shocked. I'm thrilled for you. What does your family think?'

Gemma pulls a face. 'I haven't spoken to them yet. I wanted to tell you before them, because . . . well, I just did. Whatever happens, don't ever tell Laura she wasn't the first to hear the news.'

'How do you feel?'

'Freaked out. Excited. Scared.' She squeezes my hand. 'You?'

'Mostly scared of Laura finding out you told me first.' I realize I'm trying to hide how I feel behind a joke. 'Sorry. I'm nervous. I've never been in this situation before.'

'Seriously? You've never met a woman who is pregnant with her late husband's baby?'

'Funnily enough, no.' We share a smile.

And I realize what it is that's missing from the flat. No, missing from my head. The tinnitus. It's gone, because of Gemma.

Now what? I need to say the right thing. *Come on. You can charm the birds from the trees, so why can't you do this?*

But before I can find the right words, Gemma blinks.

'Right then,' she says, her voice curt. 'I'm not here to put you on the spot, but I came because I promised I'd tell you the result. And it's cool. You've already got *more* than enough complication in your life without this.'

'Gemma . . .'

She stands up. 'But if it's OK with you, I'd like to see Casey again if she visits. You wouldn't have to come along or—'

Now or never.

'No. That's not OK.'

Gemma stares at me. 'Oh.' She looks devastated. 'That's a shame. I could ask Angelica, if you'd rather not see me.'

'It's not OK because I *want* to be there when you're with Casey, and when you're not. Because—' *Say it, you coward. Say it!* 'Because I'm in love with you.'

'Oh!' Her deep-green eyes are wide open. 'Yeah, well, I'm in love with you too. Isn't that a coincidence?'

I gaze at her. *She's in love with me.*

And now we're kissing and it's so obvious. We're in *love*.

But she breaks off almost immediately. 'Except . . . what about the *baby*?' She whispers 'baby'. 'And all the getting-to-know-each-other stuff that we won't have enough time to do properly: the gallery trips and the playlists and gigs we talked about on our first date. I mean, it's madness, isn't it?'

'I know the important things about you already. And you know me better than anybody ever has. That's taken less than four weeks. I mean, sure, we can still do the playlists and galleries. But I've waited a lifetime to feel this way about someone, and I already have the answers I need. This isn't bad timing. I think it is the *perfect* time.'

A smile spreads across her face. She sits back down and leans in and we kiss again. Even though it's gentler than our previous kisses, it promises so much that I don't want to look back, or forward.

I want to make the most of being right here, right now.

Epilogue: Gemma

Sunday 21 October

I don't know if Casey guessed where we were going, but when we drive onto the grass, her smile makes it worth all the battles we had persuading Angelica.

It's the perfect morning: crisp and clear. The baskets line up and the other passengers wait.

'We're *really* going up?'

My dad keeps hold of Bear's lead – neither is brilliant with heights, so they're staying on the ground. The pilot's a rugged man with a burnished face, from sailing a little too close to the sun. Dan helps me climb in and, although I'm capable of doing it alone, it makes me feel cared for.

I've finally hit the *glowing* stage that the pregnancy books promise. I'd been nervous that my changing body would freak us both out when our relationship turned more physical.

It hasn't been a problem . . .

'Prepare yourselves for lift-off,' the pilot says as he lets the ropes go.

The roar of the burner takes me by surprise, but that's replaced by the gentle thrill of our ascent. We hold on to each other, making a triangle: me, Dan, Casey. And, inside me, the promise of a fourth person.

We told Casey the last time she came to see us. At first she was shocked, but then she admitted that a brother or sister had been on the *secret* wish list she put together alongside the public one. And although Dan and I sat up late afterwards, worrying about whether we were raising her hopes – and ours – by talking about the future, it felt right.

Angelica was less than thrilled, but she's enjoying her weekends to herself, allowed Dan to do some emergency DIY at the chalet, and has begun counselling to help her see the world as a safe place again. Casey's progress has helped. Her tumour will always be there, but for now she's doing well: she started back at secondary school and, after a rocky few days, found friends who are allowing her to embrace her inner nerd. Science thrills her – she's talked about becoming a radiographer or a nuclear physicist, 'because I am a proton super-fan'.

We're travelling with only wispy clouds as our companions now, and I think of Andrew and the balloon flight we took to celebrate finishing his treatment, and how I feel as safe with Dan now as I did with him then.

'Look, I can see the suspension bridge,' Casey says. 'And that must be your flat down there, Gemma.'

And now we'll tell her our second piece of news.

Dan nudges me, points towards Coldharbour Road on the outer edge of Bishopston. Not as chi-chi as Clifton, or as busy as the Wells Road. A trampoline in the garden of the house next door helps us to spot the right place from on high.

'Take a look down there,' Dan says and Casey squints, looking for a landmark or something beautiful.

'What am I looking for?'

'That's our new home,' I say. 'And your home too. We're renting out our two places and moving in together.'

'Wow!' Casey hugs me first, then her dad, but the straight line of her mouth tells me she's not completely happy. 'It looks miles away from BayCaff and Pepe and the patisserie. Won't it be boring?'

'It's still close to all the things you love,' Dan says. 'But the house has a bedroom for you, and one for the baby. And it's the perfect neighbourhood for a family.'

He says the last word with a kind of awe. I've always taken family for granted, but now I can see the simple magic the word offers. Families can be a puzzle, but they don't have to rely on blood, or genes. They're formed by trust and truth and love. And once you've found yours, it will always carry you home.

Acknowledgements

The inspiration for this book came from our amazing Border terrier, who visits patients and staff on the cardiac ward of our local hospital, as well as going into universities to help students affected by homesickness and exam stress. Like Bear, she's not keen on other dogs, but loves people and seems to understand what each person needs, whether it's licks, games or the chance to rub her tummy! To find out more about therapy and care dogs, visit www.canineconcern.co.uk.

I had the privilege of speaking to some brilliant young people who shared their experiences of living with a brain tumour. Without them, I'd never have known that waffle face is a thing, or that Bob is a common name for tumours. Huge thanks to Belle, Jas, Luke, Mary, Molly and Ruby for your honesty and humour, and to Sarah Watson and her colleagues at The Brain Tumour Charity (www.thebrain tumourcharity.org) for so much help with my research. Any errors that crept in are 100 per cent mine.

I invented an entire proton beam therapy unit in Bristol for this book – the UK's two specialist centres are actually at The Christie in Manchester (thanks to Thérèse Smith for offering to help with play therapy) and University College Hospital in London.

Huge thanks to the thoughtful, insightful Tracey Sainsbury

at www.fertilitycounselling.co.uk for talking me through the practical, ethical and emotional considerations around fertility treatment, and to Sarah Rayner for putting me in touch.

Now to the rest of the 'pack' – sending wags and treats to . . .

The following cats, dogs and hamsters, and their human companions: Archimedes, Betsy, Blossom, Bluebell, Charlie, Colin, Dinx, Freya, George, Gideon, Hobnob, Jet, Lily, Liquorice, Mabel, Meg, Mina, Pabu, Poppie, Rory, Sheila, Tag and Thor.

My agent Hellie Ogden (and Lexi) at Janklow & Nesbit, for their puppy-like enthusiasm for my many wild ideas. Also thank you to Ma'suma Amiri, Kirsty Gordon, Ellis Hazelgrove, Allison Hunter, Zoe Nelson and Emma Winter.

My editor Sam Humphreys (and Lux, aka Big Dog) for sniffing out the right direction for the book, and always urging me to dig deeper. Also, thanks to Becca Bryant, Elle Gibbons, Alice Gray, Charlotte Wright, Hannah Corbett and Rosie Wilson at Pan Macmillan, and Mandy Greenfield for copy editing so, um, doggedly.

Big thank-you licks to the wonderful guardians of Stanley, Rosa and Molly. And, of course, to the person I'm lucky enough to share Vesper with . . .

My father Michael became very unwell as I was writing *Owner of a Lonely Heart*, and he died just a few weeks after I finished. From the start, I knew the book was about dogs and living in the moment – it was only right at the end that I understood it was also about fathers. Dad, I miss you. And so does Tinkerbell, who misses the gourmet dog's dinners you cooked for her.

Finally to you: thank you so much for reading this story. You can get free goodies and join my book club at www.evacarter.net or share shaggy dog stories with me on Twitter, Instagram or YouTube, where I'm @katewritesbooks – I'd love to hear from you.

Eva/Kate

If you enjoyed *Owner of a Lonely Heart*
you'll love Eva Carter's beautiful first novel

How to Save a Life

'I couldn't put it down until I reached the final page'
Beth O'Leary, bestselling author of
The Flatshare

Sometimes saving a life is only the start of the story . . .
When talented footballer Joel collapses on the eve of the
millennium, it's shy student Kerry who saves his life. But life
after death is no guarantee of a happy ending and her act of
heroism will bind the two together before tearing them apart.

Over the next two decades, their lives – and destinies – continue
to collide. They both know that their hopes for the future can
change in a heartbeat yet the past won't let them go. So what
will it take for Joel and Kerry to save each other one final time?

'We fell head over heels for this sweeping love story'
Fabulous

'Enthralling'
Rosie Walsh, bestselling author of
The Man Who Didn't Call

'Unflinching'
Jill Mansell, bestselling author of
And Now You're Back